CRIMES OF PASSION

THE COMPLETE SERIES

SHANNON JUMP

Copy Editing by Librum Artis Editorial Services
Cover Design by Shannon Jump

Crimes of Passion: The Complete Series | First edition published November 2022
ISBN: 979-8843778118 (Amazon Paperback) | ASIN: B0B8K35V5M (Kindle Edition)

Wouldn't You Love to Love Her | First edition published March 2022
ISBN: 978-0578343297 (Paperback) | ASIN: B09NGK2B7K (Kindle Edition)

Like a Bird in Flight | First edition published July 2022
ISBN: 979-8218001674 (Paperback) | ASIN: B09VVDQ585 (Kindle Edition)

Who Will Be Her Lover | First edition published November 2022
ISBN: 979-8218093679 (Paperback) | ASIN: B0B8JXLNC8 (Kindle Edition)

Content Warning: This book is intended for readers over the age of eighteen and contains mature content that may be unsuitable for younger audiences. For a full list of warnings, please visit the author's website at www.shannonjumpwritesbooks.com.

ALSO BY SHANNON JUMP

For all the times I said I wasn't a series writer.

She kissed me.
She kissed the devil.
Only a ***beautiful*** soul
like hers would kiss the damned.

~ Daniel Saint

WOULDN'T YOU LOVE TO LOVE HER

CRIMES OF PASSION BOOK 1

ALLEGEDLY, OF COURSE

Alisha

THERE'S a stain on the wall to my right. It's a dull brown that I imagine, when fresh, was once a bright shade of red. It's low enough to the ground that had I not been lying here on the concrete floor, I might never have noticed it. I stare at it now, the stain, my head turned sharply to the side, arms folded across my stomach. It's faint against the cream-colored brick wall, no bigger than the size of a pea, the edges almost jagged.

A cast-off droplet.

It's definitely blood, and probably a direct correlation to the reason I don't have a cellmate. Rumor has it my predecessor, and former inmate of cell number 154, slit her own throat with a shiv fashioned from her toothbrush.

The shiv? Currently missing in action.

I shudder at the thought, my stomach churning as I consider the amount of pressure she would need to apply to create a fatal wound like that from a piece of plastic—on her own neck, no less. Goose-

3

bumps prickle my skin, and I'm faced again with the reality that this isn't a dream. That I am, in fact, awake, locked behind a set of metal bars. A prisoner of the state.

This is my new normal.

I won't be waking up tomorrow in the comfort of my own bed, my husband snoring softly beside me as I roll over to watch him sleep. I picture his handsome face, the prominent features I've always found endearing: the tiny scar above his right eye, punctuated by a faint set of crow's feet that he always swore weren't there. The chiseled jaw, lined with prickly stubble. His head full of dark hair that I loved to run my fingers through, often disheveled from a good night's sleep. The necessary rise and fall of his chest that tells me he's alive will not be there.

A tear slides down my cheek and catches me by surprise. I want to wipe it away, but don't. I leave it there for him in case he needs it, in case he's watching.

It's proof, somehow, that I feel things, too.

Not that anyone seems to believe it. I suppose I can't blame them; it's not like I've given them much reason to. The one and only thing they think they know about me isn't something I'm particularly proud of, but what can I do?

It is the popular opinion of many that I killed my husband.

The media has a lot to do with that.

I suppose the evidence against me does as well.

That's why I've spent the last ninety-three days locked in a tiny concrete cell that on a good day reeks of urine and weeks-old body odor. Most days it's mixed with the faint scent of blood, as if it's been shed in large quantities, only to be wiped away with nothing more than cheap, unscented bar soap and lukewarm water, sure to linger indefinitely.

On the worst of days it reeks of old socks. Of sex. And sweat. And sour breath. Some of the women here seem to love it, though. Me? I don't think I'll ever get used to the stench of this place.

No sane person could.

These women…they're damaged goods. Most of them are unapologetic criminals lined up and begging for their chance at a sexual encounter with a certain corrections officer who'll go home to his loving wife and brood of children immediately afterward—as if he's done nothing wrong.

I'll be here, in this hell-hole, until my trial begins next week. At least I think it's next week; all the days have blurred together at this point. For someone like me who sticks to their cell most of the time, there's not much to break up the monotony.

Although I do get quite a bit of fan mail these days. And as if it weren't an invasion of privacy—because there's no such thing as privacy here in prison—each piece is carefully inspected, read, and analyzed by some *qualified* personnel. I don't need to mention the fact that such an act is highly illegal outside of these walls, a federal offense punishable by imprisonment, actually.

Oh, the irony.

But here? Mail is a privilege that must be earned.

Not that it matters—the one person I expected to hear from has yet to reach out, not that I blame them. And it's not like I'd care to talk to a cellmate to pass the time—if I had one. Isn't that jail house 101—not to speak with other inmates as you await trial? I'm pretty sure that's what I've always heard on those Thursday night drama shows. It's fine, though. I prefer it this way, really I do.

I can't imagine I'd make a decent friend in here even if I tried.

"Thompson, Alisha!" bellows the CO from the other side of my cell. He's not one of us—a caged animal—no, he's free to roam as he pleases. I think of him more as our lion tamer, the man responsible for this circus we're all unwillingly performing in.

He owns us.

All of us.

I'm not sure he understands he's not supposed to get high on his own supply, but he hasn't been caught with his pants down yet, and none of us have bothered to report him. So, the cycle continues; the show goes on.

Not that it matters.

He's one of the most decorated guards here, Officer Joshua Marshall.

"Present," I announce sullenly, my eyes still locked in on the shit-colored bloodstain. I hear his feet shuffle, his heavy boots dragging in the dirt that litters the floors around here. He clears his throat and taps his pen on the metal bars that protect me from the general population for over twelve hours a day.

Or them from me.

"What are you doing on the floor?" he hisses, his voice softer than the usual boom that reverberates from his throat.

"Sunbathing."

"Bullshit. What are you doing on the floor, Thompson?" he asks again, a bit more gruffly this time.

I stare blankly at the stain, focused in deep concentration. I refuse to look at him.

He likes to see the fear in our eyes.

But fear is nothing but a useless emotion, an unnecessary burden I'd rather not carry.

"Thompson!" he barks, his voice echoing in the hollow space. I shudder and finally relax—as much as one possibly can on a concrete floor—and the warmth quickly spreads through my lower extremities. It's brazened and unpleasant, the urine, as it soaks through my pale gray jumpsuit and onto the floor beneath me.

I held it in all day for this.

"What the *fuck*?" Officer Marshall says, disgust riddled across his face. "Clean it up!" He shakes his head and backs away, sighing as he makes a mark on his clipboard and moves on with his head count.

"Thorson, Francis!"

Once he's far enough down the row, I peel myself from the dank floor and strip out of my prison-issued scrubs—parts of them now a darker shade of gray, parts of them sticking to my body in ways I'd rather not think about. I toss them into the hobbit-sized sink next to my toilet before stripping the sheet from the twin mattress and wrapping it around myself like a bath towel. I yell for the other CO, the female one —Officer Marin—that will bring me fresh clothes, even though she'll mutter to herself about my inability to use the toilet. She's quite fed up with my lack of personal hygiene these days, so she tells me.

But I can't expect her to understand, not in her current state of oblivion.

Officer Marshall can do no wrong.

Obviously, I can use the toilet just fine, especially seeing as I've been awarded with my own personal commode not even five feet from the head of my bed. The thing is, I'd rather piss myself once a day than engage in another romp session with a certain CO who can't keep his dick in his pants.

See, showers are another thing that's privileged here. An inmate is not guaranteed a shower just because they pee their pants.

It does, however, make me much less desirable.

Which means I get to spend the night lying on top of a thin plastic mattress, wondering where the hell things went wrong instead of getting pounded up against a brick wall.

So, I piss myself.

It's rancid, yes, but sometimes it's the best thing I smell all day.

It is my unpopular opinion that Officer Marshall belongs six feet under alongside my husband, but that's a topic for another day.

My name is Alisha Renee Thompson, inmate number 090285, and I am awaiting trial for the premeditated murder of my husband.

Allegedly, of course.

PART I

MONOLOGUES, MELTDOWNS, & MURDER

THE VIRGINITY MONOLGUE

Alisha

I SHOULD GO BACK to the beginning, maybe tell you a little more about myself and why I'm here. Your confusion will otherwise get the best of you, and we certainly can't have that.

Let me start with a cold, hard truth, and say this: you will either love me or you will hate me. You may even love to hate me. There is no in between, no mutual understanding we can come to—even as the mature adults we are. There's no agreeing to disagree, no acceptance of opposing positions. The truth is, most people don't like me, and the ones who do are either lying to themselves or just as fucked up in the head as I am. That, or they want to sleep with me, and once they do they usually hate me afterward, so the outcome is generally the same.

This brings me back to my original point: the odds that you'll like me are not great.

I get it; it happens all the time. I don't sugarcoat a damn thing and sometimes people take offense to the half-witted shit that spews from my mouth. I won't filter my thoughts or censor my language just to make you feel better, so you'll have to get used to it or start heading for the door.

Now, let's get one more thing out on the table, shall we? I'm a sex addict. You may be a bit confused by that fact, considering my lack of interest in Officer Marshall's advances, but it's true. Of course, I blatantly denied it for years, but as of late I've really come to terms with this society-plagued, deviant-like addiction of mine. You're probably wondering how I *manage* it.

Well, in truth, I don't. Or at least didn't. Things are different now—by necessity—but for most of my adult life, I did nothing to minimize my addiction and everything to capitalize on it.

How? Well, have you ever heard of a little thing called adult streaming services? Live webcam girls? Of course you have; I don't even know why I'm asking, but whether you openly admit it or not, you've probably indulged in adult entertainment at least once in your life. Perhaps you've ventured out to a strip club, or fancied yourself a lap dance or two. You may have even dabbled in the anonymity of porn, perhaps all by your lonesome, or in the privacy of the bedroom you share with your better half. Seriously, don't kid yourself, we've all taken a peek behind the proverbial curtain.

But, we're not here to discuss *your* sexual habits, we're here to discuss *mine*, as much as I'd rather not. That adult streaming service I mentioned? It's what I do to earn a living, how I pay my bills. I run a livestream channel of adults-only content that subscribers can access for the low price of $19.95 per hour. On a slow day, I average about twenty-five-hundred viewers per hour, three days a week, three hours each day. That's it. Easy peasy, lemon frickin' squeezy.

Pretty lucrative, right? Go ahead and do that math, because once I tell you what I do on that live channel, you'll not only envy me for my money, you'll also be right back to hating me. To that I say *to each their own*.

My streaming channel is called Lisha's Bedroom. That probably tells you all you need to know, but just in case your engine is a little slow on the intake today, I'll make it a little more clear for you. Essentially, I'm a glorified stripper. But from the comfort of my own home, sans the lap dances and uninvited groping.

Plus, I get to play with toys, and nobody yells at me when I don't put them away.

The money obviously speaks for itself—and yes, I even pay my taxes like a good girl. That said, you'll wonder a few things about me as you get to know me against my will. Like why I live in a less-than-average sized house across the street from the trailer park where I grew up, even though I can (clearly) afford much better. Or why I sound like I don't give a shit half the time. Spoiler alert: I don't.

And through it all, you'll picture the man I've been accused of killing, and you'll wonder what the hell he was doing with a woman like me in the first place. You'll probably even use a few derogatory names at my expense.

It's okay, I'm not mad. People questioned my relationship with my husband long before he ended up dead, so it's nothing new. Hell, even I did from time to time. Anyway, now that I've gotten a few things off my chest, let me tell you how I ended up in the Smithson Women's Penitentiary, awaiting trial for his murder.

You may still hate me by the end of this; you were practically destined to by default. And that's fine. Or, you may surprise us all and come out loving me a little more than you already did, in which case be prepared for your friends to judge you and start asking questions about your sanity. Like I said, there's not really a middle ground for us here.

I'll start from what I consider the beginning—this may take a while, so bear with me.

I've always loved sex.

It's no secret to anyone who knows me, and I stopped giving a shit about that fact a long time ago. As a woman, sex is one of those taboo subjects we're not really supposed to talk about—even though our lovers tend not to complain behind closed doors when the freak comes out at night, right?

I digress.

Basically, you're a slut if you give it up too easily, a whore if you sleep around, and a prude if you're still a virgin after the age of eighteen. I've been called all but the latter.

I've also been called worse.

It changes nothing for me in the long run. I couldn't give two shits what someone else thinks of me. Most of the time, anyway. And I've always had a small circle of friends—often nonexistent, if I'm being honest. A partial hazard of my upbringing, but mostly due to my chosen career, which I came to terms with a long time ago.

But with sex I'm always in control. I can be whoever I want to be —or whoever *they* want me to be. That's a liberating power. It's just as addicting as any drug or the strongest proof alcohol.

As a teen, I had explored my own body quite extensively before I ever gave my V-card to anyone, and as a result, I knew what I liked at an early age. I was comfortable in my own skin before most girls even learned what a clitoris was. I could even say that word without blushing.

I made the mistake of mentioning all of this to my therapist, Kristin. We went on discussing it for seven years and still don't see eye-to-eye on the topic.

Personally, I don't think she understands what she's missing.

"There are rehabilitation centers that specialize in sex addiction," she told me during one of our first sessions together. I was taken aback, unsure how admitting one's love for sex could immediately result in a recommendation for rehab, but apparently she was going down that road and dragging me along for the ride.

"I'm not a sex addict," I argued, now on the defense.

"With all due respect, Alisha, I have to admit that I think you might be." She scribbled a note on the legal pad that rested in her lap.

"I just really love sex," I told her. She made another notation on the page and then adjusted her glasses, the thick plastic frames almost too large for her slim face.

"I think we should explore that statement."

"Why?" I asked. At this point, I leaned back on the obligatory couch, crossed my legs and folded my arms over my chest. I was making a point and therefore felt the need to convey that point with stereotypical body language. I immediately wondered what notation she might make at such childish behavior, but that didn't stop me from doing it.

"How often do you have sex?" she asked, looking at me expectantly.

At that moment, I debated ghosting her, maybe telling her to fuck off and mind her own damn business, but then I remembered that *technically* I *was* her business. I mean, I was paying her to give a shit, to ask the uncomfortable questions. So, I sucked it up and answered her question.

"On a good month? Every day. But, that's only if I'm seeing..." I paused, unsure which pronoun to use to finish the statement. "...someone," I finished, punctuating the sentence with a nod of my head.

"And, when you are seeing *someone*, is this someone you are exclusive with?"

I knew where she was going with the line of questioning; I sensed the tone in her voice. The judgment and overall condescension. "I've been known to be a bit promiscuous," I admitted, reluctantly so.

"Mm-hm," she said, her pen scribbling again. It was silent as she jotted her notes, and I uncrossed my legs before leaning forward and resting my elbows on my knees. I was certain she had flinched, but I couldn't imagine why, it wasn't like I had threatened her.

"Just say it," I snapped. Kristin looked at me apologetically, almost like she felt sorry for me.

"Alisha, I believe you have some unhealthy sexual habits."

"You have *got* to be kidding me," I said, jumping to my feet. I didn't need her ridicule and refused to sit through it any longer. Grabbing my purse and tucking it under my armpit, I waved an aggressive finger in her general direction. "Maybe *you* have some unhealthy sexual habits," I hissed. "Try getting laid sometime, maybe it'll help you pull the stick out of your ass."

I walked over to the door, prepared to make a clean exit from the chamber of hell, my hand resting on the knob. "And you know what? I don't appreciate you slut-shaming me." I huffed and puffed my way out the door, making sure to slam it nice and hard before rushing past the patrons who waited their turn in the lobby.

Despite my dramatic exit that day, since I already had the appointment on my calendar, I returned to see Kristin the following week. Apparently, I wasn't getting off—so to speak—that easily in the shrink department.

With neither of us offering apologies, Kristin picked the conversation up right where it left off. She asked the dreaded question I had seen coming, the one that subconsciously caused me to throw a tantrum and walk out of there in the first place—it's not a story I tell people, not even my late husband.

"How did you lose your virginity, Alisha?"

I decided in that moment to be *extra* diligent in answering Kristin's questions going forward. In fact, I made sure to elaborate, sharing in great detail, about the afternoon I was officially deflowered. The story goes a little something like this:

I bid adieu to my virginity back in 2002, at the age of seventeen—a little late in the game in comparison to my peers at the time, honestly. That virginal gift, in all its entirety, went to Brandon Gould, the hunky star quarterback on the varsity football team. Not that we had ever uttered a word to one another, but I'd seen him checking me out in the halls in between classes, watched him stare at my cleavage from across the lunchroom. He was dating Amy Silverton, the head cheerleader— because, of course he was, right?—so technically he wasn't *supposed* to be checking out other girls. They'd been an item since junior year and according to the rumor mill, she had yet to put out.

Poor guy.

I ran into him at the Tom Thumb gas station one afternoon after school. I had stopped in for a Milky Way bar. Brandon stood behind me at the register, a Snickers and a bottle of pop in his hand.

"I'll get that," he said, placing his items on the counter next to my highly superior Milky Way. We made eye contact as he pulled his wallet out of his back pocket—Velcro, which almost made me laugh; I wouldn't have pegged him for a Velcro wallet kind of guy.

For some reason, I found myself wondering what Brandon's dick looked like. *Is it big? Is he circumcised?* I inadvertently undressed him with my eyes while he paid for our candy bars. This was a habit I'd picked up recently, one I couldn't seem to turn off no matter how hard I tried. I often walked through the halls at school wondering how big all the boys' dicks were and whether or not they were circumcised.

I'm telling you, I don't know how men do it, because I would have been walking around pitching a tent everywhere I went if I had a penis. At least as a woman I could hide my arousal from prying eyes.

"Thank you," I said to Brandon when he handed a five-dollar bill to the cashier, a ginger with several odd-shaped freckles across his nose.

"It's no problem."

The cashier, Allen—according to his worn-out name tag—slid the change across the counter and watched us stand there awkwardly. "Get a room," he mumbled before turning away.

We left the store, me in front, Brandon behind me and likely checking out my ass, which was rounding out nicely thanks to the squats I'd been doing in gym class. I made sure to adjust my V-neck enough to display a little extra of the cleavage I knew he'd been admiring, too. I turned and thanked him again for the candy bar, waving with it in my hand as I grabbed the bike I'd left leaning against the side of the building.

"Do you need a ride?" he offered, motioning toward his single cab pickup.

"Oh. That'd be great, thanks."

He opened the tailgate and slid my bike into the bed while I hopped into the passenger seat. I was surprised to find the cab was relatively clean. Most guys that offered rides didn't keep such a clean vehicle.

"Where do you live?" he asked, buckling his seatbelt. I fastened mine as well, making sure it hugged my chest and further accentuated my breasts, which you've probably figured out by now had developed quite nicely.

Brandon cleared his throat and diverted his eyes forward.

"Just over by Lake Pulaski," I said. *In the trailer park, I left out.*

"You're, um…very pretty." Brandon managed. I pretended to blush and gave him my best version of bedroom eyes. "You're a junior, right?" he asked.

"Yep."

"I've seen you around school. Alisha, is it?" he asked, but pronouncing it "Uh-lish-uh."

"It's Alisha...like A-leesh-uh, but with an 'sh' instead of a 'c.' It's spelled differently," I corrected.

"I like it," he admitted with a coy smile.

"This is me," I said, pointing to the blue rambler on the corner. He pulled up to the curb and put the truck in park, but made no movement to open his door. Neither did I.

"I'm going to break up with Amy," he blurted.

"Oh."

"She's, uh, not my type. Not really, anyway."

"I thought all the star quarterbacks were supposed to date the head cheerleaders?" I teased.

He laughed. "Well, in this case, the head cheerleader is kind of stuck-up."

"Oh..." I said again. We sat in silence for another beat, and I wasn't sure if I should get out or stay. Brandon shimmied out of his letterman's jacket and draped it over the back of the seat before planting his hand on my thigh—sending an unexpected shiver through my entire body.

I'd never had a boyfriend, although I'd made out with a couple guys under the bleachers at football games before. But Brandon's touch was electric, pulsing. It had taken me by surprise.

"I really like you," he said, his hand snaking further up my thigh. I inhaled a breath and unbuckled my seatbelt so I could slide over next to him.

"You do?" I asked, somewhat seductively like I'd heard the women do in the porn DVDs I'd stolen from one of my mom's boyfriends.

"Yes." He swallowed the lump in his throat. I leaned back in the seat and spread my legs. I couldn't help but watch his face; he was mesmerized by my forwardness, his eyes dilated and his mouth slightly open while his tongue traced his bottom lip. When he didn't move his hand, I placed mine over the top of it and guided him to the wetness inside my skirt. I hadn't dressed appropriately for the fall weather, but it was suddenly worth having been cold all day.

"How much?" I asked.

"So much," he said before he leaned over and kissed me. His lips were soft and his tongue rough as it plunged into my mouth.

"Not here," I said, breaking the kiss. He adjusted himself in the seat, his bulge prominent in his track pants.

He drove us to an abandoned farm on the other side of the lake, and as soon as he pulled onto the gravel road, I unbuckled my seatbelt and lifted my shirt over my head. His hands were on me before he even had the truck in park, and it inadvertently rolled forward a bit.

"Sorry," he said nervously, tapping the brake and shifting into the proper gear. I reached behind me and unclasped my bra, admiring his face while he watched my breasts tumble out.

His mouth dropped, his eyes opening wide, but he said nothing. It was clearly his first time seeing boobs in the flesh.

He slid his pants and boxers down and they fell to his ankles, bunching in a heap at his feet on the dirty floor mat. He was already hard, and I gasped in excitement at the sight of him because I figured he would like that—it's what all the porn stars seemed to do, anyway. Like they'd been given a gift and couldn't contain their excitement.

"Put your mouth on it," he coached, his hand on the back of my head to draw me closer. I took him in my mouth, and the sound of his moans filled the cab of the truck. Something had come over me in that moment, and I had never felt so alive, like I possessed some sort of magical power over him.

I climbed on his lap, still very much in control, and while the whole act of sex took less than ten minutes from start to finish, when I felt his release inside me, I silently cheered for myself. I was proud of my newfound abilities, at the fact that I'd gotten him off.

Afterward, he shucked the condom out the window and then drove me home—or at least, he thought he did. I told him I lived in the blue rambler we'd pulled up to earlier, but I actually lived in the trailer pack across the street. The blue rambler belonged to Gretta Maylen, the sweet older lady whose dog I let out every day after school for ten bucks a week.

What makes this loss of virginity extra pathetic is that Brandon never did break things off with Amy. When I asked him about it under the bleachers later that week while giving him a blow job, he said they'd worked things out and that he'd deny it if I ever told anyone what happened between us. That he wasn't going to let a *girl like me* ruin a good thing.

As if it were my fault he had just cheated on his girlfriend.

After he came, I wiped his secretions off my mouth, stood up, and spit the mouthful back in his face. Before he had a chance to realize his own semen was dripping down his cheek, I shoved my tits back into my top, flipped him the bird, and sashayed my way out of there.

I'd learned the nasty truth about guys that week: they'll use a woman for her body just because they *can*, and then go home to their girlfriend, wife, or lover afterward without a pang of guilt.

And the worst thing anyone ever calls them is a player; they may even get a high five or two.

This is why I love sex, you see? Because the first guy I ever let fuck me managed to do so in more ways than one. But he taught me a valuable lesson, too. I decided that day that I'd never let another guy like Brandon use me again. That I would always be the one who would determine whether sex was a game or an act of endearment.

And I've been playing that game ever since.

THE MOST PERFECT SPECIMEN

Alisha

Growing up in a rundown trailer park was about what you'd expect. It was dirty, shady, and at times, a little unsettling. Our front door never locked properly, so one day, since my mother was too much of a junkie to do it herself, I used twenty dollars of my dog-sitting money to buy one of those locks you screw into the top of the door—I figured even if an intruder could break the door off the hinges, at least the cheap lock would give me a chance to get out of there before they managed to get inside.

I was becoming more resourceful, too, so when I got home I asked our twenty-something neighbor, Cole, to install the lock for me, even though I could have done it myself. Cole, being the nice guy that he was, didn't charge anything for it, and I felt bad, so I sucked him off as a thank you. It kind of became a thing for us after that; he'd help out around the trailer when my mom was gone on a bender, and I'd thank him with blow jobs.

And, I guess it sounds a bit ludicrous, looking back, but after my virginity-stripping romp in Brandon's pickup, I learned that sex could be a useful tool for a girl like me.

I knew I was pretty.

I knew I was well endowed in the chest region.

So why not use those things to my advantage? I didn't have much else going for me, so yes, I slept around quite a bit and was what you might refer to as a closet ho. I made my rounds through the guys in school but was never actually labeled a whore because none of their other halves ever found out. And the guys didn't talk; it was like they had some secret bro code, and they all knew about it. It worked out well for me; I got to get my jollies off and the guys whose girlfriends wouldn't put out—or did, but lacked a sense of adventure—got to stay in their idealistic high school romances but still get their dicks wet every once in a while.

I would've charged for my services had such a thing been legal. I've never quite understood how it's okay for a porn star to make money having sex just because they're considered "actors," yet it's prostitution if you charge for it from the comfort of your own home, sans the camera.

I considered getting into porn, to be honest. Why not make some money doing what I loved most? I had been blessed with the body for it, even though I rarely exercised and never had the money to eat healthily. And while stereotypically, most guys really do prefer blondes, it turns out they're also suckers for a blue-eyed brunette with thick lips and loose morals.

In college, I let a guy film me while I sucked him off. I didn't know his name, but he was drunk, and while I was ready and willing to give him the best blow job he'd ever had—for the sake of the camera, of course—the asshole couldn't keep it up, and because of that, my amateur porn debut never made it to the internet.

Anyway, I digress. Kristin says I'm a walking, talking cliche with this shit. I asked her what she meant by that, even though I knew the answer, and she back-pedaled pretty aggressively. I moved on and pretended to forgive her, but mentally I added another derogatory mark to her Yelp review.

College got more exciting once word got around that I wasn't afraid to put my sexuality to use. Eventually, I was invited to just about every party on campus, and they were *insane*, to say the least. Since I didn't drink, these parties were merely an easy way for me to experiment sexually, and just about everyone was fair game. I didn't know a single "happy" couple who didn't sleep around behind their partner's back. And they had a knack for spilling the dirt on each other, too. It's amazing what you can find out about relationships when you're lying around letting the after-sex glow wear off. Guys talk more than you'd think, and it's almost unsettling when they share their dark fantasies with you *after* you've already let them stick their dick in you. Like, thanks, asshole. Thanks for letting me know that you're a fucking creep *after* I got you off.

I started screening men a little differently after college, and while I still had my fair share of weirdos, they were fewer and further between.

But it wasn't just men that propositioned me for sex; the women were equally as horny and just as unfaithful. I tried to draw the line somewhere, though. There were enough men around campus that I didn't need to take advantage of the women, too. I hated to be a snob, but other than letting a couple girls go down on me, I enjoyed the dick too much to formally cross over. I wasn't sure what that said about my sexuality, but I also didn't care to put a label on it either.

Now, I know I claimed early on that my sex life wasn't an addiction, but these days, I'll be the first to admit that it is. And I've always had an intense addiction to porn. I couldn't get enough of it—and sometimes I watched it only for research purposes, figuring I could learn a few things from it.

And that's exactly what I was doing on that Saturday afternoon in 2015 when I first laid eyes on Dylan Thompson.

I lived alone in a one-bedroom apartment—with a sex "addiction" like mine, coupled with my habit of walking around naked, and the need to work from home, how could I *not* live alone? I had just finished getting off to some amateur porn when there was a knock at my door. I stilled, buck naked on the couch, and silently listened for a second knock. Non-residents did have a tendency to show up at the wrong apartments.

Knock, knock.

"Fuck," I mumbled under my breath. I slid my arms through my kimono robe and wrapped the fabric around my torso. "Who is it?" I yelled through the peephole-less door.

"Uh, hi. It's Dylan," the stranger answered.

"I don't know any Dylans," I said with a huff.

"Gretta Maylen's grandson? I called the other day…"

Oh fuck.

Fuck. Fuck. Fuck. I had completely forgotten he would be stopping by. Mrs. Maylen had moved into a nursing home the week prior, and her grandson, a Realtor, had cleaned out her house to get it ready to put up for sale. He'd called and said she'd left something for me and asked if he could come by. I had no idea what she could have possibly left for me, but I had agreed and given him my address. In all my years living across the street from Mrs. Maylen and watching her beloved golden-doodle, I'd never met her grandson.

I unhooked the chain from the top of the door, flipped the deadbolt and pulled the door open. There before me was the sexiest and most perfect specimen of a man I'd ever seen in my entire life.

"Oh. Um. Hi," he said. He scratched his head of beautiful brown hair and his equally beautiful brown eyes trailed up and down my body before settling on something behind me.

"Hi," I said, slowly turning around to see what he was looking at so intently.

The porn.

I forgot to shut off the fucking porn.

"Oh, my God! I'm *so* sorry! One second!" I lunged frantically away from the door, hopping over the back of the couch, and snatching up the TV remote. Never before had I jammed my finger so hard into the power button. My habit of watching on mute—on account of the painfully fake sounds that erupted from some of those women—had backfired. I stood motionless for a moment, unsure if he'd be standing there when I turned back around.

He was.

Still beautiful as ever.

"I see I've interrupted you." He pointed to my ensemble, and it was at this time that I remembered I was only wearing a silk kimono robe. It was another second later that I realized I'd never actually tied the belt of that kimono robe, and it had flown open in my haste to turn off the porn, putting all my lady bits on full display to the gorgeous stranger at my door.

I grabbed at the robe and pulled it back over my body, holding it closed with my arms since I wasn't sure where the belt had disappeared to.

"I'm having a rough day," I admitted. He laughed, and it was the most incredible laugh I've ever heard, throaty and full of bass—like he really meant it.

"I can come back another time," he offered, motioning down the hall. He was blushing, and it was adorable.

"No, no, it's okay. Really. Can you just give me a minute to throw on some clothes?"

"Sure," he said. He stood awkwardly in the doorway, not quite inside my apartment, but not quite in the hallway either.

"Is it okay if I come in?" he finally asked, and I waved him inside before running off down the hall to rummage through the clean but not yet folded basket of laundry that sat on my bedroom floor. I quickly slid my legs into a pair of sweatpants before pulling my arms through an off-the-shoulder crop-top, channeling a scene from *Flashdance* with my new ensemble. My dark hair was mussed in what I hoped was a sexy way, and as I glanced in the mirror before running out the door, I realized I had that 'just fucked' glow to my cheeks, courtesy of the porn I'd forgotten to turn off.

Perfect.

I padded down the hall and made my way back to the handsome stranger standing in my living room. His hands were in the pockets of his jeans, and he'd been unintentionally looking around my apartment, taking it all in. I could sense his nervousness; he was clearly uncomfortable, but his face lit up when he saw me coming, and for some reason, that was *the* moment for me. That was when I knew.

"You found some clothes!" Dylan cheered awkwardly.

"Would you like something to drink?" I asked, motioning toward the kitchen.

"Sure, some water would be great."

I pulled two bottles of water from the fridge and handed him one. "I'm sorry about before," I mumbled after a quick sip, although I was fairly certain he liked what he saw.

"Oh, it's no problem."

He cleared his throat and took a sip of water; I couldn't help but watch his Adam's apple bob up and down while he drank. Even *that* was sexy.

We took our seats at the table and sat in silence for an awkward beat, each of us drinking water like we'd die of thirst if we didn't take one more sip. I tucked a stray hair behind my ear before looking over at Dylan and opening my mouth to speak. But no words came out, they were stuck, so the silence continued, the air thick and riddled with sexual tension.

I'd never experienced such a loss for words.

"This is..." he said, trailing off. He cleared his throat again and visibly adjusted himself under the table.

"Are you okay?" I asked.

"I...yeah. I'm sorry, maybe I should go? I can come back another time." He stood, but didn't step toward the door, like he didn't actually want to go.

The next thing I knew, my lips were on his. I whimpered at the warmth of his mouth, and that was all it took for him to kiss me back—for his lips to travel along my cheek and down my neck, to my earlobes and then my clavicle. Every single nerve in me had been awakened.

But he pulled away, leaving me empty. I stepped back and brought a hand to my mouth to feel my swollen lips, the taste of him still lingering.

"I...I'm so sorry," he started. "I don't know what came over me. I..." I watched in a trance while he tried to make sense of the attraction between us. It was cute that he thought he had been the one to initiate the kiss. "I don't normally do this, I...wow, you're..."

I stepped forward and placed my hands on his chest, the muscles taut beneath his shirt. He sucked in a breath, and I pressed my hips into him.

"There's absolutely no need to be sorry," I said, my voice low and sultry.

"No?" he asked, his mouth only millimeters from mine again. I outlined his bottom lip with my tongue, and he released an audible sigh before our mouths collided once more. He lifted me, his hands on my ass, and I wrapped my legs around him while we stumbled down the hall to my bedroom. He threw me onto the bed and reached for his belt buckle.

Again, he stopped abruptly, looking down at me, his face wary but his eyes filled with lust. "We shouldn't do this," he said. The bulge in his pants told me his appendage disagreed.

"Okay," I whispered. I pulled my sweater over my head anyway, watching his eyes grow wide as I slowly placed it around his neck and used it to pull him toward me. He studied me for a moment before he finally gave into temptation and removed his pants.

His lips met mine without further apprehension.

Beneath him, I wiggled out of my sweats and took in the sight of him. He was perfect, and I planned to claim every inch of him, maybe even more than once.

Hours later, I lay there in ecstasy while Dylan snored softly beside me. And I realized with a start that I was fucked, in the figurative sense. I'd broken every rule I had adhered to since the day Brandon had taken my virginity.

I had been greedy by not reciprocating oral.

I had screamed his name.

I even let him stay the night.

I was no longer winning at playing the game.

NOT THAT KINDA GUY

Dylan

THE WAY I SEE IT, it's no surprise that I'm dead. Not really, anyway. I mean, we all die at some point. We all have our time to go with the gods, or however the saying goes. That's not to say that I like the way I went out, though. Multiple stab wounds to the chest? Nope, didn't care for that.

The way I went out fucking sucked.

What I *am* saying is that my life ended with no regrets. I can't think of anything I would have changed, anything I would have done differently had the opportunity presented itself.

Alisha was it for me. She was my "meant to be"—my muse. The inspiration of my life. It's cheesy as hell, I know. I was once a skeptic, like you, so I get it.

I'm sure you don't see her the way I do, based on what you think you know about her. But come on, even Ted Bundy had a love of his life, and we all know how that turned out. I know I can't change the way you think about the woman I loved. What I can tell you is how I feel—how I *felt*—about her.

I wasn't sure what to expect the day I knocked on her apartment door. My grandmother was newly admitted into nursing care and had asked me to leave her house keys with Alisha, to explain to her that the house would be hers since she was no longer able to live on her own. I'd been working on the paperwork to gift the house to Alisha, not at all surprised that it would be going to her. I certainly had no desire to move out to the suburbs, so I was happy Grandma didn't ask me to take it.

But I knew about Alisha, who she was, and how Grandma had taken her in after her mother died.

Grandma loved that girl.

I knocked on her apartment door and couldn't have predicted the events that followed. She opened the door wearing nothing but a silk robe, and I could see her nipples poking through the thin fabric. Years later, I remember thinking back to that moment and still feeling a rush of blood straight to my dick. I immediately resisted the urge to pounce on her and instead chastely remembered I was a gentleman, cleared my throat, and looked off in the other direction.

Surprise number two: there was porn playing on the TV behind her, which I figured was the reason it took her so long to answer the door.

I barely heard anything she said after that, but I pointed to the TV, suddenly suffering from cotton mouth and unable to speak clearly. She ran to shut it off, hardly as embarrassed as one might expect her to be, considering the circumstances.

When her robe flew open, I about died.

This woman was insanely gorgeous, practically dripping with sexuality. There was an air of mystery to her, and I was immediately and completely enamored. For the life of me, I couldn't stop staring.

No wonder my grandmother kept me away from her until now.

The swell of her breasts beneath the thin robe quickly caught my attention again; it didn't matter that she had pulled it closed. I already knew what was under there. It was all I could do to look away when I wanted nothing more than to bury my face in her.

But I'm not that kind of guy, even if she was that kind of girl.

Not that it mattered. The next thing I knew I *was* buried inside her, and as crazy as it sounds, I knew she was about to change my life. We may have started things off with nothing more than raw sexual attraction, but she became so much more than that.

I couldn't get enough of her.

A woman with a tragic story was kind of my *thing*. I don't know why; I honestly couldn't have explained it if I tried. But I liked the way I felt with a woman like Alisha. There was something beautiful in the way she had herself convinced she didn't *need* me, even though her body seemed to think otherwise.

Eventually her mind did, too, much to her dismay.

Truth be told, I'd like to say things started off slowly with us, but you and I both know that would make me a liar, and that's one thing I refuse to be anymore. Alisha doesn't do anything slowly, and I really don't think I would have been able to handle it if she had. I was sold from the moment she opened that door.

The woman was sure to be the death of me.

And now that I think about it, I guess she was.

ALL FOR THE NOOKIE

Alisha

THEY SAY murder is a crime of passion, often premeditated. Deliberate. Now, I don't mean to say that *they* are fucking idiots...but *they* are definitely fucking idiots. Sometimes things just *happen*; they're not always premeditated and deliberate. Passion is meant for the bedroom.

I made this comment to my highly sought after attorney, Kyle Lanquist, and he told me to cut the shit. To shut up and stop talking unless I had something case-winning-worthy to share with him.

I didn't.

So, I shut my mouth. I let Kyle talk instead. Apparently, you're not allowed to disagree with statistics when you're on trial for murder.

Silly me.

I'm sure Kyle knows what he's doing. He seems to know his way around a courtroom, and he knows the law better than his own dick, so to a point, I guess I trust him. He *probably* knows his shit, statistically speaking.

But, if there's anyone who understands passion, it's me, and the idea of *passionately* murdering someone seems a little far-fetched. I think of *passion* in sexual terms only. As in, 'he seduced me with passion'. How can the same word be used to describe murder and death? I don't get it, and that's why *they* are fucking idiots. In fact, I passionately disagree with the statement.

See what I did there?

It's currently just after midnight and I'm lying on an uncomfortable mattress, alone in the dark within the confines of my cell. Lights out was a few hours ago, and I've tried desperately to sleep, I really have. But sleep isn't coming, and I doubt that it will tonight.

There's not much to do to pass the time after lights out, and I've already masturbated twice in hopes that my nerves will settle the hell down.

They haven't.

I'm not sure what else to do.

My body needs sleep.

I need to be rested for the first day of my trial tomorrow.

But all I can focus on is my visit with Kyle earlier today. For the hundredth time, we went over my trial strategy. We walked through my statement to the police, the order of events that occurred *that* day. And as usual, the visit dragged on for hours, with just the two of us crammed together in that stale room.

The air was so thick I could smell Kyle's breath when he spoke. He had onions with his lunch, most likely white as they're the most potent, and it seems he couldn't have been bothered to brush his teeth or at the very least chew a piece of gum before hot-boxing me in the interview room.

By the time Kyle finally quit flapping his jaws, I was so frustrated I nearly came on to him. Because, yes, that's how my mind works some-times. Sex is a stress reliever for me so, despite the fact that hot onion breath radiated from his mouth for no less than three hours straight, I couldn't seem to get the idea of sucking Kyle's dick out of my head.

And let me make something clear: Kyle Lanquist is *not* a good looking man by anyone's standards.

But experience—and a long history of adults-only entertainment—proves that sometimes the least attractive of men carry around the greatest packages. How do you think some of these guys made such a career in porn? If I *had* made a move on Kyle, I simply would have adopted the no-kissing policy from *Pretty Woman*. Vivian knew what she was talking about when she penned that one.

I pondered the thought several more times by the end of our meeting, my desperate need for release nearly outweighing all of the obvious turn-offs. Plus, his dick was in close proximity on the other side of the table. It would be so easy to crawl under there and...

Who was I kidding? A CO was stationed outside the steel door, watching us from the 6x6 inch square window. There was probably even a camera.

Maybe he'd want to join in...

I needed to refocus, to clear my mind. Every time my thoughts drifted to something sexual, I did my best to refocus them somewhere else. I tried closing my eyes and just listening.

But Kyle's heavy breathing was all I could hear.

Then there was the blood. The pictures Kyle kept shoving in my face, reminding me of the gruesome scene. Of my husband's mutilated body, the stab wounds, the knife in my hand.

I've never been a fan of blood.

And there was so much of it.

An awful, awful lot.

And the smell...don't get me started on the smell of it. The copper-like aroma lingered in my mouth, on my tongue, for days. I had nearly vomited at the sight of the photos. The pool of crimson soaking into the sheets, my husband's body sprawled haphazardly on our California king bed. The cast-off splatter on the once-gray walls, the streaks on the ceiling.

"Are you with me, Mrs. Thompson?" Kyle asked.

"Yes, I'm sorry," I muttered, shaking my head to clear the cobwebs.

"Good. It's important that we get through this today." He shuffled another set of papers in front of him. Police reports, evidence logs, and stacks of crime scene photos. There was so much to go through.

"Can you put those back in the folder?" I asked, pointing to the 8x10s strewn about the table. "They're making my stomach turn."

"Sure," Kyle agreed. "But as I've said multiple times, these photos will be shown in the courtroom throughout your trial. You really need to get comfortable around them." He stuffed the glossy photos into a manila folder and set it on the far edge of the table.

I crossed my arms over my chest, annoyed by his condescension. "That's pretty fucked up."

"What is?" he asked with a crooked brow.

"That I need to *get comfortable*, as you say, with photos of my dead husband."

Kyle let out an audible sigh. He was used to my outbursts, my random mood swings. Not to say he was any less frustrated than the first time we met. His annoyance was written all over his face. He leaned over and rested his head on his hands, his elbows on the table as he looked over at me incredulously.

"Mrs. Thompson, you're on trial for your husband's murder."

"I realize that, Kyle, but that doesn't make looking at evidence of that fact any easier on me."

Kyle pointed a chubby finger at me and waved it around for dramatic effect. "Drop *that*," he said, waving his finger some more, "... attitude. We can't have that in the courtroom tomorrow."

I glared at him.

Kyle glared back.

We were at an impasse, my attorney and me. I realized right then and there that Kyle was not remotely convinced. My short, balding, thirty-something lawyer with onion breath was simply adhering to the parameters of his job description. His responsibility was to defend me, whether he thought I was innocent or not.

It was evident he did not.

Which meant that I was—yet again—fucked. But this time in the ass with no lube. Not even a thank you card.

I no longer wanted to suck Kyle's dick.

I pull the scratchy blanket up to my chin and try to remember the song my mother used to sing to me when I was a little girl and couldn't sleep. For the life of me, I can't recall the lyrics, but I still hear the melodic sounds of her voice. It soothes me, and I catch myself humming it quietly as I think of her; of her long dark hair, her deep amber eyes and sharp nose peppered with freckles. I can smell her perfume, the way the floral notes mixed with the menthol cigarettes she always smoked.

There was a time, I suppose, when she really did try to be a good mother.

It never lasted. As soon as I was old enough to do simple tasks on my own, Mom always went back to the bottle, she went back to using.

And I went off to kindergarten.

For years I wondered if she ever wished she could go back and do things differently. I never got the chance to ask her, and if I had, I'm not sure I would have. Something tells me I wouldn't have liked her answer.

But that afternoon was the start of it all—the calm before the chaos. After Brandon dropped me off at "home," I walked into Mrs. Maylen's house and let her goldendoodle, Teddy, outside for a quick pee in the backyard. Once he did his business, the two of us went back inside and hung out in the living room until Mrs. Maylen got home from work.

Her house was small and outdated—her husband, Frank, was long gone by then—but was much cleaner than our trailer and, truth be told, sitting in her house doing my homework with Teddy's head resting on my legs was always better than going home to my mom.

If she was even there.

So that's what I did for the next three hours.

Mrs. Maylen had told me on several occasions that I could help myself to the fridge and stay as long I liked, so I did. I think she had a good sense of what went on at my house and wanted to help in some small way. Not that I wanted to be a charity case, but Mrs. Maylen never once made me feel like one. So, I'd grabbed a can of pop from the fridge and made myself a turkey sandwich for dinner. It wasn't like my mother ever cooked for me anyway, and I would have been surprised if there was any edible food in the trailer.

Where things truly went wrong, and what I hadn't anticipated, was that my mother was across the street in our dilapidated, single-wide trailer, passed out on the dirty floor and wheezing through the last breaths she'd ever take. I chomped away on a delicious turkey, cheese, and mayonnaise sandwich while taking notes for my upcoming history test, and petting Teddy on his cute little fluffy head, completely unaware that the alcohol had finally taken my mother.

And because I'd done all of this with my Sony headphones glued to my head at max volume, while Fred Durst sang to me about how he did it all for the nookie, I didn't hear the sirens when the ambulance came and took my mother's lifeless body away. Her Fuck-of-the-Week had the wherewithal to call 9-1-1 when he realized she wasn't breathing, but lacked the basic human decency to stick around and wait for help to arrive.

Paramedics found her on the floor with her face in a puddle of vomit. She was pronounced dead on arrival. Darlene Hill was no longer my last living relative.

And because I didn't have a cell phone and hadn't told anyone where I was, after Mrs. Maylen came home from her nursing shift around nine p.m., I stuffed my homework into my backpack, walked across the street to our empty trailer, and climbed into bed.

The last coherent thought I had before falling asleep that night was *at least Mom isn't home to ruin my good day.*

THE TEN-DAY TRIAL

Alisha

I'LL NEVER MEET another man quite like Dylan Thompson. He was charming, in that I'm-kind-of-secretly-an-asshole way, but it worked for him. Because deep down, he wasn't an asshole at all. On the surface, he had a mama's boy look to him, but he was quick with the one-liners and one hell of a handyman around the house. He was caring and nurturing, but mostly, Dylan was a genuine soul. A beautiful mind, fused with a beautiful person.

He was also a god in the bedroom. We fucked every day—although Dylan preferred the term *made love*, but whatever. Truth is, I was impressed with Dylan's ability to keep up with me, to find ways to keep me just as satisfied physically as he did emotionally. No man before him had ever accomplished that—or even tried—not that there were many I let stick around for more than a couple times around the bases.

Dylan was rare in that regard.

I had become a quick fan of Tinder just before meeting Dylan. The dating app had simplified my hookup routine, and I had several dates on the calendar for that week. But Dylan asked me not to go, to cancel the dates, and shut down my profile entirely.

I laughed.

There was no way the man was serious. No way in hell.

Oh, but he was.

That probably makes him sound creepy, huh? Maybe a little… possessive? Yes, I can see how you might think that about him. But Dylan wasn't possessive at all. He wasn't creepy in the way you might think and didn't harbor any of the qualities of an ax-wielding murderer.

Maybe on paper, but not in the flesh.

It took me a little while to understand him. To see his love for what it was, and not what society and every horror movie plot deemed it to be.

Dylan was a simple man who proudly wore his heart on his sleeve. He trusted his gut, his intuition—which, let's be honest, got him killed in the end—and had no problem expressing his feelings. Somehow, he was even smart enough to know that the way to my heart wouldn't be an easy path, that it would require an intense amount of sex—trust me, it's not always a man's wet dream to hear that; it's a lot of pressure to burden them with—and the ability to put up with my mood swings.

But he was in it.

He wanted a chance to play his hand.

After canceling my Tinder date for the evening, I agreed to let Dylan hold me hostage in my own apartment for the next ten days.

"Give me ten days to win you over, and if you can honestly say you don't love me after ten days, I'll drag my ass through that door and never come back," he had said, pointing at the door. "I promise."

I agreed on one condition: that he put out at least twice a day, every day, throughout the ten-day trial period. You'd think I'd have thrown in something like, "and don't murder me with a chainsaw" or some shit like that, but apparently the only fear I had in that moment was that he wouldn't be able to keep up with my sex drive. He agreed without hesitation, and, just like that, I no longer required the services of my Tinder suiters.

I let them down as gently as I could, but the dick pics kept coming, filling my inbox with promises of pleasure and a generally good time. Any woman who's ever created a profile on a dating site knows what I'm talking about here. But Dylan and I managed to make a game of it, and some nights we would sit for hours looking closely at all the dick pics together, rating each of the packages. We even developed a scoring system—complete with color-coded charts—and printed the pictures out on heavy-duty card stock, taping them up on the wall above the couch. We ate delivery pizza while staring at fully erect penises and drinking black cherry pop until we declared one of them the Top Notch Dick.

Dylan even drew a crown on the winner's tip.

In retrospect, it helped that Dylan didn't seem to have a jealous bone in his body—a weight off my shoulders considering my profession, which he accepted with little concern. He liked that I didn't work more than a few nights a week, and my customers weren't the only ones that got off at the sight of my performance. Eventually Dylan even took to watching from across the room, off-camera but in perfect view from my perspective, sometimes with his dick in his hand.

I expected him to run by the fourth day.

But he stayed.

He kissed my forehead as I slept in his arms, and even helped with dishes after we cooked our first meal together.

By the eighth day, we seemed to have settled into a domesticated routine. It was confusing, but surprisingly comfortable, and I didn't know what to make of it. I couldn't believe I wasn't sick of him yet.

On the morning of the tenth day, Dylan worked from his laptop in my living room, preparing closing documents for a buyer while I watched my robot vacuum, Dustin Timberlake, clean the floors so I didn't have to. When he finally signed off and closed his laptop, he extended a hand to me and pulled me from the couch. Wrapping his arms around me, he kissed the tip of my nose and led me to the bathroom to join him for a shower.

We lathered and cleaned each other's bodies, and as soon as the last of the suds were washed away, he pushed me up against the wall and rubbed his growing erection against my backside. It had become a daily game for us, teasing each other until one of us couldn't take it anymore. And while I usually won our little torturous game, the thought that Dylan would probably be out of my life by the end of the day was enough to make me whimper in anticipation, my body begging to be taken by him.

I needed him.

He reached around, rubbing between my legs, quickly finding my clit and swirling a finger over the sensitive bud. With my tits pressed against the cold tile, I arched my back and he slid into me, claiming me from behind with slow, purposeful movements. I nearly cried out, but for the first time in my sexual history, I stifled my verbal approval.

I didn't want him to know how much my body needed him.

We moved together, instinctively building momentum, and suddenly nothing else mattered.

"Don't let this be the last time," he whispered in my ear, pumping harder and finding release quickly. He pulled out suddenly, groaning as I turned and dropped to my knees in front him, catching his load on my chest.

"My God, Alisha…" he mumbled through labored breath.

I licked the tip of his cock and stood to face him, kissing him deeply. "Let's move in together," he said with his lips still pressed to mine.

"Are you serious?" I asked, the shock surely written across my face.

"As a heart attack." He smiled deliciously, his mouth curving into a toothy grin, palm cupping my cheek. "I love you, Alisha. I have since the first day I met you, and I can't lose you."

"Yes," I blurted, the simple word taking me by surprise as it dropped from my mouth.

"Yes? As in…" He raised his brow.

"As in, yes, we should move in together," I confirmed. I searched his eyes for a tell that he wasn't serious, that he was merely acting on impulse and didn't actually want to live with me. But I saw nothing other than happiness in those eyes.

"And?" he coached.

"And, I love that we'll be able to do *this* every day," I said, wrapping my fingers around his length again. He pouted and his eyes crinkled; all I could do was look away.

Wrong answer.

"*Really?*" He huffed, pulling away and standing under the stream of water flowing from the shower head. I enfolded my arms around him and lured him back to me, not wanting to hurt him or let him believe for any reason that I didn't want this.

I can't lose you, either.

"I'm sorry, it's just that...*that*...is hard for me to say," I whispered.

"Then fucking nod or *something*," he snapped, frustration getting the best of him. "I need to know you love me back," he pleaded, his eyes searching mine. "This won't work if you don't feel the same. You know that, right?"

"I show you how I feel every day," I teased, running my hands down the muscles on his chest.

"This isn't about sex."

I sighed.

"Fine. I luh you," I mumbled, averting my eyes.

"You can do better than that..." he coaxed, his fingers trailing down my stomach. Softly and slowly, they worked their way inside me, his thumb flicking my clit, and I whimpered again, nearly buckling at the knees.

"Say it," he commanded. I steadied an arm against the slippery tile, my reserve dwindling with each flick of his thumb.

"I..."

He lowered his head, his tongue grazing my nipple as his thumb continued its reign of torture. "Love...yousofuckingmuch!" I cried out, my orgasm hitting me hard. Dylan's lips crashed down on mine, and it was everything.

Everything I never had.

Everything I never knew I wanted.

"That's my girl." He held me in his arms, under the water, where I cried silently against his chest, grateful for the mask it provided for my tears.

Like the Grinch, my heart swelled to three times its size that day.

No one had ever told me they loved me.

WHERE'D YA GIT THEM JEANS?

Alisha

"*ALISHA!*" *my mother's raspy voice yelled. I pushed my tenth-grade math books aside and climbed out of bed, turning down the hallway toward the living room. She was splayed across the torn couch, smoking a cigarette, the ash hanging off the end and about to fall onto her lap. Her dark hair was greasy, and the makeup from two nights earlier was still caked on her face.*

"*There's my girl," she slurred, a lazy smile stretching across her prematurely-wrinkled face. "Be a doll and grab your mother a beer, would ya?"*

"*Sure," I mumbled, crossing my arms and making my way to the kitchen, where a pungent odor loitered in the air. I glanced at the sink to find it stacked with plates caked in rotting food and several drinking glasses with curdled milk at the bottom.*

I had stayed at Mrs. Maylen's just about every evening after school that week, not returning home until after we shared a glass of milk and one of her famous oatmeal raisin cookies.

She never sent me home with an empty stomach.

Mom's crackhead friends had been in and out of the trailer, as if we had a revolving front door I didn't know about. I'd watched them come and go from across the street, knowing full well that whatever was going on inside was nothing I wanted to be a part of. Aside from the drugs, I wasn't naive enough to think my mother's male friends hadn't noticed me.

It was only a matter of time before one of them tried something. I did what I could to steer clear of them.

"Whatchya diddle daddlin' for?" Mom barked. I rolled my eyes, opened the fridge and snatched a generic beer from the otherwise bare shelf.

"Here," I said, handing the can to her. I pivoted as she grabbed my arm at the wrist, her bony hand cold against my skin.

"Where'd you git them jeans?"

I couldn't tell my mother that I had bought my jeans at Walmart with my own money. I'd outgrown most of my clothes in the last year, but I knew she would never waste her "hard earned" money on new clothes for me. She didn't even know that Mrs. Maylen was paying me to watch her dog, and if she had, she would've expected me to hand her the cash in exchange for room and board or some stupid shit like that.

As if it wasn't her job to provide food, clothing, and shelter for me.

"I borrowed them from Sara," I said nonchalantly, thinking on the spot with a shrug of my shoulders.

"Who's Sara?"

"Just a friend from school." I freed my arm from her grasp and gestured toward the kitchen, making sure to offer up a half-cocked smile to appease her. "I'm going to do the dishes. Do you need anything else?"

Mom's bloodshot eyes shot back at me. She studied me again, focusing in on my jeans before cracking open the beer and taking a long sip. She settled the can on the rickety coffee table and let out a loud belch.

"Nope. Don't need nuthin' else," she slurred.

"Okay," I mumbled. I turned on my heel and went back to the sink, wishing I had a bandanna so I could cover my nose and mouth to rid my senses of the rotten odors that awaited me in that kitchen. Instead, I swallowed my wishful thinking and sighed, pulling my T-shirt over my nose and getting to work.

The next morning I took a freezing cold shower, thanks to a busted water heater that we couldn't afford to fix, and then tiptoed across the hall to my bedroom, careful to be extra quiet and not wake my mom. I was hoping to slip out for school without running into her at all.

I closed my bedroom door, locking it behind me and dropping my towel. Shivering, my arms and legs suddenly riddled with goosebumps, I quickly stepped into a fresh pair of underwear before pulling a sports bra over my head and stuffing my boobs into it as best as I could. Like everything else, the bra was too small, but it was clean. I made a mental note to bring a load of laundry with me to Mrs. Maylen's after school; she never minded when I used her machines, and it sure beat dragging a garbage bag full of clothes to the laundromat.

When my boobs were finally tucked away, I reached for my new jeans, but instead of the familiar denim I expected, my fingers squished into something sticky.

The smell of fresh shit snaked into my nostrils.

I jumped to the other side of the room and flicked the light switch, holding my sticky hand out in front of me to inspect it. A brown goo was smeared between my fingers and underneath my freshly polished fingernails. I scooped my towel up from the floor and used it to wipe off my hand, realizing without a doubt that the substance in question was, in fact, human feces.

I peered down at the jeans at the end of my bed and noticed they were smeared with brown streaks, too.

My mother had taken a shit on my brand-new jeans.

SUDDENLY FEELING STUPID

Dylan

I GREW up in a decently-happy home—or homes, I should say, considering I split my time between two households—raised by divorced parents who after some-odd years apart, managed to co-parent decently together. I don't remember my parents ever fighting. Eventually, they both re-married. Dad and his wife moved out to Arizona, and I visited a couple times a year. Living with Mom full time was a bit much, I'll admit, considering that her new husband, Jim, brought along a son of his own—my stepbrother Sawyer. Once we got over the initial stepsibling bullshit, we were close for a bit, as teens and even as young adults.

Until we weren't.

Nonetheless, in retrospect, life was—dare I say it—fairly easy for me. I played on the varsity baseball team in high school, got good grades, and even had a long-term girlfriend—until I didn't. Other than getting my heart broken by a girl, I never experienced anything close to the horrors Alisha faced growing up.

They say opposites attract, so I guess it made sense that we were made for one another. My only complaint was the fact that it took so long for us to find each other.

She completed me, just as I did her. Sorry for the *Jerry McGuire* reference there; I didn't even like that movie, but the line seemed fitting. I went off to college the fall after high school, and after graduating *summa cum laude* from the University of St. Thomas, I decided to stay in the Twin Cities.

Never once did I imagine I'd be living in a small suburban town like Buffalo, Minnesota. But that's where I ended up after meeting Alisha. I loved the hustle and bustle of Minneapolis, the skyline, the expansive floor-to-ceiling windows in my condo that overlooked the Mississippi River.

But Alisha hated it.

"Too many people," she'd said. She preferred the quiet of the smaller town, the privacy of our fenced-in backyard, the ability to see the stars clearly at night. Most of all, she loved the memories of my grandmother's house, and it was that admission that had me shoving my belongings into boxes and hiring a moving company less than two weeks into our relationship. Alisha closed on my grandmother's house, and I put the condo on the market.

And never once did I regret that decision.

When Alisha agreed to marry me I told her I'd move anywhere for her. Nothing else mattered, and with my job as a freelance Realtor I had the luxury of working anywhere. My condo sold quickly—well over the asking price—and I moved into my grandmother's house to be with my soulmate.

Admittedly, the house was several steps down in terms of luxury and modernization, but Alisha had plans to renovate, to bring the home up to standard with an expansive new kitchen and dining room, an open concept into the living room, and an en suite master bathroom fit for a B-List celebrity. She put her HGTV-inspired design skills to work and singlehandedly re-purposed a home filled with character.

We married only three weeks later, in a private ceremony at the nursing home, in front of my mother and stepfather—who weren't exactly in support of the marriage. I still wasn't speaking to my step-brother, which my mother, of course, had thoughts about, but somehow managed to keep to herself. My grandmother was Alisha's maid of honor, alongside her friend, Chris, who I was growing fonder of each day. She had no one else, she had said. The thought was unnerving, but I intended to change that for her down the road.

She had only four contacts saved in her cell phone; me, my grand-mother, Chris, and her hairdresser. She was adamant that no other numbers were worth saving, and the ones she didn't have could be found through a simple Google search.

Sometimes I envied my wife's simplicity.

But I accepted her as is; my new wife was a loner, happy on her own and nearly void of friends or family. The irony always intrigued me, but it was evident she did her best to keep people at bay, and I couldn't blame her.

"It's far better to be unhappy alone than unhappy with someone," she'd told me the night of our wedding, quoting the iconic Marilyn Monroe.

"What does that mean?" I asked, suddenly feeling stupid. It was such a simple saying, a generic concept really, yet I had a hard time comprehending it. What did I know? I was a popular jock in high school, and well liked in a decent-sized circle of friends, even as an adult. Although, if I'm being honest, that circle shrunk significantly during my years with Alisha. The nature of the beast, I suppose.

My new wife simply shrugged—as if the topic was fit for noncha-lance—and continued. "Other people make me feel lonely," she admitted sheepishly. "They're just *there*, taking up space, but not really present."

I nodded as if I understood, but I didn't, not really. All I knew was that I never wanted my wife to feel lonely again.

"Do you feel lonely right now?" I asked, pulling her close. She smiled and brought her lips to mine, stopping just before we touched, her minty breath warm on my face. She was good at that—at giving me just enough to keep me wanting more.

She had this devil-like grin that sucked me in every time; a spark in her eyes. "No," she said, smiling. And our mouths molded together, our lives officially intertwined, my wife and me.

Perhaps it was destiny, who knows?

Nonetheless, little by little I learned more about her past. About her childhood and the incompetent mother who raised her. About the father she never knew, the man she had never met. Grandma hadn't mentioned how bad things were for her before she'd taken her in, but I knew enough to know enough.

And all of that, everything I learned over time, only made me love her more.

She had my heart—all of it.

Until the very end.

DECEIT'S FAVORITE ROLE

Alisha

FRIENDS ARE a rare commodity in my world. I've never had many, aside from Dylan and Mrs. Maylen. And Chris, but we'll get to him later. Everyone at school hated me—unless they were involved with me sexually, of course, and even then they often ended up hating me in the end—and I found that being alone was simply easier. There was no one to let me down, no one to judge me or drone on about the dramas of their life. No one to lie, cheat, beg, borrow, or steal.

When you grow up with a mother like mine, the silence can be comforting. I guess that kind of stuck with me.

Kyle suspects my lack of friends will be an issue of concern during the trial; there really isn't anyone left to speak on behalf of my character—not positively, anyway. Personally, I think that's bullshit, but my opinion rarely seems to matter. How is it my fault that women have always hated me? And men? Well, they only hate me when their wives are around.

So, naturally, when the story of my husband's murder hit the local news I was the first and only suspect the media honed in on, thanks in part to my perpetual loner status, coupled with the fact that the spouse is *almost* always to blame.

Plus, my alibi was horse shit.

Channel 5 News pounced first. Their overly made-up, camera-ready reporter was outside on my lawn with her news crew before I was even arrested. It didn't matter that they had yet to establish a narrative—they heard murder and came running. Public speculation was sure to do the rest of the work for them.

Let the pieces fall where they may.

Alisha Thompson, the wife of Dylan Thompson, a Buffalo, Minnesota man who was found stabbed to death in their home this morning, looks to be the prime suspect in his brutal murder.

Of course, I *was* alone during the window of opportunity, off on my morning run along Griffing Park Road. Other than a nosy neighbor who happened to peer out her kitchen window as she guzzled her morning coffee in her slippers and fuzzy bathrobe, there wasn't a single person to corroborate my story. It didn't help that I headed out for my run nearly two hours earlier than usual since I was having trouble sleeping, on account of the argument we'd had the night before.

Police say neighbors of the couple reported that thirty-year-old Alisha Thompson was seen leaving the home during the very early hours of the morning, just before five o'clock. She was described as "distraught" and one witness suggested she appeared to be "on a mission".

The house was suffocating me.

Every corner of every room was a reminder of what I'd lost. I needed to get out, to inhale fresh air into my lungs, to feel the ground at my feet. I climbed out of bed, slipped into my yoga pants and sports bra and slid my feet into my running shoes. Downstairs I stopped in the kitchen for a bottle of water, and scribbled a note to my husband—who I'd abandoned in the bed that I'd just crawled out of.

The note was just in case.

Admittedly, my choice of words, what I wrote on the back of that grocery receipt, weren't ideal. I suppose I could have written something more likely to have come from a loving wife.

It wouldn't have killed you to tell the truth.

Those are the words I chose to leave behind. The message I felt necessary to jot down on a wrinkled receipt before taking off for a run to clear my head.

I was angry.

Dylan was angry.

Our fight had been monstrous.

The note—found in our trash bin—was confiscated by investigators for evidence, and would be used against me in a court of law.

My iPhone was left behind to charge on the kitchen counter.

There was no record of my whereabouts that morning, even though the GPS tracking app Dylan had installed on it would have otherwise provided law enforcement with significantly useful information.

By my estimation, I was out of the house no longer than thirty minutes.

Thompson, former host of the popular adult streaming website LishasBedroom.com, has no other social media presence, and sources from Mr. Thompson's immediate family say she has been a quote, "thorn in their side", since the day she and Mr. Thompson met. They say she has no friends, that she takes pleasure in embarrassing them with her profession, and that Mr. Thompson was completely infatuated with her.

The general population had a hard time accepting the fact that any sane person would choose to work in my profession, a career entirely based on looks, sexual fantasies, and what they consider "deviant" behavior. I mean, why focus elsewhere when the sex-obsessed, friendless wife of the victim fits the mold *so* well?

Viewers ate that shit up—the media's notion of a jealous lover, a lonely wife. Vindication. It sure made for good TV. Hell, even I would have watched it.

To make matters worse, the most damning piece of evidence in the prosecution's arsenal is the fact that I was standing right there, in the middle of the crime scene, wielding what would later be confirmed to be the murder weapon, when the police busted through the door.

A chef's knife taken from the woodblock in the very kitchen I stood in earlier that morning.

With a gun pointed at my chest, an officer coerced the knife from my trembling hands as blood dripped from it onto the carpet.

I stood, frozen in place, unable to move or speak, staring down at my husband's mutilated body, at the seventeen stab wounds, still fresh, in his chest.

Because of me.

Neighbors also reported hearing screams coming from the Thompson family home that morning. They heard yelling in the late hours of the night, a common occurrence from the Thompson household, they said.

What the media failed to understand, and subsequently gave zero fucks about, is that sometimes people scream when they're frustrated. They fight and argue when they're scared and in need of someone to blame, because that's the only way they get through it. Sometimes it's the only immediate relief for those endorphins so they don't suffocate from within.

So, yes, I screamed.

Because I was angry.

My husband had just confessed a devastating secret.

Mrs. Thompson has declined to comment. We'll have more on this developing story. For now, I'm Lexy Dawson, reporting for Channel 5 News.

I like to eat my meals alone these days, as with any other activity in lockup. Sometimes the other women like to fuck with me—they'll cat call or grope me when I walk by. But most days they leave me alone since I don't play into their childish games.

As difficult as it is to refrain, I'm trying here.

Kyle says a clean record in lockup could lead to lesser sentencing.

Today, however, it seems I've made an accidental friend, a confidant, if there is such a thing in prison.

"So, did ya do it?" Tiffany asks. She winks and offers a coy smile as she shoves a plastic fork full of tasteless scrambled eggs down her gullet. She's beautiful, like me, only in a completely different way. Her blonde hair is chopped to her shoulders, her eyes an amber tone I haven't seen on many women. When she lifts her fork I notice the scars on her forearms, alongside a shitty tattoo of the word, *overcome*.

"No," I say, meeting her eyes.

"That's what they all say." She laughs. It's soft, almost pretty, but also mocking in a way. It pisses me off.

"Did *you* do it?" I snap.

"Yep."

I stop chewing and watch her face. She's stoic and doesn't blink as she dares me to challenge her further. I'm not at all familiar with her case, but I believe her, based on the creepy ass look in her eyes. I don't doubt for a second that Tiffany is capable of murder.

I also don't doubt that this woman is proud of whatever she's done. And I can't help myself, I want to know what she did. I *need* to know.

"Why?" I ask, and she shrugs like all I've asked her is what she wants for dinner.

"He deserved it."

I don't say anything, just spoon another bite into my mouth and wait for her to continue. It's silent as we chew, each waiting for the other to speak.

She caves first.

"Bastard liked to put his hands on me," she says. Her tone hushed, like she enjoys the mystery of it, and doesn't want anyone else to hear her confession.

"That seems to be a common theme in here."

"It's a common theme everywhere, gorgeous." She tucks a strand of stringy hair behind her ear, and I notice another small scar just above her earlobe. "Most of us are just too fucking chicken shit to do anything about it."

"If he was abusive, then what are you doing in here? Wouldn't killing him fall under self defense?"

"Sure," she shrugs. "*If* he had been the aggressor the night I killed him." She wants me to ask, and I swear I'm not going to, but I have to know, so I do.

"I'm not following." I sit back in my chair and cross my arms over my chest.

She sighs and rolls her eyes, as if she's annoyed I haven't figured it out yet. She's not.

"It was premeditated," she says. "I planned it. Thought about it for months, really." I don't engage further, just continue watching her.

Her shoulders slump, and she leans over the table, her breasts dipping into her plate of eggs. "I couldn't take the abuse anymore and knew he'd never give me a divorce. He'd never let me leave him. So, I went out and bought a gun, and then I waited for him to come home from work. Shot him when he pulled into the garage, and then went back to boiling noodles for my manicotti. I knew it'd be my last supper." She pauses for effect and then shakes her head in disbelief, staring down at her plate and pushing the food around like it had done something to piss her off. "It's a shame; I was a damn good cook."

We sit in silence again, each of us eyeballing the other. I'm not sure if she's playing me, but in that moment I choose to believe her.

"Was it worth it?" I ask.

"Yep." She picks up her tray and stands before leaning down and speaking into my ear. "A friendly word of advice? Stop claiming your innocence in here. Whether you did it or not doesn't matter. You're already here, mixed in with a group of murderers and sociopaths. Saying you *didn't* do it only makes you look weak. It puts a target on your back. So either start lying or go fucking kill someone and earn your stripes."

She straightens and turns on her heel, and I watch her walk away. I smile as she looks over her shoulder and winks, the realization that she's just fed me a delicious line of bullshit sinks in.

"Deceit's favorite role is that of the victim," I say to no one but myself.

SIMPLY HER

Dylan

I WASN'T PERFECT, okay?

Everyone kind of has their *thing*. Their guilty pleasure, the one secret they keep from everyone else, be it from embarrassment, shame, or otherwise. I was big on not keeping secrets from Alisha. I wanted her to be honest with me—even if the truth was difficult to hear—and in return, I vowed to do the same for her.

Only I didn't.

I'd been lying to her since the day I met her. Because once I met her, little to nothing else mattered more than keeping her. I no longer cared about money—although, between the two of us, we had plenty of it—or my family, my friends. Not even my career—not that it suffered, really. I just worked less.

I had my woman, the one with whom I'd spend the rest of my life, and I cared less and less about everything else. That's probably where I went wrong.

That's probably where things began to fall apart for me.

I stopped questioning things. I stopped sleeping with my eyes open, and instead, with her in my arms, reveled in the smell of her shampoo and the sensation of running my fingers up and down her toned arms. The soft skin that lined them was a newfound addiction for me.

I missed all the signs.

Every damn one of them.

Because the only thing in my line of sight was her. Did I regret it in the end? Did I beg to go back and do it all over again, to do it all differently?

Nope.

Not even for a second.

I didn't even regret the lies.

But despite Alisha's profession, despite her utter beauty and near-genius mind, my lovely wife lacked confidence. She truly had no idea how amazing she was; she didn't know her worth. I guess that's what a childhood full of bullshit and let-downs will do to a person. I worked tirelessly to prove that she was more than deserving of love. To prove she was worthy of every single thing this world had to offer.

I wooed her, even though I didn't have to.

I took her out on dates, showed her around Minneapolis, introduced her to new and expensive cuisines, because even after she grew her wealth, she still ate TV dinners and takeout and frozen lasagnas. She hated to cook. I bought her nice clothes, even though she didn't need them and clearly could have afforded them herself. I took her to get her hair done, her nails. She loved it. She had never been pampered before, and it wasn't like anyone had ever taught her these things—she didn't know what she had been missing.

And I loved being the one to show her that side of life, the joy of being taken care of. I'm sure you think I'm crazy, that I'd lost my damn mind, right? Meh. That's fine. Really. It's not like it changes anything. But I get it, I do.

Who would give up everything for a woman like that?

Me, that's who.

If you'd met her, you'd understand. She was a majestic creature you couldn't look away from him. A goddess. But my infatuation with

Alisha stemmed from so much more than sex, I promise. I'm sure you think that's a complete line of bullshit—it's really not. *I* had a hard time keeping up with *her*, so trust me, it wasn't the sex that had me wrapped around her finger. It wasn't even her strikingly beautiful face and her better-than-super-model body, either.

It was simply *her*.

And let me tell ya, if you don't know what I mean then you better question whether or not you really love your significant other. Truly. Because if you did, you'd understand exactly what I'm talking about.

You'd get it.

You'd have told the lie, too.

You won't learn all that much about me when all is said and done, because I assure you, I existed for the sole purpose of loving Alisha Thompson.

And that's what I did—until the day I died.

PSYCHO-BABBLE BULLSHIT

Alisha

MY MOTHER HAD a way with words. She was the best at spewing them, even when they made no sense in the order she chose to spit them out. She was, after all, always drunk or high or both, and only present when she wanted to be—or when her unemployment funds dried up and she couldn't even afford a pack of smokes. So, when I say my mother had a way with words, it wasn't that she was *good* with them; she simply used a lot of them.

They made good weapons.

Her favorite thing to do was degrade me, to rant about how ugly I was, how incompetent and useless I had become. As a kid, and even as an adult, these words haunted me. But at that age, as a teen, I didn't know if they were true or not; I hadn't yet tested their validity in the real world. Instead, I learned to take each spiteful word with a grain of salt and eventually realized her love of putting me down stemmed from nothing less than jealousy.

She wanted what I had.

What substance abuse had taken from her.

"I swear, you're the ugliest girl on the planet, Alisha," she once said, waving her arm around as if to demonstrate the entire planet she was referring to. I hadn't said a word to initiate the conversation; she simply blurted it out during a commercial break. *Roseanne* was no longer entertaining her, so it was time to harass me instead. I looked up from the book I was reading and debated whether or not to engage. Sometimes saying nothing is the best response to criticism.

She chugged from her beer, emptying the can and tossing it across the living room.

"Whatcha readin' for, anyway? S'not gonna make ya any prettier." She laughed at my expense, pleased with herself as if what she'd said were actually funny.

"It's for English class," I said, paying her little attention.

"Don'tcha know men prefer skinny girls? None a them'r gonna want a curvy girl like you."

"Okay." I went back to reading and considered leaving the room. I knew it wouldn't help, though. It would only instigate the situation further. She'd follow me and then lash out for disrespecting her and walking away while she was talking to me. As if respect was a word in her vocabulary.

Best to wait for the show to come back on. Then she'll forget about me.

"Git me another beer, will ya?" she asked. I marked the page in my book and got up from the frayed recliner, making my way to the kitchen. The fridge was empty, save for a half-eaten box of pizza, the beer gone.

"You're all out."

"Don't fuck with me child," she barked, sticking another cancer stick in her mouth and lighting the tip with a match. She inhaled and then withdrew the cigarette from her lips, holding it between her fingers, the smoke like fog floating around her lips as she spoke. "Well, don't jus' stand there. Go out and git some more."

"I don't have any money."

"Fuck, child, neither do I. Find some. Go sell that ridiculously curvy body of yours on the street corner or sumthin'. See if it's worth anything."

I was fourteen years old and stared at my mother blankly, trying to convince myself that she hadn't just encouraged me to sell my underage body on the street corner.

But she had.

And not for the first time.

I didn't know what to do. I wasn't old enough to buy beer even if I had the cash, but getting out of there for the night was the only thing on my mind. So, I grabbed my coat and book bag and went across the street to Mrs. Maylen's house, where I stayed for the next six days.

My mother never once checked in on me.

Mrs. Maylen took me in after my mother's overdose.

Sometimes I have a hard time understanding why she did it, but most days I'm nothing but grateful. Her own daughter had been out of the house for years, already with a family of her own and a couple kids. She said she could use the company. I had no other living relatives that I knew of—I've never met my father, and my mother always claimed she didn't know his last name so he wasn't even listed on my birth certificate. CPS didn't take issue when Mrs. Maylen offered to foster me, and I was able to move in with her right away.

It was confusing at first, having someone who cared about me. The first weekend I stayed with her, she took off a couple shifts at the hospital and helped me clean out Mom's trailer—most of which we donated or tossed in the shared dumpster—and together we packed up my bedroom. I moved across the street with little more than three small boxes. She said she didn't want me to become another orphan lost in the system just because no one wanted to foster a seventeen-year-old girl.

If I were a Southerner, this is where I'd insert the sympathetic, "bless her heart."

That also meant she expected me to go to college. I did well in school and ended up earning a full ride to St. Cloud State, which is the only reason I was able to attend college at all. My mother had left nothing behind. No life insurance, no savings. Just a rundown trailer full of ratty furniture and overflowing ashtrays.

It still amazes me how a proper parental figure can change the entire course of a person's life. For the first time ever, I had a curfew. Dinner was on the table every single night, and most nights I even helped cook. I had to ask permission to make plans, and Mrs. Maylen had to approve of them. A typical teenager and newly orphaned child likely would have rebelled at such structure, but I reveled in it.

Somebody finally cared about me enough to worry. Enough to put rules in place that kept my ass parked on the couch doing my homework instead of out on the streets experimenting with the very drugs that made me an orphan in the first place.

I didn't cry when I learned that my mother was dead. The tears never came; I didn't need them.

I wasn't sad.

I hadn't loved my mother since the day she sent me off to kindergarten and didn't pick me up because she was passed out on our living room couch. I knew, even then, that love is a two-way street, and she was driving down a one-way road.

My teacher, Mrs. Ronzon, had given me a ride home when five o'clock ticked by and she still hadn't shown. I'll never forget the look on her face when we pulled up to the trailer.

"Would you like me to walk you to the door? Do you have a key?" she asked, tentatively shifting the car into park.

"No, thank you," I said quietly, shaking my head. "We don't lock the door."

"I'll wait here to make sure you get inside, okay?"

I nodded and removed my seatbelt. "Thanks, Mrs. R."

I got out of the car and jogged excitedly to the front door, as if I were thrilled to finally be home. Mrs. R didn't need to know that I wasn't. A foul smell instantly smacked me in the face, and I spotted my mother passed out on the couch. She was sprawled on her stomach, her left arm hanging heavily over the edge and a spent cigarette in the ashtray, burned down to the filter.

I pasted a smile on my face and turned back to Mrs. R, giving her a thumbs up. I could see her sigh with relief when she placed her hand over her heart and waved goodbye before backing out of the driveway.

These days, a situation like that would've sent me straight to foster care.

Kristin and I spoke about my mother often. She was adamant my mom was the source of my detachment issues—and in hindsight, sure, she probably was. Any idiot could make that assumption. But it was Kristin's roundabout way of getting there that irked me.

"Do you feel emotion, Alisha?" she asked, her chin tilted. We were forty minutes into our session, focused only on the topic of my mother, and she'd just finished a spiel on nature versus nurture, of which I wasn't entirely sure which side of the proverbial fence we'd landed on.

"What kind of question is that?"

"Humor me. Do you *feel?*"

"Of course."

"Show me." She waved her hand, as if doing so offered some insight as to what the hell she wanted me to say.

"What do you mean?"

"Show me happy," she said, nonchalant, as if I were an actress auditioning for a play. I suppose I was a performer of sorts, considering my profession. Yet, I stared at her blankly, as I often did, and tried to anticipate where the line of questioning was going. "What makes you happy?"

"I don't know."

"There has to be something"

"Sex."

"Okay, how about sadness? Do you ever cry?"

"No."

"Do you get sad?"

"Not really."

"How do you feel right now?"

"Annoyed."

"That's fair. Do you feel angry?"

"Not really."

"Hmm…" She started writing on her legal pad. The room was silent for a few minutes while she scribbled her psycho-babble bullshit onto the page. "When was the last time you remember feeling angry?"

My face contorted, and I pretended to ponder the question. Anger wasn't necessarily my thing, despite my upbringing. I'm fairly certain one has to feel some sort of connection to something, or someone, in order to feel anger, and for the most part, I cared little about anything.

That cord had been disconnected a long time ago.

"When my mother forgot to pick me up from school on the first day of kindergarten."

"That was the *last* time you felt angry about something?"

"Probably," I said, shrugging my shoulders.

She looked at me in disbelief and then returned to her notes, her head lowered for several minutes. I cleared my throat after five minutes passed without a word. The silence was becoming awkward.

"I think that'll be it for today," she said, looking up at me and removing her reading glasses.

"We still have fifteen minutes…" I reminded her. Not that I wanted to stay, but she'd never once ended a session early, and I didn't know what to make of it.

"You did well today, Alisha." She stood and placed her notebook and pen on the desk, motioning to the door.

I left that day never understanding what made her end the session so abruptly. The following week I was preoccupied with my husband's murder.

I haven't seen Kristin since.

FESTERING BENEATH THE SURFACE

Alisha

I TALK TO HIM.

Dylan.

Sometimes it's like he's right beside me, like he's here with me. I feel the warmth of his lips against my skin, his fingers trailing my body. I don't know how or why it happens, but I cherish these premonitions, these unexpected visits from him.

I long to hear his voice, to undo what I've done. I would write to him in a journal if I didn't think it'd be used against me as evidence. I don't trust that it won't fall into the wrong hands. So, the one-sided conversation resides in my head, never to be repeated. Never to be misconstrued for something it's not.

I miss you, and I don't know what to do with that. You come to me in my dreams at night, and you're as beautiful as ever. I hold you, because I know one of these times it will be for the last time. Why did you have to break us?

I'd give anything to breathe you in, to inhale the scents of you—

your skin, your hair, your breath. I'd taste your lips, your cock. My body needs you in ways I can't explain.

It's not fair, what I've done to you. What you've done to us.

But life never is, is it, baby?

Ironically, it was my mother who taught me that, and I'm ashamed to admit I caught myself missing her the other day, too. I wasn't sure what to make of it. But I craved her honesty for reasons I can't explain. I needed her raw sense of truth.

She came to me in a dream, too—much like Dylan often does. She was the version of herself that didn't suck, before all the drugs. Before the drinking and uninvited house guests. I was a little girl, only four, and she sang to me as I drifted to sleep, running her fingers through my hair, my head in her lap. She was sober, and still beautiful in the intoxicating way she once was. Some would say I look like her in pictures. How she looked before she was no longer beautiful.

"Don't get too used to this," she says quietly.

"Why not?" I ask, looking up at her, my voice tiny and full of wonder.

"It never lasts, sweetheart."

I lay my head back on her lap, a sigh escaping my lips.

Mother always knew best, even when she didn't.

———

"Thompson, you have a visitor," CO Marin barks, stepping into my unlocked cell. Kyle didn't mention coming by today, so her announcement startles me.

"Who?"

"Dunno," she says. "Get dressed, let's go."

I pause for a moment, the idea of an unexpected visitor leaving a sour taste in my mouth. "If it's not my lawyer, I'm not interested."

CO Marin gives me a hard look, visibly debating whether to force me down to the visitor's parlor, and I stare back, unintimidated by her posturing. She sighs and stomps off, and I almost feel bad at the thought that my visitor—whoever they are—has inconvenienced her or any of the other staff here. They would have had to run them through the security screening, and I hear they're pretty swamped down there. I'm not out to piss anybody off, but I didn't ask for a visitor, either.

Not that any of the women get them often; most of their families, their men, abandon them once they end up in here.

But if it wasn't Kyle, who else would visit me here?

Officer Marshall's hand wraps around my throat before I have a chance to realize he's in the hall. I'm usually more alert, more aware of his presence. Without warning, he shoves me against the wall, and the other women scatter, like roaches in the spotlight.

CO Jones is gone, too.

He grabs my face with a rough hand and shoves his pelvis into mine, anchoring me against the wall as I turn away, my face pressed against the cold brick. "I've been watching you for years," he taunts, his tongue rough like a cat's along the length of my cheek. "And how lucky for me that you're *here* now."

My eyes bore into his, daring him to touch me again, except I don't actually want him to touch me. Everyone seems to think because of my profession that I'm free game. People here know who I am, and they've made the assumption that I'm guaranteed to lie back and spread my legs to them, inviting them in on an assembly line. What they're quickly learning is that I'd rather fuck myself with my own hand than let any of them touch me.

Officer Marshall doesn't like that. He doesn't care for my lack of interest in his pleasure toy. But there is no doubt there, in his eyes, as he stares me down. He knows nobody will stop him from getting what he wants.

They never do.

"No one will ever believe a slut like you," he declares through gritted teeth. His nostrils flare and he lets out a guttural moan, his hands tearing at my clothes, untucking my shirt, his fingernails scratching the surface of my skin. "Don't act like you don't fucking want it, Thompson. I *know* you do."

I kick at his ankles and make an attempt to scream, but his hand covers my mouth before anything audible comes out. He pants like a dog, moaning as he manages to slide my pants down my waist, further stifling my ability to kick free. He hovers there, the weight of him immobilizing my arms and pinning me to the wall. Perspiration drips from his forehead, and I try to breathe.

To mentally go somewhere else.

I loosen my muscles and succumb to his power, realizing I won't be able to stop what he's about to do. He *will* have his way with my body.

But he will not have *me*.

There's relief in his eyes when he feels my body relax, and I close my eyes and tell myself he's Dylan, that I want this. I don't want to remember Officer Marshall's face when this moment haunts me later.

"Good girl. I knew you wanted this," he says. "Fuck," he mutters, pinning me down with one arm. He flips me over and enters me from behind, wasting no time building momentum.

I'm wet, even though I don't want this.

The anger bubbles inside of me as he fucks like a wild animal in season. I try to bring myself somewhere else, but all I see is red...I see blood. *So much blood. And it pools beneath his body and drips from my hands, outwardly flowing because of me. Because of these urges I can't control, can't stop.*

Officer Marshall groans, snapping me from my reverie. My eyes pop open instinctively, though I don't want them to, and he pulls out, shaking his load onto my ass. I turn my head, still pressed against the wall, and it's Shelly Farber who stands watch at the end of the corridor this time. She's peeking—the naughty girl—watching me get fucked like she's jealous it isn't her.

She hasn't had her turn yet.

He knows how much she wants it.

I feel unclean, suddenly in need of a shower but knowing I won't get one until morning. He stuffs his dick into his boxers and zips his pants, tapping my backside to let me know it's okay to come off the wall, but he places a possessive hand on my hip and leans in, whispering in my ear.

"You've always been my favorite, Lisha."

His eyes are dark, still dilated from the high of the chase, the penetration he didn't deserve. I say nothing, although I'd like nothing more than to spit in his face. His semen still covers my ass and he hands me a wad of paper towels that he pulls from his back pocket as casually as a dog owner picking up shit with a plastic bag. I take them and he thinks I will thank him, like the others, but I'm not grateful.

I don't thank him.

He turns and makes his way down the corridor toward Shelly Farber.

He whistles as he walks.

"Let's go, playmate. Back to lockup," he calls out in a singsong tone.

I use the wad of paper towels to wipe him off me before pulling up my pants. One foot in front of the other, I follow Officer Marshall, guilt building with each step as I chastise myself for coming right along with him.

I feel that anger now, that missing emotion Kristin once spoke of. It's here, festering beneath the surface like acid.

And I fucking hate it.

UNEMPLOYMENT-VILLE

Alisha

I STILL HAVEN'T TOLD you how I ended up working in the sex industry. It's not that I'm ashamed of what I do—what I did. My work was perfectly legal and safer than stripping at a club. Is it something I ever admitted to Mrs. Maylen? No. But that'd be like confessing your darkest sins to your grandmother, and who the hell would do a thing like that? The woman would have had an aneurysm if she knew what I did to earn a living.

So I didn't tell her.

And neither did Dylan, because I'd sworn him to secrecy. I honestly don't think he would have been able to tell her even if he wanted to, though. It was hard enough when his parents found out. It was a whole thing, and awkward as all hell when we discovered that his own father was a paying subscriber.

Imagine *his* surprise when Dylan texted him a photo of us together. Dylan was so proud of his new girlfriend, and certain my profession wouldn't be an issue because no one would ever find out about it.

But they did.

Even the purest humans often can't resist temptation. And what better way to indulge in one's sexual fantasies than via the internet in the privacy of your own home?

It's no secret that sex sells. I tried to go a different route, truly I did —it just didn't work out for me. I started my first full-time job right out of college. I was twenty-two and had otherwise earned my spending money as a part-time barista, but the paycheck was no longer cutting it—I'd recently rented an apartment and had no choice but to get a decent job to pay the rent. And while an office job was sure to bore the living shit out of me, I was prepared to do it, to stake my claim in the workforce as a Monday through Friday nine-to-fiver.

It took an embarrassingly short amount of time for me to realize how unfit I was for corporate America, and my first day on the job also happened to be my last.

Drew Milner, the lucky fuck who had the pleasure of employing me, greeted me at the reception desk on the ground floor of a sky-rise building in downtown Minneapolis. My new boss, due to a scheduling mishap, wasn't the person I initially interviewed with the week earlier, so our first encounter occurred right then and there. He was visibly displeased from the moment he took a look at me as he rounded the corner coming off the elevator.

Why? I hadn't a clue, but I was determined to put my best foot forward with this job, to turn a lasting impression into a regular paycheck.

But my arms were full, and evidently the impression I'd given wasn't one he was interested in. In one hand I carried a small box of personal belongings to decorate my new desk—for no reason other than that cliches told me that's what you're supposed to do when you work in an office. In the other, a travel mug filled with coffee, and my most successful garage sale find to date—a knock-off designer purse I was quite proud of despite my disdain for expensive things. Sometimes I just wanted to fit in, what can I say? But because of this, because I cared more about filling my arms with "stuff", I couldn't shake Drew's hand. Instead we more or less nodded in each other's direction.

"Alisha Hill?" he asked with a raised brow.

"Yes! Drew? Hi, it's so nice to meet you."

"Likewise. I see you've got your hands full there. Need some help?" He reached for my box of trinkets, and as he did, his hand brushed against my breast. I hoped it was an accident, but his face seemed to say otherwise—he wasn't phased by it and didn't acknowledge the mishap, so I didn't either.

I adjusted my shirt with my now-free hand and followed him down the hall, my nerves rattled. "Thank you," I said, doing my best to ignore the incident the same way he had.

The elevator ride was awkward at best, the seconds ticking by as if in slow motion. We barely spoke, and the few times I wanted to say something, I found myself biting my tongue instead.

Once off the elevator, we reached a pod of cubicles, and Drew gestured to the empty desk that would be mine, motioning for me to step in first.

Or so I thought.

I realized my mistake when we bumped into each other, and this time he walked directly into my backside, and managed to grab my ass in the process.

"I'm so sorry—" I started, the apology rolling off my tongue as I turned to face him. He set the box on my desk and held up his hand, speaking in a hushed tone more suited for a library.

"It's fine. Listen, maybe you should run home and change? I can push your first training session out to ten o'clock."

I ran my hands over my clothes, certain I must have spilled coffee on my outfit.

"Excuse me?"

He raked a hand through his hair before shrugging and motioning to me again. "You can't dress like that here," he said. The trajectory of his eyes contradicted his words. It was evident he liked what he saw.

"Like *what*?" I asked, challenging him to grow a pair and explain himself.

"Like...*that*." He gestured at me incredulously, making an effort not to look me in the eye. "It's...*provocative*."

"Nothing I'm wearing goes against the office dress code," I argued, certain the rebuttal was accurate. "I checked." More than once actually, just to be sure I was dressed appropriately for my new job. Mrs. Maylen always told me to *dress for the job you want, not the job you have*, so I was channeling my inner Gretta by donning a pencil skirt that fell below the knee and three-quarter-sleeved white blouse buttoned high enough to hide my cleavage.

Is it the heels? Are they too high? The wrong color? Should I have worn nylons?

"Well, I happen to disagree and would be more comfortable if you'd head home and cover up. This is a place of business."

His assessment didn't sit well with me, and immediately I knew I didn't belong in an environment like that. "*You* would be more comfortable? Are you fucking kidding me?" I snapped, unconcerned with the rising volume of my voice.

I fought the urge to slap him, if only on account of the many witnesses whose heads were starting to pop up like whack-a-moles over the tops of the cubicles. Instead, I turned and grabbed my box from the desk before stomping back toward the elevator.

"So we'll see you back here at ten then?" he semi-shouted, trying not to further disturb the staff.

"Nope," I said, not looking back.

I hadn't expected to be sexually harassed on my first day of work, no less than fifteen minutes after entering the building. With my never-to-be-unpacked box of supplies tucked under my arm, my coffee abandoned on the desk, and my pride dangling by a thread, I was in the elevator on a ride straight back down to Unemployment-ville, population seven million, give or take.

To top it off, rent on my apartment was due in just over a week, and I didn't have enough in my checking account to pay it. I'd have to get a job bartending again, and that was the last thing I wanted to do. But there was no shortage of bars in downtown Minneapolis, so it seemed like the most logical option, given the short window. I hated the long drive home at two in the morning, but the tips added up quickly.

I punched the button for the ground floor and set the box on the floor—I had twenty-two floors to descend and didn't care to hold it the whole time. It was warm and stuffy in the elevator, so I grabbed a folder from the box and fanned myself with it.

Ugh, I'd give anything to be naked in front of an industrial fan right now.

And that was all it took, that one single thought, to get me riled up. I suddenly wanted nothing more than to be fucked in that elevator right then and there. I settled for unbuttoning a couple buttons on my blouse —I had already been fired, there was nothing more to lose.

I noticed on the ride up that the elevators had cameras on them, beneath the Plexiglass next to the numbered buttons. I couldn't help but wonder who watched those cameras.

Was someone manning them all the time? Was it security? Or just a recording for safety purposes in case something were to happen? The idea that someone was watching turned me on more than anything, making me wet at the thought. I fluffed my hair, licked my lips, and leaned over to shake my tits in front of the camera, more so for my own entertainment than anyone else's.

When the bell chimed on the ground floor, I picked up my box, making sure to bend over directly in front of the camera. I knew full well that my ass looked good in that skirt and figured someone else might enjoy the view.

Sighing, I made my way out of the building and into the parking lot, annoyed there wasn't even anyone at the security desk for me to wave goodbye to. Nobody gave a shit I had been there.

I reached my car and set my box of crap on the ground while I dug in my purse for the keys, the faint sound of footsteps pounding the pavement behind me.

"Hey! Wait up!"

I turned and saw a man running toward me, his arm waving in the air. It was evident by his attire that he worked security for the building I'd just stormed out of. "Hi," he said once he finally caught up with me. He wiped a bead of sweat from his brow and motioned toward my box. "Can I help you with that?"

"Oh, sure. Thanks, that would be great. It's kinda heavy," I lied.

"I'm Ryan," he said, shoving the box into the backseat of my car and closing the door.

"Alisha. You weren't at the desk," I said, pointing to the building. "When I walked out, I mean. I was gonna say goodbye, but there was no one there."

"Oh, yeah, um. Sorry. I…was distracted."

He stuffed his hands in his pockets and stood there with a gawky expression on his face. "Um, not to make this awkward, but is there any chance you'd like to grab a drink tonight?"

"I don't drink."

"Oh, sure. Yeah, that's cool." I couldn't help but notice the rejection on his face. The poor guy looked defeated and I hadn't even said no to a date, only to the drink. But he gave up so fast I was starting to lose interest.

"Thanks for your help, Ryan." I said finally. He nodded, and we stood there for another uncomfortable second, neither of us making an effort to carry on the conversation. I wasn't in a hurry, but I didn't care to stand there watching the guy sweat either. I was about to reach for the door handle when he spoke up again.

"I saw you," he spit out bashfully. "In, um…in the elevator."

"Oh, my God, I'm so sorry," I feigned innocently. "That was so inappropriate, I—"

"No, no…not at all. I liked it."

"Oh. Oh! Like you *liked it* liked it?"

He nodded, and it was suddenly clear to me why I didn't see him at the desk when I walked out. He must have been preoccupied with concealing a boner.

Yay me!

"I wasn't sure if you knew that we watch…the cameras, I mean. That one feeds to my post."

"I honestly didn't know anyone was watching. I'm sorry, I was—I got fired today. So it was kind of like a 'fuck you' to the guy upstairs, you know?"

"Yeah, sure. That makes sense. Sorry to hear that, though. I guess that means I won't see you around."

I looked at him with new eyes. With his blond hair and light blue eyes, he wasn't unattractive. He wasn't entirely attractive, either. He could stand to gain a few inches in the height department, and his security guard uniform wasn't quite doing it for me either, but something told me he wasn't as inexperienced as he came across.

That maybe he knew a few things.

"So you liked it?" I asked. "What you saw in the elevator?"

"Yeah," he answered a bit too quickly, and I couldn't help but smile. "Come on," I said, taking his hand. "You're going to fuck me in that elevator."

His eyes went wide and he stumbled over his feet as we made our way back to the building, but despite his initial inelegance, Ryan was —at the time—the best fuck I'd ever had.

Called it.

A half-hour later I was back in my car, fixing my hair in the rearview mirror when my phone buzzed from the passenger seat. I recognized the local 7-6-3 area code, but not the number that followed.

A text message.

From an unsaved number.

I'm off at five if you want me to come over and help you change out of that skirt.

Who the hell?

Then a second message.

This is Drew Milner. I figured since I'm no longer your boss…

The man was wearing a wedding ring.

After rolling my eyes, I snapped a quick picture of cleavage, making sure the lace of my bra was showing through my unbuttoned blouse, and sent it to Drew along with an address.

When he showed up at Mrs. Maylen's house around 5:45 that evening, all she could do was laugh. I didn't live there anymore, and it wasn't the first time I intentionally directed a douche bag to the wrong house just to fuck with them. She always got a good laugh out of it, and it wasn't like I was putting her in danger; none of the boner-donors knew we were connected and simply assumed they had the wrong house or quickly figured out they had been played. In this case, it didn't take long for Drew to realize his misfortune.

But the best part was that Mrs. Maylen caught on quickly and slapped a sultry expression on her face—he *was* quite handsome, if I'm being honest—and invited him inside.

She said he couldn't have high-tailed it out of there fast enough, and we laughed about it over dinner for years to come.

SEX KITTEN-LIKE MISTAKES

Alisha

I WAS jobless for over a week, impatient, and waiting to hear back from several bars I had applied to, certain at least one of them would call any day.

Bored and horny, I spent most of that week naked on my couch watching porn on my laptop, nearly picking up the phone to invite Elevator Boy over for a booty call. But when an ad popped up to join a live webcam, I came to the realization that I had been sitting—literally —on a gold mine.

I barely had to do anything to capture Ryan's attention the week before, and he was ready to blow his load before the elevator even reached the main floor. So much so that he followed a complete stranger out to the parking lot and offered to take her to dinner, as if he were interested in anything more than sex.

"You don't belong cooped up in an office anyway," he'd said as we got dressed afterward.

"No? Well, what should I be doing then?"

"Don't take this the wrong way, but..." He shrugged and looked away for a moment, his eyes downcast as he adjusted his belt. "I'd pay to watch what we just did."

"What do you mean?"

"Porn. You should do porn."

His comment threw me off at first. I wasn't about to dive head first into the porn industry, but the more I thought about it, the more enticing it became. I had spent no more than ten minutes in the presence of Drew Milner before he was so turned on he couldn't even introduce me to the rest of the team. And the fact that he was willing to cheat on his wife just for a quick taste?

But I wasn't sure porn was for me, and truth be told, I was afraid to get a glimpse of that world behind the scenes. I didn't want to know enough not to be able to enjoy it anymore. But I needed something more lucrative than bartending, something that would allow me the anonymity I craved and the ability to set my own schedule.

There *was* a job out there for me. And I was looking right at it.

Live girls.

Online.

No one physically there to grope me, shove my hand down their pants, or stick their dick in my ass.

A webcam girl—*that* I could do.

The next day I headed straight to the Ridgedale Mall, ready to invest in my future. Armed with the cash I had set aside for rent, I bought a decent webcam and then headed to the lingerie department.

I was terrible at lingerie, even worse at fashion in general. I lived for a pair of leggings and a good hoodie, and even though I knew I'd end up naked at some point during my lives, I'd have to start out wearing something.

I needed something sexy to entice the viewers, to keep them wanting more so they'd come back. And, to my surprise, after over two hours struggling to find any lingerie that I liked, I managed to make a friend. Apparently when you have no clue how to shop for lingerie, making a friend while standing in line at the checkout counter is a good way to ease the burden; it never hurts to have that second set of eyes.

"You're not wearing that for a man, are you?" the voice behind me asked. He held his hand up to his mouth, almost like he was disgusted, but his eyes told me otherwise.

He was genuinely concerned.

"Excuse me?"

"Sorry, if I may?" He reached for the skimpy garments in my hands, holding them up on full display to get a look at them, clearly oblivious to the customers gawking around us while he analyzed them with intent.

"This is the wrong color for you. Not even a straight man would go for that shit." He shook his head in disappointment and took the remaining items from my arms, setting them on the counter. I couldn't help but stand there looking like an idiot.

"Are you in a hurry?" he asked, not waiting for an answer. He took my arm and pulled me out of the checkout line and back toward the shopping floor. "You can go ahead and restock those, Jen!" he called back to the cashier. She rolled her eyes, and all I could do was offer her a shrug of my shoulders. To my surprise she laughed as I was dragged away, without even a hint of concern for my safety.

"Have fun!" she shouted instead, subsequently moving on to the next customer in line.

"Do you work here or something?" I asked, trying to keep the pace.

"I do, yep. I'm Chris. What's your name, sweetheart?" He held his hand out to me, and despite my reservations, I took it, internally jealous of his ability to talk to strangers as if they were anything but.

"Alisha."

"Ooo, love that name! So pretty." He released my hand and clapped his own together in excitement, turning abruptly and making a beeline to the sexiest of lingerie. "And it just so happens that *you*, my dear, managed to nearly sneak out of here making the biggest sex-kitten-like mistake *ever*."

"Which is?"

"First of all, nothing says 'trashy' more than a hot pink garter belt." He shuddered, his shoulders shaking as if there were a chill in the air. "You're much too gorgeous for that shit. It's not you, honey, it's him. Don't worry. Just come with me, and we'll get you in something perfect."

We rummaged through the racks, quickly picking through the inventory and avoiding anything similar to the pieces I previously picked out.

"What about this?" I asked, holding up a canary yellow thong and shimming my hips. Chris swiped it out of my hands and tossed it back on the table as my lips formed into a pout.

"Hey, I liked that one," I whined.

"No, you didn't." He shoved another garment in my direction, not bothering to turn and look at me when I took it from his hands, his nose still stuck in the rack.

"Okay, dressing room, here we come!" he finally declared after several minutes of scouring.

"What? No way," I protested.

"Way. Now, scoot!"

"I'm not trying these on for you."

"Calm down, Lisha dear, they're just boobs. Literally *everyone* has seen boobs. But if it makes you feel better, you can keep your panties on since they're already in a bunch anyway." He winked, and my jaw nearly dropped to the floor. But I followed him to the dressing rooms anyway. Because he obviously knew what he was talking about, and for some reason I valued his opinion, despite having just met him.

Caution to the wind, I wiggled out of my clothes and into the first piece of lingerie, Chris standing back and watching as I did so. The piece was snug, but I didn't hate it.

"Push those ta-tas up a bit...there. Yep, there ya go." He stepped back as if admiring his handiwork, grinning like a proud parent. His hands on my shoulders, he turned me so I was facing the floor-length mirror. "Oh, hey, girl!" he said, biting his lip and whistling.

"Wow..."

"Black is really your color! With that skin tone? Do you love it or do you loooove it?"

"I must admit, Chris," I said as I ran my hands down the lacy fabric. "You are excellent at picking out sexy lingerie."

"And don't you forget it!" he said, spinning me to take another look. "What do you need all this for, anyway? It's an awful lot to buy all at once. Oh! Wait! Did you recently lose a ton of weight?" *Gasp.* "Were you fat once?" he whispered, his hand cupped against his mouth. I laughed, despite myself, and shook my head.

"No, I wasn't fat once."

He raised a brow, his head bobbing in wait of my response. And suddenly I wanted nothing more than to tell him. To confide in him like a friend.

I hadn't had one in a long time.

"Okay, fine. I'll tell you. But you can't tell anyone," I said.

"Sweetheart, I don't even know your last name. Who would I tell?"

"Good point. Okay, so…I'm starting a livestream channel. I'm gonna be a webcam girl."

"A webcam girl? As in…like, live nudes or something?" I nodded, biting my lip.

"No…freakin'…way."

"Yes freakin' way."

"Oh, sweetheart…we need to get you some red Louboutin heels!"

Two days later I was up and running, live on the web for the first time and doing nothing but cleaning my apartment dressed in a classic French maid outfit, my feather duster sweeping the same surfaces over and over.

My apartment had never been so clean.

Viewers could see and hear me, but I couldn't hear them, not yet anyway. I knew I'd have to invest in some better equipment down the road. It was a mostly PG-13 show those first few times—just a lot of ass cheeks and a few nip slips, but I earned my rent money back within the week.

The following month I was able to pay the landlord on time, and Lisha's Bedroom was officially born. Thanks, in part, to my new friend, Chris.

THAT'S WHY I LOOK FAMILIAR

Alisha

Wᴀs it difficult for me to give up promiscuity after meeting Dylan? No. Not at all, actually. I had no issues with monogamy, I just hadn't found anyone I wanted to be monogamous with until I met Dylan, a fact that surprised Kristin, among others. Up until then, my dating life was a continuous list of disappointment, of nights out on the town trying to meet people to take me home and fuck my brains out.

Not that I walked around with a sign around my neck saying that, but the conquests were harder to come by than you might think.

When you're the only sober one in a bar full of drunk people, it's hard to see past the idiocy that can ensue. They're the ones sporting beer goggles, not me, so for them it's a win-win.

The trick was to find someone just sober enough not to be sloppy.

Nonetheless, the website helped redirect my interests. I was so busy I didn't *need* to date. Not to mention, I could call up a private session at any time and get my rocks off that way. In the beginning, I worked every day of the week. Until I no longer needed to.

But every night was something different. I loved the change of pace, the element of surprise in never really knowing what I'd get.

Private sessions quickly become a lucrative favorite. I didn't need to stream for hours on end once I started booking private sessions.

And I'd gained some regulars.

Most enjoyable were the ones I would consider straight-laced men. The ones that required little to no prep in terms of hair, makeup, and wardrobe. My first private session was awkward though, to say the least.

I dressed in a silk black robe and my signature red stiletto heels, my nipples poking through the thin fabric perfectly. I kept the thermostat low for just that reason.

My customer had a girl-next-door fantasy—a lot of them did, actually. In my experience, most men were under the impression the perfect girl-next-door was a freak in the sheets, dressing in sexy lingerie under their conservative clothes, just desperate for someone to notice.

The misconception always made me chuckle.

For this particular customer, however, I was asked to have my hair done and wear a little makeup. His "neighbor" was supposed to be getting ready for a night on the town. She would enter the bedroom, having just done her hair and makeup, and drop her robe, exposing her naked body for him to secretly admire through her bedroom window.

I straightened my hair, my face highlighted, along with a touch of bronzer and a layer of mascara. The finishing touch was the colorless lip gloss he was adamant about—as if red lipstick would have taken away the character's innocence. I turned on the camera and stood in front of it, giving him a moment to admire the view.

"Mm, yes. You are looking lovely today, Willow," he said, using his desired name for me. His camera pointed straight to his crotch, never his face—you'd be surprised how many of them are—his dick hard as he stroked it with his right hand. I couldn't tell if he was married—another hazard of the right-handed man. "Show me the back," he commanded.

I turned and bent slightly, showing off my plump derriere. He moaned and pumped a little faster.

I hadn't even taken off my robe yet.

He narrated the scene out loud, as if reading from a script. "I'm watching you through your window, Willow. It's dark outside, the breeze is blowing in and it's chilly. Are you cold?"

I slowly untied the robe, letting it fall from my shoulders, the fabric soft when it grazed my nipples. I shivered, feeling the draft, the goosebumps forming on my breasts. I played coy, my fingers raking through a rack of clothes as I stood there naked, trying to decide what to wear. All the while, I feigned ignorance of the camera, never once looking over at it.

Ope, silly me. I seem to have dropped a hanger on the ground. I better bend over and pick it up.

I hear it then, the sound of his balls slapping against his leg, against his hand. He jerks off violently, the sight of me bent over—my ass and pussy on full display for him—seemingly what he'd been hoping to see.

He clicks off without another word.

The session cost him nearly a hundred dollars.

After a quick shower, I threw on a jacket, grabbed my purse and headed out the door. I was on a bit of a high from the excitement of my website taking off, but I was bored. I needed a change of scenery and a basket of wings, so I shot Chris a text and asked him to meet me at Thirsty's on the off-chance he was free.

Once inside, I claimed a seat at the bar, the bartender approaching a moment later with a friendly but harmless smile on his face. He seemed more like Chris's type than mine.

"What can I get ya?" he asked, setting a cocktail napkin in front of me.

"Just a Shirley Temple, and a basket of honey barbecue wings, please."

"Coming right up."

The gawker spotted me within minutes, his big brown eyes drinking me in. Despite my lack of interest, I couldn't help but admire his stature, the muscles in his forearm. He sipped his drink before standing and making his way over to me.

"Hi," he said to my surprise. No one-liner. No wink. It was unusual, the lack of originality in his game. I nodded and turned back to the TV behind the bar, the local news informing me of yet another shooting in Minneapolis.

"I'm Jacob." He stuck his hand out in my direction, holding it there and waiting for me to take it. I had dated plenty of men like him. Men who think they're God's gift to women, that they're some kind of rare breed. Spoiler alert: they're not. There's one on just about every corner.

But I liked his hair. The salt and pepper look worked for him. The thought to run my fingers through it danced in my mind, but I knew better than to touch him. Touching led to kissing, which led to fucking, and that inevitably led to disappointment.

I'd had enough disappointment.

I was turning over a new leaf, and wanted to eat my damn wings in peace. "Can I buy you a drink?" Jacob asked, taking his rejected hand back and stuffing it in his coat pocket.

"No, thank you, I don't drink."

"Then what are you doing at a bar?"

"They have good wings."

He chuckled, and it brought out the crow's feet around his eyes. When he smiled, he was more handsome than I originally thought, but for some reason, he reminded me of Vincent, the guy I fooled around with for a while after high school.

Our last night together was the first and only time I drank alcohol. We had been seeing each other for a couple weeks, which at eighteen really only meant we were learning new sex positions, but definitions aside, two weeks with a guy was considered a long time for me, even back then.

Attachments weren't my thing.

We were fresh out of high school, and the summer was just getting started. I was on the hunt for a job, and Mrs. Maylen worked weekdays, so Monday through Friday I did little more than hang around the house, bored out of my mind.

I hadn't really dealt with the loss of my mother, though it wasn't like I had deemed it as such. I didn't *lose* her; I knew exactly where she was.

Buried.

Her corpse rotting in the ground of a donated cemetery plot.

Because she chose drugs and alcohol over me. Over her own daughter.

And for some reason, I spilled my guts about this to Vincent. His hair-brained idea was that all I needed was a good fuck and a bottle of vodka. "Numb the pain, just like she did," he had said.

So I did.

I took his advice, and together we got shit-faced drunk. I giggled all night, and danced naked on the coffee table in his living room. We took body shots off one another and he prank-called his buddies while I made sex noises in the background.

But as fun as it was, his master plan failed.

The next morning I woke up sore between my legs and more exhausted than I'd been when I'd laid down the night before. My head throbbed, and I rubbed at my temples. I had no choice but pry my eyes open and squint at the sunlight that seeped in through the curtains. I wanted to move, to get out of his bed and go home, but my stomach gurgled with the threat of vomit, so I stayed.

He lay there beside me, naked and lying on his stomach, his bare ass exposed to the elements. I looked under the covers to find that I was naked too. I remembered very little. Limbs pressed together, mouths on mouths, his limp dick in my hand. "Whiskey dick," he had said when the appendage failed him during round two.

He hadn't even been drinking whiskey, so it made no sense to me at the time. How was I to know it was a universal term?

I didn't understand the appeal of alcohol, the desire to repeat the cycle over and over, day in and day out. It didn't even taste good. I knew then that I'd never drink again, out of spite for my mom, if anything.

But mostly because I simply didn't want to.

"You look so familiar," Jacob said, pulling me back to the present, to the game-less stranger doing his best to impress a girl who just wanted to stuff her face with chicken wings. I sipped my drink and twirled the ice with my straw.

"Yeah? How so?"

"I don't know. I just feel like I've seen you before. Although, I don't know how I'd forget a face like yours."

"That's what they all say, Jacob."

"Oh. Wow, I'm so sorry. This must happen to you all the time."

"What's that?"

"Weird men hitting on you in bars."

"It does," I acknowledged coolly before turning to my phone. Chris had texted. Jacob pulled his wallet from his back pocket, removed a twenty and dropped it onto the bar. I knew he was about to leave, to take the hint and buzz off. And if I'm being honest, a small part of me wanted to let him take me home—I was oddly intrigued by him.

But the wedding band on his left hand was a turn off.

Men like him were part of the reason I was single in the first place. "Lisha's Bedroom," I said.

"Excuse me?"

"That's why I look familiar." I stood and grabbed my jacket from the back of the chair. His face fell in shame when recognition finally hit him. "Go home to your wife," I said, sauntering out the door and raising my phone to my ear.

"Hello?"

"Christopher..."

"Oh, God, what did I do now?"

"Nothing, I just like to freak you out."

"Well, stop it! It always makes me feel like I'm in trouble when you call me Christopher. What can I do ya for, lovely?"

"Ice cream. Bring me ice cream. I'll queue up *The Real House-wives*-of-Wherever-the-Fuck-They-Live-Now."

"Ooh, you're always so salty. I love it. See you in twenty!"

Until I met Dylan, Chris was the one and only reliable man in my life. The fact that he was gay and never tried to get into my pants made him easy to love.

YOU CAN'T FIX STUPID

Dylan

Did the website bother me?

Of course.

What kind of man would I be if it didn't?

But what could I have done? Alisha started that website long before she met me, and I sure as shit didn't deserve a say in whether or not she kept it up and running. My wife had a mind of her own, and she didn't hesitate to use it. She was a grown woman, fully capable of making her own decisions. That's not to say I always agreed with her, especially when it came to that damn website.

It did mean, however, that I had to figure out a way to help her. She deserved more than what Lisha's Bedroom offered her. Sure, the money was great, but she was already set for life by the time I met her. She didn't *need* to work anymore, she just wanted to.

So, did I ask her to shut it down? Eventually, yes. In the early days while I was busy making sure she fell in love with me and stayed there? Nope. Not a fucking chance.

She bored easily. She demanded more out of life than the average person, and when she was working, when she was performing for her customers, she was thriving. It boosted her self-esteem, her confidence. It also put money in her bank account, and after a lifetime of poverty, how could she turn that down? How could she stop once she started?

Alisha spent her life under scrutiny, being judged for her lack of wealth and her sexuality. I wasn't there to see it then, but I'd heard stories, mostly from my grandmother, but even Alisha slipped in the occasional admission every once in a while. Like the time she was asked to leave a local boutique because employees saw the backpack she carried that doubled as a purse and assumed she was there to shoplift.

Or when a theater attendant asked her to leave in the middle of *Titanic* because he thought she had sneaked in, even though she presented a ticket stub for the right date, time, and movie.

Residents in the small town she grew up in knew her. They knew her mother, Darlene, and her history with substance abuse. They made the assumption that Alisha was no different, that she'd grow up and follow the same path, stepping directly into the very footprints her mother had laid out for her.

But once she had wealth? Once they knew she wasn't an addict, that she didn't enter a store with the intent to steal? Everything changed for her.

She didn't, though; she never changed who she was to meet the demands of society. She lived her life unapologetically, because that's how she deserved to live it.

She radiated confidence, and it transpired into the bedroom, into her web show, and her customers couldn't get enough of it. They couldn't get enough of *her*.

Somehow, she even managed to keep her profession under wraps around town. Most of the locals had no clue how she'd dug herself out of poverty. And she liked it that way, the anonymity. She deserved it after everything she'd been through.

Until I was murdered and it all went to shit.

After that everybody knew our business—everybody knew *her*

business. She had been exposed, and they were fascinated by it —by *her*.

And the funny thing about that? She had gotten out of the business by that time. Yet it was the first thing the media picked up on, the first thing they pounced on as soon as the investigation began.

America ate that shit right up.

Men were enamored with her, and women hated her *because* the men were enamored with her—although, some of them secretly loved her, too. It didn't matter that she had retired from the industry. To them, she was still Lisha. She was nothing more than a porn star, and that's all she'd ever be.

She became a household name and every teen boy's wet dream.

If I weren't dead, I'd be on my soap box every single day trying to show those fuckers who she really is. But here's the thing: you can't fix stupid. You can't change someone's mind when they're set on believing a misguided truth. I mean, that's the whole premise of politics, right? Nobody ever switches sides; we're all either Republicans or Democrats until the end. That's it, that's all.

The same goes for life, really. Most people don't get a second chance to make a first impression.

And when it comes to Alisha, as she's always said, you're either with her or against her.

KYLE IS A DOUCHE

Alisha

I MEET with Kyle at 10:00 a.m. every Tuesday. Sometimes Thursdays, too, depending on the week. He tells me we'll meet more frequently as the trial draws nearer, which is fine. It's nice to sit and chat with a man from time to time; the women in this place are so fucking catty.

But Kyle's kind of a douche, too, so I'm not sure which is worse. And today it seems both Kyle and I are in a mood, which is never a good thing.

I know this meeting isn't going to end well before it even starts, and while I brace myself for impact, Kyle unpacks the contents of his briefcase. I take a seat across from him at the table and watch as he opens several folders and spreads their contents out. The paperwork seems to have multiplied since the last time he was here.

He finally stops pulling shit out of his briefcase, and looks up at me, leaning over the table and lacing his hands together as if he has something important to tell me. "Hey," is all he says.

"Hi."

"How are you holding up?"

"Fine."

He looks as if he's about to explode, and we haven't even started talking about my case yet. I can't say I feel any differently—tensions have been high between us for weeks—but you'd think my thousand-dollar-an-hour attorney would be able to keep his shit together—or at least fake it well enough to make me believe he knows what the hell he's doing.

I can't help but hold my breath in anticipation of what he's uncovered since his last visit.

"Look, here's the deal, Alisha. We need to go over a few things." He shuffles through one of the folders and pulls out a newspaper clipping. When he slides it across the table, his uses his sausage finger to point at the provocative photo of me. "*This* is what the media thinks of you. What the public sees."

Personally, I find the photo quite flattering, but I shrug and cross my arms, leaning back in the chair and not caring for his tone. "And?" I ask.

"And what?"

"What's the problem?"

"Really? I show you a nearly nude photo of yourself—that made the front page of the *Star Tribune*, mind you—and *that's* your response?"

"It's no secret what I do for a living."

"No, it's not. And that's part of the problem."

"I'm not ashamed of my profession, Kyle."

"Great. By all means, be *proud* of the so-called *work* that you do. But get this through your head. You're a porn star. And the media knows it. The general public knows it, too. And juries? Juries have little to no sympathy for sex workers. So you're fucked at the gate, and not the way you like it. They'll form an opinion of you before the DA even finishes his opening statement. Do you get what I'm saying to you?"

"None of that should matter, considering I didn't do this. I didn't kill him, Kyle."

He sighs and turns back to his paperwork. I see the frustration in his eyes, in the way his lip turns up when he doesn't hear the answer he wants to hear. I know he's trying.

But he needs to try harder.

"The evidence is bigger than you think. It's stacked. There's not much to work with in terms of a defense. Our best shot? To create reasonable doubt. You really haven't given me anything that will allow me to do more than that."

I nod, despite myself. I don't want to accept this, his assumption that a jury can't see past sexuality to find a semblance of innocence. But his words hold weight. There's truth behind them, whether I like it or not.

"Let's go over the morning of again," he says, as if it's only the second time we've discussed it and not the fourteen-hundredth.

"Why?" I ask, annoyed again and rolling my eyes.

"Because I still don't understand it."

"You're a well-educated attorney, Kyle. What's not to understand?"

He pulls a face and twists his mouth into a tight grin. I can practically see the smoke coming from his ears. "Enlighten me."

"Fine. Cliff notes, then." I lean forward on the table, getting real close to Kyle and doing my best to match his demeanor. "I woke up. I peed. I brushed my teeth. I went for a run. I came home. My husband was dead. I puked. I pulled the knife out of his chest. Police busted through my door before I even understood what was happening. They brought me to the county jail, fed me cardboard, and delayed my phone call. Then, *magically,* two days later"—I smile as if this is the best part of the story—"I got to meet *you.*"

"You're charming as usual, Alisha. Anyone ever tell ya that?"

I lean back in the plastic chair as Kyle runs his hands over his thinning scalp. I think of Dylan's full head of hair and suddenly wish I could run my fingers through it. I miss the scent of his shampoo. "Tell it again," he says.

"What?"

"Tell it again."

"Why?"

"Fill in the margins for me...no more abstracts."

"Fuck this, Kyle! No. All that matters is that I didn't kill my husband!"

"No? What if you blacked out? Do you drink?"

"No."

"How's your mental health? Before all this, I mean..."

"I didn't black out." I say through gritted teeth. "And I'm not fucking crazy." He shrugs with nonchalance, as if he doesn't believe that either.

"You said the two of you argued the night before. What about?"

"I already told you I didn't want to talk about that."

"No? Well, I do. Tell me what you argued about."

"No."

He slams his hand down on the table, the pen jumping up like a popcorn kernel. "Here's the thing, Alisha. I think you *did* kill your husband. I think you stabbed him repeatedly until he bled out. And then you got caught. Does that matter? No. Does it change the fact that I'm here, representing you to the best of my ability? No." He points a chubby finger in my direction. It's much less threatening than he thinks. "But it does mean that you don't get to sit here and fucking lie to me anymore. Tell. Me. What. Happened."

"Fuck you, Kyle!" I hiss.

After a moment of silence and an intense stare down, Kyle stands and starts shoving paperwork back into his briefcase. My heart rate increases at the realization that he's about to walk out on me. He may even quit.

I'd have to start all over with someone new.

And there's no time for that.

"What are you doing?" I ask quietly.

"Leaving. I have other clients to see. Clients who actually give me the information I need to represent them in a court of law."

They hurt, his words. The memory of what I've lost. All of it just fucking hurts. And it's taken too long for me to realize that Kyle's right. If I have any shot in hell of getting out of here, I have to tell him everything. But I'm not sure I can do that.

97

THE MASKS WE WEAR

Alisha

ALL THIS TRIAL prep is killing me.

I can't take it—Kyle's insistence that I "practice" looking at the crime scene photos, his need to walk through every minute of that day over and over, even though there's no possible way I could share something about it he doesn't already know. Yet, it's the first thing he asks me every time I see him. *"Walk me through the day of the murder,"* he always says.

And even though I know it's coming, I fight the urge to stab a pen through his eye every time.

I'm worn out, my patience is thin and soon to be nonexistent, but every visit from Kyle means the trial is getting closer. I'm either reaching the end or approaching the brink of darkness, should I end up with life in prison. That thought is terrifying. That part makes me want to crawl into a hole and die. I need to get the fuck out of here.

I'm not sure if that will ever happen.

So I go through the motions. I appease Kyle and—with a good

amount of attitude—I answer his questions. I try to fill in the gaps so he can use them to poke holes in the prosecution's case.

Today is no different than last week, except we're opening a brand new can of worms. One I hadn't expected to tap into, yet here we are. Why I ever thought I could keep anything from my attorney is beyond me; he always knows, and if he doesn't yet, he will find out.

"Why didn't you tell me about your court-appointed therapy with Dr. Lindsay?" he asks, massaging his temples. Only two days have passed since we last met, and already he's managed to dig up more dirt on me.

I can only imagine what the state has found.

"Kristin? Why does that matter?"

"Why *wouldn't* that matter? It's public record, and you didn't think to tell me?"

I shrug, mentally unprepared to discuss anything to do with Kristin. I nearly ask about patient confidentiality before it occurs to me that she could be asked to testify.

"Has she turned up on the witness list?" I ask with an upturned brow.

"What happened that got you sent to her office?"

"Has she?"

"Yes."

Fuck.

"It wasn't just one thing...but none of it was my fault."

"Right," he drawls. "Continue..."

The first time I met with Dr. Kristin Lindsay, my mind raced as I tried to make sense of why I was in her office to begin with. I didn't choose to be there. I didn't voluntarily sign up. And while I'd done everything to fight it, there I sat, pissed off and ready to argue with a complete stranger about why I am the way I am and how I didn't deserve to be there.

But as irritated as I was, I couldn't get over how good it smelled in that office. Like lavender and vanilla and chamomile or something to that effect. An array of essential oils meant to calm my nerves, strategically fermenting in the room for no purpose other than to trick me into relaxation so I'd spill all my secrets.

I wanted that smell. I needed it, craved it to the point where I hopped online the second I got home and ordered enough of it to supply a small country.

And the fucked up thing is that I never used the oils. All they did was remind me of Kristin and that damn office I could never get out of fast enough.

And the reason I had to go there in the first place? Complete and utter bullshit, although I seem to be the only one who thinks so. I'd run into a client at a coffee shop. It was rare, but it did happen from time to time. And this particular client had a thing for submissive women. During our cam sessions, he liked to put me in my place, to give instructions I didn't particularly care to follow, and my refusal to do so only turned him on more.

He was the kind of man every woman steers clear of in the real world, and as luck would have it, he was standing right next to me.

"Lisha!" he beamed, a shit-eating grin on his face as if we went way back, as if we'd ever met in person.

Brenner Dixon.

I smiled, my own camera-ready grin always in my back pocket and ready for use at any given moment, despite my growing lack of people skills. "That's me," I admitted, raising a finger to my lips to quiet him. "But let's keep that between us." Why I didn't think to feign complete ignorance is beyond me.

I should have excused myself and walked away, pretended like I didn't know who he was and there was no way he could possibly know me.

But I suppose once someone's seen every inch of you, it only gets harder to conceal your identity.

Brenner winked like he was in on something, leaning in and placing a hand on the small of my back. "I do love a good secret," he said. "In fact, why don't we head to the bathroom and share one of our own?"

Two seconds.

That's about how long it took for Brenner to proposition me in public for the first time.

But I wasn't one to mix business with pleasure, especially with locals, and my only intention was to let him down gently, grab my coffee, and be on my merry way. "I'm sorry, I'm actually in a bit of a hurry."

"Hmm, playing hard to get, huh? I like it."

"No, I'm not actually," I corrected him. "I really do have somewhere to be." I didn't, but that fact was none of his business. I had a right to refuse his services without reason.

"Tight pussy like yours? Trust me, it'll be quick. Let's go." He took hold of my forearm and pulled me in the direction of the bathroom.

"I said no," I snapped, yanking my arm from his grasp.

"Fucking bitch," he hissed, reaching for me again. His fingers were rough as they dug into my skin. Fortunately for me, I'm left handed, and he'd taken hold of the wrong arm. I took a swing before he had a chance to take another step.

Brenner ended up with a broken nose.

And then gifted me with assault charges.

Which led to court-ordered anger management, despite the fact that I was the one who'd been sexually harassed. The punishment for him failed to stretch beyond the bill he received from his lawyer.

After that, he did everything he could to trash my name in the forums, but it did nothing to harm my career. If anything, I gained clientele. Nobody in those forums gave a shit, they just wanted a show.

And that's what I continued to give them.

But my run-in with Brenner wasn't my only offense. A couple months later, I met an angry housewife. The woman—a mother of three, and honorary neighborhood soccer mom, slash chauffeur—claimed her husband was cheating on her.

With me.

Because he subscribed to my channel, which she'd caught him jacking off to by way of a nanny cam strategically hidden in their bedroom.

Apparently that's considered cheating by some standards, though I'd never seen the man face-to-face. What I learned that afternoon is that oranges make great weapons.

But a wife scorned makes an even greater one.

And as was my luck, her husband happened to work at a law firm, and the fact that I'd pitched an orange at her face, hitting her square in the jaw, made me the perpetrator once again.

And sent me straight to court-ordered therapy on account of my "rage."

On that first day in Kristin's office, our intake session, I claimed residence on the love seat, and she looked at me with expectant eyes. I presented as a confident woman, one who knows her shit stinks but isn't bothered by the fact.

Everyone's shit stinks.

"Good morning, Alisha. I'm Dr. Kristin Lindsay, but you can call me Kristin. I'm proud of you for coming in today." She took a seat in an executive leather chair across from me. She was petite, wearing black trousers and a button-up that was so tight I found myself wondering if it was intentionally snug or perhaps she'd recently put on some weight. Why the thought crossed my mind, I wasn't sure, but I brushed it aside and nodded, saying nothing in response to her introduction. I was there to answer her questions, not to offer up information on my own free will.

"I thought we'd start by getting to know each other a bit. Does that work for you?"

"Sure."

"What brings you in today? Let's pick at the scab, so to speak," she said, smirking at the cleverness of her analogy. I didn't find it as clever as she did and instead wondered how often she used it with new clients, playing it off as she'd said it for the first time.

Already I sensed her judgment of me. I felt it in the way she studied me, my mannerisms and reactions. I heard it in her tone, the condescension and vague introduction—like she didn't want to be there with me any more than I wanted to be there with her. In her profession, she was supposed to be a neutral party. She was supposed to be Switzerland against the world.

But we were both guilty, she and I.

I didn't care for her either.

So I guess that means I judged her a little, too. She came off weak, but in control. Confident in an unfamiliar way—as if her confidence only resided on the outside. As if she, too, wore a mask.

"I'm required to be here." I replied to her question. She looked at the page of notes in her lap, pulling her glasses down her nose. I wondered if they were just for show or if she actually needed them.

"Yes, it says here you received a court order."

"Right. So, that's why I'm here. Some asshole in a choir robe told me I had to be."

She pulled a face, and it was evident my response wasn't what she'd expected. She looked disappointed, as if she knew me well enough to be disappointed in me.

"I don't think that's a very constructive comment. Do you?"

"Nope."

"Let's start over then. What brings you in today?" she asked again, and all I could do was outwardly sigh. I'd met my match, and I wasn't sure what to make of that. But appease her I did, because what else were we going to do for the next hour?

"So, that's it?" Kyle asks when I finish.

"That's it."

"How often did you see her?"

"Weekly. Until I came here."

"And how are you doing? With the, uh…the addiction."

I scoff at the fact that Kyle suddenly thinks he understands me, that he discovered my sex addiction diagnosis without my consent. I don't feed into his concern. Instead, I look him in the eye, teasing him with a smirk and an unsolicited air kiss. "Everyone has a vice, Kyle. Even you, I'm sure."

"Right. I'll see ya in a couple days," he says, picking up his brief-case. He stands, his chair knocking against the wall behind him.

"That's it?"

"For today, yes."

And I almost want to cry.

The clock ticks loudly on the wall above the door, and as much as I don't want to look over at it, I do. I don't want to shoot the shit with Kyle longer than necessary, but I'd rather be in here with him, talking myself out of propositioning him with a blow job, than back in the pod.

But back to the pod I go.

Because this time, Kyle doesn't sit back down.

HOW'S THE WIFE?

Dylan

I WARNED Alisha that her career choice would come back to bite her in the ass one day. All those men, and even the women she entertained, whom she had essentially teased during her days with Lisha's Bedroom, were bound to grow angry at some point. They were bound to lash out and find ways to take claim to Alisha.

Everyone wants what they can't have.

Not that I was an expert on the subject, but her run-ins with that asshole, Brenner, and that other schmuck's angry wife were proof that jealousy can spark anywhere, even in a virtual environment. The majority of her customers were ignorant enough to believe they were the only ones—that Alisha performed exclusively for them.

It was no surprise they were obsessed with her; it was easy to fall under her spell, especially if you took her personality out of it and focused on her physical attributes. But none of them knew her the way I did. They only knew the side of her that she presented to them, the character she portrayed on screen.

When we met, she told me she was an actress. Which I suppose is accurate, although somewhat misleading. I knew what she did for a living, though. I knew Alisha worked in the porn industry. I just wanted her to be the one to tell me.

And she did, after a few days.

Not that I ever admitted I'd known all along.

I mean, I benefited from it, too. I loved to watch her perform for the camera, to touch herself in ways any man would blow a load over. It worked for us for a while. She pleasured herself with her toys, viewers paid money to watch her in a private session, and I dove in tongue first to finish the job when the cameras went off.

The fact that none of them were able to touch her made the pill of jealousy a little easier to swallow, and eventually I didn't think much of it anymore.

Until the strange phone calls started coming. Her number was unlisted—for obvious reasons—so it was clear someone was desperate to track her down and had succeeded in doing so. She had to change her number because the calls were coming so frequently.

"You're making a big deal out of nothing," she said when I expressed concern for the umpteenth time. It was a Friday morning, and I was exhausted from a long week of showing houses, but the conversation needed to be had. The coffeemaker beeped, and I poured its contents into a travel mug, topping it off with cream and sugar. I'd debated playing hooky for the day, but I'd been doing that more often than I cared to admit and needed to get back into the swing of things. I wanted Alisha to shut down the site; in my opinion, it had run its course and was turning into nothing but a nuisance.

Plus, I was gearing up to address the topic of a baby. I had no fucking clue how *that* would go over with Alisha, but I did know I didn't want my future child's mom working in porn. Sharing her with anyone—virtually or otherwise—would no longer be an option once that seed was planted.

"No, I'm not," I said, twisting the lid onto the tumbler and turning to her. She looked beautiful in one of my white T-shirts, her bare legs exposed. I stifled a groan and watched a smirk form on her lips; she knew what those legs did to me, how they shot a current straight to my dick just at the sight of them. I felt the friction against my pants as she hopped off the counter and pulled the shirt over her head, the perfect mounds of her breasts on full display, her nipples perky in the chilly room. I couldn't help but stare. I was putty in her hands, and she knew it. Without another thought, I abandoned my coffee on the counter to ravish my wife. She needed my cock just as I needed her pussy.

And I'd fuck her ten ways to Sunday if she asked me to.

It wasn't until later that morning, after I'd showered for the second time, that I realized Alisha had played me again. She didn't approve of our topic of conversation.

Husband wants to discuss your poor career choice? No problem! Let's distract him with sex, and he'll forget what he was talking about in the first place. Ready, set, go!

I made a mental note to table the discussion for later. It wasn't over.

On my way in to work I found a parking space at Caribou Coffee because, in my haste to love on my wife, I forgot my coffee on the kitchen counter, and I was officially overdue for a caffeine fix.

I pulled open the door to the lobby, stopping dead in my tracks as I took in the face in front of me.

My stepbrother, Sawyer, who stood just as motionless, his fingers wrapped around a to-go cup of coffee.

I hadn't spoken to the sorry excuse for a man in years, on account of him sleeping with girlfriend, Ivy. The two of them shared similar interests, and at the time, I was working a lot, trying to make a living and saving for a ring. So, like a careless idiot, I suggested they hang out. I sent Sawyer in my place when I couldn't attend an Aerosmith concert with her. I subbed him in for our bowling league when I was busy with a closing that resulted in a huge commission. So, I didn't question it when they started making plans without me.

Really, I was just a sucker and fell for the whole we're-just-friends bullshit, I trusted my brother. And I trusted Ivy even more. Sure, I should have found it weird that my own brother was growing so close with my girlfriend, but truthfully? I barely had the time to notice.

Until I walked in on them fucking.

In *my* apartment. On *my* couch.

Last I heard they were separated and he was living somewhere in the Twin Cities. Why Sawyer's ugly mug was standing in a coffee shop in the middle of fucking nowhere was beyond me.

"Hey, man," he said when he spotted me. He looked about as confused as I felt, but he was the one out of place there. Not me.

"I have nothing to say to you." I shoved past him and made my way to the counter, confident he didn't have the balls to try another hand at conversation.

I was wrong.

The sound of his voice felt like a knife to my back. "Come on, Dylan, don't be that way. It's been long enough, don't you think?"

"Has it? How's the wife?"

"Okay, you know what? I don't need this shit. Yes, I married Ivy. I'm sorry I slept with your girlfriend and ended up happy. For a while, anyway, but she's gone now. So, fuck you, man! You're married, too, remember? And from what I hear, you're pretty damn happy with *your* wife. At some point, I'd like to think you'd get over it!" He pivoted and walked out the door, punching the air—or fist-fighting a mosquito, who knows—once he stepped outside.

Several sets of eyes bore into me as I watched my brother stomp off. For a second, I debated leaving too, but I wasn't about to forgo my morning coffee a third time. I stepped up to the counter, ignoring the prying eyes, and placed my order, nearly convincing myself to call it a day and head back home.

I found Sawyer in the parking lot on the way out. Apparently he hadn't had enough yet.

To my surprise, the words out of his mouth were, "I'm sorry." He shook his head, almost in disbelief, and I saw it then—the regret in his eyes. The knowledge that what he took from me could never be returned, gift receipt or not.

I didn't want Ivy anymore, but I couldn't forgive my brother either.

"I know, man. I know," I said. With a turn of the heel, I headed off in the direction of my car, ultimately deciding to go straight home. The day was shot anyway.

"That's it?"

"What's it?"

"I say I'm sorry and you just hop back in your car and leave?"

"I don't have time for this today," I said with a sigh, despite the fact I was about to head home and sit in front of the TV.

"No, of course you don't. Just like you didn't have time for Ivy back *then*."

At lightning speed, I slammed my coffee to the ground and clocked Sawyer in the jaw before I had a second to reconsider my actions.

The reflex was unexpected; I wasn't really the fighting kind.

He stumbled and brought a hand to his mouth, dabbing at the blood that dripped from his bottom lip. I thought he'd fight back, at least throw a punch or two.

But he didn't, the coward.

Instead he backed off without another word. I didn't even bother to watch him walk away.

It was the last time I ever saw my brother.

Why I couldn't let it go is beyond me. Did I still love Ivy? No. But that wasn't the point. The point was that my brother, the one person I was supposed to be able to trust, betrayed me.

Loyalties may run thick, but so does bullshit.

And no one wants to step in that.

AFTER-SEX SNUGGLES

Dylan

YOU KNOW THAT PHRASE, "you never know what you've got 'til it's gone?" I never knew I wanted to be a father, how much I wanted to start a family with Alisha. I thought it would always be just us. Kids were never really on our radar—at least not in the beginning. We were enamored with one another, and nothing else mattered for the longest time.

Until it did.

Part of me wants to admit it took some convincing for Alisha to realize she wanted a baby, too. But in my heart, I knew better. She wanted a baby, and she always had. She just couldn't admit it to herself.

The first time the conversation came up, we had just made love— Alisha hated it when I called it that—and even though she wasn't a fan of after-sex snuggles, she let me hold her. We always joked that our roles were reversed, but it never bother me. I knew I wasn't less of a man just because I wanted to cuddle with my wife.

"Do you ever think about having kids?" I asked her. I felt her body tense in response; of course, she tried to hide it, but I felt it when every muscle in her body tightened and her heart rate increased.

"I can't," she said after a minute. I didn't know what that meant; whether she physically couldn't because of some medical reason or if it was emotional. Something in her psyche that told her she couldn't be a mother.

"What do you mean?" I asked, running my fingers softly up and down her arm.

"I just...I don't think I could do it."

"Oh, babe...I know you could. You'd be a great mother." She pulled away from me and sat up, pulling the sheet over her chest to cover her breasts.

"Is that what you want? Kids?"

"Well, of course. You don't?"

"No. But hear me out. I know I'm *supposed* to want kids. To dream of babies and shitty diapers and nursing until my nipples are raw. But I don't. I don't want that, because..." She paused, as if the words were foreign on her tongue, their taste bitter. I squeezed her hand, my fingers laced between hers. "I don't want to turn out like her," she nearly whispered.

"Like your mother? Alisha, you are *not* your mother."

"I know that. But the potential is there. It's always there."

"Baby, come on. I know you. You'll never be her."

"No, I won't. But that doesn't mean I'll be a good mom. My career alone should tell you that. How is that fair to our child, Dylan?"

"You'll have to quit eventually, right?"

"Right. But the internet won't. It will always be there."

"So? You changed your last name when we got married; the business is set up under Hill. How would anyone ever know? Just think about it. Somewhere, deep down, I think your heart feels the same way."

And it did.

After that we played fast and loose with condoms, and Alisha's

IUD expired a few weeks later. So, I knew she wanted a kid; she wouldn't have let her IUD expire if she didn't.

When she got pregnant, those double lines suddenly became everything. We were excited, and nervous. Her anticipation was palpable. But neither of us had a fucking clue what we were doing.

THERE'S NO MUSIC

Alisha

I WASN'T sure why Dylan never went to work that morning, the morning of his caffeine-less nightmare. I didn't ask. I figured he'd tell me if he wanted to, and he never did offer up a reason.

I did see the blood on his knuckles, however.

Nonetheless, we spent the day binge-watching Netflix and eating junk food. Neither of us were expecting company, but the doorbell rang anyway.

And there it was, another gift with my name on it.

An edible arrangement from my apparent secret admirer.

"Maybe it's time to give up the website…shut it down a little earlier than we planned." Dylan suggested, his hands massaging my shoulders and sending shivers down my spine.

"You're distracting me with words again," I muttered in a daze. I was under his spell; the heat of his touch seemed to do that to me.

"We don't need the money," he reminded me.

"I know."

"So why don't you just shut it down? Let me have you all to myself." I didn't disagree with his logic, but I wasn't afraid to let him sweat it out a bit either. Give him a chance to think he had some convincing to do.

He didn't.

And the truth is, I'd already made the decision to shut it down earlier that morning. I was ready to hang up all the sexy lingerie and save it for a rainy day. "Is somebody jealous?" I teased anyway.

"Yes," he said with raw conviction. My head shot up from his chest at the unexpected admission. I brought a hand to Dylan's cheek, the desperation in his eyes nearly enough to bring a tear to my own. "Baby, I...I'm so sorry," I said.

"You didn't know, I get it."

"No, I didn't...I didn't know it bothered you. Why didn't you tell me?"

"I wanted it to be your decision. But I don't want to share you anymore, Alisha. I'm ready to have you all to myself."

"No, you're absolutely right. I'll shut it down tomorrow and refund the unused credits. I'll dissolve the business."

"Really? Just like that?" I smiled at the shock on his face.

"Just like that," I confirmed.

"Wow, I kind of expected an argument there." He pulled me close as his lips curled into a smile.

"It's time. I'm almost embarrassed to admit it, but I think I've grown out of it. All the dressing up and make-believe role play is getting old. Now I can sit around in sweat pants!" I pecked a kiss onto his cheek, amused at his attempt not to smile.

"Wow, you're really giving me something to look forward to in this marriage," he teased, and I playfully shoved him.

"You know what I mean! Plus, it's not like I'm getting rid of the toys...who says we can't still enjoy those?"

"I do like the sound of that."

"You just have to be able to keep up with me," I said with a seductive wink.

"I think I can do that." He smiled and gave my ass a quick squeeze. "Dance with me?" he asked.

"There's no music."

"Oh, there's always music, my love…"

While I left that afternoon full of excitement and potential, my trip to Kristin's office knocked me ten steps backward.

"How are things at home? With Dylan, the website? He still has yet to express concern over it?" she'd asked. Admittedly, it'd been a while since I'd made it to a session, so she was a little behind in the saga of my life. But the question had uncovered what I considered to be the last scoop of dirt she'd throw in my face.

"Actually, I shut it all down. The website. Dylan and I want to start a family, and it's just not practical for me anymore. Of course, there's this whole other pregnancy porn trope I guess I could pursue, but—"

"Oh, my. Wow, this is…unexpected, to say the least!" she beamed, cutting me off. She'd looked at me with what I could only assume was pride, her eyes lighting up in my presence for the first time. "I have to say, Alisha, I am *utterly* impressed." She made a check mark of sorts on her notepad, clicking the pen a few times before dropping it onto the page.

But I was nothing more than a deer in headlights, just waiting for the semi-truck to slam into me. Her sudden change in demeanor caught me off guard. "I'm sorry, you're impressed with what, exactly?"

"With *you*! Surely, you can understand how unprecedented this is. Your progress is remarkable."

"…I'm still not following."

She adjusted her glasses, and crossed her legs, tucking one behind the other like a proper lady. "You've come from virtually nothing, making a name for yourself in a lucrative and competitive industry. You built an empire of financial stability, and now you're in what I would consider your first monogamous relationship. And you're finally willing to give up your career to start a family." She paused for effect, and I imagined the perplexed look on my face alerted her to my continued state of confusion. "Don't you see?" she continued. "You're nothing like her—your mother. And, I know I shouldn't make that assumption without ever meeting her, but what I see in you, Alisha, is compassion. I see heart, and the will to not only love yourself, but to *be* loved in return."

She sat back in her pretentious chair, crossing her arms over her chest and smiling like the fucking idiot that she is. Of all the derogatory remarks she made over the years, I think that one stung the most.

"Yeah? Well, all I hear is your long-awaited approval, not *because* of all I've overcome, but rather a direct result of my decision to leave the porn industry."

She sucked in a breath and waved a corrective hand in the air, not having realized her mistake until it was too late. "No, no, that's not what I said. I just meant—"

"You didn't have to. Trust me, it was implied." I stood and threw my purse over my shoulder, the sudden tension in the back of my neck sure to develop into a headache later. "Ya know, at the end of the day, I'm still a sex addict. I still like to fuck and *be* fucked. And I'm not ashamed of that—despite your attempts to convince me I should be. I mean, you told me yourself that I'd never be able to escape the title, so why not wear it proudly? And seeing as I'm all *healed* now, I'll no longer be in need of your services."

At that, I stormed out of Kristin's office for the last time.

Seven years of her bullshit was more than enough for me.

THE KIND OF PERSON WHO ALWAYS
LOSES THEIR KEYS

Alisha

I WAS NEVER much for holiday shopping, but Christmas was fast approaching, and while I didn't have many people to buy for—just Mrs. Maylen, Dylan, and a little something for Chris—I wanted to make sure their gifts were meaningful. If it weren't for them, I'd have no one to shop for in the first place, and I'd never bought a gift for a significant other, so I was stressing over what to get for Dylan. To make matters worse, thanks to my mom, I was a horrible gift-giver by nature.

But I was determined to change that.

I'd scavenged the outlet mall for nearly two hours, and was annoyed at the sheer volume of people in my way at every turn, the long checkout lines, and the fact that I couldn't for the life of me figure out what the hell to get for Dylan. Finally admitting defeat and throwing in the towel, I headed back to my car, the vibration in my pocket alerting me to an incoming phone call as I stepped off the curb.

The words *Restricted Number* scrolled across the screen. I should have let the call go to voicemail, but curiosity got the best of me, and I answered it.

"Hello?"

"Lisha?"

"Who's this?" I asked tentatively. Nobody other than my subscribers—and Chris—called me Lisha. None of them had my number, and Chris's would've shown up on the caller ID. I froze in place, standing in the middle of the walkway, my eyes scanning the parking lot while my heart hammered in my chest.

I recognized the voice on the other end.

"It's Lila!"

Fuck.

"Lila, hi." I spun around to get a look behind me, certain she was near but unable to prove it. I felt her presence, as sure as day. The thought that she might be watching me sent a shiver up my spine.

"Did you get a new phone number?" she asked, clearly aware that I did.

"Yeah." *How did you manage to get it?* I wanted to ask.

"I miss you," she admitted with a longing in her voice. I wasn't sure what to say, so I listened to the sound of her breathing instead. After a moment she asked, "Do you miss me?"

"Listen, Lila, I'm not sure how you got this number, but I have no interest in seeing you. Please don't call again." I disconnected the call, annoyed that I would have to change my number again. There was no way she'd be able to resist using it again.

I wasn't sure what to make of the intrusion, but I knew I didn't like it. One should never mix business with pleasure, and Lila—despite her attempts to prove otherwise—was nothing more than a former business partner, a colleague of sorts.

And she was chaotic; the kind of person who always loses their keys or can never remember whether or not they unplugged the curling iron. I didn't do well with chaos. I didn't do well with clutter or dust or people who buy frivolously.

And Lila was all of those things; the kind of woman whose brain rattles whenever she turns her head.

Sliding into my car, I chided myself for judging her; I hadn't meant to be catty. But I'd told her before, and my patience was running thin.

We couldn't see each other anymore.

I'd met someone.

That's what I'd told her when I called her following my ten-day trial with Dylan. House calls were officially a thing of the past—and not just for her, but across the board. I was going back to live streams only, no more private sessions, no more in-person hookups. It wasn't like I was under contract with anyone; I wasn't tied down in any way.

And I certainly wasn't about to ruin a good thing.

I'd told Dylan the same. He was on board, and even accepting of the fact that I'd still work. "I'm just glad you won't be doing those private sessions anymore," was all he'd said the morning I told him. He'd poured a cup of coffee, gave me a kiss, and headed off to work. I hadn't given it another thought; in retrospect, I should have payed attention to the underlying subtext, the snicker in his response. The upturn of his lip.

He didn't want me to work anymore.

He just didn't have the balls to tell me.

MY DARLING, LISHA

Dylan

STANDING up to Alisha was never my strong suit. Not that I *couldn't*—I just wasn't *good* at it. Sometimes I left her to her vices. I wasn't afraid to admit she knew better than I did when it came down to it. But there were definitely times I felt the need to butt in. She never saw herself the way others did.

The way others saw her started to matter, though. I hated to be the bearer of bad news, but it really did. After Grandma passed, Chris and I were the only two people who gave a shit about Alisha.

That fact would concern any husband.

Nobody cared about her wellbeing, whether or not she had a roof over her head, food on the table. A loving and safe relationship. They didn't even want to know anything about her, and once they did, they immediately judged her by appearance alone. Or, by her profession, if they happened to know what she did for a living.

People are dicks, they always have been.

But for some reason this was a surprise to Alisha. She cared so little what people thought of her that she truly had no idea how much they hated her. We all want what we can't have, and when we meet someone who has *it*, we instinctively despise them. We inadvertently wish them misery.

We want them to suffer.

And then we watch from the sidelines as they do.

I tried to explain this to Alisha. But as you may have figured out, my wife is quite stubborn—she never listens.

The day the flowers came, I admit, I lost my patience with her. Not at first, though, not right away. No, the argument took a while to heat up. I tried dealing with the situation politely, giving Alisha the opportunity to do the right thing without being told.

Does that make me sound a bit controlling? Oh well. Had you been in my shoes, you may have handled things the same damn way I did. When you marry a woman like Alisha, sometimes the jealousy creeps up when you least expect it. One day it's there, the next it's gone.

But it never goes far.

And when another woman sends your wife two dozen long-stemmed red roses, you better fucking believe you'll have some suggestive questions.

"She's becoming a bit obsessed with you, don't you think?"

"It's not like that," she protested. I approached the topic with a subtle urgency, because that's how I had to approach all things with Alisha. By calmly implying she was in danger and strongly suggesting she allow me do something about it.

"It seems like it is, Alisha. This woman is sending flowers to our house. She shouldn't even know where you live. It's…stalker-like." I plucked the card from the table and gave it a quick read.

To my darling, Lisha.

"She's just lonely," she said in flippant rebuttal. Almost like she felt sorry for this woman.

"She has a husband…" I reminded her.

"She does." She rearranged the flowers on the table and stood back to have a look at them. I couldn't tell what she was thinking, whether she liked the flowers or not. "They're separated, though." She turned and grabbed the card from my hands, placing it at the base of the bouquet. "Not *every* husband is as wonderful as you are, Dylan." She stroked my cheek with her hand, her fingers tracing the edge of my mouth before the pad of her thumb slid across my bottom lip.

And just like that, the spell had been cast.

Her seduction began.

I wrapped my arms around my wife, pulling her close and pressing my erection into her hip. Her body responded, her arousal evident in the depths of her eyes, the beat of her heart against mine. She rolled her tongue along her bottom lip and slid her hand into my jeans, taking me in her palm and stroking slowly, taunting me without breaking eye contact.

Hurriedly, I backed her up against the dining room wall, my hands gripping her thighs, and lifted her until her legs wrapped around me. I pulled her panties aside—the fact that she wore only my T-shirt giving me easy access—and slid into her with ease. I took advantage of that moment to just *be* inside her, claiming her with everything I had to offer.

Then her mouth met mine, her tongue begging for me.

So I fucked her until she came.

Then I fucked her again.

Because those flowers sitting on our kitchen table reminded me that if I didn't keep my wife satisfied, someone else would.

The fight that ensued later that night knocked the wind out me. To be honest, it was our first major blowout. The one that changed the tides and ruptured the dam. The culprit?

A simple question, really.

I asked my wife how many people she'd slept with.

Curiosity had been eating at me since the day I met her, and I couldn't stop the inquisition from falling out of my mouth.

Talk about a mistake, a big whopping clusterfuck of a mistake on my part. Word to the wise: don't ever ask your wife how many people she's had sex with. If you're planning to ask that question, do it while you're dating, but don't expect an honest answer, even if you give one in return. Everybody lies about how many people they fucked before they met their spouse. But should you feel the need to ask such a question, definitely do it before you get married and the answer that casually flies out of their mouth breaks your fucking heart right in two.

And most importantly, don't do it after sex, when she's sore and tired from riding you like a damn bull.

"Why the hell would you ask me that?" she snapped, popping up from the bed and stripping the sheet from the mattress. She wrapped it around herself like a toga, tucking the corner at the top.

"I can't ask how many people you've slept with? Is the answer *that* terrible?"

"Yes, as a matter of fact, it is. But thank you. Truly. For making me feel like a piece of shit just so you can take pride in being the final notch in the belt."

"That's not at all why I was asking. It was just a question."

"And why does it matter to you? Hmm? You're the one that's here now. I already gave up my fucking job for you. What more do you want?"

Her blaming me for shutting down the website was the kicker.

She'd said it was a mutual decision.

Apparently, that was only the case until she needed something to throw back in my face.

A WEAPON MADE OF PAPER

Dylan

IT WAS OFFICIAL—MY wife had a stalker. A full-on, stage-five clinger.

And a woman to boot.

First the edible arrangements, then flowers, and the never-ending phone calls. The so-called accidental run-ins would come next; it was only a matter of time before she showed up at the house looking for her. I hoped it wouldn't come to that, but then again, I kind of hoped it would.

I went from turned on to straight-up freaked out in a matter of minutes and wasn't sure what to make of any of it. My concern was Alisha's safety, of course, and I was committed to ripping apart anyone who jeopardized it—man or woman.

So many thoughts raced through my mind...the first? Was she hot? And yes, I'll admit that probably wasn't the best first thought to have on the matter, but it is what it is.

Sometimes a man can't help but think with his dick.

Anyway, my second thought was a general curiosity as to what this woman wanted—what her end game was. Was she in love with my wife? Did she want to hurt her? I wanted to know what kind of stalker we were dealing with.

I had a hard time asking Alisha any of these questions, so for the most part, I asked none of them. Not because I lacked a backbone and harbored some unexplainable fear of my wife, but to be honest, I wasn't sure I was ready to hear the back story.

And I wasn't in the mood for another argument.

I assumed this woman—Lila, apparently—was either a former customer of Alisha's or a former…girlfriend? Lover? It didn't matter. All I cared about was getting her the fuck out of our lives.

"At some point, you might want to consider a restraining order," I'd suggested. Alisha huffed and brought her hands to her hips. I knew she was pissed at me, but all I could think was how adorable she looked when she was mad. The way her nose crinkled up, her lips in a pout.

"It's too late for that, Dylan," she snapped back. "She won't quit. What good is a weapon made of paper?"

"I don't know, but we can't keep doing this, Alisha. She's *obsessed* with you. How are we going to bring a baby into this world with that woman popping up everywhere?"

"I don't know," she snapped again, this time with more of an edge to her tone. She threw her arms up in the air and sighed. "I don't *fucking* know."

"Hey, hey…babe, it's okay. Come here," I said, pulling her close. She rested her head against my chest, and I inhaled the scent of her hair as I rubbed her back.

"Stop smelling me."

"I can't help it." I nipped playfully at her ear, and she giggled, despite her mood, the sound of her laughter somehow erasing the stress of the day. I wrapped my arms around her like a claw machine. "You're kinda cranky this morning," I teased, my hand sliding under her shirt to her stomach. It was still flat, but the pooch would come soon.

The baby would be the change we needed; it would fix everything.

"What's your point?" She pushed my hands from her shirt and picked a sweatshirt off the floor before pulling it over her head.

"No point. More of an observation, really."

"Well, your unsolicited observation is noted," she said, smiling in that cute way that made me want to jump her. My heart melted, and all I could do was pull her into my arms and plant kisses on the top of her head. Those moments of vulnerability were so few and far between with her. I took advantage of them when I could.

A crack formed in my heart the following afternoon when Alisha suffered a miscarriage. She was only a few weeks along, but the loss hit us just as hard.

ONE HELL OF A GIVER

Alisha

I HAD ARRIVED at the hotel exactly thirty minutes early, as instructed.

A small suitcase in tow, I stopped at the front desk and picked up the room key. He'd said there was a surprise waiting for me inside, and the familiar chills of anticipation quivered in my bones.

The bed was littered with rose petals—a cliche I could've done without—and a bottle of non-alcoholic champagne chilled on the bedside table. Next to it was a small gift box and a card.

Put these on and wait for me.

With the blindfold in place, I laid on the bed naked but for a skimpy pair of edible, crotchless panties. Even before he arrived, it was a high like I'd never experienced. A sensory overload of sorts. Everything was heightened without my sight.

The draft of cold air on my nipples.

The sound of footsteps in the hall.

Then, a soft knock on the door. I sat up, propping myself on my elbows.

"Are you ready?" he asked. "Did you follow the instructions?"

"Yes."

"Good girl."

Only a minute passed before the removal of his coat, followed by his shoes. I heard the sounds, was able to picture the scene play out, down to the color of his suit. Then, the slap of his belt being pulled through its loops.

A zipper.

A shifting of weight on the mattress as he joined me, his leg brushing against mine. I shivered at the contact, my heart rate rapidly increasing.

His fingertips grazed my body, from my breasts and down my torso. And I anticipated their touch on my swollen folds, where I expected them next, but instead it was his mouth, and it was—oh, it was fucking beautiful. My body writhed at the motion of his tongue, and I fought the urge to cry out.

And at the height of it all, there was something missing. There was something I couldn't hear, couldn't feel. And I was fairly certain that was against the rules.

Lila.

―――――

Fully showered and satisfied some time later, I exited the bathroom in the suite and met Grant in the sitting room. His iPad on his lap, he wore nothing but a pair of boxer briefs, and my heart skipped a beat at the sight of him.

He looked up and smiled when I stood beside him, and I couldn't help but smile back. The shit-eating grin on my face had been difficult to wipe off after what I'd just experienced.

And as much as I didn't want to ask, I found myself doing it anyway. "Where's Lila?" He shook his head, but I couldn't place the expression on his face. "Is she coming?"

"It's just us this weekend," he said with an even tone.

"What about the agreement?"

"I didn't sign anything. Did you?"

*Aside from your marriage certificate...*I wanted to say. "No," I said instead.

"Do you plan to tell her about our indiscretion?" I shook my head. "Good. Neither do I." He motioned for me to join him on the couch. And I'd like to say the thought of having Grant all to myself for the weekend didn't excite me.

But it did.

It excited me a whole hell of a lot.

I'd wanted nothing more than to get him alone since the first night I laid eyes on him. And now that I had?

I had to admit, Lila's husband was one hell of a giver.

ASSETS TO WORK

Dylan

So, the truth is, I'd seen Alisha coming out of the hotel that weekend. I didn't know *who* she was, but I knew I wanted to be close to her. I was attending a Realtors' conference at the same hotel, and aside from sitting in on all the seminars and panel discussions, I'd essentially spent the weekend jacking off in my room and drinking from the mini bar.

Like a goddamned teenage boy.

Except that I was a thirty-four-year-old man simply hung up on his ex. For the life of me, I couldn't seem to pull myself together long enough to do anything about it. I certainly wasn't ready for another relationship—don't even get me started on my list of grievances about dating—and meaningless hookups had never been my thing.

I checked out of the hotel by eight that morning, taking a seat in the lobby to scarf down a pistachio muffin and a mediocre cup of coffee before hitting the road.

But then, there she was—the most strikingly beautiful woman I've ever seen in my life. She towed a small suitcase behind her, her other hand stuffed in the pocket of a long coat as she made her way out the door. Her heels clicked on the floor when she walked by, and I watched —almost as if in slow motion—while the sight of her burned its way into my brain.

Then I saw him follow her out the door. I saw her stand on the tips of her toes, despite the height she'd gained from the heels, to kiss him goodbye.

And yet, days later, I still couldn't stop thinking about her, and that was becoming a problem, because the chances of ever seeing that woman again were sure to be one in a fucking million.

There was no chance the two of them had done anything in that hotel other than engage in an affair.

That's when I turned to the internet. In hopes of finding her? No. I wasn't a fucking idiot—I knew I had nothing to go by, nothing identifiable to use in the search field. I stared at it, the blinking cursor taunting me.

So I set out to find someone who *looked* like her. Call it a fantasy if you will; I'm not entirely proud. Next thing I knew, I was searching through porn sites with key words like "brunette bombshell." Not because I had any inkling that I'd find *her* there, that *she* was a porn star herself—no, that fact was far beyond my imagination.

But sure as shit, there she was.

This goddess of temptation, right there on my computer screen. Lisha's Bedroom, the name of the site that I bookmarked and couldn't get enough of—but just the streaming and prior content videos, though. There were no private sessions for me, no one-on-one time with her.

Not until I met her, anyway.

All this to say to you—to *beg* for your understanding—that I had no idea this mystery woman was the same woman my grandmother had taken in all those years ago. I had no fucking clue of that fact when I knocked on her apartment door for the first time a few months later and found her standing there in that kimono robe.

But after that? After that I knew the only way to win this woman over was to take that secret to my grave.

"So, when are you going to fill me in on the whole Lila back story?" I asked Alisha one night after dinner. We were snuggled together in our underwear, watching some cooking show, and the question just leaked right out of my mouth.

Like spilled milk through the cracks of a kitchen table.

Did I have intentions of asking such a stupid question?

Nope.

Still kinda wish I hadn't, but it was out, and it was too late to put it back. So I did the only thing I could think to do, which was to ask a follow up question before she even answered the first. "What's the deal with her?"

She shrugged, and even from my position on the couch, it was obvious she wasn't in the mood for a game of *Twenty Questions*. "There's really nothing to tell," she said, her eyes never leaving the TV. Her nonchalance didn't sit well with me, though—I knew there was more to it. Something she didn't want me to know.

To my shame, I asked no further questions, knowing full well that I should have. Instead, I stood abruptly in outward annoyance. Her lack of interest in the discussion pissed me off.

But, as she often did, Alisha put her assets to work.

We'd been arguing a lot lately, and neither of us wanted to go another round. To my surprise, Alisha slid off the couch and onto the floor, dropping to her knees in front of me, where she pulled out my cock and took me in her mouth.

The act was effective in shutting me up—and very clearly let me know that the conversation was over.

We never did get a chance to revisit the issue.

REJECTION REALLY IS A BITCH

Alisha

I SPOTTED her as I left the candle store, her blonde hair peeking out under a red beanie. Her disguise was subtle, but still enough for me to do a double-take.

She either frequented the same places as me, or she was following me again.

My money was on the latter.

I felt her presence, her footsteps behind me. I ducked into a coffee shop and walked straight to the ladies' room, locking the door behind me and pulling out my smart phone. Why? I'm not entirely sure, but I felt threatened, so I did.

I fired off a text to Dylan. **HELP. COFFEE SHOP. NOW.** He'd know which one.

The heavy door creaked melodically when she pushed it open, the lock turning a second later. The click of her heels, the stilettos she always wore, seemed to echo in unison with my heartbeat.

I silently sucked in a breath, sure to pass out as I held it in for fear that I'd make a sound.

"Lisha?"

Oh, God.

My heart pounded so hard in my chest, I was certain she could hear it thumping. That the very thing to ruin me would be the one thing meant to keep me alive.

She's looking under the stall doors.

She knew I was in there, despite my lack of response. Despite the fact that I hovered over the toilet, my ass planted on the tank cover. I fully anticipated her busting through the stall door, ready to assault the shit out of me, but to my surprise, she turned and left.

I hunkered down in that awkward position for a good half hour, hopeful Lila would have left the coffee shop entirely by the time I re-emerged. No one waits around in public that long when they're stalking someone, right?

Wrong.

Her eyes were the first I locked in on when I eventually stepped out of the bathroom. My legs went numb at the sight of her. She was perched on a stool at the coffee bar, patiently waiting for me and sipping an espresso.

She had ordered one for me, too.

"There you are," she said calmly, tauntingly. "You were in there a while. Tummy issues?" she asked, placing her hand on her stomach. She refused to accept the idea that I was hiding from her on purpose.

I nodded, almost grateful for the out but careful not to appear as terrified as I was. A woman like her thrived on fear. "Something like that," I managed to say.

"I saved you a seat."

She pulled her designer bag off the stool next to her and placed it on the counter. I stood in awe for a moment, quickly realizing I had no choice but to sit with her, to join her for a cup of coffee that—now that I think about it—she very well could have drugged or poisoned.

That kind of stuff didn't happen in real life, did it?

"You haven't been taking my calls," she said quietly, looking down at her cup. I avoided her eyes when she finally looked up. The sadness in them couldn't be real. It wasn't warranted.

"I've been busy."

"We're all *busy*, Lisha." She waved her hand in the air as she spoke, and I'm nearly certain I saw her eyes roll. I wasn't sure how to respond, so I didn't.

She waited a few awkward minutes, letting me sweat it out, and then reached over and took my hand. I fought the urge to pull it back, to break the skin-to-skin contact she had been so desperate to establish.

"Grant has been asking for you," she admits. "He—*we*—miss you." She paused for a beat, seemingly offering me a moment to take in her admission. "We'd like you to come back."

"Lila, I can't—" I started, but she cut me off before I could get in another word.

"Why not?" she snapped, her face oddly pain-stricken.

I sighed, allowing my growing frustration to overtake the fear that squirmed in my belly. *She's harmless,* I reminded myself. Lila was just a woman in love with the idea of opening her marriage to another woman. She was nothing more than a wife trying not to disappoint her husband.

I'd seen it more times than you might think, women forcing themselves into a ménage à trois to keep their husbands happy.

It rarely does, and most often results in divorce. Especially when neither party follows the agreed upon rules.

"Look, it's not your fault," I started, taking my hand back. "It's nothing against *you* or even Grant," I continued. "But I'm with someone now. I've gotten out of—" I paused, unsure how to phrase the statement. "*That* lifestyle."

I saw the tears well up in her eyes before the first one rolled down her freckled cheek. She was hurt. I couldn't blame her; rejection really *is* a bitch.

But you can't force someone to love you, and if you think you can, in the end it's not really love anyway. I reached up to wipe the tear from her cheek, but she swatted my hand away and abruptly stood from her chair.

"You can't just toy with people's emotions like that, Lisha. It's not fair to us." She spat the words like they tasted sour and scooped her bag off the chair. She didn't bother to wipe her tears as they fell. She had no qualms about crying in public, about making a scene over a lover's quarrel.

She was weak like that.

"Lila, come on," I argued, pulling a twenty from my wallet and tossing it on the counter. I had no idea if she'd already paid for our coffees, but I wasn't one to make a scene in public and leave without some form of condolence, so the barista was welcome to keep the change for a tip.

I followed Lila outside, running into Dylan just as I stepped out the door.

"Babe? Is everything okay?" he asked, pulling me into his arms. I could do nothing but watch the back of Lila's head as she stomped briskly down the sidewalk. At the end of the street, she turned and looked back, her eyes locking with mine as Dylan held me close.

How quickly the look in her eyes had changed from love to hate.

LIKE A DYING CAT IN HEAT

Alisha

ONE WORD RINGS in my ear.

Over and over, on a loop it plays. Like none of the other words in the dictionary matter anymore.

Murder.

Why it's there, I don't know. But it's there. It's loud, it's boldly written in all caps and highlighted in yellow.

And I fucking hate it.

I even caught myself humming a makeshift tune for it, as if an entire song could be derived of this one stupid word. But there it is, swimming in my head like that annoying jingle from the National American University commercial.

And I've always been a terrible singer.

Dylan used to say my singing voice sounded like a dying cat in heat. I wasn't sure what that sounded like, but figured it couldn't be good.

"The fuck you hummin' over there, Barbie?" Ronnie asks, looking up from her lunch tray. She's been getting into some trouble lately and hanging around Tiffany a lot. I'm not sure how she ended up at my table, but she's here now, so I have to answer her.

"Hm?"

"You're humming something. I don't recognize the song."

"It's nothing," I say in attempt to wave her off. It'd be nice if she went back to opening her mouth only to stuff her face. But I seem to be down on my luck today.

She pitches a face and curls her lip in a half-cocked smile. "Ohhh, damn, girl. You...you wrote it, didn't you?" She makes air quotes as she speaks then laughs, throwing her head back like the idea of me writing a song is a stand-up-worthy joke.

"Not exactly," I say.

"Oh, cut the shit," she snaps, pointing a threatening finger in my direction. "You're losing it." She pokes at her temple with the same finger and stands, lifting her tray from the table. "Happens to the best of us."

I watch her leave, chuckling to herself as she dumps the remains of her lunch into the garbage bin. She hums my tune while she wanders off, waving her hands in the air like a dedicated choir director.

"I'm not the one losing it," I mumble to myself.

"Don't let her get to you," Tiffany says with a wink. I didn't see her sit down, so I don't know how much of the conversation she overheard, but I'm guessing all of it.

She's sneaky like that.

"I'm not," I say in defense, my tone flat. I stand and gather my garbage, deciding it's time to head back to my cell, but Tiffany grabs my forearm, anchoring me in place as she leans in close.

"I saved you a seat, you know."

"Where?"

"Over there." She points to a small table across the room, the loner table I used to sit at when I first arrived here. Most days no one sits there.

"Okay..."

"Next time, join me. It'll be good for your sanity in the long run."

And I don't know why I say it out loud, why I can't just keep the thought to myself. But the words are out of my mouth before I can stop them. "I don't know about that."

She digs her fingernails into my arm this time, a devilish look playing in her eyes. "Hey, ya know, I've been nothin' but nice to you since you got here, Thompson. The least you can do is acknowledge me when I'm in the room. I'm the only fucking friend you got."

And this is why women don't do well in prison, why emotions run hot. We're too needy, too high strung and territorial. It's like everyone's periods sync up and it's all we can do not to drown in the cesspool.

"Sorry," I mumble in response to Tiffany. She releases her grip on my arm, her fingernails leaving tiny crescent moons behind.

She stands and awkwardly leans in to kiss my cheek. I flinch when she reaches out and taps my crotch before she palms it and accosts me with her finger. "Just remember, there's no room for pretty people here. Prison makes everyone ugly. It levels the playing field," she says before walking away.

And the ugliest ones are always guarding the net.

CHANNELING OUR INNER DEXTER

Alisha

Time stands still in here.

Like I'm suspended in life, just waiting around until I'm allowed to go outside and play again. The day-to-day I once knew continues to fade away, the comfort of my simple life nearly long gone. I sleep. I eat. I shower. I piss and shit. I masturbate. Sometimes I meet with Kyle. And occasionally someone sexually harasses me. That's it, the daily cycle guaranteed to repeat again tomorrow.

Sometimes it feels like I'm drowning in the silence. I've been alone most of my life, but it's nothing compared to this. Childhood was a cake walk next to what I'm facing here.

I've never felt so unnecessary.

I don't know how to matter in here.

Maybe I never will.

During rec, I make my way to an empty table and sit down with a book. I've read it before, but I'll read it again just to keep busy. There isn't much to choose from here, and certainly no new releases.

But minding my own business keeps the other inmates at bay. Most days, anyway.

Lately it feels like they're all ready to eat me alive, though. Officer Marshall sure likes to take a bite every now and then. And that's part of the problem—he favors me, and they know it. They're never top choice anymore, and they can't take it. They need the dick, and Officer Marshall seems to be the only one willing to give it to any of us.

Not that I've resorted to asking for it.

My heart remains with Dylan, and I can't bring myself to engage in sexual activity with anyone here. Not willingly anyway. I *could.*

But I won't.

I can't focus on the words on the page. They blur together and my mind drifts again, back down Memory Lane, where it often likes to sneak off.

And then I'm with him again, with Dylan. Back at Mrs. Maylen's house right after it became mine. I remember the way his eyes sparkled when he laughed. How his lip twitched when he was aroused. Everyone has those little endearing quirks, and sometimes it's all I can focus on when I think of him.

I was a sucker for his lips, always had been.

"Dylan? I'm home!" I'd shouted as I walked through the door. I'd just dropped Chris off at the airport, sending him on a flight to Wesley Chapel, Florida, to meet the man he hoped would turn out to be his soul mate. I wished him well in his online dating adventures, but internally, I already missed my friend.

I was kinda pissed he left.

"In here!" Dylan called from upstairs. I took the stairs two at a time, anxious to see what he was up to, and why the house smelled like paint.

"Whoa, what's going on in here?" I asked. The expanse of our bedroom was covered from floor to ceiling in clear plastic. I mock searched for blood splatter, but found none. "Are we channeling our inner *Dexter*?"

"We're painting!" he confirmed, his mouth stretched into a wide grin. "Surprise! I thought we could get started on some projects since you're not working anymore. I know you're getting bored. Do you like the color?" I nodded and smiled at my husband's thoughtfulness, at his willingness to put my needs before his.

He knew I would struggle to occupy myself without working, to find a new hobby of sorts so that I didn't sit around masturbating all day. And Dylan's suggestion was to inundate myself with projects around the house.

"Come here," Dylan said, setting the paint roller in a tray and stepping over it. I held my arms out to him, suddenly wanting nothing more than to roll around naked with him in the wet paint.

"Hi," I whispered against his mouth.

"Hi back." His hand found my own, his fingers mindlessly twirling the diamond band on my left ring finger. "Feel like painting a picture?" he asked.

"Mm, I do," I replied with a hint of seduction. I pushed to the tips of my toes and met his lips, his hands already tugging at the hem of my shirt.

We were naked within seconds, our bodies molded together as I rode him in the middle of the floor, covered in gray paint, plastic wrap crinkling beneath us.

It's memories like this that make it hard to move forward here. Sometimes I forget he's gone, though, and that helps. That makes it easier to get through the day.

I'm not sure I have anything to look forward to otherwise.

BE THE TEQUILA

Alisha

THERE'S an old saying my mother used to repeat that drove me crazy for years—I didn't understand what it meant. I was thirteen, and far too young to properly place the reference, but for some reason I liked the way it sounded when she said it. Like she knew it was the most clever thing to ever come out of her mouth.

Maybe it was, who knows? I'd never admit it to her, but I kind of thought so, too. And, for some reason, it felt like motherly advice in a way, as odd as it sounds. As if there were a rare validity to her words.

While I made a point not to spend much time at home, I found myself stuck in the trailer over the holidays. Most nights I did my homework at Mrs. Maylen's with Teddy snuggled up to my side, his head on my lap as I studied. But over winter break my freshman year, Mrs. Maylen left for a week to visit her daughter and grandkids. Teddy went too. I had my own key to her house, but it didn't feel right staying there while she was out of town, so I didn't.

And a week at the trailer with Mom wasn't something to look

forward to. Not only did she have nothing planned for us, there was also no Christmas tree, and no gifts to put under it if we had one—not that Christmas was about the gifts. I would've been content with just about anything, but what I wanted most was a normal day with my mom. The way things were before she found the bottle. I wasn't sure what everyone else's Christmases looked like, but mine were just like any other day, the only difference was that I didn't have school.

On the morning of Christmas Eve, I woke up to a quiet trailer, and sat at our kitchen table eating scrambled eggs and hand writing a research paper for history class. Mom had been decent company the night before, but it was a new day, and I never went into those expecting much.

She came out of her room around nine that morning, wearing a tattered bathrobe, a pair of crew socks that had seen better days crooked on her feet. "What'cha working on there?" she asked, her voice gruff from sleep.

"History paper."

"On what?" She grabbed a packet of instant coffee from the cupboard—probably stolen from the run-down motel she sometimes worked at—pouring it into a mug and adding water before placing it in the microwave. She stabbed at the buttons with a bony finger.

"The Great Depression."

"Ugh, story of my life," she joked, chuckling to herself. "I don't know why you're wasting your time with that shit anyway. It ain't like it'll get ya into college. Lord knows I won't be paying for it."

"I plan to go to college," I said with conviction. I didn't care that she didn't believe me, I believed in myself enough for the both of us. I had a chance at a scholarship *somewhere*. It didn't matter where, as long as it got me out of there.

"The fuck you wanna do that for?"

"So I don't have to live like *this* for the rest of my life…"

"Ain't no such thing as a good life, comin' up like this, child. You were fucked from the moment you came outta me. Nothin' to do about it now."

Her words stung, and I wasn't sure why I let them. I tried not to value her opinion, but for some reason I did. I needed her approval more than I cared to admit.

The microwave beeped, and she pulled out the coffee mug and took a sip, her face souring at the taste. I wondered if she had any idea what a good cup of coffee tastes like.

"The cycle has to end somewhere, Mom," I mumbled, turning back to my assignment.

"For God's sake, Alisha, be the tequila, not the lime. Stop chasing a dream that ain't worth chasing."

Mom's words rang in my ears for hours that day. I may not have understood their connotation then, but I knew they held weight I wasn't ready to carry.

When I finally did graduate from college, she wasn't around for me to rub it in her face.

It took meeting Dylan for me to see just how wrong my mother was, and after that, I wished I hadn't spent my entire childhood—and let's face it, years of my young adult life—believing half of the convoluted bullshit that came out of her mouth. Sure, I took everything my mother said with a grain of salt, well aware that most of it was nonsense. But I was never entirely sure where the needle landed on the bullshit meter.

I had digested her insults into my heart and soul.

And they lived inside me like a demon, like a devil sitting on my shoulder.

Solitude is a strange thing. If you're anything like me, you don't mind being alone. You can live with yourself without going crazy. The quiet is cathartic, peaceful. It gives us time to reset.

But our minds like to play tricks on us, too.

Sometimes there are voices. Other times a general feeling that someone else—some*thing*—is in the room with you. You may even talk to them, have full-on conversations. And that's when you know you're going fucking crazy.

When the solitude starts to feel like a best friend.

I have nothing to do but sit alone with my thoughts, and my mother has been on my mind often. She had me convinced at a young age that I was unlovable, Mrs. Maylen was the first to suggest otherwise. She'd never came out and said it until the end, but I'll never forget when she did. I cherish those words, the truth behind them.

"Gretta?"

"Yes, dear?"

"Do you ever wonder what would have happened to me if you hadn't take me in?"

"All the time."

"Do you think I would've been stuck in that trailer forever?"

"No, not you, sweet girl. You were always meant for bigger things." I smile at the thought that she never failed to see something in me. That she didn't think of me as the burden my mother told me I was.

We sat in silence playing a hand of Rummy 500—she won, like always, her mind still sharp enough to kick my ass in any card game. I picked up the cards and shuffled them in case she wanted to go for another round. But her hand covered my own, and I set the cards off to the side of the table.

Instead, she held my hand, squeezing as if with all her might. Like the thought of letting go meant she'd have to say goodbye. "I love you like a daughter, dear. I hope you know that," she said before closing her eyes.

And I couldn't move. I held her hand, and sat there by her side, unable to do anything more than stare at the deck of cards on the table.

We were still holding hands when she drifted off to sleep, and it was Dylan who finally pulled me away from her a few hours later, when he came to pick me up.

It never was quite the same after she passed.

SO MANY DAMN QUESTIONS

Alisha

"FORMER SEX WORKER, *Alisha Renee Thompson, has been charged today in connection with her husband's brutal murder. Sources say the wife of Dylan Thompson, a freelance Realtor, has lawyered up. She'll face Judge Wyman for arraignment on Thursday. More on this developing story on Channel 5 News at 5:00.*"

It happened quickly.

My arrest.

I was confused at first, my mind racing as the cruiser headed down the street. I watched my house disappear from sight. The home that I'd known for so long, now forever tainted, its memory tarnished.

At the station, the arresting officer escorted me to an exam room to be processed—searched and prodded for evidence, and photographed like the very crime scene they'd dragged me away from. They swabbed my hands, under my fingernails, the inside of my cheek. The cotton left a dry taste in my already sour mouth.

I could still taste the vomit.

I swallowed hard as the final swab was placed into a test tube, capped, and slid into an evidence bag. I wasn't sure what those swabs would say about me.

How much damage they'd eventually do.

"Hold out your hands," the technician instructed. He took my fingers one by one and clipped the nails, catching each of them in an evidence bag. I couldn't help but notice how ugly my hands looked. The absence of my long, manicured nails left my fingers naked. They looked like man hands.

Dylan had great hands.

The best hands.

I'd give anything to feel his touch.

After processing, I'm taken to an interview room and left alone, the lead investigator taking their time. I stare at my hands in a daze. They no longer looked like my own, not after what they'd done.

I stifled my surprise at the sight of a woman walking through the door, a no-nonsense look printed on her face. She took a seat across from me and slid a cup of coffee across the table.

I could tell it was burned without even tasting it.

"I'm Detective Adams," she said as she shuffled papers around in front of her. I wondered what was on them, considering we'd only just begun. How much could they possibly know this early into their investigation?

She looked up as if she was expecting a response to her introduction, but I wasn't sure what to say. "Mrs. Thompson, you understand why you're here, right?"

I nodded.

"Okay, well, considering the fact that you're about to be hauled off to jail, I suggest you start talking." She sat back in the chair, suddenly looking smug, like she was putting on a one woman show of good cop, bad cop.

But still I said nothing. I was at a loss for words. Even if I wanted to share any, I couldn't. After a fifteen-minute stare down, she huffed and left the room, meeting her captain in the hall, neither of them bothering to speak in hushed tones. I heard every word as clear as day. Maybe I was meant to.

"The arresting officer said she isn't speaking."

"Make her speak then, Adams! I've got a dead body full of stab wounds, and I want answers. This should be an opened and closed case here, Detective. Open it…and then fucking close it."

The captain's footsteps echoed as he walked away, Detective Adams taking a minute to re-enter the room, probably trying not to lose her shit after being spoken down to that way. I cast my eyes downward, determined to avoid a too-close-for-comfort eye contact battle.

Cops love that shit.

Alleged suspects, however, do not.

And that's what I was to her. An alleged suspect.

"Mrs. Thompson, I need you tell me what happened."

I picked at a cuticle, the skin somehow still caked with dried blood. *Dylan's blood.*

The detective sighed, her frustration increasingly more evident. I knew she didn't like me. She knew what I'd done— what I was accused of—and that's all that mattered to her.

"Mrs. Thompson," she began again. "We can do this all day."

I knew next to nothing about the law, but there was one thing I *was* sure of: I needed a lawyer.

"I'd like an attorney, please," I said. There was no tone, no emotion in my request, just a stated fact. They were the first words I had spoken since arriving at the station, and while they were meant to protect me, apparently they were the wrong ones.

"Sure you would," Detective Adams grumbled, not even looking me in the eye as she rolled her own. She gathered her papers into a pile and stood, heading for the door.

Her mind was made up about me already; I didn't need to answer any of her questions.

It wouldn't do any good.

"I didn't do it," I said softly.

The door unlatched and she paused, holding it open and turning back to me. "That's what they all say." She exited the room, letting the door slam shut behind her.

I sat in that stale room for hours, waiting to be brought back to a holding cell. My mind raced as I thought of how I would've answered all her questions had I bothered to respond. But I was fucked no matter what I said.

What happened to your husband, Mrs. Thompson?

Did you have an argument? Catch him in an affair?

Did he put his hands on you? Maybe knock you around a bit?

Tell me about the knife. Why seventeen stab wounds? That's pretty excessive…a crime of passion…can you hear me, Mrs. Thompson?

Officer Jones finally returned at what I could only assume was an ungodly hour. He cuffed me, offering no leniency with the cuffs; they cut into my skin and tugged the hairs on my wrists.

"Let's go," he said, guiding me out of the room. He shoved me into a holding cell, and removed the cuffs again.

"What about my attorney?" I asked, well aware I should've been able to make a phone call.

"What about 'em?"

"I need to call one."

"So do it."

"There's no phone in here." He knew that, of course, and he chuckled to himself as he headed down the hall.

"You can call someone when I get back from lunch."

Kyle arrived later that afternoon. He didn't do much, other than ask a few questions and fill out paperwork.

"What happens now?" I asked, my curiosity growing with each passing minute.

"You'll face a judge for arraignment tomorrow."

"What does that mean?"

Kyle looked at me incredulously, offering no further explanation. I felt like an idiot for my lack of understanding of the legal system. As if I should've been familiar with the proper handling of a murder suspect.

"So, that's it? I just sit here?"

"Yep."

He gathered his papers and shoved a form and a pen in my direction. "For the retainer."

I grabbed the pen and signed my name as best as I could with my hands cuffed, the twenty-thousand-dollar retainer sure to be used up within the week.

"Don't talk to anyone in there," he reminded me. "Your case is already very high profile, and the media is in a shit storm right now trying to gather information. Say nothing."

Why the hell the media would give a shit about *me*, or why my case would be considered high profile, was beyond me, but I found out the answer to that question the following morning when an officer brought me something to eat, slipping me a newspaper in the process.

My face was on the front page.

Apparently, people have an interest in murder cases when the main suspect is a porn star.

I'm denied bond at my arraignment.

In addition to the nature and severity of my crime, the judge considered my financial means a flight risk. Kyle didn't even bother suggesting house arrest.

He looked anything but surprised when the judge advised I was to be transported to Smithson.

SLIM TO FUCKING NONE

Alisha

THE HECKLING STARTED ALMOST IMMEDIATELY. It didn't matter that I was sporting a bleak prison uniform, or that the makeup had been wiped off my face and my hair hadn't been washed in two days.

They all stared anyway.

Like vultures.

I pulled at the scratchy uniform, grateful, at least, that it wasn't orange, as Corrections Officer Marin led me to my cell. I tried to peek into the others as I walked past, but the preview did nothing to settle my nerves. It didn't matter what the cells looked like.

It was a cage, no matter how they decorated it.

I'm cat-called as we walk, my hands cuffed to my waist.

"Well, hot damn, look what the warden brought in for us today, ladies!"

"Did you see the ass on that one, Tiff?"

"Oh, shit, dibs on the new girl!"

A low whistle echoed in the space, and CO Marin chuckled at my expense as we approached the cell that would become my home for God-knows-however-long. "Looks like you already have some fans," she said, shoving a key in the lock. She twisted it, and the lock disengaged with a click, making me jump. "Step in, please." I did, and was instructed to turn and face her, to hold my arms out in front of me.

"Uniforms, toiletries, pillow, and blanket are in the cubby to your left. Head count at eight forty-five, lights out at nine." She unlocked the cuffs on my wrists and took a step back, on the other side of the yellow line that was painted on the floor.

I knew what it meant, what would happen next.

And it terrified me to my core.

She said nothing as she re-engaged the lock and carried on about her afternoon.

My hands trembled, and I pivoted to the toilet to vomit up my breakfast.

Kyle made an appearance two days later. He was my first visitor, and a small part of me was happy to see him. He was the only person with the potential to punch my ticket out of here, my one and only lifeline.

"How are you holding up?" he asked.

I nearly laughed at the question. At the notion that I'd give any answer other than, "Fucking peachy."

"Ah, what's eating you?"

"What's *eating* me? *THIS!*" I made a wide circle with my hands, motioning to the tiny ass room we were cramped into. "I'm in fucking prison."

Kyle rolled his eyes, compassion decidedly not one of his many endearing qualities.

"Beyond the fact that you're in prison against your will," he started, the sarcasm already heavy on this tongue, "you're okay, I assume? No one's physically hurting you? You're fed? Have a working shitter in your cell?"

"Fuck, Kyle, really? Is this how you treat all your clients?" He winked, avoiding the question entirely as he moved on to the next.

"Do you understand the charges against you, Mrs. Thompson?"

"Alisha."

"Fine, *Alisha*. Do you?"

"Yeah."

"Great, then you understand that this trial will be anything but a walk in the park. As I instructed the other day, you will speak to no one —not one single person in here, other than me—about your case. You confess to anyone, and it's over."

"*Confess*? Are you kidding me? I didn't kill my husband, Mr. Lanquist, and I sure as shit won't be caught dead talking to anyone in here."

"It's Kyle," he said, throwing my words back at me, and it takes everything in me not to crawl across the table and wrap my hands around his neck. "We have eighty-seven days to prepare for trial. That means you'll be seeing a lot of me, so I suggest you get comfortable. Don't expect any favors from me, and don't fucking lie to me. You lie to me, we lose the case, and you get to spend the next twenty-five years in this concrete palace. Got it?"

My posture deflated, the wind knocked out of me at the notion of spending what could very well be, the rest of my life in prison. And it hit me then, the realization settling in the pit of my stomach. "Oh, my God…"

"What?" he snapped.

"You already knew who I was."

"Excuse me?"

"You've seen my work. You knew who I was before you took on my case, didn't you?" The smirk on his face grew wider, his cheeks reddening just a bit.

"No comment," he answered evenly, and he's stoic as he crosses his arms, daring me to push the issue further. But I didn't. Kyle pressed on. "Sex sells, right?" he stated with a shrug. "Why else would you have benefited so greatly from your choice of profession?"

"My choice of profession is none of your damn business. My job is perfectly legal."

"It *was*, yes. But, for one, you no longer have a job, and two, a certain set of consequences come along with a career in porn—former or otherwise. Surely you know that by now?"

"What I do behind closed doors is nobody's business but mine."

"See, that's where you're wrong. *You* chose to put your life out there for the world to see—that's what your career did for you. Had you chosen a less public career, nobody out there would give a shit about you, and you'd be lucky to get a one-paragraph story on page ten of your local paper. But since you're a public figure, your life is *everyone's* business right now, Mrs. Thompson, and like it or not, everyone out there is completely infatuated with you. And not in the way you're used to, either. They want *you* to go down for this. They believe you killed your husband. And if you walk into that courtroom with a giant chip on your shoulder, your chances of proving even one of them wrong are slim to fucking none."

At the conclusion of his monologue, Kyle officially became my one and only ally. For reasons unknown to me, all that managed to do is turn me on.

And that's an admission far more embarrassing than the invasive strip search I'd endured forty-eight hours prior.

"Hey, pretty lady, you lonely yet? Looking for some companionship?"

Ronnie.

The inmate in the cell two down from mine. I was sick of hearing her talk within the first few hours of arriving here. Sick of trying, and failing, to tune her out.

"Don't engage," CO Marin muttered, and I couldn't help but wonder if ignoring the peanut gallery did nothing more than put a target on my back. Still, I bit my tongue, my feet shuffling forward as we headed back to my cell. I didn't know my way around the prison yet, and while I wasn't sure my assumption was accurate—things had been a bit of a blur those first couple days—I thought I was on some kind of first-week probationary period or something.

I seemed to be the only one unable to move around freely, and always had a CO at my side.

"Don't ignore me when I'm talking to you, baby!" Ronnie continued, and I made the mistake of looking over at her. "I'm taking applications for my next in-house relationship. You gay for the stay, sweetheart? 'Cuz I can bump you to the top of the list if you ask nicely." She winked, and it sent a shiver down my spine.

I don't think she realized how little temptation her proposal held. Or, perhaps she did, and that explained the opening at the top of the list —maybe there wasn't even a list to begin with.

I looked away as CO Marin unlocked my cell, and that's when I heard him for the first time. I hadn't even been introduced to him yet, but the sound of his voice still made me cringe.

"Who do we have here?"

"Your newest inmate, Officer Marshall," she advised, rattling off my inmate number, name, and alleged charges. She'd memorized my rap sheet, almost as if to impress him, but I didn't hear any of it.

Because all I could focus on was the erection Officer Marshall was trying to conceal as she spoke.

TWELVE PEOPLE WHO GIVE A SHIT

Alisha

THE PROSECUTION IS SET to begin today in the trial of Alisha Thompson, the adult entertainer accused of murdering her husband, Dylan Thompson, a local Realtor. Channel 5 correspondent Lexy Dawson is live at the courthouse. Lexy?

Thank you, Cindy. I'm here at the Hennepin County Courthouse, where Judge Conwell Wyman, a twenty-two-year resident of the bench, will hear opening statements this morning, the trial expected to begin just after nine o'clock. I spoke with the District Attorney, John Hedland when he arrived, and he says the state is confident in their case against Mrs. Thompson. He expects a speedy trial, and anticipates justice will be served. We'll have more on this story after court concludes this afternoon. For now, I'm Lexy Dawson for Channel 5 Morning News.

I have no path to follow. No order of operations for the remaining course of my life. I'm not sure what to make of that, but today I'm taking things one hour at a time.

I can get through one hour at a time, right?

While I hardly slept last night, I still managed to wake from a nightmare, dripping in sweat and nearly hyperventilating.

A darkness had flitted over Dylan's body.

He lay lifeless on the bed that we shared, the knife still in the shadowy stranger's hand. I tried to make sense of the figure but couldn't. When it turned, I gasped, the air stripped from my lungs.

It was my own face that I saw, as if looking in a mirror. It was my hand that harbored the murder weapon, my arm that drove it over and over, into my husband's chest.

As if the rage had taken over from the inside, desperately attempting to free itself from my soul.

I couldn't help but feel like I'd had the same dream once before.

"The media is going nuts. You wouldn't believe half the shit they're saying about you," Chris says over the phone. It's my last phone call before I'm transferred to the courthouse jail for trial, and his voice is the only one likely to calm my nerves.

I hadn't expected him to take my call.

"I don't give a shit what anyone thinks of me," I remind him.

He scoffs, his voice firm as he puts me in my place. "Well, it's time you start," he says. "Because those twelve seats in that courtroom are filled with the asses of people whose only job is to judge the living shit out of you. *You* are the only person who can win them over. Not me. Not your fancy-pants lawyer. *You.* That's your only job, Alisha. To give a shit about the twelve people who give a shit about you."

"Wow, Chris...I'm impressed. That was pretty good," I tease, while digesting his words.

He drains a sigh of relief, and chuckles a little. "Thanks, I am, too!" We laugh weakly before falling into a comfortable silence. It's been so long since I've heard his voice.

"So, only twelve, huh? No thirteenth person on that list?"

"Shut up, bitch, you know I love you."

And it's everything I need to hear. Chris's voice, his relentless ability to see the good in me, even when he shouldn't. As we hang up, I walk away with a smile on my face despite the charges I'm facing.

Because no matter what happens, at least I get to see his face in the courtroom.

"How are we feeling this morning, Mrs. Thompson?" Kyle asks as he enters the holding room. I already want to punch him, to deliver a heartfelt "fuck you" in the form of my fist to his pretentious face, but for now I appease him and settle for a snarky comment.

"How do *you* think I'm feeling today, Kyle?" He's not at all phased by my verbal assault—likely used to them by now—and I shouldn't be surprised, but I am. I hope this is a sign that Kyle can hold his own in the courtroom, but my faith in him wavers by the minute, so I let the thought go as soon as it comes.

"Any questions before we head in there?" he asks, digging in his briefcase. I take a step back and get a good look at him. Somehow he manages to look almost handsome in a dark gray suit and navy tie. He's usually more of a khakis and button down kind of guy.

I'm impressed, but don't admit as much to him. "No," I say.

He stares at me for a beat before an odd look settles in his eyes, like I've finally done something to please him but he doesn't quite know how to feel about it. I don't want to ask, so I raise my eyebrow and cross my arms over my chest.

"It's good, you looking like that," he finally says, waving a hand in my direction. "I like the subtle makeup, too. Makes you look more..." He trails off, apparently unable to settle on whatever insulting phrase is about to roll off his tongue.

"Don't bother finishing that sentence," I say. And even though I wish I didn't know what he meant by the comment, I do. Black slacks with a three-quarter sleeve blouse, a pair of boring flats, my hair wrapped in a low chignon and nothing but a layer of mascara on my lashes.

Quite unlike the pictures that have been in the newspapers and evening news. And oddly comfortable in comparison to my wardrobe as of late.

My image matters in the courtroom—just as it does in my prison cell and just as it did with Lisha's Bedroom. Each is a uniform representative of its own unique character, a persona enabling me to adapt to my surroundings for the purpose of survival.

The bailiff arrives and escorts Kyle and me to the courtroom. We're seated at the defendant's table, and once my ass is parked in the chair, my handcuffs are removed.

I'm no longer sure what to do with my hands.

Kyle pulls out several folders before pouring water from a pitcher into a plastic cup, and handing it to me at the precise moment I realize I'm salivating and about to pass out.

I take the cup and chug the water as ladylike as possible, already aware of the beady eyes boring into me from all angles of the room.

Within a few minutes, the prosecutor, John Hedland, arrives with his team of associates, each taking a seat at the state's table. I'll admit, they're as intimidating as they intend to be. I feel like a mouse playing a game of chicken with an elephant.

I don't find myself afraid of a man very often, but there's something about the way he looks at me that makes me want to crawl into a hole. His green eyes are piercing, but it's his stature that draws my attention. He has to be at least six-foot-seven—better suited for the NBA than the courtroom.

He and Kyle exchange greetings before Hedland turns to me, tipping his head in my direction as a means of hello because he's not allowed to shake my hand. He's looking at me funny, and I don't like it.

"All rise for the honorable Judge Conwell Wyman," booms the bailiff's voice through the courtroom. I stand along with the herd as the judge enters from his chambers.

Even *he* manages to intimidate me.

When we're allowed to sit again, Hedland smirks and glances in my direction, and it takes everything in me not to flick him off. If this is how the rest of the trial is going to go, I am most definitely fucked.

Just like old times.

HIVE FIVE, HEDLAND

Alisha

IT TURNS OUT, Hedland and Kyle have faced each other in the courtroom a total of six times.

Kyle has never won.

This fact would have been helpful three months ago when I hired him, but here we are.

As opening statements begin, I can't help but glance over at the jury, despite the fact that Kyle has instructed me not to. They are an interesting mix of jurors, almost like a modern-day *Breakfast Club*. I inadvertently make eye contact with two of them.

I don't tell Kyle about it.

For the most part, everything about the state's case turns out to be solid. If I were a member of the jury, I'd probably give Hedland a high five for taking another murderer off the streets.

Kristin's testimony kicks my ass.

As a witness for the prosecution, she provides expert testimony explaining, in great detail, the so-called signs and symptoms of sex addiction, the formal diagnosis she documented in my file at the demise of our one-sided relationship. Her professional opinion is even a matter of public record on account of the HIPAA authorization I erroneously signed at the start of our court-ordered therapy sessions.

Go fucking figure.

Her testimony is the first time the jury hears of my sexually deviant behavior—as Hedland likes to call it—but certainly not the last. The whispers and less than subtle glances my way were a clear indication that their judgment of me had officially begun.

Kristin is poised and confident as she answers the rapid-fire questions from Hedland, and later from Kyle. To be blunt, she fucking killed it.

Which is a shame.

She avoided my eyes while she spoke, and as much as I love a good stare down, I can't say I blame her. After all, I never did make a good therapy patient. Not only did she throw me under the bus with her expert testimony, she even managed to give Hedland the space he needed to run me right over with it.

To his credit, Hedland asked all the right questions.

Kyle, however, did not.

Cross examination does not go as well.

Dr. Lindsay—or Kristin, as I've always known her—is escorted from the witness stand. She keeps her head down as she passes by, and the realization that I have no ill will toward the woman lands right in my lap. I sure thought I did, but even though her testimony does nothing to help me, in the moment, I feel none.

She had been right about me all long; how could I possibly hold that against her?

Amongst others, Dylan's mother also testifies for the state. The show she puts on is equally as damaging, although she isn't on the stand more than ten minutes. After she's sworn in, Hedland is unable to ask any more than two questions. She's unstable, constantly dabbing her face with tissues as she sobs like a fucking baby on the witness stand.

And that's the only reason Hedland needed her.

To show the jury the poor, old, grieving mother of the deceased, and make sure she says the one thing that is sure to simultaneously break the hearts of all twelve of them: *"No mother should have to bury their son."*

Kyle instructs me not to look at her as she's escorted from the box.

But I look at her anyway. I watch her the whole time.

Because I can't help but think what a great actress she would've been.

POISON IVY

Alisha

"THE STATE CALLS Ivy Rogers to the stand," Hedland says, making a show of shuffling papers around on the table.

This is the final witness for the prosecution, and Hedland's last chance to prove the state's case, to convince this jury of my supposed peers that I'm guilty of murdering my husband.

And after that Kyle will try to earn his paycheck, although he gets to cash it either way.

A woman stands in the gallery, smoothing the pencil skirt that seems to hug her curves in all the right places. She's nervous, I can tell, but I doubt anyone else will notice. She saunters to the witness stand, her blonde locks draping down to the middle of her back. I can't help but salivate as I watch her, and my physical reaction takes me by surprise.

She's enticing in that girl-next-door kind of way. Like, the kind of woman who looks innocent enough for a man to take home to his parents, but once he gets her behind closed doors, all bets are off.

I've seen her type before; I've *been* with her type. And maybe I've been around women too much lately, because it isn't like me to pine over one, but for some reason, I can't stop staring at her ass as she takes the podium.

She turns and faces the courtroom to be sworn in, and my eyes instinctively fall to her neck. To the small mole just above her clavicle.

I've seen that mole before.

As if in slow motion, her ocean blue eyes settle on mine; they're vivid and startlingly intense as they bore into my soul with a desire only I can see. A seductive smile plays on her cherry red lips, and I suck in a deep breath at the realization that I know this woman.

It's her.

"Stop," I mumble, my body suddenly frozen in place, unable to move a muscle.

"What?" Kyle whisper-shouts, leaning in closer.

I raise my arm slowly and point to the witness on the stand with a shaky finger. "Stop," I say again. My mouth fills with sand, my knees weak, and suddenly I'm sinking, like I'm drowning in quick sand.

Judge Wyman bangs the gavel three times.

The echo reverberates in my ears.

"Control your client, Mr. Lanquist," the judge warns. Kyle tugs on my arm, which is hanging loosely at my side, a tingling sensation traveling through it and settling in my spine.

I can't take my eyes off her, and I swear she's glaring at me in the most provocative way.

Just like she used to.

She winks, and it's subtle, but I know I saw it. I hope someone else did too, because if not, I am truly, truly fucked.

I'm sweating and hot all over, and I let out a piercing scream before I drop to my knees. Kyle is at my side, his arms around me, trying to pull me back to my feet. The bailiff sprints over from his post, a hand on his service weapon.

The last thing I hear before the lights go out is Lila's voice.

"Tell me you love me," she pleads.

I met Ivy months before Dylan first knocked on my door, only her name wasn't Ivy.

And she wasn't blonde.

I'd met her through one of my regulars, Grant. His was a sugar daddy fetish, the need to provide for his woman financially, to watch her earn her monthly stipend through sexual favors.

It wasn't uncommon, but Grant was different than the others. He was sexy, and mysterious, and I couldn't help but look forward to our private sessions.

"Will you touch yourself for me?" he asks, a throatiness to his voice.

"Mmm, always." I bring my hand to my breast, pinching the nipple through the lacy lingerie; the skimpy fabric, that leaves little to the imagination, is one of his favorites. I make a mental note to thank Chris for picking it out.

"See what you do to me?" Grant groans, his strong hand wrapping around his cock as he strokes. "I wish I could touch you."

And he's said it before, how much he wants to have his way with me. They all say it, but when Grant says it, his words settle into my bones. I lean closer to the webcam to show him my cleavage as I press my breasts together the way he likes. He moans and it sings in my ear, the bass from his voice sending a tremor straight to my pussy.

"What would you like me to do for you?" I ask with puckered lips.

"Show me your tits," he says, swallowing hard.

"Oh, these?" I tease with a shimmy. I slide the straps of the garment down and slowly pull my arms through, my eyes never leaving the camera. My breasts tumble out, my nipples hard as the lace falls to the floor.

"You're so fucking sexy."

"Only for you."

"Mmm...show me."

"Show you?" I ask with a raspy voice.

"Yes."

"What do you want to see, baby?"

"Come join us," he says, and I raise a brow, the request unexpected. I didn't realize there was anyone there with him.

"Us?"

"My wife and I. We watch you together."

Oh, fuck.

"She's about to take my cock in her mouth," he admits, and I see her then, the back of her head as she slithers into view. "We want you to...ughh, yes, baby, just like that...we want you to join us."

My pussy soaked, I can't help but bring my hand to it as I watch her head bob up and down. "What would I do for you?" I ask, my mouth going dry.

"Play."

The following evening, I knock on the front door of Grant's luxury high-rise apartment, my pulse racing and a tingling sensation between my legs.

I can't believe I'm about to do this.

He answers the door in jeans, his toned chest on display, and I suck in a breath at the sight of him, at the divots in his hips. His dark hair is mussed, and I pick up the woodsy scent of his aftershave. His eyes trail my body, and he licks his lips. "Lisha," he says.

"Grant."

He steps back, pulling the door open further, and I walk in, my red Louboutin pumps clicking on the expensive tile.

"Take your coat off," he instructs, stopping abruptly in the foyer. I untie the belt and open the trench coat slowly; there's nothing underneath except the lingerie he sent me: a scalloped trim garter in white lace.

"Mm, good girl," he says approvingly.

He drapes my coat over the back of a chair before taking my hand and leading me down the hall. My heart is hammering against my chest, the anticipation intense, and I take a breath as we come to a stop at a closed door.

"She's ready for us," he says, and his fingers graze my chin, the contact sending a chill straight my nipples. I'm so turned on I can hardly keep from pouncing.

"Lila?" I ask, my voice gruff.

He nods, and pulls me to him, bringing his lips to mine. His bulge is prominent against my thigh, and I know this is against the rules we established earlier, but I can't stop myself from kissing him back.

We are not to fornicate independent of one another.

Grant pulls away without warning and turns the knob of the wooden door, pushing it open. It's dark in the room, but there's just enough candlelight that I can see her.

Lila.

She lies on the bed, naked but for a pair of black stilettos. She looks up as Grant and I enter the room, and brings a finger to her mouth, sucking it and biting her bottom lip.

She is stunningly beautiful.

Her dark hair is curled and loose around her face, her blue eyes coated with a layer of mascara and nothing more. And her lips...a dark shade of red that I know it will be all over my body by the end of the night. The thought drives me crazy.

She takes my breath away, and I don't know what to make of it. I've never been so attracted to a woman before.

Grant closes the door and comes up behind me as I walk slowly toward the bed. I feel his eyes on my backside, confident he likes what he sees.

Lila crawls to the edge of the bed, and I watch her breasts drag against the sheets, my own nipples hardening in response. She stands and walks toward me, and I can't help but admire the curves of her breasts, the sway in her hips as her heels click on the hardwood floor.

"Kiss her," Grant commands, and she does. She brings her lips to mine, her tongue dipping into my mouth, her hands already exploring my body. They're the softest lips I've ever felt.

"Yes, good girls," he says, unzipping his pants and stepping out of them. Lila's manicured fingernails trail down my stomach and make their way to the wetness between my legs. She finds my clit and rubs it *gently before sliding two fingers inside me. I let out a groveling moan that she silences with her mouth, and all my senses are awakened, the heat of seduction sparking a fire between my legs.*

I hadn't expected things to move so fast.

But I don't want to slow down either.

Grant takes Lila's hand, and they explore my body together. They touch, and knead, and caress in unison. He plants kisses on my back and along my shoulders while she kisses my breasts, and I'm in complete ecstasy as they worship me together.

They bring their lips together, me between them, and I lean into Grant, his cock hard and ready, brushing against my ass.

"Lila," he says in a throaty voice.

"Yes, baby?"

"I want you to pleasure Lisha while she services me. Can you do that for me, sweetheart?"

"Yes," she agrees, and her pupils dilate; she wants this as much as I do. I take Grant's cock in my hand and stroke it slowly. He moans, his breath hot on my neck. Without warning, he lifts me and lays me on the bed, spreading my legs and standing back to admire the view. Lila joins him at his side, and he gives her ass a slap before pulling her in and kissing her hard.

They stand at the end of the bed, watching me, the tension pulsing throughout the room.

"Isn't she beautiful?" Grant says to Lila, but she doesn't answer. Instead she climbs onto the bed and seductively crawls between my legs. He smacks her ass again, slapping his dick on it before burying his face in her. She squeals as a look of absolute pleasure spreads across her face.

I can't help but want what he's doing to her.

I tangle my fingers into her hair and shove her face between my legs. I need to feel her there, for her to taste me. She licks and sucks with greed, her fingers inside me as I buck my hips against her tongue.

And he's next to me in an instant, throbbing and ready for me, and I take the length of him in my mouth. He moans and squeezes my breasts, and I suck faster, my lips wrapped tightly around him.

Lila climbs on top of me while he fucks my mouth, and her breasts rub against mine. She kisses every inch of skin she can find, and I moan against Grant's cock. He pulls out and moves to the other side of the bed, stroking himself as he watches Lila make her way back down my body.

He enters her from behind, and she calls out when he takes a fist to her hair and pulls. I sit up, bringing my lips to hers, the sudden need to feel the smoothness of her lips again taking over. When she pulls away, she bites down on my shoulder before bringing her mouth to my ear.

Her breath is heavy as Grant pounds into her, her fingers reaching out and finding my clit again, and I feel the heat in my belly, the orgasm taking over everything in me.

She brings her fingers to her mouth, licking the taste of me from them, and I barely hear her when she speaks.

"Tell me you love me," she whispers.

And her eyes bore into my soul, the desperation in her voice lingering in my ears and swallowing me whole.

She sucks her bottom lip into her mouth and starts to cry as Grant fucks her harder...then she lays her head down on my chest, wrapping her arms around me like she's holding on for dear life.

PART II

ROLE PLAY, ROMANCE, & REVENGE

ONE HELL OF A HARD-ON

Dylan

I KNEW Ivy long before I ever met my wife. Did I realize at the time that Ivy was the same person obsessing over her? No. I never could have guessed, and I sure as shit didn't make the connection until much later, and by that time, it was too late. I had no idea she was the same psychopath narcissist who was stalking Alisha. And we've already established the fact that I overlooked a great deal after meeting my wife, so does it really surprise you that I missed all the signs?

I didn't think so.

Look, love can certainly be blinding. It fucks with your psyche. Makes you see shit that isn't there, and overlook the shit you *should* be concerned about.

And it makes you do some idiotic shit, too.

Like lie to your wife about your knowledge of her connection to your piece-of-shit stepbrother.

How was I supposed to know that Sawyer's wife—my ex-girlfriend —was the same psycho claiming to be in love with Alisha? All I knew of her was that she was an ex-lover of some kind—I knew Alisha had a habit of swinging in either direction, and I didn't have a problem with that. But I assumed this woman was a former friend, maybe an acquaintance of some kind.

Fuck if I cared to ask questions.

I just knew there was a woman.

And she had one hell of a hard-on for my wife.

And Lila? Where the hell did that name even come from? Ivy had turned into a fucking train wreck, like an accident on the side of the road that you can't peel your eyes away from no matter how badly it burns.

Ivy, once thought to be the love of my life—the first woman to poke a permanent hole in my heart—was now my stepbrother's estranged wife, and also happened to have fucked my wife, accidentally falling in love with her in the process.

Alisha had slept with *all three of us.*

This realization started the bleeding that would eventually kill me.

Because every man knows a broken heart never heals. It can be fixed temporarily, sure, but the holes will still be there when you look closely.

Ivy had always been beautiful: a petite blonde with the prettiest blue eyes I'd ever seen, a few freckles splattered across her nose. I thought she was the one. I thought we'd get married and have kids and run off into the sunset.

Then I caught her with my brother.

And six months after that, I met Alisha.

Ivy no longer mattered, and I hardly gave her another thought. Had I known she was the same woman harassing my wife, I'd have done something to put a stop to it. Although, I'm not sure I would have realized her jealousy was directed at Alisha.

The common fucking denominator between us all.

EVEN COCKROACHES

Alisha

A MONTH INTO OUR RELATIONSHIP, and just a couple weeks before we were married, Dylan took me to meet his parents. Well, his mother and stepdad, to be more accurate. I had yet to meet his father, but we'd planned to take a trip out to Arizona after the wedding.

We never did.

Dylan told me to dress conservatively, so we stopped at the mall on the way, and I bought a pair of dark jeans and a loose-fitting sweater appropriate for an eighty-year-old. Dylan laughed at my expense, and despite the playful connotation, it pissed me off.

I'd done what he asked, pulling myself straight out of my comfort zone, and he couldn't even stifle his amusement.

We arrived at his mother and stepdad's Tudor-style home, with its well-maintained lawn and new cars in the driveway. It was obvious when we pulled into the driveway that they were the kind of people who flaunt their money instead of using it for good. I'd made a mental note to share a list of the charities I donated to each month

—in hopes that they would consider doing the same—but I knew within minutes of meeting them that the gesture would not be well received.

"It'll be fine, babe, just be yourself," Dylan coached when we approached the door. I didn't bother reminding him that being myself was the one thing he'd asked me *not* to do, but I chalked it up as an inadvertent slight on his part.

His stepfather answered the door, pulling Dylan into an immediate hug while I stood behind them awkwardly. Bev stepped in from the kitchen, her privilege dominating the room like a fox in a chicken coop.

I wanted nothing more than to run, but my feet were planted to the floor. A fox could outrun a chicken any day of the week, even on Sundays when they met their future mother-in-law for the first time.

"We missed you at church this morning, son," she said in place of hello. Dylan nodded, neglecting to acknowledge her snide comment, and while he'd never admit it, I could see his disdain for his mother just as clearly as I felt toward mine. Their relationship was tainted just the same; they simply had different grievances eating at them.

"Mom, Jim, this is Alisha," Dylan said, placing a protective arm around my shoulders, as if he knew it were necessary. I willed my hands to stop shaking. My pits were wet with evidence of the nervous sweats I'd been suffering with all afternoon.

"It's great to meet you," I said, reaching out to shake Jim's hand, a mistake I hadn't thought twice about. I'd later learn secondhand that Bev found it disrespectful I didn't go for hers first. To this day, I'm not sure I did anything more than that to displease the woman.

"That woman is garbage, an utter embarrassment to our family," she'd said to the press. *"My son's good name has been dragged through the mud because of her."*

"Alisha, nice to finally meet you," Jim said as his wife's expression settled into a glare. It was obvious who wore the pants in that house.

"It's a shame your brother can't be here," she said, the jab landing as intended. I squeeze Dylan's hand to silence him, impressed when he managed to let it go without a word.

Little did I know the brother in question would turn out to be Grant.

Bev finally addressed me with a nod of the head when we sat down to eat, following what I can only refer to as a formal announcement of the dinner menu, a meal she had prepared entirely from scratch *as the Lord intended.*

"Alisha, may I ask what you do for work?" Jim asked.

Of all fucking questions, Jimbo.

I cleared my throat before dabbing at my mouth with a napkin, determined to pretend I had a semblance of table etiquette. "I run a streaming channel," was all I could think to say.

Dylan and I—in our haste to change my wardrobe—had neglected to discuss a backup career in the event that this very question came up in conversation. "What's a streaming channel?" Bev asked, her face turned up in confusion.

"It's just a website, Mom. Nothing exciting," Dylan chimed in. He placed a hand on my thigh; I'd said too much, gone against his wishes to keep my profession quiet. In my opinion, it was better to tell the truth from the start than to have it come out in the wash later.

But come out in the wash, it did.

Channel 5 loved nothing more than to air my dirty laundry.

My own father finally made an appearance after I ended up here; once my face was all over the news and in the papers. He even provided a copy of the paternity test to prove he was who he said he was.

Thirty years it took for the fucker to step forward.

And to my surprise, he'd known all along.

My mother knew damn well who he was—and so did he.

She was such a piece of work that my own father chose to make a run for it before she had a chance to ruin him, too.

Talk about a hit and run.

He has a family, my father. A wife, and two daughters in their twenties. Owns a construction company that's quite successful. I'm not sure what to make of any of it, what to do with this newfound information. All these years, he had the potential to save me from my mother.

And he chose not to.

His is the first letter I've received in prison, aside from the fan mail that never seems to cease.

I wish it had never come.

But even cockroaches find their way through the cracks sometimes.

GRAB A PEEK AT HER LADY BITS

Dylan

For Alisha, the icing on the cake was when my father—not Jim, but my birth father, Weston—stumbled upon Lisha's Bedroom.

Look, it was an honest mistake, completely unintentional and an unfortunate happenstance. Did I have any idea that my dad watched porn?

No.

Should I have guessed?

Sure, probably.

But give me a break. I hardly ever saw the man. Was I supposed to bring it up casually in conversation? And who talks to their dad about porn, anyway? I highly doubt that's a topic for the dinner table, let alone a fireside chat.

And really, I should have known something was up when he called, practically whispering into the phone so his wife wouldn't hear him from the other room.

He'd made sure to mention that she didn't approve of his habit.

"It's not right, son. She's your wife, and everyone out there can grab a peek at her lady bits whenever they want."

"Dad, come on, that's not fair."

"What if it were your mother? Hmm? Think about it. A man cannot bring a child into the world with a woman like that. She's not mother material. Hell, she's barely even wife material. Trust me, that miscarriage was a good thing."

He'd said it so casually I almost didn't pick up on it.

I should have ended the call right then and there. I should have taken a stance against my father and put him in his place for disrespecting my wife like that. He had no right to speak ill of her, no right to judge her for the decisions she made long before we met.

And God knows my father made plenty mistakes of his own.

The fact that he was still, at his age, secretly streaming porn behind his wife's back was a prime example of one of those mistakes. I should have reminded him that every single one of those women was somebody's daughter. Somebody's wife, or mother. Who was he to think less of them for the very thing that made him so fond of them in the first place?

But what came out of my mouth instead was much worse than anything I *should* have said.

I didn't stand up for my wife.

I didn't tell my dad to fuck off.

Instead, I said, "I know, Dad."

Three words, morphed into a simple sentence with one comma and a period. That sentence caused more damage than the insult it was said in response to.

Because Alisha was standing right there in the doorway.

She'd heard the whole conversation.

THROWING EXPENSIVE SHOES

Alisha

I REMEMBER how she used to watch me, like she was in a trance, her eyes glossed over and slightly closed in that intense way that almost made her look high. I wish I had seen it then, all the signs.

Ivy is *Lila*.

The same Ivy who had an affair with—and subsequently married— my husband's stepbrother was *the* Lila who had been stalking me.

Grant is Sawyer.

My husband's stepbrother.

With this knowledge, I'm left in a constant state of confusion, my heart heavy and only growing angrier as the pieces slowly come together—at the understanding that everything I thought I knew was wrong.

That Dylan knew Grant. He knew Lila.

Lila and Grant weren't who they said they were.

And that possibility had never once crossed my mind, just as I had never suspected Dylan of his ill intentions.

But he had played me, too.

My perfect husband had kept a secret of his own.

He'd known all along who I was, had subscribed to my website, streamed my live events. Only, when he finally confessed, he didn't tell me the whole story—he told only the side of it he thought he *had* to tell.

The part he knew I'd already figured out.

But he left out the fact that he was well aware I'd fucked his step-brother—that the first time he'd seen me was not the day he knocked on my apartment door, but rather at the hotel where I'd stayed with Grant.

And Grant? Well, he wasn't just a customer who had invited me to his room to play with him and his wife. He was a fraud, just as much as Ivy.

The Grant I thought I knew didn't even exist.

Sawyer did.

And *that* I didn't have the pleasure of finding out until after Ivy Rogers first took the stand.

Dylan made sure to leave that part out of his confession.

"I should have told you, I know. I'm so sorry, babe," he'd said the night he spilled the first intricate details of his deception, the night before his death. It was the cause of the argument our neighbors reported to police after his murder, the one that's been in the papers and all over the news.

There was yelling.

And shoving.

And throwing of expensive shoes like they were nothing. I had screamed, and cried, and demanded that he leave. But he didn't. Dylan never left during a fight.

Maybe this time he should have.

"I can't look at you right now," I said through gritted teeth, my words like ice. He stood there, suddenly looking out of place in our living room, his face sullen and eyes puffy. They pleaded for forgiveness that would never come.

I had none to offer.

"Alisha, we have to talk about this. Don't shut me out."

"I have *nothing* to say to you!" I screamed, the words echoing in the expanse of our open-concept home. He stomped over from the kitchen, his face riddled with anger as if I were the one to have wronged *him*.

"Stop screaming at me!" he shouted, bringing his hands roughly to my shoulders and shaking me. "This doesn't change anything about the way I feel. Did I intend to fall in love with you? No, I *didn't*, but it happened, and I'm so fucking glad it did, baby. I love you with every part of my being." He pulled me to him and I shoved against him, pounding on his chest in hopes that he'd let go.

But I couldn't stop the tears by that point. The man who promised he'd never break my heart had singlehandedly managed to do just that.

My arms stopped moving, fists forming and resting against his chest, my voice barely above a whimper as I gave in and let him hold me. "You lied to me, Dylan...*this whole time*."

He had won me over under false pretenses.

"I know...and I...I'm so, so fucking sorry. That's why I came clean, why I confessed."

"No!" I shoved myself away from him again, his words nothing but bullshit. "You confessed because you got caught!" His face fell at the legitimacy of my statement.

My husband had admitted to his betrayal, yes. Not because he wanted to, but because he had no other choice. He would have gotten away with it, too—had I not stumbled across Lisha's Bedroom saved in his bookmarked links. The search history on his laptop had given him away.

The link had been saved to his computer months before we ever met.

Had I managed to piece together the rest—the fact that Grant was his brother—he may not have had to die.

So in a way, I guess that's on him.

NURTURING THE SEED

Alisha

LILA'S OBSESSION had blossomed like a flower in spring, one I unwittingly nurtured. I'd watered the seed and gave it room to grow into an unfathomable being of destruction.

And by that time, it was far too late to stop her.

I chew on the inside of my cheek, the nervous habit seemingly new and about as ineffective as all my other nervous habits. I pace the expanse of my cell and find myself counting my footsteps as my feet shuffle along the floor.

One.

Two

Three

Four.

But that look, it's stuck with me. There was something about it, as if Lila was trying to tell me something and I was too self-absorbed to pick up on it.

Her eyes.

Glossed over.

Squinted, the slits narrow.

Almost like she was in pain.

Like she'd been hurting for too long and just wanted it to end.

That's why, despite my lack of desire, I found myself out in bars with her at night. Grant worked long hours sometimes, and Lila's call would come through without fail, every Thursday and Friday evening. I don't know why I gave in and joined her; it wasn't like I used the opportunity to drink, but the atmosphere was nice.

And, for the most part, I didn't mind her company either.

I didn't feel as alone with her as I did around other people.

"Come home with me," Lila suggested one night after she'd had a few drinks. Her voice was low and seductive, like she thought she might be able to convince me with the same tone she often used on Grant.

"I can't tonight, I have a client in…" I checked the time on my phone. "One hour." She pouted and her eyes dropped to my cleavage, my breasts pushed together in a black halter top.

"I promise I'll be quick," she said, brushing my arm.

"Lila…"

Her face settled into a sour expression, her shoulders slumping. "You always have a client," she whined.

"Well, that must mean I'm good at my job."

"It doesn't have to be your job, you know."

"Well, I suck at everything else and have no desire to work in the world of corporate assholes. So, yes, it does have to be my job. I'm too young to retire."

"You could quit. Grant would take care of you."

I wasn't entirely sure what she meant by that, but I had no desire to play house with Lila and her husband on a full-time basis. The sex was incredible, sure, and yes, I was openly enjoying extracurricular activities with each of them—without the other's knowledge—but no relationship needs a permanent third wheel, and I refused to be that person.

A third wheel isn't necessary when you know how to ride without it.

Not to mention, I wasn't looking to get caught in the crosshairs, and I intended to keep them both in a state of blissful unawareness about the amount of time I was spending with each of them.

I said nothing as Lila continued to stare me down, her face filled with dismay and disappointment.

"Whatever. I get it. Have fun," she finally said after an awkward minute. She stood and grabbed her clutch, tucking it under her arm. I couldn't help but roll my eyes; these kind of theatrics were one of the reasons I never cared to entertain female friends.

I watched Lila stomp out of the bar, never once turning back to see if I cared enough to watch her leave. I didn't, not really, but I couldn't help but watch her anyway. I wondered how Grant managed to put up with her.

Turning back, I raised a finger to flag down the bartender, realizing with annoyance that she hadn't paid her tab.

DON'T THANK ME YET

Alisha

I TELL KYLE EVERYTHING.

Everything I can think to tell him about Lila, about Grant. And for the first time since I met the prick, he actually looks like he feels sorry for me. Like he believes the words pouring out of my mouth like vomit —that I didn't kill my husband. That I've been set up.

He looks sick, his face ashen like he might pass out or, at the very least, barf all over the floor.

"I'm going to request a continuance," he says after a minute, as if a continuance will magically fix everything. It's no more helpful than applying a bandage to a bleeding wound after the bleeding has already stopped.

He's too late.

"What will that do?" I ask, willing my hands to stop shaking. I pick at the cuticles, at the dry skin that now covers my hands. I can't get the image of her out of my head, that hateful look that was in her eyes.

"It'll buy us some time," Kyle says. He runs his hands through what's left of his hair and breathes heavily.

"Time for what, exactly?"

"We need to investigate further. See what we can find out about Lila—or Ivy—whatever the fuck her name is. Her past. Look into her alibi. Our defense is built entirely on reasonable doubt, and now we finally have it." He avoids my eyes as he speaks, rattling off his to-do list while he scribbles it on a sheet of lined paper. His pen moves frantically, and I can't help but wonder what the hell happens next.

He can't save me.

"Kyle?"

He stops writing and looks at me with apologetic eyes. To my surprise, I place a hand over his. "Yeah?"

"Thank you." It's all I can think to say, these two tiny, insignificant words that mean nowhere near enough.

"Don't thank me yet," he says, suddenly popping up from his chair and leaving the room. I stare at the stale gray door, my mind suspended in time, remembering that first night I met Lila and wondering how the hell I never considered the fact that she and Grant would give me fake names.

Lila.

Ivy.

Grant.

Sawyer.

The pieces fit together like a lock and key.

How did I miss so much?

Dylan had known all along—he *knew* Ivy was dangerous. That she would ruin me. Ruin us. I was well aware that she was crazy, sure, but I never suspected she was capable of *this*—of murder. That she'd take my husband from me.

He tried to warn me.

I try to make sense of everything I've learned, of this new information that probably isn't all that new when I think about it hard enough.

Dylan was naked when I found him.

In our bed.

Traces of semen—Dylan's—were found in the blood specimens, which I'd learned in court during the prosecution's testimony, the shock probably written all over my face for the jury to see. For them to misinterpret along with all the other evidence against me.

Did she fuck my husband?

It's the only logical explanation. Dylan always slept in his boxers—said the sheets tickled his dick when he slept in the buff.

So, why was he naked?

He would never cheat on me, not Dylan. Never in a million years, especially with the very same woman who'd done it to him.

Right?

Kyle returns less than twenty minutes later, sweat slick across his forehead, his shirt partially untucked.

Judge Wyman has denied our request for continuance.

LIKE A MONSTER UNDER MY BED

Alisha

ALL THE AIR deflates from my lungs when Ivy is called back to the stand. She's sworn in as Kyle's pen slithers on the page in front of me, and I don't want to look at the words he's written, but I can't help it, so I do.

Calm down, he writes, underlining it with a final swipe of the pen.

But the words seem to have the opposite effect on me. Ivy's presence in the courtroom is too much. I want to crawl under the table and hide. She's like a monster under my bed, a demon I can't escape no matter how hard I try, not even in the dark.

Hedland approaches his witness. He smiles, and she smiles back, tight-lipped, so she doesn't show her teeth. She knows they're sharp and doesn't want the jury to see.

She's filled out since I last saw her. I hadn't noticed it the other day, but I do now. She looks different somehow, and it's not just because her hair is a different color. Maybe it's the fit of her skirt, the way it sits on her hips. Maybe it's the loneliness that's gotten to her.

I've never been as equally afraid of, and attracted to, a monster, but that's the pull I feel in my chest seeing her up there. I want to run full-on in the other direction, yet I can't fucking look away.

"Can you please state your name for the record?" Hedland asks.

"Ivy Rogers, sir."

"And your relationship to the defendant, Mrs. Rogers?" Her eyes reach mine, and it's all I can do not to blink. To hide behind the fear. She's nervous, despite the perversity behind her eyes. Like she wants to please me, or make me proud, even now.

"We're former lovers," she says, and a hush falls over the room—over the jury—and even Judge Wyman is outwardly taken aback by Ivy's confession.

It wasn't what I expected to hear either.

"Could you be more specific? Had you and Mrs. Thompson entered into a formal relationship?"

"Not exactly."

"Help us understand."

"Alisha—I mean, Mrs. Thompson—" she corrects herself, clearing the frog in her throat. "Was involved...sexually...with me and my husband."

"Your husband," Hedland starts, making a show of looking at the sheet of paper in his hand, even though he probably doesn't need it. "...is Sawyer Rogers. Is that correct?"

"Yes," she says, nodding. The jury doesn't pick up on the significance of it yet. They can't possibly know, because the last names are different. They're not related by blood.

It's one of the reasons I missed it, too.

"Tell me, Mrs. Rogers, is your husband here today?"

"No."

"And why not?"

"My husband and I are separated."

"Why is that?"

"Objection, speculation."

"Sustained."

"When did you and your husband separate?"

"About two months after Alisha ended our arrangement."

"And what exactly was your arrangement?"

"Sawyer and I invited Alisha into our bedroom under the agreement that she would engage—sexually—but only with *both* of us present."

"And did all parties stick to that arrangement?"

"No."

"Who strayed?"

"We all did," she admits, looking down at her lap. She's playing the jury, acting as if she's ashamed, but I know she's not. She was the first to stray.

"So, is it safe to say your marriage was jeopardized as a direct result of Mrs. Thompson's involvement? That perhaps she was the cause of your marital problems?"

"Objection again, Your Honor. This is ridiculous." Kyle says smoothly, gesturing at Hedland with a flippant hand.

"Overruled. You may answer the question, Mrs. Rogers."

"Yes."

"Tell me, were you aware of your husband's relation to Dylan Thompson, the deceased?" She freezes, the question seemingly startling her, as if Hedland had phrased it differently during trial preparations.

"I...yes, I was."

"And what was the relationship between Dylan Thompson and Sawyer Rogers?"

"They were stepbrothers."

The tone in the room has changed at Ivy's admission of Dylan and Sawyer's relation. I see the apprehension in the jury, in their newly stiffened body language. Their notebooks readily open on their laps. They see this turning point for what it is—a potential redirect of opinion.

Kyle approaches the witness stand with a swagger I haven't yet seen from him. He appears confident for cross examination, his eyes like daggers as they bore into Ivy's. He's rehearsed these questions so much that he doesn't even open his folder, just leaves it sitting on the table next to me. I shuffle in my seat, the nerves swimming in my belly.

"How did you come to know your husband, Mrs. Rogers?" he asks with an even tone.

"I met him through his brother, Dylan."

"And, if I understand correctly, you were involved in a long-term relationship with Mr. Thompson, and later with his stepbrother, Sawyer Rogers?"

She nods tentatively, swallowing slowly. She knows where Kyle is headed, and she doesn't like it.

"I need a yes or no, Mrs. Rogers."

"Yes."

"And did you end the relationship with Mr. Thompson prior to pursuing a relationship with his stepbrother?"

She glares suddenly, the break in her resolve palpable. "No."

"So, is it safe to say you're well-versed in the art of deception?"

"Objection!" Hedland bellows from the opposing table.

"Sustained."

"Rephrase, Your Honor. Mrs. Rogers, how long did you pursue a relationship with Sawyer Rogers behind his stepbrother's back?"

Ivy looks to Judge Wyman as if to ask if she's required to answer the question. Wyman nods and waves a hand, encouraging her to proceed. "Um…I'm not sure," she finally says.

"I'll wait, if you need a moment."

"I think it was about four months."

"Four months. That's an awful long time to engage in an affair."

"The court is not the place for opinions, Mr. Lanquist. Ask a question," Wyman says with annoyance.

"I'm sorry, really quick—can you remind the jury of your first name, Mrs. Rogers?"

"Objection, the witness has already stated her name for the record."

"Overruled."

Ivy squirms in her seat, beads of perspiration forming above her brow. She knows what's coming, and she doesn't like it, but it won't matter.

"Ivy."

"Hmph. That's odd, my client seemed to be under the impression you went by a different name. Lila, was it?"

She pauses, taking her time before replying through gritted teeth, "Yes."

Kyle waits for the jury to react. Several of them make note of the response, and anticipation knocks in my chest. I lace my fingers together, holding my own hands to prevent them from shaking.

"It was a safety precaution. My husband and I didn't feel comfortable sharing our real names."

"And how long were the two of you involved in a sexual relationship with my client?"

"A few months. Give or take."

"During that time, did you ever confess your real names to her?"

"No."

"Did you ever inform my client of your husband's familial relationship to Dylan Thompson?"

"No."

"Even though it seemed likely you might run into her outside of the nature of the relationship? Perhaps at family gatherings, holidays?"

"Correct."

"Why not?"

"Sawyer and Dylan hadn't spoken to one another in several years. We didn't attend family events where Dylan and Alisha were present."

"Why were Sawyer and Dylan not speaking?" I expect an objection from Hedland, but it never comes. He looks about as entranced as the jury. He's not even taking notes.

Ivy swallows hard, and I see the change in her eyes. The moment the fear changes to anger. She sees red, the fire in her eyes enough to burn a hole through Kyle's head.

"They hadn't been on speaking terms since Dylan discovered our affair."

"Ah. Okay, that makes sense. So, essentially, you tore the family apart, did you not?"

"Objection!"

There it is.

"Sustained. Mr. Lanquist, you're on thin ice with this line of questioning."

"My apologies, Your Honor." Kyle pauses, casually brushing a palm across his forehead. "Just one more sequence of questions here. Mrs. Rogers, at what point did you begin stalking my client?"

Hedland erupts, and all I can do is relax into my seat and fight like hell to suppress a smile. I'd give anything for a bowl of popcorn right now; this is turning into quite the show.

I can't help but commend Kyle for his resolve in the courtroom today. Never once did he mention that I'd met Ivy and Sawyer—*Lila and Grant*—because they were paying clients. And that was a good thing; any time we could help the jury forget what I did to earn a living was a point for the defense.

Apparently I'd given Kyle much less credit than he deserves.

He's even managed to steer the jury away from the notion that my profession was the cause of their separation, instead focusing on Ivy's expert ability to maintain her deception.

He was fucking brilliant in there.

Suddenly I find myself fighting the urge to drop to my knees and take Kyle's dick in my mouth. He deserves appreciation for his hard work today.

It seems Ivy Rogers has finally met her match.

SPELL IT OUT FOR THE JURY

Alisha

MUCH TO MY CHAGRIN, Chris is never called to the stand; Kyle has decided not to question him as a witness for the defense, even though I'm adamant we need him. I fight Kyle on this, on the fact that, without Chris, there is literally no one else to speak on my behalf.

We have no other witnesses.

And that's when Kyle decides to tell me that he's putting me on the stand.

The whispers from the gallery grow louder as I'm sworn in and take a seat in the box. My testimony under Kyle's line of questioning is smooth. There are no surprises.

It's short and sweet, like when I lost my virginity.

The true dance begins when Hedland stands, making a show of his presence in the center of the room, buttoning his suit jacket slowly while everyone else waits for him to start.

The first few questions aren't too bad.

But they grow increasingly more difficult—more damaging—as he goes on.

"Is it safe to say you've earned your living by seducing people?"

"Objection, Your Honor!" Kyle's voice booms from the table. He looks funny over there all by himself, different from this angle for some reason. He's objecting a lot, but Judge Wyman keeps shutting him down, and even when he doesn't, Hedland just finds new ways to ask different questions that result in the same damaging response as the original.

"Sustained."

"I'll reword. Mrs. Thompson, what do you do for work?"

I look to Kyle, his expression unreliable, but I read it anyway.

You're fucked.

But I can't break down now.

"I run a website—a content channel."

"What kind of content channel?"

"Not the kind that's kid-friendly," I admit, and at least one member of the jury scoffs at the response, a reminder that I need to reel in the sarcasm.

"What's the basis of the show?"

"Well, it's not a show, per se."

"What is it then?"

"A live stream."

"Of?"

I suck air into my lungs, ashamed of my career for the first time since its inception; Kristin's testimony was nothing compared to this. Hedland's about to put me in my place, and I'm not sure how to stop him. "Adult content," I finally say, certain it comes out more like a mumble.

"Adult content...as in porn?"

"Not exactly."

"Enlighten us, Mrs. Thompson. Spell it out for the jury." He smirks, and I want nothing more than to slap his lips off his face. I have no doubt that Hedland himself is well-educated on the meaning of adult content. Kyle objects but is overruled. Hedland turns to the judge, flippantly explaining the line of questioning.

"Your Honor, the defendant's profession is an intricate part of this case. It establishes not only her questionable character, but her compulsivity and perverse nature."

And this is where Kyle's lack of witness coaching gives Hedland an upper hand.

I push to my feet.

In the witness box.

Pointing a finger right in the prosecutor's smug face.

"So, you're implying that because I work in a *legal* sex industry, that I have no character? Is that what you're saying, Mr. Hedland?"

The bailiff approaches as I realize my mistake and sit back down.

"There will be no further outbursts from you, Mrs. Thompson. And you are to stay seated while you're on the stand, is that understood?"

"Yes," I say, slumping in the seat.

"Mr. Lanquist, you will advise your client to speak only when spoken to. The attorneys will ask the questions around here." Kyle shoots me a look, nodding to Judge Wyman in the process.

"The defense would like to request a short break, Your Honor," he says to my surprise. Wyman rolls his eyes and makes a show of checking the clock.

We're grateful when he allows the break.

In the holding room, Kyle kindly tears me a new asshole. "You absolutely *cannot* react like that on the stand, Alisha. The jury will hang you in a heartbeat."

"What am I supposed to do, Kyle? Put on a nun's cloak, strap on the rosary, and say my fucking prayers?"

"That's funny," he says mockingly. "Stick to the script. We discussed this, remember? You can't lose your cool up there, not after all we've accomplished. That jury is unsure, I can see it in their eyes... and do you know what that means?"

"That we have a chance?" I say tentatively.

"That we have a chance," Kyle confirms with a nod.

TELL ME YOU LOVE ME

Alisha

"HAS THE JURY REACHED A UNANIMOUS VERDICT?" Judge Wyman asks the jury foreperson. Her nerves are palpable throughout the room, and she clears her throat as she approaches a microphone. "We have, Your Honor."

There's a hush over the courtroom as the clerk asks for the reading of the verdict. I forget to breathe as it's read, the words seemingly spoken at a snail's pace, but no matter how fast or slow they come out, they're still the same in the end.

I fight the urge to scream, to kick and punch and throw myself onto the floor in a tantrum of epic proportions.

My body wants to protest when the bailiff approaches with handcuffs.

I hear nothing but the click of the locks as they slide into place. And it's as if the sound is nearly a thousand decibels louder than anything else in this room.

It may as well be a noose.

I've just been convicted of murder.

The courtroom doors open and the media are allowed back in, their cameras' red lights taunting me from all angles now. Everything suddenly seems too loud.

The shuffle of feet, a throat-clearing cough, the ticking of the clock.

Until everything eventually blurs together, and I can't move. As if I'm suspended, floating in the air above me, watching this scene play out like I'm the star of the movie.

Kyle's head falls into his hands—he knows he has failed. He's let me down.

I scan the room in search of Chris, of the last of the thirteen people who might still give a shit about me. But it's Bev that I see instead, and that hatred behind her eyes is devastating. The upturn of her lips that tells me she thinks I got what was coming to me, that she, too, is without a doubt that I murdered her son.

"This way, Mrs. Thompson," the bailiff says, and Kyle stands. Looking into his eyes is painful; I feel his remorse in my bones.

He should have done more.

He should have tried harder, believed me a little sooner.

We would have had more time.

"We'll appeal," he says with little confidence. I say nothing as I'm dragged away, back in the direction of the holding cell.

I see her then, just before the door closes, and I can't tell if she's happy or sad. She's just there. Present, but aloof, a single tear rolling down her cheek.

"Tell me you love me," she whispers.

THOMPSON, MURDER FOR ONE

Dylan

SHE SHOWED up out of nowhere, crawling into our bed as if she belonged there. As if I wanted her there. Half asleep, I didn't register that it was her. I knew Alisha had left for her morning run, but I thought she had come back early. That maybe she wasn't up for a run that morning after all.

But it wasn't Alisha.

It was a blonde woman, one I recognized, and for a moment I about shit myself when she grabbed hold of the duvet and yanked it off the bed and onto the floor. "What the fuck!" I yelled, realizing with a start that she'd cuffed my hands to the headboard as well.

"Don't be alarmed, Dylan. I'm just here to have a little conversation with you," she crooned, her lips shaping into a crooked smile.

I was about to ask what she was doing in my house, in my bed, but the sound of her voice made it clear: she had come for revenge. And it was finally clear who had been stalking my wife.

"Lila?"

"Oh, *good*, she did tell you about me!" she said, pleased with my answer.

Her hand trailed over my stomach and I shook it off, an edge to my tone as I said, "Of course she did. I just...didn't think it was you."

"Ah, and I bet you probably never mentioned how *you* know me either. Did you?"

I said nothing, unable to admit I'd been too cowardly to come forward with the whole story.

Ignoring her question, I writhed on the bed, attempting to wake the muscles in my forearms enough to crack the headboard and pry myself loose.

But Alisha and I had invested in a sturdy headboard right from the start—we'd tested its strength many times.

It wasn't going anywhere.

And these weren't those cheap fuzzy cuffs you'd buy at a sex store —they were the real deal, and it was at that point that I started to get a little worried.

But despite the fact that I was restrained against my will, I couldn't hide my apparent arousal. I willed my cock to shrivel up and go back into hiding, but Ivy was a beautiful woman. And she was taking her clothes off, folding them neatly and placing them in a duffle bag. My confused cock raised to a full stance, on high alert and ready to play.

She stripped naked.

Then she climbed onto my lap, rubbing her wetness on my leg as she positioned herself. My dick throbbed at the sight of her, and I knew I was screwed. The last thing I ever wanted to do was cheat on my wife, but I couldn't seem to get that memo to my stupid dick. Ivy leaned down and kissed the tip of it, and for some fucking reason I moaned.

That only turned her on more.

I tried the age-old trick of thinking of something else—*Grandma. Dog shit. Rotten milk. Vomit.* Nothing worked...and then her tongue...*oh fuck, I forgot how good she is at that.*

"It's your fault she left us, you know," she said, her lips coming off my cock as she looked up at me through sultry eyes. Her breath teased my dick as she spoke. "You took her from us, Dylan. The three of us could've been something."

"You deserved it," I mumbled through labored breaths. "For what you did to me..." Her tits brushed against my thighs, and as if it wasn't enough that she'd taken me in her mouth again, she brought a hand to her pussy.

And then she was on top of me, and I knew she was about to sit on my cock, and despite myself—despite everything I knew—in that moment, I wanted it. I wanted to be inside of her, and the guilt that accompanied that thought broke my heart.

"Oh, Dylan...you poor, sweet man," she said, the tip of my dick entering her. And all I could think was how much I wished my hands weren't locked up so I could sit her the fuck down. "You'll never understand, will you?"

And finally, the torture stopped, and she rode me, and I watched her tits bounce like a fucking idiot. She held me down with a hand to my chest, the other reaching behind her cowgirl style. I knew I should close my eyes, maybe do my best to picture Alisha's face instead, but I couldn't stop watching her.

I couldn't.

I'd never entertained the thought of a threesome with my wife, but in that moment, I wanted nothing more than to see her walk through the door and sit on my face.

I relaxed beneath the beautiful lunatic before bucking my hips and driving deeper into her. She squealed, and we were back to fucking just like we used to, *before* she decided she'd rather have my brother.

A small part of me still expected Alisha to come out and yell, "Surprise!"

I had no clue what Ivy's end game was, but I was in it, nonetheless. She'd won, and if all I had to do was fuck her and get it over with, then that's what I was going to do.

"Get off, I'm about to cum," I said through gritted teeth. But she didn't get off, she only rode me harder. "GET OFF!" I screamed, but still, she didn't move, and there was nothing I could do to stop it from happening.

I filled her with all of me, with everything I had to offer, and the shame hit me harder than a tidal wave. "What the fuck is wrong with you?"

Ivy smirked, her eyes rolling to the back of her head. I felt her tighten around my cock, all the while looking me in the eye as she brought herself to orgasm.

And I couldn't help it. The next thing I did was ask if she was still on birth control.

"There's no need to worry about that, Dylan," she said, climbing off me and sauntering slowly to the bathroom. I even watched her walk away. She came out a few minutes later, fully clothed in black leggings and a dark sweatshirt, the hood pulled up over her head and a washcloth in her hands.

"What are you doing?"

She winked, but said nothing, just leaned in and kissed me deeply before pulling away.

And then I saw something in her hand—shiny and...*is that a knife?* I was about to scream as the blade slid into my chest and a spike of pain coursed through my body, sucking the air right from my lungs.

She struggled to pull it out, but managed, only to drive it in a second time.

And a third.

And a fourth...

Until it was dark, and I could no longer breathe because my lungs had filled with blood.

Her face was blurry—almost like an illusion as she faded away.

But her face isn't the last I see.

Alisha, sweetie, I'm so sorry.

My love.

EVEN IN DEATH

Alisha

I RETURNED from my run to find the door off the kitchen slightly open. I couldn't remember locking it, so it was possible it had blown open from the wind. That, or we had an unwelcome rodent roaming the house.

I entered, and this time I locked the door behind me, grabbing my cell off the counter where I left it charging. I'd forgotten to plug it in after my argument with Dylan the night before, so it had run out of battery.

My music-less run did little to clear my head. The note I left him was still on the counter, so I crumpled it up and tossed it in the kitchen trash.

It wouldn't have killed you to tell the truth.

A small part of me was relieved he hadn't seen it. But if Dylan was still asleep, he was sure to be late for work, because I didn't even hear him moving around upstairs. *Maybe he decided to take the day off.*

We did have a lot to talk about. Decisions to consider, apologies to make. And while I was still angry about what I'd learned, the secrets he'd kept from me all that time, I'd realized none of that changed the fact that I loved him. I believed he loved me too, and would do his best to prove it to me every day forward.

His admission hit me hard, but we would be okay. Everything would work out, and we'd be back to normal in no time. The makeup sex was sure to blow my mind—probably his, too.

"Dylan?" I called. "Are you up?"

No answer.

I made my way up the stairs, surprised to find the bedroom door cracked open. I was certain I closed it all the way; I didn't want him to wake before the alarm went off.

"Babe?"

I pressed my hand flat against the door and used my fingers to push it the rest of the way open. My breath caught in my throat when the smell hit me and I gasped, bringing a hand to my mouth.

The sight of him on the bed brought bile to the back of my throat. It bubbled up, despite my attempts to hold it down, and I ran to the bathroom to be sick. I retched, the muscles in my stomach contracting and leaving me breathless. I wiped my mouth on the back of my hand, chunks of vomit still floating around inside.

I didn't want to go back in there.

There was so much blood.

The copper scent clung to my nostrils and made me want to vomit all over again.

I shouldn't have gone back in there.

I stared at his mutilated body from the bathroom floor, the rising sunlight peeking through the windows and reflecting in the exposed metal of the knife that was sticking out of his chest. The cornucopia of colors seemed out of place with its surroundings.

It didn't look right.

And I couldn't stop myself from going to him. I wanted to take his hand, to feel his fingers between mine one last time. I needed to hold him before he went cold.

For a moment, I stood over him, staring as if paralyzed, somehow suspended in time.

When the feeling passed, I lunged forward, wrapping my fingers around the handle of the knife and pulling with every muscle in me. I didn't want it to be in his body. I couldn't stand to see it there, taunting me. I didn't want to see him that way, to remember my husband as a lifeless corpse.

With the knife out, I pulled the white sheet over his torso.

The blood seeped through the fabric, the Egyptian cotton surely ruined. Why that thought crossed my mind, I wasn't sure—it was just a sheet. I could replace it.

But not Dylan.

I reached out and touched his face, my fingers grazing the stubble along his chin. I knew he couldn't feel it, but I took his hand in mine, leaving a kiss on his forehead. His skin was still warm, yet already cold, too.

He was lifeless.

But he was still that same beautiful soul I'd fallen in love with by nothing short of happenstance. And he was beautiful, even in death.

The pounding on the door startled me. I didn't know who it could at that hour, but the shouting came next. I think it surprised me even more than the pounding.

"Police, open up!"

Because how did they already know?

I didn't want to open the door. I didn't want to leave Dylan, and I couldn't answer any of their questions, because I didn't fucking know what happened to my husband.

So, I froze.

I stood there, at my husband's side, covered in his blood and tightly gripping the knife that had been used to kill him, that I'd later learn had been driven in and out of his flesh a total of seventeen times.

Ironically, the same age I was when my mother died.

The same day of the month Mrs. Maylen left us.

The same number of times I slept with Lila and Grant.

I recognized the knife from the wood block in our kitchen. Even if I hadn't been holding it at that moment, my fingerprints would've been all over it, despite the fact that I rarely cooked.

Fear never settled in.

Not when the officers kicked down my front door.

Not when they stormed through my house.

Not when they pointed their service weapons at my face.

Not even when they cuffed me and read me my Miranda rights.

There was no fear left to be had.

Because everything I was afraid of losing was already gone.

GROW A PAIR, CINDERELLA

Alisha

I COUNT the divots in the bricks on the wall.

One.

Two.

Three.

There's nothing else to do while I await sentencing for the crime I didn't commit. It's been six days since my trial ended, since the verdict was read, my fate decided and publicly announced. Six days since I've done anything other than lie by myself in the confines of my cell, back in the very penitentiary I swore never to return to.

I wasn't supposed to come back here.

And now that I have? It's worse than before. It seems like everyone here is prepared to eat me alive, Officer Marshall included. I've been sent back to the same pod, the same COs overlooking the unit.

A lone enemy in a sea of allies.

So, for now, I stick to my cell, where I can wallow in my misfortune privately. I wallow, and I sleep, and I think. My mind is a constant loop of memories and what ifs and everything in between.

I can't stop thinking about her, about Lila. Wondering how she did it. How she managed to pull off a setup like this. For some reason, that matters more to me than understanding *why*.

I couldn't give a fuck *why* she did it. That knowledge doesn't change the fact that she did. It doesn't change the fact that I'm here. That I'll probably never live beyond the confines of this prison ever again.

I just want to understand how she did it.

She had to have been following me for some time, much longer than I realized. Studying me. Watching Dylan. It had been so long since I'd seen her loitering around the places I frequented, so long since I'd heard from her. But it makes sense in a way, I suppose.

She was always there, I just couldn't see her.

Lila lost her husband; he left her, so in her mind, I had to lose mine too.

Only it doesn't add up. It was me she claimed to love, not Dylan. Not Grant—er, Sawyer. So why not kill me instead? How does killing Dylan and framing me for his murder make everything right for her?

I can't help but wonder if perhaps I wasn't meant to go down for it. Maybe she didn't know I'd come back to the house, that I'd walk into that room and pick up the knife. Maybe she planned to find me afterward and force me to run away with her.

I don't know anymore.

I'm grasping at straws here.

But I have all the time in the world to sit around and think about it, so that's what I do.

"You just gonna rot in there forever, Thompson?" Tiffany asks, rapping her knuckles on the open bars of my cell. I haven't moved from the bed and can't say I plan to. Rec time be damned.

"Yep."

"It doesn't have to be so bad, you know," she says. I can see it in her eyes, that she wants to touch me, maybe put a hand on my arm or something. As if it would offer me comfort.

I already know it won't.

And I sure as shit don't want her touching me.

"Yes, it does," I say. She scoffs, not liking my attitude.

"Oh, grow a pair, Cinderella." She drops to half her size, leaning over with her elbows on her knees, her face inches from mine. Her breath stinks, and I resist the urge to pull away because that's what she wants. "Accepting it is the only way to get back at whoever did this to you."

She shoves off and disappears down the hall, not another word spoken between us. I still don't know if the story she fed me was true, whether she murdered her husband.

Part of me still believes it is, but I'm not about to chase her down, as I'd hate to give her the impression that we're friends.

But once again, she's left me with more insightful words to ponder, and now I'm more annoyed than I was before she stopped in to chat.

Too bad I have no fucking clue what the hell she meant by it.

I'm still pondering it forty minutes later when I'm blessed with another visitor. "You've got mail, Thompson," CO Marin announces. She pulls the mail cart toward the door and passes me a clipboard. I sign my name with the attached pen and take the envelope from her.

It's another letter from my father.

I toss it onto the stack with the others, plagued with a lack of desire to open it. I can't bring myself to read them yet haven't asked to have him removed from my mailing list either. I haven't decided what I want to do about him.

Instead, I pull out a notebook and pencil, and decide to write a letter to Chris.

I never got to see him in court when the verdict was read, but he was there, standing in the back of the room crying, and ducking out early so he wouldn't have to see me hauled away again.

Dear Chris,

I can't believe you left the sunshine state to come visit me all the way back in Minne-snow-duh—if only I could have seen you, too. I'm sorry I wasn't able to make the wedding, but as you know, it's kinda tough to get out of the office these days.

To be honest, I'm not sure if you even care to hear from me, but I'm writing to you anyway. It brings me comfort to feel like I'm talking to another human, and while you know I hate sappy ass emotions, I owe this to you. I want you to know that I'm okay. That you're the best friend I've ever had.

Oh, quit crying, you big baby…I'll be fine. And I'll understand if having a convicted murderer for a BFF is too much for you… although, who the hell am I kidding? This is some straight-up Real Housewives shit, and you love it.

Thank you for being you, for not giving a shit what anyone says about me, and for showing up in court. Not just because you had to on account of the subpoena, but because you wanted to show your support. I'm not entirely sure whose story you believe, but I hope that somewhere in your heart, you know the truth.

I'll keep this first letter brief, but I'll write to you again…

Take care, my friend.
Love,
Alisha

P.S. The potatoes here suck. I wish you could smuggle me some. Since you can't, please send me some good books to read.

A KILLER'S TEARS

Alisha

IT'S KINDA FUNNY, isn't it? How deep down you thought I did it. That I killed my husband. It's okay, I'm not mad, it's what I expected of you from the beginning. Like I told you before, the evidence was against me. Hell, I probably would have believed it, too, had I been in your shoes.

Lila made sure to secure the nail in my coffin just as surely as she did Dylan's. We didn't stand a chance once she sunk her teeth in, once she set her sights on destroying us.

And he knew all along.

He could have stopped it.

But he didn't. The lie was just too big.

I miss him every single day. A heavy brick has taken the place of my heart, resting in my chest like a tumor since the moment I found my husband stabbed to death. Since I found him mutilated on our bed. But tears won't bring him back. I know this. I learned that the hard way back when I realized my mother was too far gone to ever come back.

I was reminded of it when I lost Mrs. Maylen.

Everyone I love dies.

See, that's why it really doesn't matter that I'm here for the long haul. As I said before, there's nothing left out there for me. The irony is that I've been here all this time for the wrong reasons—for the wrong murder. And maybe that doesn't matter, maybe this is where I was always supposed to be. Statistics favor such an argument, if you think about it.

Absent father.

Drug-abusing mother.

Poverty.

Sex addiction.

The cards were stacked against me since the day I was born, my fate sealed the second my mother decided not to abort me.

"My little tax deduction," she used to say. Until I was old enough to know better, it always made me smile when she'd call me that, like the child in me thought it was a term of endearment or something.

Childhood made me hard. These walls I keep up were erected a long time ago, built of concrete—of brick and mortar—and meant to withstand the tests of time.

They're unbreakable now.

But the misconception of a heart protected by concrete is that it never had room to love. It's hard for a jury to believe your story when you're labeled as heartless and—how did they say it? Oh, yes. *A sex-crazed lunatic.* Kyle says I should have cried in court, that I should have shown more emotion during the trial.

I wasn't sure how to do that when everything I've ever loved is gone.

Taken from me.

Prematurely stripped from my life.

Erased like a white board.

You see, my love, it never mattered who killed you. There will never be justice, or even closure. Nothing has mattered since I lost you.

Nothing.

There will be no life on the outside for me after this, even if I'm paroled down the road. Kyle wants to file an appeal, now that he finally believes in my innocence. I'm not entirely sure what changed his mind, but something did, and I guess that's good enough for me.

At least *someone* believes me.

But there's no point in being out there without you.

I'm done fighting. I'm tired.

So, my love, that's why—although I know you won't agree with my logic—it's time for me to earn my stripes. To live up to the sentence that was given to me by performing the very act I was convicted of, the crime that put me here.

Murder.

I can't stand the idea of living out the rest of my life in here otherwise.

———

I see him approaching, rounding the corner like he's on a mission. It's too late to turn and run—the others are already clearing the hall, migrating to their watch posts, readying themselves for the live show.

He's come for me again.

"I wish I could see you in one of your outfits," he growls into my ear as he shoves me against the wall. His arousal digs into my hip, his tongue slick as it trails along my earlobe. His breath is hot on my face, frantic. His excitement builds quickly, more so than usual, and he runs his hands up my thigh, pushing greedily between my legs.

But today I don't give him the win.

I don't relax and pretend he's Dylan, I don't give him the satisfaction he's come for. Today we're going to sing a different song, play a different game.

"Spread 'em," he says into my neck, his hands suddenly rough when he realizes I'm putting up a fight.

I shove against him, pushing off the wall for momentum and knocking him backward. He stumbles, and it's just enough leeway for me to slide the makeshift weapon from my pocket. I turn before he has a chance to realize what's happening, and drive the point of the shiv into his carotid artery.

I pull it out and jam it in once more.

Then again.

His eyes bulge, and he brings his hands to his neck, trying to cover the holes, as if he can stop the blood from pouring out. He opens his mouth and tries to speak, but the words don't follow, just the sound of him gurgling. I smile, my eyes locked on his, watching while he stumbles backward, the color already draining from his face. The blood is everywhere, pooling at my feet, and soaking into my uniform.

This time, it doesn't make me sick.

This time, it's absolutely fucking beautiful.

I exhale heavily, relief coursing through my veins, and I slide down the wall and onto the floor, my hand landing in the crimson puddle beside me. I relax against the wall, my leg now draped over his, and watch in a daze as the motion in his chest finally stops.

A rogue tear rolls down my blood-stained cheek, and I swipe it away before the cavalry arrives and finds me whimpering like a child. But Tiffany is there, leaning nonchalantly against the wall, a sadistic smile playing on her lips.

"A killer's tears bring no mercy," she says.

She leans down and kisses my forehead, taking the blood-soaked shiv from my hand and sliding it into her pocket. I had to give her a taste just to agree to let me use it, but an orgasm is a small price to pay in exchange for one's sanity.

The security alarm sounds above us, the shrilling blast deafening, but I tune it out and close my eyes. Sometimes you have to set the alarm bells ringing just to turn down the noise.

LIKE A BIRD IN FLIGHT

Ivy/Lila

ALISHA, Alisha, Alisha…how dare you do what you've done to me.

To *us*.

You truly do deserve everything that's come your way, don't you? It does pain me a bit to think that—to say it—but our true colors do tend come out in the wash. Certainly you should know this by now.

Sex has been your weapon your entire life, like a nuclear bomb sure to explode at any moment. But it won't work for you anymore, my love.

Not.

Anymore.

People like you are users. Maybe not of drugs, but certainly of other people, and that's the worst kind if you ask me. You use people to get what you want. You prey on women like me. We are the weaker sex, after all, right? Isn't that what makes it so easy? I really should have seen it coming, that you'd shatter this fragile thing we built together. So carelessly, too.

Imagine that, huh? Well, I'm tired of being ignored. Of being shoved to the back burner because I was never good enough for top choice. But you had no problem holding on until someone better came along. Until *he* got in the way. And what about me? Who was I supposed to get in the end?

Certainly not Sawyer.

Not even you.

I loved you, you know. I loved my husband, too. But you took him from me. You ripped his love for me straight out of his chest and kept it all for yourself. And the worst part is, you didn't even need him. You already had your person, Alisha. You had Dylan.

Why the fuck did you have to take Sawyer, too?

I warned him you would do this. That you'd leave us. That idiot was so pigheaded, he refused to believe me. Until he saw you with *him*.

His own fucking brother.

And it made sense, really. Of course it did. An eye for an eye. Tit for fucking tat. But you know what? *Our* story was supposed to be different. It wasn't just about Dylan catching Sawyer and me in the act all those years ago. The truth is, I simply didn't love him anymore. He practically pushed me into Sawyer's arms when he chose his career over me. So don't go feeling sorry for him.

The heart wants what it wants, right?

Our real problems started after Dylan made you shut down Lisha's Bedroom. He always was a coward, never did have much of a backbone. Your dear husband wasn't as wonderful and perfect as you made him out to be. He didn't even have the decency to be honest with you —not even *after* he talked you into marrying him.

And who do you suppose had to make up for what Sawyer lost after your channel went down?

He made me dress like you. Made me wear a wig the same shade as your hair, the same length, the same style. I did my makeup like yours, stuffed my bra so my breasts would look bigger—like yours. But the worst part of it all—the thing that broke me—is that he made me answer to your name. Lila was gone, her persona no longer in service. No longer of use to him.

And Ivy? Ha! She—*I*—died long before Lila was born.

Even as you, I wasn't good enough for him. He knew I was a fake, a stand in. So, what did I have left in the end? My husband certainly didn't need me anymore, didn't want me. He wanted *you*. So it looks like that left me with no one.

Poor Ivy draws the short end of the stick once again.

That's why I had no choice but to seek you out. Why I tracked you and followed your daily schedule, ended up in the same places at the same time. Did you really forget that I don't like coffee? That shit is disgusting. Seriously, I don't know how you drink it. Anyway, I studied you, your mannerisms, your moves. I honestly couldn't figure out what was so special about you that I didn't have. What I was completely blind to was that you were just *you*. Some magical fucking creature; a rainbow-colored unicorn in a field of white horses.

And damn it, I wanted my unicorn back.

I fell for you in the process of losing Sawyer.

And I wasn't about to lose you too.

We could have been so good together, you and me. Even with Sawyer as the third wheel. Even if he wasn't around at all. I could live without the dick if I meant we could be together. Could you?

I suppose you have to now, being in a women's prison and all. It kinda makes me laugh a little bit inside, the thought of you in there with no one to take care of your needs.

You poor thing.

It's really too bad Dylan had to die. It's not like I hated him; there just wasn't room for him with what I had planned for us. You know he never would have accepted me into your bed, and that just wouldn't have been fair. He was nothing like his brother, and unlike Sawyer, Dylan never would have shared his most prized possession.

I had to show you, Alisha. I needed you to understand what you've done to me, how you've changed me, what you've taken from me. I needed *you* to change, too. To feel the same gut-wrenching pain I've felt every day since I first caught Sawyer watching your fucking website. Since the day he chose you over me.

Since *you* ruined him. See, you're not so innocent in all this either.

At least now I know neither of them can stick their dicks in you anymore. Thank God, because the thought of you fucking someone other than me at this point? It makes my damn stomach hurt. Jealousy does run thicker than water, you know.

So, here we are, my love. It's you and me now. I know you don't see it that way, but you will. You'll need a friend to visit you in that hell-hole soon, to put money in your commissary and write to you from the outside. I'm sending this first letter today, in fact, and I've enclosed a photo of me that you'll be able to tape up on the wall next to your government-issued bed. I'll send the racier ones your way once you prove to me that you deserve them.

And you will.

You'll see.

Of course, I have a photo of you next to my bed, too. Sometimes it helps me sleep at night, seeing your beautiful face. You were supposed to be here, sleeping next to me.

But that mistake is on you, not me.

Anyway, you're probably a little confused about the second photo I've enclosed.

The bump is really starting to show, and I can't wait for you to see it, what Dylan and I created together. I wonder how often you think about the fact that I had him last. How he died with the taste of me on his lips.

Does that upset you?

I know it's hard to see in the sonogram, but we're having a boy. I'm sure you'd never deny Dylan's son a chance to see his other mother, would you? I imagine you'd like to watch him grow up, to see whether or not he looks like his father. I'm thinking I may even give him the Thompson name, that way he'll be a part of all of us.

Dylan Sawyer Thompson.

It sure has a nice ring to it, don't you think?

I know one day that boy will be my ticket back to you.
And together?
Well, we'll soar like a bird in flight.

LIKE A BIRD IN FLIGHT

CRIMES OF PASSION BOOK 2

PORN STAR

Alisha

I'VE IMAGINED killing her at least a dozen different ways.

Not that I'm proud to admit that, but she deserves to be punished for what she's done. Some days it's all I can think about—her death and how I'd do it…how I'd kill her.

The options are endless, really. Up close and personal, a stranger-like attack, a random incident or accident. But nothing would be more satisfying than extinguishing her up close and personal.

Slowly.

Painfully.

A kitchen knife, although messy, would certainly do the trick. It'd be fitting even, if not for the irony, considering she once used the same weapon to murder my husband, Dylan.

Got away with it, too.

I imagine shooting her would feel pretty good, but I don't own a gun, and forensics can usually trace a bullet back to the gun that fired it and therefore the shooter.

Too risky.

I suppose that part doesn't matter, given my current predicament.

No, if I were to do it—I mean *really* do it—I'd probably drug her. The other options would be fun, sure, but they're too merciful, if not predictable.

Certainly way too easy.

I think I'd enjoy it a lot more if I were to go the drug route; maybe inject her with some paralytic drug like succinylcholine or vecuronium, rendering her muscles useless. She'd be fully conscious and alert, but immobilized. Defenseless. *That* would be gratifying—stimulating—maybe even empowering in some fucked-up way. I'd be free to do whatever I wanted to her after that. I could take my time, savor the moment.

Choke her.

Smother her.

Torture her.

Honestly, with all the new "friends" I've made here at the Smithson Women's Penitentiary over the last year, it'd be easy to get my hands on whatever I'd need to do the job. A walk in the park, really. In here, everyone knows someone (who knows someone) who can get their hands on anything (or anyone), for the right price.

Fortunately for me, I have plenty of money to spare; I've saved millions, thanks to my former life as a porn star.

I lie back in my bunk, sinking into the thin mattress that does little to separate me from the metal frame, and fold my arms behind my head as I stare at the ceiling. I have nothing but time in here. Time to think, time to daydream. For what this place lacks in comfort, it makes up for in that regard. But even as a bit of a loner, life on the outside for me was a constant ebb and flow, chaotic. Every day a never-ending list of to-dos without the time to actually *do* any of it. But here?

Here it's like a clock with no numbers, a series of light and dark, night and day.

An endless routine of monotony.

The mind has free rein to wander…to conjure.

I picture myself jamming a needle into the fatty meat of her arm, the injection quick but effective. I'd watch as her eyes go wide, as she starts to feel the drugs make their way through her veins, as she loses control of her limbs. The effects would kick in before she'd realize what was happening, that her life was about to end. That I was going to be the one to take it from her. I'd want her to know, of course. Revenge always tastes sweeter that way.

That's the beauty of it, you see?

I'd finally get to watch *her* suffer.

I've waited a long time for that.

Problem is, I'm a convicted murderer. So, despite this over-whelming desire to kill my former lover turned nemesis, Ivy Rogers, I'll be waiting a hell of a lot longer for *that* day to come. You knew that, though, didn't you? You couldn't possibly have forgotten all about my little situation; how I'm stuck in prison for a crime *she* committed. You probably even think I deserve to be here, and that's fine. That's your opinion, and you're entitled to it.

But you're wrong.

I suppose it *is* a little silly of me to daydream about killing someone on the outside when I'm stuck in here doing hard time, though. It's incredible how guilty an innocent person can look under the right lighting.

Shadows sure can be deceiving.

Not that I'm all that innocent anymore. There's still that other murder I *did* commit, the one I *am* responsible for, that's preventing me from living out this incredible fantasy. I'm not getting out of here any time soon, despite my wrongful conviction.

Doesn't mean a girl can't dream.

Still, everyone knows the incarcerated need something to look forward to when they get out. Something that drives us, entices us to roll out of these makeshift beds every day, to eat the food that tastes like cardboard and often smells like a toilet seat. There's usually an end goal—family, money, revenge. And when there isn't? Well, I'm sure you can figure out what happens to *those* inmates.

All hope is lost once a person loses their will to live in here.

This place is such a mind fuck.

CLUSTERFUCK

Alisha

IF I COULD GET my head to stop spinning, that'd be great. You know that feeling you get when you're about to pass out? How your hands get all tingly before they eventually go numb, followed by your feet, your legs? The next thing you know, you're hot all over, feverish, lethargic. Clammy, possibly even breaking a sweat.

The room becomes hazy.

The space around you caves in.

And you know—you just *know*—that you're about to go down, that you're headed straight to the ground and you're not about to take the fall gracefully, either.

Drop and flop, more likely.

So classy.

The physical reactions are so similar to fear. And that's what I go through every single day; that's my life now. I feel like I'm about to pass out, only seconds away from the edge, at any given moment on any given day.

And I always eat shit.

I always land on my ass.

There's really no other way.

Three hundred seventy-two days. That's how long I've been here. It feels like an eternity already, but my time has only just begun. The days tick by in slow motion, the images of a past life fading one by one; soon they'll be gone entirely.

Forgotten.

Erased.

And I see the face of a complete stranger, remembering the moment she locked eyes with Judge Wyman and uttered the word "guilty" among a courtroom of spectators. She couldn't even make eye contact with me, couldn't bother to look *me* in the eye when she sealed my fate with that one single word. Almost as if she herself didn't believe the verdict that had been rendered.

I often wonder if she was the one juror who wasn't quite sure. Kyle Lanquist, my attorney, had said there was one; that they probably caved from the pressure, from the vindictive eyes of the eleven others, eventually.

Just one.

But if that's the case, if she *was* the one, she must not have felt too strongly one way or the other, because that jury was only out for three hours and twenty-six minutes. Certainly not long enough to decide the next twenty-five years of a person's life, if you ask me.

The American judicial system at its finest, my friends.

What a clusterfuck.

It replays in my mind daily, alongside snippets of Ivy—*Lila*—and Sawyer—*Grant*. But mostly I see images of Dylan. I see him smiling —*my husband*—laughing, loving me. I long to breathe him in, to smell his scent and feel the warmth of his body against my skin.

It almost seems unfair that he's gone.

But sometimes it feels like I deserve it, too. Like I'm *that* shitty of a human that the best I'll ever get from here on out is three mediocre meals a day, semi-clean prison scrubs, and a twice-daily orgasm at the direction of my own hand.

And now there's this letter.

Would you like to meet our son, Lisha?

My stomach turns as I read her words, not for the first time either. I've read this letter more times in the last couple weeks than I care to admit—the paper is worn from repeated folding and unfolding. But it still doesn't sit well with me.

How could it?

He looks a lot like his father, his namesake. I bet you'll appreciate that. I suppose I do, too. It's really too bad you had to go and get yourself convicted. If only you'd listened to me, Lisha...

She's been taunting me like this for months, sending letters just like this one—with just enough semblance of truth, but not enough for anyone but me to know—some with sonogram pictures, others with photos of her showing off her baby bump, updates on her prenatal appointments.

But this time it's a picture of him.

She's had a baby boy. Named after his father, and she's managed to rub it in my face—even from the outside.

My husband is the father of her son.

And I picture her there, smirking to herself as she writes these letters, her hand so heavy it bubbles the ink on the page as she writes. I take in the scribbled words on these crinkled pages, knowing she once touched them, and I soak them up like they're scripture to live by.

She played me.

Just like she played Dylan.

Just like she played Sawyer.

I see the irony in her words, in the accusations hidden within them, that all of this is somehow my fault. That I had it coming. She follows them blindly, accepts them like a brainwashed cult member or a child in church singing along to "Jesus Loves Me" and actually believing that He does. And it's fitting, almost—her oblivion. Her lack of regard. It *has* to be, because I can't bear the thought of her knowingly being this conniving, this intentionally motivated.

I have to kill her.

Sometimes I think I humanize her too much, forgetting momentarily who she is, how capable she is of destruction. It helps to think about taking her life. She's already taken mine.

I need to get Dylan's son away from her.

But I don't know how to do that while I'm stuck in here.

Kyle was working on an appeal.

Key word: was.

He's not anymore.

The whole Shiv-Meets-Officer-Marshall's-Neck incident kind of blew that for me. That was my bad, I guess. But, come on. That prick deserved it, and you know it as well as I do. He needed to be stopped, and I had no choice but to take that matter into my own hands.

I get why Kyle's pissed, I really do. I can't expect my attorney to work miracles. We had a chance—albeit a very small one—and now we don't. As if this is really a "we" thing and Kyle is actually affected, right? What a joke. Even if he could exonerate me of my husband's murder, it still wouldn't get me out of here. Not after what I've done.

There were new charges. For my actual crime, the one I *did* commit, and to say Kyle was unhappy to hear I'd taken the prison rape matters into my own hands would be an understatement. The man was truly livid, more so than I've ever seen him.

But what was I supposed to do? No one else would have done anything about it, and I was stuck here, merciless to the man. He stuck his claws in and refused to let go. And me? I was never getting out of here; I had nothing to lose and a chance to prove myself to the only people left who mattered.

My fellow inmates.

Or so I thought.

Now, with two very public murders on my rap sheet, I'm probably (definitely) stuck here for life, likely without parole or the ability to pass *go*, which means my intentions of avenging my husband's death and taking out Ivy Rogers may never see the light of day. It almost makes me wish Minnesota were a death penalty state.

Some days I can't bear to soak in the misery buried within these walls.

Some days I just want it all to end.

But for now, I dream.

I plot.

I spend the core hours of my days suspended in time, locked in an eight-by-six cell with a woman who talks to herself and considers masturbation a sin. Whoever assigns cell mates in this place clearly had it out for me.

There isn't much reprieve outside of lockdown hours, either. Tiffany still has me wrapped around her bony little finger, but I'm forever indebted to her, whether I like it or not. And desperate times called for desperate measures, so it is what it is.

At least no one bothers me anymore; no one catcalls or corners me in hallways and shoves their hand down my pants. There are always consequences for those who do, now that I've shown my true colors— now that Tiffany has made it clear who's hiding the shiv—and that's more than I can say for most of the women in here. At least I was resourceful enough to come up with a contingency plan; I knew what I was getting into.

But this fucking letter.

Ugh.

My husband has a son.

And *she's* his mother.

She'll get what's coming to her, though.

She *has* to.

Right?

PART III

COUPLE SEEKING FEMALE

PLAY THE VICTIM

Ivy

SHE WANTS TO KILL ME.

I know it, and you know it. Sure, maybe one day that'll work out for her—who knows? For now, I wake up every morning and revel in the fact that she's locked up and I'm not. She can't touch me from where she's at. She doesn't have the connections she thinks she does, despite her wealth. Nobody even likes her enough to help her.

Her, being Alisha Thompson, federal inmate, local public enemy, and envy of soccer moms everywhere.

It's my fault she's there, in that prison. I admit it. But that's beside the point.

She thinks she's the victim here, but she's not. No, *I'm* the real victim. She hurt me first. And an eye for an eye goes a long way when the trip itself is just a short jaunt.

Trust me, she got what she deserved.

Do I feel bad for what I've done to her? No, not really. She left me, so there was nothing more for me to lose. And Dylan? Ex-boyfriend of mine or not, it wasn't like there was any love left between us. That ship had long since sailed, and the animosity from him was getting a little old, if you ask me. He took her from me.

So, no, I don't feel bad for what I've done.

This way works for me.

This way, we play by *my* rules. I set the tone, run the show, and write the script. Dylan's out of the way now, and Alisha can only run so far with her ankles chained together.

I haven't been by to see her yet, in the prison. Not for lack of trying; she simply refuses to see me. But she will. One day I'll take up residence at the top of her very short—if not otherwise non-existent—visitors list. She'd be a fool not to want to meet her husband's son, and I'm the only one who could make that happen for her.

One phone call.

That's all she's given me in the time we've spent apart. Over a year now, and that's all I get. I'm sick of the cold shoulder act she's playing.

The boy will change all that eventually, though; he *has* to.

He really is a cute kid; looks a lot like his dad. Nothing like *her*. Which is a shame. But he's *our* son, despite her lack of contribution to his DNA. And he may have been conceived out of spite with her now-dead husband, against his will—although, he sure seemed into it until he saw the blade of the knife that killed him—but the boy's purpose has always been medicinal. He'll fix us. That baby is the one good card I have left in my hand.

And I intend to use it.

Did I intend for Alisha to get pegged for Dylan's murder? Not really. That was a bit of an accident.

Oops.

I simply wanted the man dead and out of her life.

Out of my way.

And I wanted *her* to suffer, to feel his loss the same way I've felt hers since the moment she walked away without so much as a glance over her shoulder. I suppose that's where my little plan went a wee bit south; I didn't quite think that part through, and that's on me. See, I wanted to catch her after her run. We'd pack a bag, grab some of her hard-earned cash, and off we'd go. But she came back early, while I was busy hiding evidence in a rented car down the street, and I didn't get a chance to explain. And that nosy neighbor of hers just *had* to go and call the cops—being the *concerned citizen* that she was.

She heard Alisha's screams, after all.

Not that her testimony in court was all that damaging in the long run. Alisha kind of hammered the final nail herself, if I'm being honest.

Everything just happened so fast—a true crime of passion, if you will. Although, something tells me Alisha would disagree with that logic; she prefers to save passion for the bedroom.

Trust me, I know.

What I didn't know was that she would come home early. That she'd walk right into that bedroom, pull the knife from her dead husband's torso, and hold it in her dominant hand while she stared down at his lifeless corpse. One may have even expected her to cry, but nope. She couldn't be bothered to do that, either, because the woman was about as emotionless as yours truly. That's part of the reason we were so good together, not that it helped her in court.

And everything would have been okay if she would've just listened to me. We had time, we had means. Everything would have been fucking fine if she'd have kept her cool.

If it wasn't for that piercing scream.

I almost went back in there, you know; I wasn't planning to leave the murder weapon behind. I just hadn't gotten to it, is all. But that scream changed everything.

That scream stole minutes from us, and now years.

It was silly of me to assume she'd be able to get herself out of it once the cops showed up, but I did—I made that assumption. I thought they'd know right away, that they'd see a distraught housewife and rush out the door in search of her husband's killer; the man was still warm, for Christ's sake. They *had* to know she didn't do it, right?

Oh, how wrong I was.

Good thing I used gloves; fingerprint evidence sure would have been tough to explain. Without it, they had nothing.

And she was dead in the water, floating like a buoy without so much as an anchor to tie her down. I tried to tell her, to show her that I'd be there for her. That with just a little more planning, I'd get her out of the mess she'd gotten herself into.

But she denied me. Wouldn't let me see her while she was in county lockup, wouldn't take my calls. And then, of course, completely lost her shit when I showed up at the trial to testify. As if she hadn't expected me to be there.

The initial plan was to lie.

To muck up the prosecution's case and make sure that incompetent lawyer of hers got the acquittal. But she fainted as soon as she saw me. Dropped right to the floor like a bird in flight shot down from the sky. There were simply too many witnesses by that point; she was a lost cause.

I had no choice.

Her reaction had given away the fact that we knew each other, that we weren't the virtual strangers I was otherwise happy to portray on her behalf—nothing more than sisters-in-law who had never met due to the tumultuous relationship of the brothers we'd chosen to marry.

And she ruined it.

At that point, I did the only thing I could think to do—I looked out for myself. Me, Myself, and Ivy. The only reliable trio I've ever known.

She gave me no choice but to revert to Plan B, to play the victim.

If Alisha managed to put two and two together after that, at least there was a good chance no one would believe her when she spilled her guts. I'd be free to go, and she'd be hauled off to prison for my crime. So, I showed that jury of our peers how Alisha's desire to play house with my husband and me did nothing but ruin my once-loving marriage —as if it remotely resembled that. My husband left me, he'd fallen for our mistress. So sad.

Poor Ivy.

As much as it pains me, it was incredibly easy portraying her as the vixen, the home-wrecking whore who stole my husband. The DA liked to think—and he didn't hesitate to share this scenario in his closing statement—that Alisha had probably found out about her husband's affair with his ex-girlfriend—*me*—causing her to lash out, and thus murdering him in a heated crime of passion.

And let's be real, that's exactly what it looked like.

Of course, I made sure to leave out the part about the ménage à trois being *my* idea in the first place, and that I'd fallen deeply in love with her. We both did, my husband and I.

How unexpected *that* was.

I did my best to paint her as a flawed character and hoped each and every one of the jury members would see straight through her.

And they did.

She was the wife scorned, the porn star turned housewife. It wasn't a pretty picture, no matter how you colored it.

Nor was it hard to convince them; they'd all seen her work. They saw the nude pictures of her, the videos, and even Dylan's dead body all mangled and bleeding on the marital bed they once shared.

The evidence really doesn't lie, does it?

Poor Alisha.

FUCKED-UP-NESS

Ivy

I SUPPOSE it would only be fair for me to share my side of the story now. Alisha did get to tell hers, after all. You probably didn't even believe her at first—when she told you she didn't kill her husband—did you? I can't say I blame you; outwardly, she really *was* the likely choice. But how many times have you been told not to judge a book by its cover, hmm?

Tsk. Tsk.

You should have known better.

And yet, here you are again, doing the same thing to me. You don't even know me. I'm sure you think you do, but really, all you know about me is what you think you've learned from Alisha. So you're biased. We can fix that, you and I.

Before you go making the rest of your assumptions, let's back up. Let's make sure you have all the facts so you can make that informed decision you're so desperate to have.

First things first.

There's a common misconception that all fucked-up people come from tragedy. That somewhere within their history lies a disturbance:

signs of abuse, abandonment, addiction, mental health. The list goes on.

I, however, come from none of these things.

And I'm pretty fucked-up.

Which means it was probably the opposite in my case, right? My parents must have loved me *too* much. They must have put way too much of their energy into my education and extracurriculars, and generally hovered like a helicopter over the scene of an accident, thus creating a narcissistic, entitled monster. Was *that* the thing that broke me?

Nope.

That wasn't it either.

I happen to come from a family of middle-class Americans—a working mother *and* father, a younger sister, Erika, who for the most part, annoyed me no more—or less—than the expected amount. My dad even wrote the occasional bounced check on pizza night because for some reason, he felt his family deserved delivery pizza even though he couldn't afford to pay for it.

What a guy, huh?

We lived in a three-bedroom, split-level home in a cul-de-sac on Rich Street in suburban Minnesota—and yes, we recognized the irony of this. There was a family dog, Stanley; two goldfish, Gil and Bob; Monopoly nights, snowball fights, and church on Sundays—the whole shebang.

Daddy didn't abuse me, Mommy didn't have a drinking problem, and Erika didn't make out with any of my boyfriends under the bleachers at the homecoming game. She never accidentally shrank any of my favorite sweaters in the wash or stole my CDs.

So there was nothing abnormal about my upbringing that would explain why I'm such a shitty adult. My husband, Sawyer—well, soon-to-be-*ex-husband,* actually, if the papers ever show up—was deter-mined to solve the mystery of *why Ivy is the way she is,* and even vowed to pay whoever he needed to ensure I "got over" my unex-plained mental health issues. His words, not mine.

The thing is, I wasn't depressed, and I didn't have some diagnosable *thing* that could be treated with a regimen of pills and twice-weekly therapy. I tried to tell him this, but he's never been the greatest listener. Not to mention, his desire to fix me outweighed his inability to actually give a shit. I was nothing more to him than a wet hole to fuck and a piece of suckable candy to put on his tongue whenever the craving so hit him.

Too harsh?

Meh. It's fine, really. I was happy to play the part. It's not like I didn't benefit greatly from our arrangement.

But I'd be curious what the shrinks would have to say about me if given the chance; I do imagine they'd consider me an interesting case study. It doesn't make sense, this *anomaly*. Not statistically speaking, anyway. Scientists love data; they live for it. But my numbers are skewed; they're the outliers in what is otherwise an expected result.

I'm a motherfucking phenomenon—*yay me!*

At some point, I simply came to terms with the fact that I'm not like everyone else. Why I happened to be the apple that fell so far from the tree is beyond me.

All this to say, I'm well aware that *something* is off in my head. Do I care? Not really. I live life on my own terms—always have, always will. If you ask me, my fucked-up-ness is my most endearing quality.

The way I see it? The fact that I'm broken doesn't need to be justified by reason; I just *am*. I do find it interesting, though, and thought you might too. Again, trying to give you all the facts here. Does this understanding change my day-to-day? Make me more compassionate toward others? More self-aware?

No.

In fact, I may lack compassion almost entirely, and I have seemingly zero tolerance for liars and betrayers. That's why I live for vindication and revenge.

And I always come for it.

Always.

[LACK OF] PARENTING SKILLS

Ivy

I SMELL TOAST.

The semi-pleasurable, almost intolerable, distinct scent of burned breadcrumbs in the bottom of a toaster wafts into my nostrils as I come to. I'm also certain someone is pounding on the door, but when I roll over, I realize it's just in my head. I squint and try to make out the time with a one-eye-opened peek at the bedside clock before remembering I no longer have a bedside clock. Everything is all about the smartphone now, you know. Only old people use digital alarm clocks, and I'm certainly not one of those.

At this realization, the day of my thirty-fifth birthday—yesterday— you better believe I promptly stripped my own digital clock from the wall and permanently relocated it to the garbage bin.

The things we do to stay young.

I'm having a bit of a hard time accepting my birthday this year. I know, I know, it happens to the best of us. But it's not supposed to be *my* time yet. I'm not supposed to be turning thirty-five, on the cusp of divorce, and still leaking from my tits.

Yet, I am.

Lucky me.

When I finally roll out of bed, I pad down the stairs, somehow drawn toward the sound of baby coos and Teflon pans. Why anyone would require a frying pan to prepare breakfast for a newborn is beyond me, but I suppose that's what I pay her for. She knows best, of course.

She being my new nanny, Caramie.

She's been a godsend, and it's only her fourth week here. While I can't say I'm a fan of pushing eight-pound babies out of my vagina, it turns out I'm not much of a parent, either. But, come on, are you really surprised?

Seven days.

That's about how long I lasted on my own before enlisting the full-time assistance of a nanny. Yeah, yeah, I get it—you're over there scoffing at my selfishness, ready to point your pretentious fingers in my direction and tell me to suck it the fuck up and start taking proper care of my child.

To that I say, *no thanks.*

That's why Caramie is here.

If you think about it, her presence is really in my son's best interest. He's better off with her, trust me. So, let's go ahead and get over your disapproval of my [lack of] parenting skills, okay?

Besides, I have other shit to do.

I see the kid every morning—as long as I manage to crawl out of bed in time to pat him on the head before Cara takes him to do whatever the hell they do every day—and again in the evenings if I make it home before his bedtime, which if I'm being honest, I tend to overlook. I have a hard time remembering what time the little guy goes down, and it's not like I have some sort of biological clock to remind me either. My milk is drying up, and he's been feeding from a bottle for weeks now. If I see him, I see him.

And when I don't, Cara has it covered. What does she need me for?

Her presence has been great, though; she's a life saver, and I'm kinda patting myself on the back for hiring her. And not just because she takes care of the kid. She's on top of the household chores, too.

Before her, I had a housekeeper, yes, but Sawyer had hired her years ago, and the woman was a bit of an eyesore. I took the opportunity to class up the place a bit while I was at it.

Two birds, one stone.

Voilà!

What I *am* struggling with, aside from the dreaded birthday I just experienced, are two things:

1. Alisha is still in prison, and as you know, it's sort of my fault she's there in the first place.
2. Caramie is hot…like, really hot. (And, okay, fine, there's one more problem I need to take care of.)
3. Sawyer.

The only other person on the face of this earth with any inkling as to what really happened to his stepbrother–slash–my ex-boyfriend–slash–former lover's husband. It's complicated, I know. Don't worry, I remembered to update my relationship status on Facebook.

Let's chat about problem number one, shall we? Alisha.

I still think of her at night. I hear her voice, smell the lavender scent of her shampoo, and find myself longing for the softness of her touch, her kiss.

To taste her.

And that's confusing, because, well—feelings. I hate feelings. They suck, and I don't have time for them. That's what was so great about Sawyer. See problem number three above. The man was a steel vessel in human form. The only emotion he had was arousal, and is that even an emotion?

Probably not.

But he had it.

Insert problem number two: Caramie. What to say about her, huh? I found her on one of those nanny websites—and I don't mean the ones you go to after hours to find anything *but* an actual nanny. No, this was a reputable website where families in search of nannies can put in a bid in hopes that the nanny of their choice will agree to an interview in their home. There was a pamphlet on my bedside table at the hospital, and I happened to grab it *just in case.*

Did I intend to hire the first nanny I interviewed? No. And to tell you the truth, she was probably a little under-qualified for the job, being that I needed her to moonlight as a housekeeper, and the only thing on her résumé was reception related. Did I hire her anyway?

Yep, sure did.

She was easy on the eyes, what can I say?

"Good morning, Mrs. Rogers," Caramie says when I round the corner into the kitchen. She's wearing Sawyer's "kiss the chef" apron over her pajamas, stirring oatmeal on the stove while my son sleeps strapped in a bouncer on the island countertop. She simultaneously stirs the oatmeal while rocking him with her other hand, and I can't help but wonder what made her think to do that.

It seems almost...ingenious, and I chide myself for not having thought it before she was around. The baby even looks happy, unlike the mornings he and I were on our own and all he did was scream his face off.

"Caramie, I've told you, it's Ivy. Please. When you say 'Mrs' it just makes me sound old."

"Got it, sorry! Anyway," she says cheerfully, reaching in the cupboard for a bowl. "Is there anything you need from the grocery store? Dyl and I will be running errands today."

"Dyl?"

"Dylan, sorry," she corrects herself, patting my son on the head.

"Right. If you don't mind, let's not make *Dyl* a thing, okay? He wasn't named after a pickle."

She laughs, her button nose wrinkling in a way I'd rather not admit is adorable. But it is. And suddenly I can't help but think of myself as a cougar; I'm ten whole years older than her.

"You're not a pickle, are you, Mr. Dylan?" she says to my son.

And yes, I *did* name him after my former lover's deceased husband in hopes that she would see that as a sign that we are meant to be together and the so-called legacy of the child's father will live on.

It was a peace offering, what can I say?

I sit and watch Caramie for a moment, grateful she recently moved in. I'm in awe of how gracefully she moves around the kitchen. Everything seems like second nature to her. She slides a bowl of maple oatmeal to me, the spoon clanking on the side of the dish. I pull it out and set it aside to cool, placing my elbows on the marble countertop and making a steeple with my fingers.

"How are your accommodations? Are you comfortable in your room? Have everything you need?"

"Oh, yes! It's great, Ivy. I honestly can't thank you enough."

I'm sure I can find a way for you to thank me.

When the thought creeps into my mind, I stifle it and decide to grab a cup of tea and take it upstairs with my oatmeal. I need to behave—at least for a little bit. I can't afford to lose Caramie so soon, and I have a feeling hitting on her—without Sawyer's appendage hanging around—won't do me any favors.

Something tells me this one likes the dick.

"Good. Well, I'll leave you to it," I say. "Can you stop for the dry cleaning while you're out?" I hand her the slip from the refrigerator, too embarrassed to acknowledge the spark I feel when our fingers touch.

"Sure thing," she chimes.

Back in my room, I forgo the oatmeal and reach for my vibrator instead. Hungover or not, I need to get the nanny off my mind.

The last thing I need is another crush.

PSYCHOTIC WOMEN FOR THE WIN

Sawyer

PSYCHOTIC WOMEN TURN ME ON.

What can I say?

Ivy's crazy was the fuel that kept my fire burning. And she knew it. She was well aware of the power she possessed over me. She thrived on it and went out of her way to remind me how quickly it could be taken away.

See, that's what you probably failed to realize before; I didn't leave Ivy. *She* left *me.* For *her.* Alisha Thompson, the former star of Lisha's Bedroom, and object of our affection. I believe you've met, yes?

She's the one who changed Ivy—the reason our marriage failed.

Okay, fine, I *was* technically the one who walked away, but Ivy had already checked out, so can you blame me? I knew where things were headed and wasn't about to get caught up in the crosshairs.

I'm no idiot.

Now, I don't know about you, but I watched that entire trial play out. I consumed every second of media coverage every day for weeks. I saw the way Alisha reacted when Ivy took the stand, the shock on her face when she realized her name wasn't Lila, the name we'd agreed to give her all those months before. You can't fake a reaction like that.

Ivy wasn't who Alisha thought she was.

And neither was I.

But that was by design, the way it was supposed to be. That anonymity was crucial; it shouldn't have surprised anyone, especially Alisha.

I considered coming forward, taking the stand and telling my side of the story. Part of me wanted to come clean to those twelve jurors, to the judge, and that lawyer of hers—who very clearly had a thing for her, let's be honest—and everyone out there watching that trial on television with the same level of interest that I had.

But I didn't.

Ivy would have had my balls in a sling.

She would've killed me.

I know it, and you know it. That woman would have ended me the same way she ended my stepbrother. Seventeen stab wounds to the chest? No fucking thank you. Sorry, brother, but I'd rather not take my chances.

I suspected her the moment I found out about my brother's untimely death. Murdering her ex-lover, the husband of the woman she loved but couldn't have? That was right up Ivy's alley.

So yeah, I ran. Like a damn coward, I stuffed my tail between my legs, packed my shit, and left in the middle of the afternoon while Ivy was off spending my hard-earned money on baby furniture.

I don't regret it, and no, I'm not the least bit ashamed.

Do I feel bad for Alisha? Guilty that she's off rotting in some prison for a crime that we all know she didn't commit? I mean, sure. I did have a chance to stop it, and selfishly, I wanted her for myself just as much as Ivy did. Just as much as Dylan did. Alisha was the epicenter of our hurricane, and I think it's safe to say the three of us were nothing more than debris left behind after the storm cleared.

But let me tell you…it wasn't always this bad.

Ivy and Alisha were each crazy in their own way, yes, but it didn't start out that way. In the beginning, it worked…just the right amount of crazy.

And what's better than one crazy woman in your bed?

Two.

I just never expected things to turn out the way they did.

DICK, MEET VAGINA

Ivy

I HAVE AN ADDICTION.

Well, several, if I'm to be fully transparent, but we'll focus on just the two for now: sex and booze.

The extent of my sexual desires, my first self-diagnosed addiction, is not as severe as I imagine Alisha's was, but it's there, nonetheless. The booze came after I lost her, then again once the baby was born and Sawyer moved out.

I suppose that's to be expected. We all have our vices, and after a breakup—hell, *two* breakups, simultaneously in my case, if you think about it—sometimes we need a little assistance in the coping department.

Sometimes we need a stronger vice.

Like sex.

And booze.

So, that's the current state of my life. Orgasms and drunkenness. If it helps, I do think of myself as high-functioning in both regards, but I suppose you'll establish your own opinion.

So be it.

Really, the booze is a buffer. It helps me feel better about all the sex, masks the variants of guilt that linger in the back of my mind every time I spread my legs to a new stranger.

And the brothels, which I may have forgotten to mention? Well, those simply feed both addictions. The vice is no longer just sex, or booze; it's the thrill of what could happen when the two mix together. The calculated risk, so to speak.

I crave it.

Need it.

Want it.

So I take it, every chance I get. I take from others to benefit my own desires, my own narcissism. I blame my husband—not simply because he chose to leave. Not because I'm lonely—I am—or to make him jealous, though I'd love to.

But because he made this happen.

He turned me into this.

Lila and Grant—*remember them?*—stemmed from that evil genius's mind. And I have to admit, I was all for it. The personas presented an opportunity; a general desire to spice things up in the bedroom. Sawyer and I were...adventurous, if you will, when it came to sex. The spice had been there from day one. Really, it never left. We just got bored. Sex was too predictable.

We needed a hotter sauce.

We had sex so often that eventually it was the same old "Dick, meet Vagina" saga. The routine just wasn't cutting it anymore; it was like our sex organs knew what to expect and suddenly wanted nothing to do with each other. And don't get me wrong—we tried. We got creative—handcuffs, role play, sex in public. Then, the dominatrix phase, which, I'll admit, was my favorite.

Each "new" thing was great until it wasn't. We were a once-and-done couple, to no fault of our own. But the driving force in our marriage was sex, so what choice did we have but to work out the kinks?

Without it we had nothing.

The swingers' club was Sawyer's idea.

Because, yes, we went down that road, too. Of course, he'll deny it if asked. That's what the man does. Always claims to be so innocent when he's most often the instigator. And he gets away with it, too. A handsome man like that? Wealthy, emotionally unattached, smooth talker. Yeah, he's a real sweetheart.

"Don't take this the wrong way," Sawyer had said after a year of frustration. The tentative tone to the words that would follow did nothing but set me up to do exactly that—take it the wrong way. "But what if we try an open marriage?"

I couldn't conjure up an immediate response, so he continued under the assumption that my interest was piqued by the suggestion, when really, I was still a little hungover from the night before. It took a few minutes to digest what he'd suggested, and in the meantime, he just kept talking.

"There are these events we could try," he said. "Swingers' parties, brothels, wife swaps. That sort of thing."

"Isn't *Wife Swap* that reality show where the wives switch houses and have to take care of each other's unruly kids and clean their dirty toilets?"

He smiled, more so for my benefit than to confirm actual amusement. "No, Ivy—I mean, yes, it is, but you're getting off track. I'm not talking about a reality show."

"I know…" I shrugged, the need to explain suddenly lost on me.

"Okay, so…?" he continued expectantly, as if my delayed response might send him into respiratory duress should I continue to withhold an opinion. "What do you think?"

I paused before throwing back the covers and climbing out of bed. "I *think* I have a headache," I said, sauntering off toward the bathroom to take a hot shower.

"Ivy…"

"Sure, whatever you think is best, Sawyer. Sign us up for the PTA bake sale while you're at it, too," I replied flippantly.

"If you don't want to do it, just say so," he barked. I'd irked him. *Oops.*

I stopped in the doorway, my arm draped along the trim, and

looked at my husband. His hopes were up, I could see it—the need to try this one last thing prevailing over all else. "Do I get fucked?"

"Huh?"

"At these parties. Will there be dick, and do I get to play with them?"

"Jesus, Ivy," he said, scoffing at my bold response. But his eyes were hungry, I could see it. The thought of someone else boning his wife turned him on. It always had, and I'd known all along.

"Well?"

"Yes. You can have all the dick your horny little heart desires, Ivy," he confirmed, a grin on his lips as he followed me into the bathroom. I winked and pulled my T-shirt over my head, dropping it to the floor.

"Then let's do it," I agreed before stepping into the shower.

Sawyer stripped and followed, wasting no time showing me just how grateful he was that he'd married such a cooperative woman.

"So, how does this whole thing work?" I asked later that evening. I'd been making a mental to-do list all day, taking account of everything I'd need to prepare for our new adventure. Get waxed, a Brazilian, a massage to loosen my muscles, probably even a facial. I'd need to shop for some new lingerie too, of course...maybe some new heels.

"The swingers' club?" he asked, doing little to hide the excitement in his eyes. "I think we just show up. There's an initiation process of sorts, so we just watch at first. We can play with each other, but no other members until we're officially invited in. There are rules."

He's already done his research.

I nodded, increasingly more titillated with the idea.

"We can come up with fake names, too. Think of it as an acting gig or something, I don't know," Sawyer suggested. I shrugged.

"If you think it'll help."

"Who should I be?" he asked, and *of course* he would put the assignment on me. Picking fake names for a sex club? How hard could it be? Pretty people get fucked all the time; it doesn't matter what their name is.

"You be Grant, I'll be Lila."

And that was it.

Fuck if I know where the names came from. It didn't matter anyway; we were in agreement. Sawyer had been given his cue to sign us up for a revolving door of sexual partners.

I may have been ambivalent in my agreement at first, but I suddenly couldn't wait to get started.

SOCIAL NORMS

Ivy

DESPITE OUR WELL-THOUGHT-OUT plans and new names, Sawyer and I didn't *look* like the kind of couple to frequent a brothel, or any swingers' club, for that matter. Not that there's a certain *look* per se, but I'm sure you know what I mean. We were clean-cut, with normal jobs and a yard we kept cut and weeded.

And that was the beauty of it; that elicited anonymity was crucial, something we both needed. There's a time and place to look the part, and we pulled it off well, Sawyer especially. The man has that soft-spoken-nice-guy kinda thing about him; people fantasize over that shit.

We were different people once we set foot through those doors, and all social norms went out the window.

These events aren't well-received by the general public. The average Jane or John Doe would disapprove at the very thought of walking through those doors, let alone give the opportunity serious consideration.

It's certainly not traditional to share your spouse with a third party.

But that's kind of what made it special, too. We had each other, but there was a certain pull that came from watching my husband fuck another woman. He said the same of watching me, too.

Unlike everything else we'd tried before it, group sex wasn't something either of us had the willpower to quit.

Not that I expect you to understand; I'm sure you're over there rolling your eyes, and that's fine. You'd have to experience it to understand it. People are judgmental by nature, always sticking their noses where they don't belong, giving unsolicited opinions, unwarranted advice. They can't help it; it's just what they do. How is our sex life anyone's business but ours?

We made sure it wasn't, that it stayed private at all costs.

Sawyer's job—our livelihood—depended on it.

His social circle has always been expansive, definitely more so than mine. More lucrative, too. That's what happens when you're a likable human. From clients, to investors, partners at the firm, any minor acquaintance, really—Sawyer immediately turns into a people pleaser. He schmoozes with the wealthy leaders of the finance industry most often, desperate to stick a hand into their deep pockets and come out with a little extra for himself. But I'm sure he'll tell you all about his little side hustle, so I'll leave him to it.

Meanwhile, we played it cool and acted the part. We were always good at that.

It's easy to show people what they want to see.

We're a good-looking, wealthy couple with a lust for life, successful, and admired in the community. At least, that's what our social media presence made it seem.

And the internet doesn't lie, does it?

But my husband's dark secret, his closed-door guilty pleasure, will make its way into the light soon.

I'll make sure of it.

A WORLD-CLASS IDIOT

Sawyer

Look, I didn't think she'd go for it, okay?

I didn't.

But I wanted to get into that club and figured it wouldn't hurt to ask. And I didn't do it just for me, either. I did it for *her*. For us. I'm sure she's told you otherwise? Maybe even on the verge of convincing you that *I'm* the sex-crazed lunatic of this story?

Fine.

Whatever.

I'll step into those shoes and wear them like a man if that's what it takes. But know this: Ivy is one hell of an actress. The woman spent the first half of her life in community theater. That's where I found her, you know. Well, actually, that's where my stepbrother, Dylan, found her. I guess I can't take claim to that one since she wasn't officially mine until a good year later.

I'm just saying, don't believe everything that comes out of that woman's mouth. I may still be married to her on paper, but that doesn't mean I'd take a dip in the pool again any time soon, if you know what I mean.

The acting thing never did go her way, and I suppose that's why she goes the extra mile to fuck with people in the real world. It's like a challenge for her, playing a character. When Dylan met her, she was the lead in some musical. One of those ones everybody knows the name of and has all the cheesy songs memorized and stuck in their heads for days. Not me. I can't stand those productions. Which is probably why I can't remember what the show was called to begin with.

Either way, she was an actress. Lead role in the play. Dylan had a pair of tickets some homeowner had gifted to him—perks of being a Realtor, I suppose—and he took Mom to the show. Well, *his* mom. My stepmother. Dad and I respectfully sat that one out and played nine holes at Bunkers instead.

But Dylan had this knack for locking down unobtainable women. First, it was Ivy, and then when that went south for him, Alisha. I don't know how he did it, but apparently, I made a habit of going after the same women for sloppy seconds. We've shared at least two in this lifetime, and I imagine that number would have gone up if he were still around.

My brother was a world-class idiot, though.

He chose work over Ivy. All the time, every time. Sure, he was trying to make a name for himself, get some cash in the bank. And Lord knows Ivy needed a man with financial means. She's a bit of a spender, that one.

It was the weekend of his first big commission; he'd finally sold a house. That's when it started, my affair with Ivy. When he sent me off with her for the first time and had me stand in for him at an Aerosmith concert. Great seats, too. He'd given her the tickets for her birthday, but didn't make an effort to see the show with her.

Like I said, a world-class idiot.

Ivy and I had some drinks, took a cab back to Dylan's place where she was staying at the time, and thanks to an unexpected malfunctioning furnace, ended up taking a dip in the hot tub to warm up. In the dead of winter and on an unspoken dare, we stripped naked, tip-toed through the freezing snow, and climbed into that hot tub, where we wasted no time fucking like rabbits.

Twice.

It became a near-daily occurrence after that, us hooking up.

I don't know that either of us ever planned for it to happen, it just *did*.

And then it didn't stop.

She kept showing up at my place, or Dylan would ask me to meet up with Ivy at his place for some event he, *unfortunately, wasn't going to make it home in time* for.

It was never challenging to sneak around—the man had enabled us entirely—and as much as it pains me to admit, I didn't feel all that bad about it either. Dylan never would have been able to keep up with Ivy long-term, and if it hadn't been me, it would've been someone else.

I'd have been a fool not to have swooped in and taken her off his hands.

DRIPPING FROM HER CHIN

Sawyer

IN THE BEGINNING, Ivy and I made a game of our affair. Dylan was so oblivious that there were times we even managed to get it in while he was in the house. See, Ivy had been living with Dylan for a few months by then. I think she gave him some sob story about not being able to renew her lease so, like the nice guy he thought he was, Dylan offered to let her stay with him.

He figured their relationship was moving forward, getting serious, so why not?

But since he was never around, I took it upon myself to take care of his girlfriend—in all aspects of the word. Sneaking around wasn't necessary since he knew she and I hung out—he *encouraged* it. And the weekly poker night he hosted at his place? Often canceled at the last minute.

But you know, being the planner that I am, I always arrived earlier than the stated time anyway. *Before* my brother's group text would come through to let the guys know he was stuck at the office, that poker night wasn't happening. I knew Ivy would be there all alone, waiting for me.

I'm a bit of an opportunist, what can I say?

No, man, it's fine. Don't worry about it. Yeah, I'm at your place already. Ivy's here, so we're just going to grab a pizza and catch up on Breaking Bad.

Always so easy.

Always *too* easy.

About a week before we got caught, I accidentally told her I loved her. I have no idea what the hell I was thinking—I really wasn't the type to fall in love—but something had come over me. I think I was more in love with the idea of her than I was with her as a person.

But I ran with it, mostly because I had no choice once it slipped out.

I wasn't ready to walk away.

Now, if you haven't guessed by now, let me be the first to tell you: Ivy isn't the type of person to take that kind of sentiment lightly. But it was easy for me to say, just three words, followed by some moaning and a deep kiss. She didn't even say it back.

Not with words anyway.

"We shouldn't be doing this," she had teased in between kisses, her eyes deliberately telling me otherwise. I dropped the towel I'd wrapped around my waist after a dip in the hot tub, my dick already standing at attention, ready for her.

"He'll never know." I pulled her closer, kissing her as my hand palmed her ass and squeezed a yelp out of her.

"Oh, *but Sawyer*, what if he finds out?" She giggled when she said it, the sarcasm practically dripping from her chin, almost like a prelude of what was to come.

It was fun for her, pretending she was worried we'd get caught. She wasn't though, not at all. In fact, I wouldn't be surprised if she *wanted* to all along, given her acquired taste for drama.

"I love you," I'd said.

Yep, that's where it slipped out.

In the heat of a passionate moment, while we poked fun at what we were doing behind my brother's—her *boyfriend's*—back.

The room fell silent despite our heavy breathing.

But it was only a moment later that she dropped to her knees and took me in her mouth right then and there, her tongue swirling in all the places she knew I liked.

And that's how I knew she loved me, too.

She looked so good with her ruby red lips wrapped around my cock, her lipstick smudged along the length of my shaft. She winked and I lost it then, nearly coming down her throat.

But I needed a taste of her, more than anything, I needed to worship her right back. I pulled out of her mouth and helped her up from the floor, only to throw her right back down onto the bed and spread her legs. She squealed, as she often did when she got excited, and I ran my fingers softly down her thighs. Goosebumps prickled beneath them, and she smiled up at me with her signature "fuck me" smirk.

Her body writhed under my tongue as I licked. She bucked and moaned, and I continued to taunt her, keeping her close to the edge. When I knew she was ready, I pulled her to me and buried my cock inside her.

That was the last time I ever had sex with my brother's girlfriend.

After that, she wasn't *his* girlfriend anymore.

She was mine.

Despite the initial excitement of our affair, I could tell Ivy was bored the moment she moved into my place. We hired help, of course, to get her possessions from point A to point B—from one brother to the next —and she was entertained for a couple months while she turned my house into a *Real Housewives*-esque monstrosity. She spent thousands redecorating every room on the ground floor and half of the upper level, too. But her happiness, her contentment, didn't last. I should have known it wouldn't, but I guess I was surprised.

Still, we christened every room in my house, every countertop, every surface. It didn't matter what time of day or whether we were alone in the house or not—in fact, I recall an entertaining bathroom romp during an investors' dinner in our early days.

Still, there was something missing.

And, let's face it, Ivy and me? We've always been perfect on paper. We knew that—it's part of the reason we got married in the first place. And we did everything we could to bring that perfection to everyday life—or at least a semi-believable version of it.

Some days it felt like all the words in our story had been erased, like we'd lost our history and all we had left was the eraser dust scattered within the blank pages.

But then, the whole threesome thing got started, and after that, Ivy went batshit crazy. She became *obsessed* with Alisha.

And that was unheard of.

My wife obsessed over no one, not even me. Things, yes. But, people? Fuck no.

I really should have taken it as a warning sign, an SOS, maybe dialed things back a little, let life slow down. Maybe things were just moving too fast. We never got a chance to get comfortable as a couple, let alone a committed partnership. But put yourself in my shoes, okay? When the pussy is right there in front of your face, how do you not reach out for a taste?

I certainly couldn't resist. And the two of them together—*Lila* and Alisha—were like fire and ice, naughty and nice. Yes, I went there. I couldn't turn Alisha away no matter how hard I tried, no matter how much I loved my wife.

She'd finally done it; Ivy had found my weakness.

I just didn't expect it to be hers, too.

BODY PARTS

Ivy

PEOPLE ARE SO easy to manipulate.

It really doesn't take much to convince someone of something they wanted to hear in the first place. A feigned interest, a soft touch of the hand, maybe even an inconspicuous brushing of body parts. It does happen. People use their sexuality to get what they want all the time.

I should know.

That's how I caught Dylan's attention. See, I knew exactly who he was, I knew of the Thompson family and their wealth. His mother, Bev, had earned substantial wealth as a real estate developer. See, Dylan was a trust fund baby, even before following in his mother's footsteps.

She's a smart woman, that Bev. Wise enough to push a prenup with both of her marriages, yet dumb enough to set so much of her fortune aside for her ungrateful son.

And Dylan? He had a hell of a soft spot for a beautiful woman, especially one who needed him. I knew I had an in, that I could grab his attention.

The fact that he ended up at one of my community theater performances was a lucky accident. I had been working out a way to get some face time with him, and he just happened to speed things up for me. The thing is, I didn't think the stepbrother had access to the trust. I *should* have assumed, but Sawyer's own fortune managed to escape my radar initially. I would've started with him, had I known.

If you haven't figured me out just yet, you'll notice I excite easily. Sometimes I act before I get all the details worked out. That's what happened with Dylan.

How was I to know his trust had a marriage clause?

Five years.

That's how long he would need to be married before his wife would be entitled to any part of his fortune. And I couldn't do it with Dylan, I really couldn't.

That's why Sawyer and I ended up in bed together. That's why I picked *him* instead of Dylan. He was easier to get along with, more attentive and better suited to my sexual desires. Easily manipulated, if you will. A pushover.

A woman has needs, you know, and Sawyer was more than willing —more than *capable*—of meeting mine in Dylan's frequent absence. I would have been crazy to walk away from such an opportunity.

The thing is, while my initial intentions were to tap into Dylan's bank accounts, I didn't have the patience to wait for the man. He may have been wealthy, but he was dragging his feet on commitment—even more so after I moved into his condo—and awfully stingy with his cash.

I didn't have time for penny-pinching.

But finding out Sawyer's pockets were deep, too? That was a good day. He certainly wasn't a trust fund baby like his stepbrother, but *some* of that money was his, thanks to his father's bartering. Plus, he was working in the financial industry by then. He had man-made wealth on top of the trust allocations, and let's be real—that's a hell of a lot better. That's stability.

So yes, the opportunity to seduce him was enthralling, and when it finally presented itself?

Easy peasy.

What I didn't expect was his temper.

Sawyer could be nasty—and he was quick to show that demon, to remind me of its existence. It didn't take long for me to realize that the best way to tamper that anger was to simply appease him—to go along with his plans, feed into his desires, and essentially submit to him.

Fortunately, for me, there were many benefits to this approach.

Sawyer wasn't the only one with desires, and I planned to stop at nothing to remind him of that. Little did I know, he would come up with a prenup of his own.

With the same five-year clause that Dylan's had.

And we've only been married for four fucking years.

NOT QUITE A CALL GIRL

Ivy

Was it a shit show when Dylan finally found out about Sawyer and me?

Yeah, sure.

But it was kinda hot, too. I couldn't help but imagine the three of us together, both brothers worshipping me, bringing me to ecstasy with the flick of a thumb, a tongue here, the tip of a cock there. A girl can dream, right?

Too bad it didn't go down that way.

Dylan was never into that sort of thing—he didn't like the idea of sharing his woman—and even if he did, I don't think he'd have gone for it, considering the third wheel was his own stepbrother. There was the whole betrayal aspect of it, too, I suppose.

The poor guy's ego was hurt, and rightfully so. No man wants to bear the brunt of that embarrassment.

There was yelling.

Some punches thrown.

Name-calling.

You know, the usual caught-in-the-act type stuff. They were proud, testosterone-filled brothers on the verge of destruction. One had betrayed the other by stealing his girlfriend right from under his nose.

Honestly, are you surprised? This kind of stuff happens all the time. Dylan and Sawyer were two very good-looking men; anyone with an appreciation for the male form would be happy to go home with either of them.

I'm lucky to have had the pleasure of experiencing them both; albeit not at the same time.

Whatever, I'll take the win.

The truth is, I was already looking for a way to end things with Dylan anyway. He simply beat me to it, which is fine. I'm not upset it went down the way it did.

It would have been too awkward if this had been a smooth transition. Holidays with his family would have been a nightmare. The fight between the brothers was reassurance I'd never have to worry about seeing Dylan—possibly not even his parents—ever again. Sawyer soon strayed from the family, and I got a fancy house in Minneapolis complete with a custom mistress's room, top-of-the-line sex swing, and private bath. Everything worked out as planned.

What neither of the brothers was privy to, however, is the fact that I wasn't as innocent as I seemed. And despite my initial shock when Sawyer mentioned the swingers' club a couple years later, I may have had a *little* experience dabbling in group sex before I met either of them.

To admit this to Dylan would have been a deal-breaker long before my affair with Sawyer—he was a little too vanilla, if you know what I mean—and I decided it best not to let Sawyer in on that secret either. He really did get more enjoyment out of it later at the swingers' club when he thought it was my first time riding the bull in front of an audience.

I was happy to play into his fantasies, to let him think I'd done it for *him*.

What bothered me, though, was that they both assumed I've never worked a day in my life. It's not true. In fact, I had been working as a Lady Ann escort for two years before meeting Dylan. Acting surely wasn't paying the bills, so I had to do *something*. And unlike Alisha, I had no preconceived notions that I was meant to work in a corporate office. I knew I was entirely capable of taking my clothes off for money.

So I did.

I was a lot better at concealing my identity than she was, too. Lady Ann's was discreet; the regulars were elite members of society, their bank accounts padded well enough to keep tips in the thousands even on a slow night.

The acting gig? I gave it a go for a bit, tried my hand at smaller productions. But it wasn't long before Mom and Dad decided they were done supporting their oldest daughter, tired of paying my rent and hearing excuses about why I couldn't afford gas for my car.

That's when it started.

I was on my own for the first time, fiercely seeking independence in a way I'd never imagined I would. I left home and never went back.

The party circuit turned out to be quite lucrative. I worked the bachelor parties and private events, stuff where the money was easiest because the clientele was mostly just a bunch of married dudes looking to cheat on their wives and pretend they hadn't. Because, you know, it was *just a stripper*.

Fucking idiots.

But, to each their own, right? I didn't care who they were or why they were there, as long as they paid cash and didn't have a choking fetish. The johns had money. Lots of it. And if you were good? If you did just a *little* bit more than hang on their muscle-y arm in a short, sexy dress, they always threw a little extra your way.

And I wasn't afraid to toe the line.

At first, it was just hand jobs. A happy ending in a dark corner of the room? *No big deal, happy to help.* And hey, every once in a while one of them would finger me while I jerked them off, so it worked out for me, too. But once I got a taste, I wanted more.

And so did they.

Hand jobs turned into blow jobs, which turned into straight-up fucking—it didn't even matter that there were other people in the room. In fact, it was encouraged that everyone join in, especially the ladies.

We earned more that way.

We got invited back that way.

Eventually, the calls kept coming, and I kept showing up. Showered, waxed, and ready for anything, I was a Lady Anne escort. Not quite a call girl, too classy to be a hooker, and nowhere near enough junk in my trunk to strip on a stage for singles.

It was the best paycheck I ever earned.

And I gave it up for a while, just to see if I could. Then I met Dylan and Sawyer.

I didn't need the job anymore, not really. I missed it, sure, but for a while, things were just fine without it. That is, until Dylan decided his job was more important than me, but even then, I had Sawyer's attention to fall back on. Our affair kept me satisfied, entertained.

Until it didn't.

It wasn't long before Sawyer was off doing the very thing he'd chastised his brother for—working longer hours, attending lavish parties with his business partners to earn his keep. And I was okay with it at first; what he lacked in romanticism he made up for in cash and gifts.

But when Alisha came into our lives, everything changed. It wasn't about me anymore; our attention was on her. On keeping her.

It was when he started seeing Alisha behind my back that triggered things for me, that set things in motion. He'd broken the very code he himself had written to ensure our marriage remained intact when all was said and done.

I figured, why not? Why not get a little something more out of this myself? I went back to the swingers' club, then to a few underground brothels, and I had some fun of my own. Even opened a new bank account in my name, throwing every dime and ass-crack-crinkled dollar I had saved into it, and still continued to collect my monthly stipend from my loving husband. And despite his reservations, Sawyer was generous with his wallet, let me tell you.

So trust me when I say I had no problem getting back into the swing of things after Sawyer left. I didn't even wait for the dust to settle. Instead, I downed a pint of vodka and worked a bachelor party the first chance I got. Made a good chunk of change that night, I did.

Take it from me, the best cure for a broken heart is sex, even better if you mix in some booze.

My one complaint? Alisha wouldn't come with me; she was wrapped up in Dylan, ready to settle down and give it all up to start a family. She wasn't even returning my phone calls at that point, and that was really the start of the downward spiral that got me here: her selfishness.

Like I said before, I live for revenge.

And in my eyes? I've been betrayed.

TIDE ME OVER

Sawyer

THERE SEEMS to be some contention around my former relationship with Alisha; I'd like to clear that up, if you don't mind. Ivy seems to be under the impression that our marriage failed *because* Alisha left us. It's partially true, sure, but it's not *the* reason. Ivy and I tried to make it work without Alisha for a little while, even reacquainted ourselves with the swingers' club for a bit, although I had a feeling there was a little more going on there than she was willing to admit.

And it worked for a while. But Ivy was off her game; she wasn't really *in* it because the other person in our bed wasn't Alisha, and that was all that mattered to her.

She let it get in her head, if you ask me.

We were tainted—she and I—after Alisha left us. I didn't know how to fix us, didn't have a single fucking clue, and no idea where to start.

So, I did the only thing I could think of—after months of exhausting every other effort, I asked Ivy to try role-playing for me. Was it wrong for me to ask her to dress up like Alisha? To *be* her in hopes that it would save our marriage? Sure. I'll give you that.

Look, despite what you might think, I do have a conscience. I offered up the suggestion anyway; nothing else was working, and I had nothing more to lose. She could have said no, but she didn't.

She had a choice.

And she made it.

But she played the role terribly, unconvincingly.

The wigs never looked right on her. It was too obvious she wasn't who she was trying to be—I knew what was underneath just as well as she did. Ivy couldn't seem to cover that mole on her neck, either. Alisha didn't have a mole.

And let's be real fucking honest here—she didn't taste like her either. The fact that Ivy was an impostor was front and center in my mind, and my dick knew it, too. She lacked her usual confidence.

Some actress she was.

The thing is, nothing compared to the feeling that came over me— came over us—when the three of us were in a room together. We were electric. Intense. Born of another element. Even Ivy would agree there was something special there.

We were lost without Alisha.

Our sex life suffered. *We* suffered. And Ivy got angry. My wife wasn't one to let shit go. She knew what her body wanted.

And she set out to get it.

It was Ivy who decided to try and win her back.

Hell, it's not like we loved each other anymore, and if she tells you otherwise, she's full of shit. The thing is—and my brother would roll over in his grave if he knew this—Ivy and I only got married to piss Dylan off. Sure, we had a vested interest in one another, even liked each other for a while there. And at the time, the sex *was* cutting it. She was a dirty girl hiding behind a thick head of blonde hair. All it took was a little persuasion to get her to come out of her shell.

And I knew she had it in her, I really did.

I just didn't think she'd make such a colossal mistake.

In the beginning, finding Alisha was nothing more than a simple twist of fate, a happy accident. I kept her to myself for a bit, but knew I'd eventually introduce her to Ivy, too.

The swingers' club was fun, don't get me wrong, but Ivy and I hadn't been formally initiated yet and things were moving a little slower than I would have liked. Sometimes I needed a little extra to tide me over. Ivy knew this; I'd been upfront about my sexual desires from the start of our relationship.

It was an honest mistake, finding her, though. I was online, looking for live orgies to watch or one of those XXX websites where you can tell the actors what to do and they'll do it in real-time.

I found Lisha's Bedroom instead.

And my God, she was gorgeous.

I mean, Ivy was hot, yes, but Alisha? *Fuck.* Alisha was in a class all her own. I caught her live stream every day for at least two weeks before I told Ivy about her.

That's when the private sessions started. They were expensive, yes, but worth every penny, every minute.

Ivy and I watched her together after that, most often with my dick buried inside of her. She was just as turned on as I was watching Alisha, fantasizing about the three of us together; the ecstasy, her eyes glued to Alisha on the laptop screen.

It was Ivy's idea to let Alisha in on our little secret, to invite her over to play with us.

How was I supposed to know she'd actually show up? I didn't think she'd agree to it, but apparently, the idea of a threesome was appealing to her too, so she did.

And it was fucking magic.

From the second she walked through the front door, I was addicted. She was a drug I was ready and willing to get high on, regardless of the ramifications, marriage vows be damned.

Honestly, if you were to ask me if I'd go back and do it again, the answer would be a resounding yes.

It wasn't long before Alisha and I started our little side gig, and that's when I started to see the change in Ivy—the jealousy, the obsession. She knew, but I told myself she didn't.

And while I kind of tricked Alisha into meeting up with me alone that first time—she was under the impression Ivy would be there, too —the hotel getaway weekend probably never should have happened. Although, I think if you were to ask Alisha, she'd agree it was worth it. She would've shown up either way.

Was I surprised when she asked why Ivy wasn't there?

No.

The arrangement was clear—we were not to engage in sexual activity unless all three of us were present. We had all agreed, and I understood the rule—hell, I was the one who wrote it.

And Alisha? She was the unbiased party; what did she have to lose by overlooking that one simple rule? She got fucked either way, and that was the only end goal for her.

That weekend was the start of it all really—it also happened to be the first time my brother laid eyes on the woman he'd eventually talk into marrying him.

I didn't see that plot twist coming.

It really was bullshit that he'd take her right from under my nose. But then again, I suppose Ivy and I did the same to him.

Karma really *is* a bitch.

UNINTENTIONALLY VULNERABLE

Ivy

THE WHISKEY GOES DOWN smooth despite the trail of fire it leaves on the way down. It numbs me from the inside, and I welcome the protective shield it offers; use it to mask the pain.

Life is easier to manage with blinders on, especially the shit no one wants to think about. Like relationships and threesomes gone wrong.

That'll getcha every time.

I've been drinking too much lately, I know this. I would slow down, maybe take it easy with the alcohol, but every time the thought crosses my mind, I only want it more.

I like to think this newfound crutch is still temporary, just a necessary distraction from the atrocities of the life I'm currently living, but even that sounds like an excuse.

This too shall pass.

I tip my head and throw back another shot before paging through the thick document in front of me. Anger bubbles in my belly alongside the whiskey, and I catch snippets of the rubbish within the pages.

Dissolution of Marriage.

I didn't think he'd go through with it.

Call me naive, but I really thought we could fix this, that Sawyer just needed some time to cool off and we'd be fine after a little break, maybe even come out stronger in the end. A little time apart to reflect never hurt anyone, right?

I thought I had nothing to worry about.

We would live separately long enough to come to the realization that we can't live any way other than together. And once we did, we'd be monogamous—no more outside partners, no more threesomes, no more Alishas. Just us.

I was so wrong.

I guess it's true what they say—the sanctity of marriage really *is* lost. After all, a binding contract can be torn to shreds in an instant, so where does its true value really lie? Nothing is set in stone until we die, and by that point, the only stone being set is the one used to mark our own grave; completely useless to the dead, a benefit only to the living.

I drain the rest of my drink and set the empty glass on the marble counter with more force than necessary. It breaks and slices through the skin on my palm, the broken shards scattering to the floor. I watch as if in slow motion, as they sparkle against the ambient lighting. They're so small, yet so hazardous.

Unintentionally vulnerable.

Like me.

It hardly seems fair, this divorce. *I* made all the scarifies here, not *him*. And maybe that's why we are where we are now. Maybe I bent him a little *too* far, gave him a little too much freedom.

Maybe Sawyer needed a little more pushback every now and then; a wife who fought for him, not against him.

Irreconcilable differences.

Sawyer would say we never really loved each other to begin with, but I'm not so sure that's true. Maybe for him, but it's not the case for me. I think I was only meant to fill the void until he found someone else, someone better suited for his public image.

But even that doesn't make sense, not really.

Alisha certainly can't service him anymore, not in her current predicament, so I know it's not her he's stuck on. And the odds of him finding another woman like me, someone who's willing to marry him *and* let him fuck other women on the side? *Please.*

My hand throbs, and tiny droplets of blood land on the counter in splotches. I reach for a napkin and examine the cut; it's not deep, just enough to keep bleeding.

Suddenly exhausted, I stand, leaving the mess on the floor, the napkin wrapped around my hand and the unsigned papers on the counter.

For now, they don't exist.

"Good morning, Mrs. Rogers. Sleep well?" Caramie asks when I make my way to the kitchen the next morning. I give her a nod and nothing more; the Susie Homemaker look on her face is enough to make me gag. She plays the part almost *too* well lately, and I can't stand the new air of confidence around her.

No one should be *that* good at life.

"Tea? Just boiled a fresh pot of water," she says, reaching for the kettle. "Although, I'm not sure why you haven't switched to one of those Keurig things yet. They're much more efficient for a single party."

"I'm not single," I mutter, the edge in my voice making me sound like a pack-a-day smoker.

Cara points to the papers on the counter.

Oh yeah, that's right.

I forgot to take them to my office before heading to bed last night. Shame on her for reading them. Though, I suppose I would've, too, had I been in her position.

I fight the urge to remind her nothing is official yet, that I haven't signed a damn thing. She knows about my situation, but only in pieces. I don't like the thought of trusting her with anything that important. She still thinks Dylan is Sawyer's son.

Hasn't met him yet, either, but I've talked about him plenty, mostly while under the influence and therefore against my will, but it still counts. I don't want her to get the wrong impression of my husband; I still think he'll be coming home eventually.

I grab a mug and hold it out to her as she pours water over the teabag. "Where's the baby?"

"Asleep," she answers semi-smugly, like it were something I should already know. I swear, the kid's schedule changes by the week. How am I supposed to keep up with so much on my mind?

I take a seat at the breakfast counter, not at all surprised to see that Caramie has cleaned up the glass from last night's spill. She catches me staring at the floor.

"All cleaned up," she says, and I swear I hear a glint of pride in her voice, like I should be proud she did her damn job. There's condescension seeping from her pores this morning, and I can't say I care for it. I'm not sure I want to know why, but I ask anyway.

"What's with you today?"

"I'm sorry?"

"You're in a mood. What's up?"

"Nothing at all, Mrs. Rogers. Just a beautiful day."

It's Ivy, thanks.

"Right."

We sit in silence for a few minutes, the tension festering for reasons that remain unknown. "Your son is sleeping well lately," she says, not that I needed the update.

I don't say anything, just nod.

"Will you have a few minutes to visit with him when he wakes up?"

"When will that be?"

"Around eight."

"I'll be gone by then. Appointments today," I say, suddenly realizing the excuse means I'll need to leave the house. Caramie nods with a judgment-riddled expression; it's subtle, but I know I saw it. I equally want to slap her and kiss her, but I don't care for her tone this morning, so I do neither.

"I'll take this upstairs," I say, gently tipping the steaming mug in her direction. She smiles and pours some for herself, a look of contentment on her face as she brings the mug to her lips and takes a sip.

I'm not sure what to make of it, her new attitude, but at this point, I'm far too hungover to worry about it.

DICK IN MY HAND

Sawyer

I DIDN'T WANT to send the papers.

I knew Ivy wouldn't react well to them, but what am I supposed to do? Sit here with my dick in my hand while she raises my dead brother's son on *my* dime? No, this divorce is necessary. I've worked too hard to get where I'm at, to build my clientele and make a name for myself. It's time to cut her off. Ivy doesn't deserve my money, not after the shit she's pulled.

I'm done supporting her.

And hiring a nanny to take care of her love child, no less? I'm not about to support another man's kid, okay? I didn't knock her up, why should I have to suffer the consequences?

Kids were never in the cards—never even on the table—for us. Ivy knew that; she still *knows* that. We discussed it *ad nauseam*—she even agreed she wanted nothing to do with dirty diapers and snot-nosed kids. So whose fault is this divorce, really?

Ivy remains convinced our demise has everything to do with Alisha, with my stepbrother. But she's wrong. This divorce is the result of her trying to trap me with that damn baby.

And she tried, believe me.

She thought she had me, too, that she could play it off like I was the one who knocked her up all along. Little did she know.

I hate kids.

That's why I had a vasectomy when I was twenty-five, a birthday gift to myself, *thank you very much*. And no, I didn't bother to share that little fact with my wife. Why would I when kids weren't part of the plan? I kept her in the dark on the subject until *after* she told me "we" were expecting.

The fact that she went out of her way to feign happiness, to tell me how excited she was when she made the announcement, wasn't lost on me either. She thought she'd finally secured her cut of my wealth, that there was no way I'd deny "our" child the life of luxury they deserved.

And I'm not gonna lie, the look on her face when I not only announced my inability to conceive a child, but produced documentation to prove it, was priceless.

Talk about an elephant in the room.

When the truth finally came out, when she told me what she'd done, that she'd fucked Dylan and the kid was the seed of my stepbrother, that's when I knew for sure.

She had killed him.

I knew what it meant—why she did it—and can't say it surprised me. She was determined to take it to her grave, too.

She wanted Alisha back.

Having Dylan's baby was her royal flush.

But she'd shown her cards too early and look where that got us, where it got Alisha.

And the thing is, I doubt Ivy even considered our prenup while she took advantage of my brother. It's void now, invalid, washed away like a turd on the sidewalk. She'd had an affair and was pregnant with another man's child. She wouldn't stand a chance at alimony under those circumstances. I would've been an idiot not to get the hell away from this shit show before the crowd started booing.

This is for the best.

For both of us.

On Tuesday I head to the office early, my stress level rising with the knowledge that Ivy has been served with the divorce papers. I know she won't go down easy. I get that. I can't say I blame her; we had a good thing going there for a while. It'll be tough to let go of that, but she's given me no choice.

The kid is a deal-breaker.

My assistant, Krissy, hasn't arrived yet, so I drop a muffin at her desk—banana nut, her favorite—for later, knowing full well she'll return the favor down the road. It's what we do, what *normal* people do for their coworkers.

It's important for me to appear normal, to maintain my white-collar image if I intend to remain in this industry. My side gig depends on it.

But it's a struggle some days, today especially.

By ten a.m. I'm more anxious than I was on the way in. I'm pacing my office, wearing a path in the carpet while I try to make sense of everything that's happened over the last year. My thoughts won't settle, and for some reason, all I can think about is making love to my wife. Making love to Alisha.

The images play like a movie in my mind, and oh, how I wish I could see them in the flesh. That they were real, tangible, and happening right here and how.

Visions of Ivy as she licks Alisha's pussy.

I miss that, the three of us together.

I think I always will.

And now I'm trying to scare away a boner like a teenage boy. Apparently, my dick is making all the decisions today. I mumble a curse word and shove my laptop and some documents into my briefcase. I can't concentrate; there's no point in being here.

"Heading out for the day, sir?" Krissy asks when I step out, the muffin I left her now a mere pile of crumbs left behind on a napkin.

It feels like a metaphor.

"Yes, my apologies. I'm fighting a migraine today. Clear my calendar, will you?"

"Yes, sir. See you tomorrow." I wave and close my office door behind me.

"Thanks for the muffin!"

Twenty minutes later I'm home, stripped naked, and ready to rub one out on the couch. I grab my laptop and pull up the video, the one I saved for occasions such as this.

I'm not supposed to have this footage, but I do, and I watch it often: the night my wife and I were initiated into the swingers' club. They said no phones, no cameras; it was a well-communicated rule, but there was no way I was going to miss out on the opportunity to look back at this.

It's all about who you know and how much cash you can slide under the table.

I tap the play button on the video and lean into the couch, the leather cool beneath my ass.

"Do you want me to fuck your wife?"

I look over at Ivy, and the way she's rubbing herself and sucking her bottom lip is almost enough to make me cum right here and now. She wants it, she wants that dick, and she wants me to tell her it's okay to have it.

I nod, and he summons her with a finger, pointing toward the ground, motioning for her to drop to her knees, to pleasure him. And she does, she takes his cock like a champ. I sit back in the armchair, pumping my own fist slowly, watching in awe while my wife deep-throats another man's cock.

She looks so fucking beautiful.

I had no idea she'd look so good with someone else's dick in her mouth.

. . .

Watching my wife with another man was a high like I'd never experienced. And I've been high plenty of times, so I'm not just saying that. It was the pleading look in her eyes as she took that dick that really did it for me. The way they rolled back in her head every time he pounded into her.

She liked it rough.

And she was grateful when I admitted I paid to have the session recorded. We watched it together often in the beginning. We even tried bringing it back once after she was gone, when we struggled to find each other again, but Ivy said it wasn't as much of a turn-on as it once was.

That was upsetting.

It still turns me on just the same.

I guess nobody ever tells you that once you get involved in group sex, one-on-one will never be the same, never as satisfying. That's what made that night so monumental; it was the start of everything that broke us.

Why I continue to torture myself by re-watching it, I'll never know.

But it makes me come every time, and right now it's the release that I desperately need.

LASH OUT

Ivy

I DON'T EXPECT IT, the day she calls.

It's late afternoon, and I should be getting ready for a night out, but I can't seem to get motivated enough to climb out of bed. Something has felt off all day, almost like a premonition of sorts, like I knew something big was about to happen.

My heart pounds in my chest, the anticipation nearly unbearable as my cell vibrates in my hand. If I stare at it too long she'll be gone, so this is it. *The* moment I've been waiting for.

"This is a prepaid call from an inmate at the Smithson Women's Penitentiary…"

"Hello?"

The line is quiet, but she's there, breathing softly into her end of the phone. I'm sure it must be hard for her, making this call, so I wait patiently for her to speak. I don't want to rush her, not after all this time.

"I got your letter," she says finally.

Not the first words I expected, but they're words and they've come from her mouth, so I take them greedily. She sounds different, harder somehow. More reserved, closed off. I've been sending her letters for months now, sometimes two a week, and she's never once written back, let alone picked up the phone and called. I knew she needed time. I've respected her boundaries; it's the least I could do.

I knew she'd come around.

"Which one?" I ask, although I hope she's been reading them all, admiring the pictures I've shared with her, the words I've written on the pages.

"All of them."

I nod as though she can see me. I'm trying to rein it in, to not get upset, but my broken heart is fragile, and it wants to lash out. I need explanations, nurturing. Something to show me that what we had wasn't nothing.

That I did what I did for a reason.

"So, why now then?" I ask, an accidental edge to my voice. My intention to be nice, to be patient with her, already dissolved. "It's been a year—an entire *year*—and you're just now calling me?"

"I didn't know what to say," she admits, her tone soft but unapologetic. This is the start of *her* revenge, her chance to wrong me right back. In a way, I suppose I owe her this; I deserved her silence, and now her harsh words.

"And do you now? Know what to say, I mean."

"Why'd you do it?"

"Ah, come on...I think you can do better than that."

"Why did you do it?" she repeats, and this time the words hold weight—they're an arsenal of pain, and she tosses them in my direction with purpose.

"Lisha—"

"I have a right to know!"

"Last I checked, you no longer have rights to a damn thing," I snap. "You're in *prison*."

"Yeah? And whose fault is that? You can't expect me to just move on, Lil—*Ivy*." She pauses, and I picture her leaning against the wall, her forehead nestled against cold brick, a tear rolling down her cheek. "My husband is dead because of you."

She says the words now, possibly out loud for the first time. I bet it feels good to say them, to know I've heard them and maybe even been hurt by them.

But I've expected this.

I've waited for this call, to feel her anger, her resentment.

To understand her pain.

I miss her, but I don't tell her this. I can't. She's not ready to hear it. She just needs more time.

Silence is truly the only way, as hard as it is to give it to her. I sigh and say the only other words I can think to say. "You made your bed, Lisha. What happens next is up to you."

"Wai—"

I end the call, my body shaking as I stare at the silent phone in my hand. I didn't mean to hang up on her, but what was I supposed to do? I know they record these calls, and I'm not about to say something stupid and get myself in trouble. She baited me. She *wanted* me to say something incriminating.

I'd thought we were past that.

But this phone call changes things, and I'm sure she knows it, too. We're speaking again, and that's the first step to getting her back, to finding *us* again.

I'm still so angry, but this fight, this feud of ours, is in our blood, coursing through our veins like a virus that can never be cured. This history between us is terminal unless we overcome it together, and soon she'll realize it too. She *has* to.

Alisha loves me.

She *will* come back to me.

SCHMOOZE, YOU LOSE

Sawyer

THERE'S a lot of schmoozing in the finance industry.

I should know, I'm a finance guy.

To be honest, sometimes I hate it, but the money is good, and we all know that's what makes the world go 'round. What they tell you in business school—and that I've found entirely accurate, by the way—is that people want to invest their money with guys they trust. They want a solid character, someone who has more than a little stake in the game, something to lose: a family man.

I'm not a family man, not by any means, but I'm good at pretending to be.

My job depends on it, so I do it. That means Ivy did, too. Now, if you haven't figured it out by now, my wife doesn't like to be told what to do, let alone abide by societal norms. She can be a challenge, but she listens when she has to, when I tell her it's time to put on a show.

She likes money.

She'll do anything for it.

Our arrangement worked for us, for a while anyway, living a privileged life in the public eye, so to speak. I mean, we're not celebrities, not by anyone's standards, but we've become pillars of the community. I'm the guy that invests in the small local business. The guy who throws money into charitable causes whether he believes in them or not, goes to church on Sundays despite his many sins. There are eyes on us even when they're not looking. It's the nature of the game, so we do it.

Ivy, being a former "actress," knew how to turn it on when necessary. She even helped me land one of my biggest accounts—not to say I agreed with her methods, but she secured a once-in-a-lifetime deal for me. I think that's why she feels entitled to my money now that things are less than kosher between us.

It was innocent at first, our approach at the investor's luncheon. A garden party at the home of our firm's president, Alexander Bookman. Unbeknownst to him, I had insider information on the client, and that's why I fought so hard to be put on the account. Luckily, my boss, great guy that he is, went out on a limb by letting me take the lead.

As we waited for our guests to arrive, I stood locked in conversation with Bookman, a frosted glass of beer in my hand. It was my fourth of the day, although I'd drunk the first three before the catering crew had arrived, so to everyone else, it was my first, and I was nursing the shit out of it. Secret of the trade for you there.

Bookman had been yammering on for a good twenty minutes about some new investment opportunity with an up-and-coming sports agency in Minneapolis, and I had grown bored just a few minutes into his spiel. It wasn't that I was uninterested, just that I'd heard the same monologue from him a week earlier.

And he wasn't the target I was after, anyway. He knew my mind was elsewhere, and didn't take offense when I politely excused myself to meet with the head of EHC.

The Ehrens-Havenbrook Corporation was expected to make a killing for anyone involved, and more so for me if I played my cards right.

I wanted in.

I'd studied the business model for ten days straight, and from what I could tell, on paper they had a justified business—with plenty of means to launder a shit ton of drug money on the side. Now, I'm not going to assume you're one to approve of such a thing, but here's a little newsflash for you: I'm not against money laundering. I'll take my cut and never lose a wink of sleep.

The business cover was good, the paperwork and financial accounts solid—untraceable.

That's why Ivy was across the yard flirting with the only guy there who mattered, *the* reason we made an appearance at the dog and pony show.

Connor Ehrens.

The man who was going to make me rich.

I had heard Ehrens had a thing for petite blondes, liked the way they flirted with him, and that was a category my wife fell into easily. The rest of her body worked in our favor, too.

I told her the plan over breakfast that morning, and she was on board. "Whatever you need," she'd said. What I needed was to land that fucking client.

I watched Ivy place a hand on Ehrens's chest. She giggled at something he said that I doubt she found remotely funny, and batted her long eyelashes at him. His face softened, but I imagine other parts of him hardened right up.

I hadn't meant to watch it go down—the suspense was nauseating —but I found myself hiding behind a well-manicured hedge like a peeper while she worked him over.

She flirted.

She flattered.

Eventually, she took him upstairs to the guest bathroom, and that's where I lost sight of the target. I suppose it was to be expected, given the circumstances, so I wasn't upset. I'd seen my wife with other men plenty of times by then. My biggest complaint was that I didn't get to watch.

It was later, though, after the party, when I realized the small kink in our plan.

Sending Ivy in to hook the shark was a mistake, a rookie move on my part. We played our hand awfully early, and I should have known they'd take advantage of her involvement after that, that they'd want to keep her.

I should have seen it coming.

She did give one hell of a blow job.

We landed the client.

But only if Ivy was willing to work for Ehrens, too.

"You may have outdone yourself with Ehrens today," I told her later that evening. I undid my tie and slid it off my neck, fingering the material and watching Ivy remove her heels, my eyes locked in on her toned legs.

"I did what you asked me to do."

"And then some," I muttered with a smirk.

"Don't do that," she snapped, pointing a finger in my direction. "Don't patronize me. *You* sent me in there."

I managed a laugh and took her hand, positioning it over the growing bulge in my pants. She gasped and massaged me through the material before shoving me down onto the bed.

I welcomed her need to regain control, to put me in my place.

She took the tie from my hand and wrapped it around my wrists, knotting it tightly through the slats of our headboard. My dick throbbed as her hands found my belt and went to work.

My wife knew she had the upper hand.

She had earned her reward.

And it was going to cost me.

ATTENTION-SEEKING

Sawyer

IVY NEVER DID MANAGE to fit in with the other wives.

And she knew it, of course. I think it's safe to say her awareness of the issue caused more damage than good. She tried too hard, always going the extra mile, but being overly fake about it. They saw right through her act, and I can't say I blame them.

Sometimes I think she did it on purpose, but there's no sense in arguing a point I can't prove.

One of the wives, in particular—Bethany—seemed to have it out for her. She and Ivy despised each other—and boy did they make sure the rest of us knew about it.

I don't know what it is about men in finance, but we tend to marry the attention-seeking-housewife types, those beautiful women seemingly placed on God's green earth for their beauty and little else. Don't scoff at that—you know it's true, that they're out there.

Ivy certainly dressed the part; she did her best to keep up with the status quo, but eventually, Bethany managed to tear her down. Right down to the stump.

And you can't fault her for it, either. It happens with the weak ones sometimes. When they're not careful, those loose cannons have been known to sink ships.

Ivy was never careful.

She was reckless, acting with abandon when she should have kept her shit together. It was bad before it was ever good, I guess.

The attention from Alisha's trial didn't help either—why would it? These women wanted the inside scoop. They wanted Ivy to spill the beans about her involvement, but all that did was set her up for further ridicule. The gossip started and ended with my wife, but what she didn't realize—what she *couldn't* possibly have known—is that she was slowly digging her own grave.

All she had left to do was jump in.

Lie down flat.

They'd shovel the dirt in right on top of her the first chance they got.

I tried to fix it, I did. Little chats with the wives here and there at cocktail parties and dinner nights, a comment to one of the partners— the husbands who did their best to rein in their wives. I'd hoped it'd clear the air, show everyone Ivy wasn't the conniving temptress she came across as.

You and I both know she is.

So did they.

My attempts had a tendency to make things worse for her in the long run. My kind words and stories about her good deeds within the community—how she organized the church bake sale, sat co-chair for the annual fundraiser—all seemed to have the opposite effect.

Ivy does whatever her husband tells her to.

That's the only way she gets to collect her allowance, you know.

Damn, those women were ruthless.

I can't say I blame them; Ivy's drama is nothing if not entertaining.

"Sawyer?"

I'm in the grocery store, grabbing stuff for dinner when I see her.

Bethany.

She's looking pristine as always, even for the grocery store, as she tucks a strand of hair behind her ear with a freshly-manicured finger. *Just the woman I didn't care to see today.*

"Bethany, good to see you," I say, careful of my tone.

"I thought that was you...didn't realize you do your own shopping these days. How have you been?" She tips her head in faux empathy, her hand embracing my forearm.

"Hanging in," I say, aware that while I don't want it, I need her sympathy. I have an image to uphold here, and my soon-to-be-ex-wife isn't making things any easier for me, despite our time apart.

"Listen, about Ivy," she continues before I get another word in. I nod, but don't bite. I know whatever I say will make it around the block when she starts running her mouth the second she walks out of here.

"I'm in a bit of a hurry."

"Oh, sure. My apologies. Don't let me keep you." She pats my arm, her fingers lingering longer than they should. "Before you go?"

"Hm?"

"The girls and I would like to put together a care package for Ivy and the baby. You know, since she wasn't so keen on the shower idea. Anything, in particular, you guys need?"

And there it is.

The question I'd hoped to avoid.

Our social circle is still under the impression I fathered Ivy's son.

It's time to let the cat out of the bag and give these women a new reason to talk behind my wife's back. This time she deserves it.

"He's not my son," I say.

And then I abandon my cart in the store and make a beeline for the door.

I don't need this shit today.

KATY FUCKING PERRY

Ivy

I TYPE out a text to Sawyer and press send before I can talk myself out of it. I know I shouldn't be contacting him, but I can't help myself. I want to hear from him. See him. He rarely responds, but I know he loves the dirty messages I send him, the naked pictures. He's a stubborn mule, but a sucker for a wet pussy, and I have no problem reminding him how wet mine can get for him.

The hope is that he can't resist, and that he'll show up at the front door, all his belongings in tow, and come crawling back to me.

That he'll forgive me.

Sometimes a man just needs to be reminded of what they have and what they're about to lose if they follow through with their dumb decisions.

Sawyer is one of those guys.

I still don't think he'll follow through with the divorce. I haven't signed the papers, and it'll be months before a judge will force me to. Even then, it won't be the end of us.

There is no end to us.

I set the phone on the counter and nurse a glass of Moscato. The day has gotten away from me. A lot of days seem to be getting away from me lately. But it's fine.

I don't have a problem.

It's not like anyone is around to notice most of the time, tonight especially. Caramie left hours ago for a night out with her friends. She doesn't have much of a social life, which bodes well for me given our current arrangement, but I'd be lying if I said I don't miss her tonight. I feel her absence. Good thing baby Dylan is such a good sleeper; not a peep all night.

I like to think I'm okay being here alone, but when I hear her come in through the garage entrance, my pulse picks up a smidge. I sit up straighter on the bar stool and try to look less drunk, a little less depressed, as I plaster on a smile.

"Ivy? Are you in here?" Caramie's voice calls around the hall corner. She steps into view and manages to take my breath away. She's gorgeous in a tight little black dress, her blue suede pumps elongating her toned legs.

All the wine goes to my head as I stand.

I can't help myself.

I walk to her, my breath heavy when I reach out and touch her hair. I see the confusion on her face, but she's intrigued, I know she is. I see that, too, feel it in my soul. She doesn't push me away as I move closer, and I wonder if maybe she's been expecting this all along, if she feels the attraction, too.

I intend to use words, but none come out.

Instead, it's her hand I feel on my hip, drawing me closer, as if letting me know this is okay. That she wants me, too. Her lips meet mine, and, *oh—they're so fucking soft.* She tastes like strawberries and mint and wine coolers, and I want more.

I whimper, and she does, too.

Our bodies relax into one another, a crash of heat between us.

But she pulls away after just a moment and brings a hand to her mouth, her eyes left searching my own.

"Cara…" I whisper. She takes a step back and I can see her nipples poking through the fabric of her dress, like proof that she liked the way it felt—our kiss, our bodies together. She wants more, but I'm not sure she'll allow herself to take it.

"I'm sorry, Ivy, I…" She scurries off down the hall, the click of her heels echoing on the hardwoods beneath her. I watch her leave, soft brown curls bouncing against her back as she does.

And it's clear then, what just happened, and what's about to happen when I eventually follow her down the hall and sneak into her bedroom. She'll give in, because that's what women do. It's what we need to feel human.

Except that when I go to her, she doesn't give in at all. She doesn't let me have her the way I want to, the way I need her. Because she's not like me.

I've been a fool to think she'd want me.

But it's not the first time I've been wrong.

I slept like shit.

Rejection tends to do that to me.

You'd think I'd be used to it by now, but the sting is fresh, another wound in my weakening armor. My eyes are puffy, but I'm not sure if it's from crying or the bottle of wine I consumed by myself. My guess is both, but if Caramie's downstairs when I grab my morning tea, I'll need to go with the wine excuse.

She's used to that one by now.

And she's there, as I knew she would be, sitting at the table nursing a cup of coffee while Dylan sleeps in the playpen beside her. The tension is as palpable as ever, but I drop a tea bag into a mug and pour hot water from the kettle over it before joining her at the table.

"Listen, about last night—" I start, but Caramie silences me with a hand in the air, her face softening like she knows just how much last night hurt me but isn't sure what to do about it.

"Don't even mention it," she says. "It was my fault, really, I shouldn't have—"

"No, don't do that to yourself. I was the one who initiated it, and I'm sorry, but it was nothing. I was just drunk and horny."

I'm not sure if she sees through my feigned nonchalance or not, but I give it a try anyway. The last thing I want is for things to be awkward between us. I need her here, with me, with Dylan.

"It's just that...I would understand if you want to fire me. I shouldn't have—"

"Oh, Cara, no. It was just a stupid kiss. A *kiss*. It was nothing, trust me."

"You sure?"

"Positive. And really, it's *my* fault. I should be the one apologizing. I shouldn't have taken advantage of you like that."

"You didn't take advantage..."

"No?"

She shakes her head, her cheeks suddenly coloring with blush. "It was kinda nice," she says. "I've never kissed a woman before."

"Oh, honey...you really don't know what you're missing, do you?" I tease with a wink.

We sit in silence for a moment, and it's not awkward. Just quiet, a peace offering of sorts. Until a moment later when her laughter fills the room, and she's giggling uncontrollably, her eyes crinkling in that cute way they do when she's amused. "I can't..."

"What is it?"

"It's that...stupid Katy Perry song..." she says between breaths. She clutches her stomach, the laughter apparently giving her an ab workout. The look on her face is priceless as she finishes the thought. "I can't get that fucking song out of my head!"

Cara had kissed a girl...and she liked it.

LADY ANN

Ivy

I SAID I wouldn't do it.

That I didn't *need* it.

Apparently, I was wrong, so here I am.

I've returned to Lady Ann's. I know, I know, it's stupid, and I know what you're thinking. I need to move on from my past, start fresh, maybe in a new town, a new home. The problem is, I'm not ready to let go of my old life, of the thrills, the excitement.

The pleasure.

This is the hit I crave.

Things will be different this time around, though. Unlike before, I'm not a paying member of the club. This time it's a career. A business opportunity. Lady Ann herself is paying *me* to be there, on top of the fees and tips I'll make off the customers. I like to think of my newfound employment as an investment opportunity in myself.

I'm not too naive to realize the irony in that statement, but I'll take it, considering. Against my will, it seems I'll soon be past my sexual prime, so why not? How long can I keep this up, and at what point will I start *looking* like the cougar I think I am?

My clock is ticking.

Thank God the money is good.

Who knew there was a lucrative side to this business? That it wasn't all orgasms and living out sexual fantasies? Turns out, once you've been in for a while, once Lady Ann trusts you and sees you're good for business, she'll want to use you. She sees your value, the one good card you bring to the table.

So, I work for her now. I'm officially back in the escort business.

And I'm loving it.

I'm still thinking about my shared kiss with Caramie when I head out to Lady Ann's two nights later. There's something about my son's nanny that's been keeping me awake at night. I can't put my finger on it.

Literally.

She's so different from Alisha, from all the other women I've been with. There's an innocence about her. I think I want to take that away from her.

I'm a good fifteen minutes early for work, so I park and kill the engine before unbuckling and grabbing my phone from my purse. I tap the icon for Instagram and head to Caramie's page. We follow each other, more or less so I can ensure she holds up her end of the bargain, which is not to post pictures of my son on social media. My page exists merely to keep tabs on other people, Cara being one of them.

She's kept her word, I don't see any photos with Dylan, nothing suspicious at all really. I run my finger along the screen, scrolling leisurely as I take in the selfies and food-related content. She's not one to post often, but when she does it usually falls into one of those two categories.

I don't understand the purpose, but that must be me showing my age again. Closing the app, I drop my phone back into my clutch and check my makeup in the visor before heading inside.

I'm not inside for long before Lady Ann hands me a slip of paper with an address on it. It takes me by surprise; I'm always assigned to house duty. I'm still new here.

"You and Pen have a pickup tonight," she says. I don't ask questions. That's not what we do around here, but this is a new development; she's never sent me on a house call before. Not that I question her judgment. Lady Ann knows our interests better than anyone; which clients we'll go for and which we won't. She even knows how far we'll go sexually. That's part of her job and why she's so good at it.

But she's never assigned me—or Penelope, for that matter—to a pickup.

It's no surprise that we run drugs through the house; hell, I've helped Sawyer launder money through this place. I just didn't think I'd find myself fetching the goods for her. I can't say I'm against a little bump every once in a while, though, especially considering how well my life is going lately. It is what it is, I guess.

Our driver delivers Penelope and me to the location, well aware that showing up alone for a drug pickup with a vagina under your dress is strongly frowned upon. We all know this. It's Whoring 101, right there on the top of the syllabus.

Not that our armed driver will be following us through the door. We're on our own once we get in there.

"Are you nervous?" Pen asks, flipping her long dark hair over her shoulders. It cascades down her back in waves, the curls loose and bouncy. I imagine a john with his fingers wrapped in it, tugging just enough to excite her.

"Earth to Ivy…" she says, snapping her fingers.

"Hm? Sorry, I was thinking about something."

"What's with you?"

"I'm not sure. What did you ask me?"

"I asked if you're nervous."

"Oh. No, why? Should I be?"

"It's our first pickup together. I've never done one before. Have you?" I shake my head, although I didn't necessarily want her to know it was my first job. Why Lady Ann would send two virgins out on a supply pickup was beyond me. But I suppose that's why I'm not the one in charge. I just do what I'm told; the payouts are bigger that way.

But this house looks familiar, like I've seen it before. "Where are we?" I ask the driver; he just shrugs. He's not supposed to speak to us, but it was worth a shot.

"I hear this guy hand-picks his girls," Penelope whispers beside me.

"Is that so?"

"Mmhm, and he's *insanely* wealthy. Older guy, probably forties or so. Doesn't take shit from anyone," she says as we climb out of the car. "I'm happy we're the chosen ones, he's quite the tipper."

I'm hung up on the fact that she considers *in his forties* older as we climb the front steps and pause at the top. "Ready?" she asks, raising her hand to knock on the expansive wooden door. It opens with a creek and I recognize him right away.

Connor Ehrens.

No wonder I was assigned to pickup tonight.

"What have we here?" Ehrens asks, winking at me.

"Lady Ann sent us for pickup," Penelope says.

"Did she now?"

She nods and sucks her bottom lip into her mouth. She looks like the amateur that she is, but I refuse to be the one to tell her. Ehrens doesn't seem to mind, though. He seems to appreciate her innocence. He brings a hand to her chin, his fingers snaking along her neck. "What's your name, gorgeous?"

"Penelope," she says stupidly. She was supposed to give a fake name.

You never forget the fake name.

"Pretty. First time?"

"Yes." She nods.

So much for Plan A.

"Then we may need to show you ladies how things work around here, hmm?" He taunts her, walking slowly around her like she's his prey. I spot another man at the staircase, a handgun attached to his hip, and I recognize him as Michael Havenbrook.

I wonder if he knows I can see his erection through his pants.

Dibs, I think.

We step further inside the house and the door closes behind us, a guard standing against it with his arms crossed.

"Lady Ann filled us in," I inform him, sticking to my it's-not-my-first-rodeo charade, despite the fact that these guys likely know otherwise. His eyes dart to mine, his fingers still making their way down Penelope's neck. She drapes an arm around his shoulders, the other resting on his chest.

"Glad to hear it," he says. "Show me what you have for me, Lila."

The mention of my stage name is unexpected; he knows who I am. He could have blown my cover if he wanted to. I take the bait and play along.

"Product first," I say with a teasing tone. "We know how this works."

Ehrens pulls a small bag from his pocket and passes it to me, a conniving smile playing on his lips. "As you wish." He pulls out a second pouch, opens the small baggie, and pops one of the pills onto my tongue. I consider spitting it out, maybe hoarding it under my tongue, but I don't mind the idea of forgetting tonight and decide to swallow it down instead.

"Good girl," he says.

And I hear it then, the sound of his belt buckle. As if on command, I drop to my knees and take his cock in my mouth, Penelope kneeling down beside me. She reaches over and pulls the top of my dress down, exposing my breasts, and my nipples immediately perk up. The sexy stranger at the staircase *(Havenbrook)* joins us, freeing his cock from his pants as he comes up on the other side of me. I take him in my mouth while Pen works on Ehrens; he doesn't take long to finish.

The "stranger" comes quickly, too, and I'm unexpectedly grateful because the E is starting to kick in, and I think I need to lie down.

"Here," Ehrens says, tossing me another bag before shoving his dick back in his pants.

"What's this?"

"A little extra for you. Since you were both so generous with your payment tonight." He winks and opens the door as I stand and struggle to put my tits back into my dress. "I'll see you in a couple days?"

I nod, even though I have no idea whether or not I'll ever be back here. That's not my call to make.

It's amazing what a couple good blow jobs can buy, though.

We walk with swagger back to the town car, Penelope giggling as she says, "I don't think we were supposed to suck them off." She snakes an arm through mine, and I laugh with her.

"No, I don't think so either." I'm not opposed to cutting corners, though—never have been. My moral compass rests easy as always.

"Should we keep the extra E for ourselves?"

"No, we can't. It could be a test," I say, and she pouts, seemingly bummed to miss out on the high.

But I don't feel an ounce of guilt when I pocket the extra pills for later.

BETWEEN MY LEGS

Ivy

I DIDN'T WANT to dress too casually. Didn't want to overdress, either, if I'm being honest. I think the outfit I chose is rather modest, especially in comparison. Simple skinny jeans and a white blouse. Flats, minimal silver jewelry. My blonde hair now cut to my shoulders, styled in a bouncy bob.

I feel good; pretty even, but not *too* pretty.

She has refused to see me since the day she was convicted, so my efforts will likely be for nothing, save for a few empathetic glances in my direction from strangers I'll never see again.

I don't know why I keep subjecting myself to this, but I do. I'm here, waiting for her, hoping today will be the day she changes her mind.

"Can you check again, please?" I ask the intake officer. The partition window is covered in fingerprint smudges, and I can't help but want to clean it. Surely, this place can afford a cleaning service, right? At least to hide the fact that things aren't what they seem once you get through the heavy doors.

The admin removes her hands from the keyboard, a sympathetic tilt of her head telling me she's less sympathetic than she is annoyed. This isn't the first time I've shown up here uninvited for visitor's day. She's turned me down before.

"Mrs. Rogers, you're not on her call list. You're not on her visitor's list. I'm sure she'll let you know if that changes." She pauses, waits for me to step out of line and walk off with my tail between my legs. I don't move, just stand there processing, trying to understand why she won't see me. "Next!" she calls, waving a hand in the air.

"Ma'am? Let's go, come on." A corrections officer takes my elbow and pulls me aside, so they can assist the next person, someone with an inmate waiting to see them.

My chest hurts.

It shouldn't, not after going through this so many times, but it hurts, nonetheless.

Why won't she let me see her?

I drive home in a cycling state of confusion.

I can't be the only one hurting here. Has she even considered what this will do to our son once he's old enough to understand her rejection? He deserves to meet his other mother, he does.

"Fuck!" I scream, the vibrato of my voice rattling my throat. I slam my hands against the steering wheel, the car veering into the other lane, but it's okay because there's no one there. I'm the only car on this deserted road, the only idiot that was sent away before visiting hours were over.

All I want to do is breathe the same air as her; to look at her in the flesh and tell her I'll find a way to get us out of this.

I just want to get us out of this.

BORROWED TIME

Ivy

SAWYER STOPS by unannounced around the lunch hour, looking dapper in a three-piece suit, as if it isn't a Friday afternoon in the middle of a Midwestern summer. He doesn't even break a sweat. Meanwhile, I'm sunbathing in the backyard—sweat pooling in all major crevices—when I hear the alert from the Ring camera. Caramie's entertaining baby Dylan under the shade of an umbrella, her modest one-piece suit working wonders for her curves.

"I'll get it," I say uncharacteristically. She gives me a look, but I shoo her off. "I need to grab some water anyway."

She nods and I step inside, padding barefoot through the house as I wrap a shawl around my torso. When I open the door to him I can't help but feel under-dressed, grateful that my tits look good in this bikini top. I can't say I'm ready to see him, but he's here, and I need to decide what to do with that. There's a pang in my chest as I drink in the sight of him.

"You shouldn't be here," I say, the conviction hidden somewhere far beneath the words when they make their way out of my mouth. It's always been hard to say no to him, to turn him away, but I have to or he will bury me.

"I just need to grab a few things, Ivy," he argues, his eyes lingering on my chest.

"No." I shake my head, no longer trusting my voice.

"This is still my house."

"Not for long," I snap, as if those words hold any weight. I know they don't; nothing I say does anymore, but Sawyer doesn't know that yet, so I keep pushing. I have to make his life without me as miserable as possible so he'll come home to me. And yes, that means I'm hoarding his shit.

"Ivy, have you been drinking?"

"What? No, of course not," I lie, wishing I'd had a chance to pop a piece of gum into my mouth. But Sawyer thinks chewing gum is classless, so I rarely have it around.

"I can smell the booze on your breath," he says, leaning closer as I back away. "Just let me in."

I stand there silently, watching Caramie through the window out of the corner of my eye. She scoops up the baby and heads toward the house. He's gumming the noise-making toy he's been playing with that's better suited for the bottom of the garbage bin, his arms flapping and a smile turning up on his face, the drool dripping down his chin.

He's teething.

Which means he's not sleeping well. I imagine that leaves Cara pretty tired these days, considering she's the one getting up with him at all hours of the night, and rightfully so. Better her than me.

"Are you going to let me in?"

"Not today."

"Come on, Ivy, this is ridiculous!"

This isn't how things were supposed to be, I know that. But I can't forfeit now. I can't let him win.

"Cara, put Dylan down for his nap, would you?" I ask, providing the instructions without taking my eyes off Sawyer, despite the fact that I have no idea when my son's nap time actually is.

"Are you sure, Mrs. Rogers?" Cara asks, adjusting my son on her hip.

I nod, the gesture more than enough to send her and Dylan up the stairs and out of earshot. The last thing I need is for Sawyer to set his sights on her. But he wastes no time laying into me, his eyes quickly shifting in anger as soon as Cara's gone. He points a threatening finger in my direction.

"See, *that*, right there is why you and I will never be 'us' again. You don't get to fuck my brother, pop out his kid, and then just expect me to be okay with it. We said no kids, remember?"

I feel it then, the shift between us. The notion that *his* word will be the final word, that he's putting his foot down and all is said and done, right here and now. I smile, a contortion I don't play with often enough these days, but it's there now.

My blood thrums from the alcohol, just the way I need it to. It does little to stop the anger from bubbling alongside it, though. I'm festering, I know this. It's like I'm walking too close to the edge of a cliff, well aware I'm going to slip and fall, but not giving a damn if I do.

I take a quick step back and slam the door, securing the deadbolt in place before stomping down the hall. It's cute, really, how Sawyer thinks he can walk away from all this unscathed, unharmed.

But he's on borrowed time.

He just doesn't know it yet.

JUST FOR YOU

Alisha

THERE'S a certain feeling you get when you know the shoe is about to drop. It's like a sudden pull in the atmosphere, a changing of the tides, a gut feeling that something big is coming. That maybe it could fix everything.

This battlefield we stand on is built on love, destroyed by it just the same. We're all merely pawns in a life-sized game of chess, like tiny soldiers taking the first bullets on the front lines, and if we're lucky, one of us will still be standing in the end.

There's no telling who it will be.

> *Roses are red,*
> *I watched as he bled.*
> *Violets are blue,*
> *I did it just for you.*

Ivy's latest declaration of love settles into my core.

This poem, this tiny piece of paper derived from fifty-seven letters to form seventeen words, is the admission of guilt I've been waiting for. And it's the closest she'll ever come to a confession.

I read through it at least a hundred more times, soaking up the meaning of the prose, the not-so-well-hidden connotation buried within. I won't allow myself to make too much of it, I know I'm the only one who'll understand its value.

At least for me, these words bring closure. They give meaning to what I've put in motion, give me purpose again.

It's just a matter of time now.

The storm is coming.

PLANNED INTRUSION

Ivy

I'M HUNGOVER AGAIN.

Sawyer's impromptu visits tend to do that to me, regardless of how they turn out.

The fog in my head is thicker this time, but that isn't what startles me, what leaves me rooted to the kitchen chair, momentarily suspended in time. If I sit still long enough maybe the unrelenting knocker will take the hint and go away.

I haven't had enough caffeine to welcome this kind of chaos, and it doesn't help that Caramie doesn't seem to be around to answer the door.

What am I paying her for?

Do I answer it? Appease whoever feels the need to interrupt my morning so rudely? The banging continues; it looks like I'm getting up.

Against my will, I abandon my still-steaming cup of tea on the table and pull my robe closed before padding to the door. The flashing lights through the pained glass window stop me in my tracks.

They swarm through the foyer in a kaleidoscope of blue and red.

A set of uniformed officers stand perched on my doorstep, hands hovering over their holstered service weapons as they peer inside. Hesitantly, I take a step forward, unlocking the door and pulling it open just before the bigger of the two officers pounds on it again. His arm hovers in the air like he wasn't expecting me, despite the planned intrusion.

"Do you mind?" I bark, my voice gravelly and thick with irritation.

"Are you Ivy Rogers?"

"Who's asking?"

"Officer Dettmund, ma'am." He gestures to the female officer beside him. "My partner, Officer Jarron. Are you Ivy Rogers?"

"Yes."

"Can you step outside, please?"

"What for?"

"You're a person of interest in a cold case. We'd like you to come to the station to answer a few questions."

"Wha—no." I shake my head vehemently. "No, you have the wrong house." I motion to slam the door in their faces, but a steel-toed boot blocks the way, and a deep voice cuts through the tension.

"It's entirely your choice whether we take you in cuffs or not, ma'am, but this isn't an optional request." The politeness in his face from a moment ago is gone, replaced entirely by an all-business don't-fuck-with-me exterior.

My throat drops into my stomach.

I know what this is about.

But how?

How could they possibly know, and why are they here?

I stare in contention, my feet planted firmly to the hardwood floor, my heart hammering a beat in my chest. "May I get dressed first?"

"You can have some clothes delivered to you at the station. Is your purse nearby?" He peers into the foyer behind me, and I lift my bag from the console table next to the door, attempting to clutch it to my chest. The officer pulls it away, takes a quick look inside. I'm not sure he's allowed to do that, but I do nothing to stop him.

"Any weapons in here?"

I shake my head and step out of the house and onto the concrete slab, the soft padding of Caramie's footsteps approaching behind me. The officer takes my arm; his hands are rough, but he's gentle when he guides me down the stoop and across the lawn, as if he can't see the sidewalk.

Sawyer hates footprints on his lawn.

The cuffs go on despite my compliance, the metal clinking as it's locked into position. I guess he was bluffing when he said the cuffs were optional.

"Ivy Rogers, you are under arrest for the murder of Erika Lacey. You have the right to remain silent... "

"Mrs. Rogers? What's going on? Who's Erika?" Caramie finally steps out of the house, my son attached to her hip. And because I know I won't be returning home anytime soon, I ask the one question worth asking at a moment like this.

"What do I need to do to grant temporary custody of my child to his nanny?"

"We can work that out down at the station," he says, turning to Caramie. "Miss, are you okay to maintain care of the child for the time being?"

Caramie nods reluctantly but says nothing as she hugs Dylan closer to her chest.

"Call my lawyer, Cara. Her information is in my address book in the office."

I suspect this must be traumatizing for her. But she just nods, as if I'd told her I'll be home soon and asked her to have dinner on the table, maybe reminded her to pick up the dry cleaning.

Why isn't she more concerned right now?

I'm assisted into the back of a squad car, my arms awkwardly bound behind my back so I can't even lean properly against the seat. The door closes, and the officers take a moment to confer before separating and folding into their separate cruisers. Officer Dettmund, my apparent chauffeur, says nothing as he fastens his seatbelt. I catch his eyes in the rearview.

It's clear right away that he doesn't like me.

He pulls a pair of sunglasses over his eyes and enters something into the computer before putting the car in gear and steering it away from the curb. I turn and look through the rear window as we drive away, as my home becomes smaller, the two bodies on my front lawn seemingly shrinking into nothing.

An unexpected tear slides down my cheek.

I can't wipe it away because my hands are indisposed, so it lands on my thigh.

But it's not my son's face that brings this wave of emotion. It's not the fact that the neighbors are watching and this is embarrassing beyond belief.

It's the look on Caramie's face that alarms me, and I don't know what this means for us. I don't know why it hurts so much or why I care that she's not in tears right now.

She's smiling as we drive away, holding a cell phone to her ear, my son still glued to her hip.

She certainly shouldn't be smiling at a time like this.

PART IV

DECEPTIVELY CHARMING SOCIOPATH

THIS IS AWKWARD

Ivy

THIS IS AWKWARD.

I was really hoping you wouldn't find out about Erika. I feel like I've ruined things with you now, and that's really a shame because I thought we were off to such a good start, becoming friends and whatnot.

I've worked so hard to show you I'm a good person, that I'm not the monster Alisha has made me out to be, that Sawyer wants to prove I am.

See, the thing is, I left out a few things earlier. Omitted *some* of the truth, if you will. It's kind of a thing I do. I probably should have warned you. I'm not exactly proud of this oversight, but here we are. I do tell the truth more often than not, just not always the complete story. More of a partial tell, really.

What I've told you *is* the truth.

I just left out some parts.

Contrary to what I told you before, my sister Erika—*remember her?*— was a royal pain in the ass. She was—*how do I say this politely?*—a manipulative bitch. Two-faced. Arrogant. We got along just fine when we were kids; that's why I said I grew up relatively *normal*.

But things change, as you know.

My little sister turned out to be a deceitful rat. I liked her less and less the older we got. She was a Daddy's girl, Mom's handy helper, and their homegrown live-in spy. Erika criticized everything I did, and anytime I did something morally wrong in her eyes—which was often —she wasted no time running to Mom and Dad to tattle on her big sis.

They'd put her up to it, too, not that either of them will ever admit to it.

But Erika was the reason I got grounded for shit I would've otherwise gotten away with. And it wasn't because I confided in her, I knew better than to do that. We hadn't been close in years, not since she became the clear favorite in our household. No, it was because she was a lousy sister, with no respect for my privacy.

I found her going through my things all the time, reading diaries she shouldn't have been reading. She was good at finding ways to get into my hiding spots.

Those diaries were all I had, my private thoughts, and they were ammunition to her once she ransacked my dresser drawers and my backpack. Anything to get me in trouble so *she* could stay in Mom and Dad's good graces. So she could get everything her little heart desired.

She was precious to them, could do no wrong…their little angel miracle baby that arrived a couple years after me. She was never supposed to be born in the first place.

And she hated to be reminded of that.

Now, you're probably over there thinking *that's no reason to kill your sister, Ivy*. And, you're right. I don't disagree. That's not why I killed her.

And I did kill her. No sense in beating around *that* proverbial bush. I simply had other, more pressing, reasons for doing it.

PRETENTIOUS TAPPING

Ivy

THE INTERVIEW ROOM IS SMALL, a glorified closet, really.

I can't help but imagine Alisha in a room like this, maybe this exact one. I wonder if she found it as suffocating as I do right now.

Officer Dettmund—and the lady cop he's probably banging behind his wife's back—have officially turned me over to the homicide investigations team, or HIT as they apparently prefer to be called. It doesn't sound very intimidating until you end up in my seat, a baseball bat's length away from a burly detective who's been investigating your sister's cold case for most of his adult life. Detective Wes Raylen, they call him.

A tiger shark disguised as a teddy bear.

I cast my eyes downward and stare at the worn table, at the chipping plastic that's been picked at, prematurely aged by the anxious criminals who sat here before me. For a second I mull over how many of us have been in this seat, simultaneously terrified and excited at the same time.

Detective Raylen can't seem to sit still, like he's suffering from ADD or something. Not that I'd think less of him if he were; I'm sure he's a great detective. But I'm the one being put out here, not him. He doesn't get to play the annoyed party role, I do.

He taps a pen while he reads my case file, the beat likely mimicking whatever overplayed country song is stuck in his head this morning, but I don't listen to the radio often—certainly not to country—and can't seem to place it. He definitely looks like the kind of guy to enjoy today's latest and greatest hits: simple-minded, a follower, not much of a leader.

Tap. Tap. Tip-pity tap.

The intimidation factor wears off the longer we sit here in silence; I'm not sure he realizes that, but if he reads any slower, surely I'll start to question his intellectual ability. And shouldn't he already be familiar with everything that file has to say?

"Should I come back at a later time?" I ask, disrupting his pretentious tapping. Not that I'm confident I have the option to stay or go, but at this point, I'll say just about anything for a break in his rhythm.

He looks up and pushes the folder aside, leaving it open on the corner of the table before reaching for a Styrofoam cup on the other side. He slides it toward me as if demonstrating the definition of slow motion.

"For you," he says, his brows raising, hand motioning to the cup. "It's probably cold by now."

"You actually expect me to drink that?"

"Thought you might be thirsty."

Tap. Tap. Tap-pity tap.

"You thought wrong. Are we done here?"

"Quite the opposite, actually. I'm just getting started with you." He winks, and it's all I can do not to shudder. He's managed to reinstate his manliness with little effort, and now the room suddenly feels cold. Goosebumps prickle my skin despite the warm temperature and the moderate sweatshirt I've been gifted from the lost and found (since I've yet to receive the fresh set of clothes I was promised earlier). The cheap synthetic material itches against my arms. "I need to know where you were the night of August 4, 2006," he says.

It's a statement, not a question, but it's clear he expects a definitive answer, which is the last thing I'll be giving him.

"How do you expect me to remember that? It was sixteen years ago."

"I would think it'd be pretty easy to remember, actually, seeing as it's the night your younger sister was *killed*. Most people would remember their exact whereabouts on a day like that."

"Hmm...ya know, come to think of it, you're right. I *should* be able to recall what I was doing the night my sister *died*, but..." I lean in real close, an accidental smirk playing on my lips. "Sorry, I don't."

"Mrs. Rogers, do you understand what kind of trouble you're in here?"

"I understand what kind of trouble you *think* I'm in, yes. But you're wasting your time and the taxpayers' hard-earned money. Don't you have better things to do than harass the family of a girl who's been dead for sixteen years?"

"That's odd."

"What?"

"The file I was just reading? You know, the new *evidence* that's come to light? Well, it seems to tell me a different story than what you're depicting here. That perhaps I'm not wasting my time—or the taxpayers' money—at all."

Sure, I'll bite.

"And what evidence would that be?"

"We'll get to that. First, tell me where you were that night. It's rather *important* to the narrative here."

"I don't recall."

"I have a feeling you do."

"Yeah? Do you like to talk about your feelings, detective? Sounds to me like you'd make a great therapy patient. Maybe you should see someone."

Tap. Tap.

"It's just interesting to me, you know?" he continues. "That I would tell you there's new evidence in your sister's case, and you immediately ask what the evidence is, as if you know there's evidence to be found."

"What's your point?"

"My point is that you should either be excited or scared by this new evidence. You know, depending on your level of innocence, whether you give a shit. But you seem a bit nonchalant about it. Aloof, if you will."

"Yeah, well, she and I didn't get along the greatest. What can I say? I came to terms with her death years ago; I don't need to relive it."

"Well, I'd like to be able to offer your parents some justice, wouldn't you?"

Tap. Tap. Tip-pity-tap-tap.

My butthole puckers at the mention of my parents, and just like that, this conversation is officially over. My arms fold across my chest and I lean back in the seat, prepared to sweat it out on mute for the duration of the interrogation.

I refuse to discuss those assholes.

"I'd like to call my lawyer now."

And there he goes with the tapping again.

A QUICK FUCK WILL HELP

Sawyer

IVY'S ARREST is a bit shocking, to be honest. I can't say I didn't see it coming, but she's always been so good at staying under the radar and playing the system. Nearly five years together and I had no idea my wife had a sister. That her parents hadn't been killed in a car crash as she'd previously stated. She'd told such a convincing story.

Always so clever, that Ivy.

Imagine my surprise when the faces of her loving parents—Sebastien and Cristina Lacey—flash across my television screen.

Not just in picture either, but in motion.

Speaking.

Crying.

Very much alive.

"We just want justice for our daughter."

I really should have looked more closely into my wife's background, I see that now, recognize my mistakes. How unlike me not to cover my bases, to protect myself. I trusted her.

Maybe I *am* an idiot after all.

But the pieces will fall where they may. It's not my responsibility to save her anymore. The past does tend to catch up with us sooner or later.

It's likely, I suppose, that I'll be making a court appearance in the near future; there's no way whatever expensive law firm she hires won't want to have a chat with me, her legal husband.

Not that I have more information to share.

These thoughts flutter through my mind while I work on tonight's dinner, the television still set to the local news station as I prepare salmon and wild rice with asparagus. My lady friend should be arriving any minute now, so I need to get my mind off my wife and her extracurriculars.

But I've burned the salmon.

The rice is overcooked, the asparagus still raw.

This news is just too mind-boggling, and it's taking a minute to sink in. When my date finally knocks on the door, it's so soft I barely hear it, but I abandon the burned fish on the stove and punch the power button on the remote to turn off the TV and dissolve the images of my previously presumed dead in-laws.

I need company tonight.

A quick fuck should help me relax.

It always does.

I turn the deadbolt and pull the door open. For some reason she looks hotter today than usual, more…grown-up, sophisticated. And I must admit, it's nice. Sure, she's a little young for me, but she's damn good in the sack and, surprisingly, a near-perfect partner in crime despite my initial apprehensions.

What more could a guy ask for?

"Hi, baby," she says, stepping inside and delivering a peck on my cheek. "You took forever to let me in. Is everything okay?"

"Yes, sorry. I was cooking dinner." I flash a smile, tell myself to shake off the thoughts roaming through my head, and take in the sight of her.

My new mistress.

At her long, toned legs in those hot pink stiletto heels, the curve of her ass beneath her khaki coat. From the looks of it, there's not much under there, and she officially has my attention.

"Oh, how sweet, Grant! You didn't have to…"

Why she still calls me Grant, I have no idea. She knows my real name, has since the beginning. It's just a thing between us, I suppose. I can't say I mind, really. I feel less like Sawyer every day as it is.

That life seems to be behind me, preserved for nothing more than the memories that came of it.

"Yeah, well, it's uh—it's burned, the salmon. So…we can't eat it." She pouts, and somehow it's sexy despite its childish connotation. But she recovers quickly, untying the belt of her trench coat and sliding it off her shoulders. It drops to the ground, and *my God, she's beautiful.* All innocence is lost at the sight of her in *that* little number. It's sheer lace everywhere but between her legs.

Just like the outfits Alisha used to wear for me.

Yes, a quick fuck will definitely do.

"I assume you've seen the news?" she asks, dismounting me. She rolls onto her back, pulling the covers up to her torso, but leaving her tits exposed. I reach over and work a perky nipple through my fingers, my heart rate steadily decreasing. It always takes a moment to come down from the high of her.

"Right before you arrived, actually. That's how I managed to screw up dinner."

She giggles at my expense, and it's adorable the way her nose crinkles up. "You're quite the little investigator," I tell her.

She knows what the headlines said, the accusations behind them and what this means for me. For my wife, now that the world knows she's a killer.

"It wasn't hard," she admits with a wink. "The woman is almost *never* home, and when she is, she's usually passed out in her bedroom with the door locked. Hardly sees her kid—don't even get me started there."

"I can't say I'm surprised. She never wanted to settle down."

She rolls onto her side, burrowing under my arm and bringing a soft hand to my chest. "Trust me, babe, this will all work out. We did good."

"I have no doubt you'll make sure of it," I say. With my hand on her chin, I pull her to me and bring my lips to hers. Her lipstick is smudged, the remnants of the cherry red still trailing down my chest from our first go around.

"Round two already?" she asks, lifting the sheet and taking a peek at the tent I'm re-erecting.

I'm hard, what can I say?

It's the way she works those fingernails on my stomach, the playfulness in her eyes, the twitch of her upper lip. Maybe even the idea that this woman is nearly fifteen years younger than me and I can keep up with her, please her the way she deserves to be pleased.

Or perhaps it's the excitement of knowing she helped me put my wife behind bars.

The fact that she didn't ask any questions when I told her what I needed her to do.

"See what you do to me?" I growl, and she pulls me on top of her this time, yelping when I bring my mouth to her nipple and nibble it with my teeth. I can't help but moan myself when she grips my cock in her hand, wasting no time as she guides me to her still very wet center.

And I know I shouldn't do it, but I close my eyes, and for just a second I'm almost convinced it's not her I'm inside of. I shake the thought away, guilt gnawing at me from the inside.

This is not the time to be thinking about Alisha.

Not when this woman has done so much for me.

It's amazing what a woman will do for a little cash, though, isn't it? Stability often comes at a price, and she was willing to pay it, to go along with the plan I'd laid out before her. That's what this is about, after all: a plan.

Because my wife was a liability.

A wrinkle in an otherwise crisp bed sheet.

And who better to help me take her out of the picture than the nanny I delivered right to her doorstep? I just didn't think we'd end up in bed together, me and Caramie, but I guess we can chalk that one up as a perk of the job, hmm?

Oh, yes, she's definitely a perk of the job.

FIVE-STAR NANNY

Sawyer

Now, I know what you're thinking—I shouldn't be sleeping with my wife's twenty-five-year-old nanny, yeah, yeah. I'm a pig and I shouldn't have gotten involved because it couldn't possibly do any of us any good. Right? Am I close? Getting warmer?

I thought so.

But you don't know the whole story. It's not your fault, surely, you couldn't have seen this coming. See, the thing is, sometimes the obvious answer is right under your nose.

Sometimes the only way to keep the enemy close is to give them exactly what they want.

Fun fact: I've known Caramie a lot longer than my wife has.

In fact, Ivy has *me* to thank for her five-star nanny.

Of course, my intentions for bringing the two of them together were not good. Not in your eyes, anyway. But it needed to be done. Cara works for *me*—or *worked* for me, I should say, as my office manager at the firm. She didn't last long, not for lack of skill set, mind you; she performed the duties of the job just fine.

I simply saw potential in her…needed her for bigger and better things.

It was easy to see that she was more than capable of playing a much larger role in my continued success, from inside my estranged wife's home instead of the desk outside my office.

It helped that she's so easy on the eyes. The flirting between us started right away, within the first week if I remember correctly, and it wasn't long after that we were fucking on top of my desk in between meetings. We're a classic grumpy/sunshine story, Cara and I, but that's not what's important here.

The important thing is not to get caught.

It was planned before Ivy had the baby, while she was pregnant and doing everything she could to get me to stay. But I'd already moved out, started seeing Cara after hours, and things spiraled from there. There was a lot on the line for me; my reputation at the firm didn't need the kind of scrutiny that follows an office affair. And Caramie certainly deserved better than to look like a homewrecker, should the news travel back to the wrong party.

But she knew my predicament, how Ivy wanted to ruin me.

She offered to help, and I told her how she could. I'd earned her trust, then enticed her with some money. And that's when the plan came together.

Like I said, I didn't think she'd be so quick to jump on board, but she was all in. Ready and willing to help me cut ties with my wife for good. To take her out of the game even though I knew she'd go down swinging.

By the time Ivy had the baby, we were ready. The plan was in motion; Cara had been let go from the firm—things *just didn't work out*—and we'd put together her profile on the nanny finder website.

Which is why she's now employed by my wife, which technically means I'm the one paying her, but it's legit on paper, despite our cruel intentions.

She even got a pay bump and a place to stay. I needed her eyes inside of my house, to watch Ivy, to watch the safe in my office until I could get in there and empty it out. I'd left so quickly when shit hit the fan that I didn't take much with me. I wasn't able to get the safe cleared, and there was useful information in there.

And that's where Cara initially came in.

The plan was for her to work for Ivy for a bit, and when she'd had enough of Ivy's bullshit, she'd quit. It was simple, sure, but believable, considering the situation. My wife is not an easy woman to get along with, as you may have figured out.

The thing is, I didn't necessarily trust her with the safe yet. I couldn't bring myself to give her the key code right off the bat. She needed to prove herself first; show me she could pull off the illusion.

It wasn't long before I realized Cara was nothing like Ivy. She wasn't about to screw me over. In fact, Caramie came up with a better idea, something that would work even more in our favor, give us a little more bang for our buck.

Why not have her work for Ivy a little longer and see what she could dig up on her while I wasn't around? I knew our divorce would be messy, I just didn't know *how* messy it'd be and I wanted a bigger insurance policy.

Ivy expected alimony, and a bite off my trust fund, despite the five-year marriage clause and the fact that she had another man's baby. Her lawyer was working on a way around that, apparently, as confirmed by Cara last week. Ivy thinks she's entitled to everything, but she's not. I just have to make sure she doesn't find a loophole; there's always a loophole. I mean, the woman hasn't worked a real job a single day in her life, but somehow she'd be entitled to *my* money, even once we split? Sorry, but really? No fucking thank you.

Caramie's plan was brilliant, it really was.

We'd build a case against her. Prove to a judge—if necessary—that Ivy's nightly activities made her not just an adulterer, but an unfit mother.

See, Ivy was working for Lady Ann again, and this time she wasn't keeping things kosher by any means. She didn't know I knew about her prior affiliation with the escort agency either, but the thing is, I'm pretty resourceful when I need to be; I was more than well aware of her transgressions in the bowels of that brothel.

What I hadn't expected was that she'd return to work for Lady Ann once we'd split, after Alisha's trial. I guess rejection will do that to a person, but who am I to judge?

It was Cara who thought well enough to share some additional information with me, when she started to question Ivy's whereabouts, her frequent absences at home.

"She leaves every night around seven and doesn't return until morning most days," she'd said.

"Where does she go?"

"I don't know, she's never said one way or the other, but she usually looks a little…disheveled…when she strolls in the next morning."

"Is she seeing someone?" An unexpected bout of jealousy slithered in my stomach as I asked, but I ignored it, told myself it didn't matter.

"Not that I know of."

I knew Cara would come through for me, I did. Her obsession with my cock bodes well for me in more ways than one, and well, can you blame her? She's dedicated, let's just say that.

But I had no idea she would uncover what she uncovered, what she'd find.

She's even brighter than I gave her credit for.

And it'll come to light, very soon it will.

"We should follow her. See what she's up to," I suggested. My curiosity was more than piqued; I needed to know what my estranged wife was up to.

"How am I supposed to do that when I'm taking care of her kid all the time?"

"Oh, that's easy."

She raised a brow, the obvious answer not quite there for her yet. "We hire a babysitter," I said.

"*I'm* the babysitter."

"Right. But who says you can't babysit Ivy instead?"

.   .   .

So, we played house. Cara brought baby Dylan to my place, and together we pretended to be the doting mother and father in desperate need of some time out of the house. We interviewed a few local teenagers looking to make some extra cash.

Then we hired one.

And we followed Ivy to Lady Ann's that night, straight to the place where it all began. Of course, I neglected to let Cara in on that little secret, that I had ties to the place, too.

She waited in the car, on lookout in case Ivy came out early. Really, it was more of a way for me to maintain my cover; people would recognize me in there. They'd know who I was. Hell, I still had the credentials to get in, too.

I put Cara on camera duty. She stayed busy securing the evidence as I went through the main doors. Masquerade night, to my surprise. The easiest events to get into and subsequently back out of, should anything go wrong.

Once I was through security, I made my way around the rooms in search of my darling wife, hopeful she didn't spot me in the sea of sex addicts among us. It was clear within minutes that Lady Ann had found some more lucrative ways to run her business in the time since I'd been gone. Security had been upgraded, the women sexier than ever, more daring, more bedroom doors intentionally left open. The men were going from room to room, taking their turns without reprimand.

And I tried to resist, I did.

But my cock was hard, fighting against the zipper of my trousers, and there was little I could do to stop myself from participating once the arousal hit me.

I managed to find the room, the one she was in.

I watched her.

She looked stunning as always; orgasms had a tendency to do that to her, to bring light to her eyes. Dark corners do a gawker like me wonders in that place, let me tell you. It was easy to hide in the shadows, to observe. The hidden camera in my masquerade mask captured all the ammo I needed.

And once I had her face on video, her transgressions documented from inside the house, the deal was done.

With the camera switched off, I saw myself out of the room and entered another, this time releasing my cock from my pants and taking a turn on a blonde in a pair of black leather boots.

The only thing I did that Ivy didn't bother to do that night was close the door.

I shoved my guilt aside, proud of my night's work. Cara would be none the wiser to my little mishap, and with the video evidence I'd captured, surely no judge in the world would grant Ivy alimony after witnessing proof of her illicit affairs, right?

I had her.

WE GOT BOOBS

Ivy

I HAD A BEST FRIEND ONCE. I imagine that's a little hard to believe, perhaps even sounds a little fictional given what you've learned about me, but it's true. Her name was Joy, and she was the very definition of the word. A bright light in my otherwise dark world.

In the grand scheme of things, I suppose our friendship wasn't all that life-changing, but back then? Back then it felt like we were destined to be friends forever, attached at the hip, and I pictured us old and senile in our rockers, still causing trouble into our old age.

We'd been inseparable since kindergarten, having been assigned as table partners in Ms. Olsen's class, and decided that meant we had to do everything else together, too. Joy came from a good home—an *actual* good home, not the kind I pretended to be from—and she was an only child without the clichéd, spoiled rich girl attitude to go along with the title. The Tiernan family was the epitome of every '90s sitcom ever written.

And I wanted in.

I spent as much time at the Tiernan household as I could. Joy and I baked cookies with her mom on Sundays, and I often tagged along to family outings. Valley Fair, shopping trips to the Mall of America, the Minnesota State Fair, movie nights, day trips to one of Minnesota's ten thousand lakes. It didn't matter where, as long as I didn't have to be at home with my own family.

Joy felt more like a sister to me than Erika ever did, and that meant something in my book.

In sixth grade we both got boobs.

In ninth grade we shared our first cigarette—and hated it.

In eleventh grade she got her first boyfriend, and later that year, I got drunk and had sex with him at a party. We vowed never to tell her, promised each other it was a one-time thing and would never happen again.

The thing is, I was upset, hurt.

I'd been rejected, and I didn't know what to do with that.

Earlier that week, I kissed Joy.

It was stupid and I don't know why I did it. I knew I shouldn't have, but I did it; I couldn't take it back, and it ruined our friendship. Joy didn't understand; she didn't feel what I felt when I looked at her. She wasn't curious like I was.

She wasn't confused.

My lips were on hers, and I never wanted to break them apart. But her palms pressed heavily against my chest as she shoved me away, like she had no idea who I was and why I was there.

"Gross, Ivy! Why would you do that?" she'd barked in disgust, literally wiping the taste of me from her lips, smearing her Dr Pepper lip balm all over the sleeve of her sweater.

"I'm so sorry," was all I could think to say. She was crying then, actually *crying*, the tears streaming down her cheeks like her grandmother had just died.

A person should never cry like that over a kiss.

A kiss is supposed to be a happy moment, like fireworks in the summertime.

But she cried, and that made everything worse—the embarrassment, the shame. It was all too much.

It hit me then, the reality of the situation. The finality of our friendship after so many years. My best friend was homophobic. How had I let that fact slip by? I should have known, should have noticed the warning signs, but I was too immersed in *her* to see them.

"Don't ever talk to me again!"

And just like that, she was gone. Joy had been sucked from my life, eliminated, all because I couldn't keep my stupid feelings to myself. Our friendship, the memory of her and all the firsts we'd shared, would forever be tarnished.

That should have been the end of it.

But it wasn't, not by a long shot.

Because it was later that week, at Savvy Drayer's Valentine's party, that I saw her again. We locked eyes across the room, and she glared at me with such disdain that I couldn't look away. I saw something change in her eyes.

It didn't help that she was there with my bratty, fifteen-year-old sister who was supposed to be at home writing a paper for her government class. They stood there together, watching me, both of them giggling behind cupped hands as they sipped from their Solo cups and shared secrets that weren't theirs to share.

I balled my fists, squeezed tightly so the fingernails left little crescent moons on my palms. The pain was good—necessary—because without it I didn't feel human.

I needed to feel human.

That's when I went upstairs to find Trevor, the aforementioned boyfriend.

I didn't think, just took him by the hand and drug him into an empty bedroom. He didn't ask questions, didn't harbor any more remorse than I did, so what did we have to lose?

The sex was quick, sloppy and awkward, as it always is at that age. But I'd done what I set out to do. I took my revenge, and I'd do whatever I needed to do with it when the time came.

They continued dating until evidence of our betrayal found its way to the internet later that summer. Somehow, overnight, I became the star of a show I didn't know I was performing in, and my do-no-wrong sister was both the director and producer.

That's right, my own flesh and blood sold me out and uploaded a video of me having sex with my best friend's boyfriend onto the internet.

She'd followed me—*us*—into that bedroom, and recorded the whole thing on her flip phone through a crack in the door.

Erika was smart about it, too.

She held onto that video clip for months, somehow managing to keep it a dirty little secret until she saw just the right opportunity and took it.

That's when it all started really, the beginning of the end.

When I made the decision to kill my sister.

That sex tape didn't just expose my most intimate moments and body parts; it exposed my sister's true colors, her ill-intent. She was more dangerous than she looked.

She was the enemy.

Before school started in the fall, my senior year, the entire school had seen the video, probably even saved it to their desktop computers, their flash drives. The eyes could not unsee.

Same went for my parents.

And Trevor's, and Joy's, and the school principal. The list goes on and on.

I no longer had a best friend.

I no longer had a sister.

And unlike Trevor, who was high-fived by his chauvinistic friends and only mildly reprimanded by his parents because, hey, *we're just glad you didn't get her pregnant*, I was ruined.

Disowned by every single person I knew, including my parents. Grounded for the foreseeable future, likely until I turned eighteen, even longer if I chose to stick around.

The only thing left on my mind after that was revenge.

My sister was going to pay for what she had done.

I'd known long before then that Erika had a problem, that her soul was no less dark than my own. Her heart had filled with hate long before mine did, so I like to think she had it coming in the end.

She did this to herself.

345

DEAR DIARY

Ivy

IT NEVER DOES TAKE MUCH for a sane person to come unhinged. Not much at all. The screw can wiggle loose right under your nose, and you won't even realize it until it's too late. A snide comment can be made softly under someone's breath, a dirty look shot in your direction. If done at just the wrong moment, watch out.

I don't recall the exact moment I snapped. I *want* to—I think it could be helpful to know—but I don't. All I can say is that one day I was okay, and one day I wasn't. I could sit here and blame any number of things like I tend to do, but the truth is, deep down I always knew something was *off*, that I could lose it at any moment.

I could feel it in my bones.

There was a storm brewing, and I was ready to unleash it.

The cloud had hovered for far too long.

The dam was bound to break eventually.

And it did.

It broke, and there's one hell of a crack in the facade.

They've found something, the police.

I don't know what, but it feels big, maybe even monumental.

They've brought me back in for questioning, out of the cesspool that is the county jail, for what I imagine will be another several hours of curious word play.

I can't say I'm in the mood for any more today.

Jail is exhausting. Nobody really tells you that, that it's mind-numbingly boring to the point of exhaustion, and by the time you realize it, it's too late. You're there and you can't leave, no matter what you do or who you know.

Detective Raylen finally joins me and my lawyer, Kelly Moon, in the interview room, his usual smug expression plastered on his face. He carries in a white file box, my name and case number scribbled on the side of it.

I'd think it were a scare tactic, just an empty box for show, if it didn't make such a thump when he set it down.

"Care to explain these?" he asks, opening the cardboard lid and pulling several books out of it. It takes a moment to sink in, to realize what he's holding in his hands, but when I do, I can't hold back my surprise. The sharp intake of breath, the hand to my chest.

They found my diaries.

I'd like to say I'm baffled, shocked even, but I'm not. It's a surprise to see them after all the time they've been missing, but the fact that they've come into the possession of the police isn't that unexpected, considering. Sure, I'd have locked them in the safe if I'd known they were on to me, but that opportunity never presented itself. I was preoc-cupied; it all happened so fast.

Sawyer.

He's the only explanation, really. He would know where to look, was well aware of all the little nooks and crannies of the home we once shared. I wonder how long he's had them.

"I didn't even know you kept a diary," he'd said when I asked him if he'd seen them.

It had to be him.

Fuck.

I've written some questionable things in those diaries—damning things. And those words are all in the wrong hands now. The proof in the pudding.

I know I should say something now, but the words are lodged behind my lips, stuck like taffy on the roof of my mouth, and all I can do is savor their flavor before I eventually swallow them.

"Mrs. Rogers, I asked you a question," Raylen says, pulling the first book from the pile and running his fingers along the colored tabs sticking out of the pages. He flips to a yellow tab, exposing one of hundreds, maybe thousands, of private entries in a book I wrote but never intended to share.

"I heard you," I finally mutter.

There, I've said something. I'm not mute after all.

"Great. And?"

"And...I didn't realize you were such a book nerd."

"I'm not. But I did find this one rather interesting," he taunts, waving the book in front of him. "I'll read you a passage."

"That's not necessary."

"Oh, I think it is. Unless you'd rather summarize it for me? I'm sure Kelly will be interested in what we've found here. You may be familiar with the content, though, yes?"

"Why do you ask a question when you already know the answer?"

"So, you *do* know what these are then? I don't need to explain them to you, read them verbatim until we're all blue in the face?" Raylen's eyes roam the room, and I see Kelly make eye contact with him before writing something in her notebook. She knows I'm guilty; any doubt she may have had is surely gone now that my diaries have been exposed.

It probably changes things, but she has to defend me anyway. I'll remind her of that if I have to. Can't let her forget who she's working for, can I?

It's slow, but I shake my head no in response to Raylen's final question.

The wheels in my head turn rapidly.

There's no positive way to spin this.

I'm fucked.

IVY ROGERS DIARY ENTRY
SEPTEMBER 4, 2004

It's hard to say what normal is any more. Were we all born "normal," only for some of us to later turn insane, or did a select group of us just start out this way? Maybe the beast festers all along, ready to awaken at any given moment, for any given reason.

Maybe there's one inside of all of us.

I like to think so anyway.

The thought is oddly comforting, but I'm not sure why.

Mom says I have too many mean bones in me, that sometimes they break. I don't think that's a thing, but I overheard her say that to Dad last night after I was sent away from the dinner table. My attitude, apparently, wasn't on their agenda for the evening. And that's fine, I don't care. She's a shitty cook anyway, and I'll just sneak out to McD's or something after they go to bed.

But it's all bullshit, because Erika's attitude was way worse than mine, and she wasn't asked to leave, so I think that tells me all I need to know.

She was at that party too, fucked in the head just enough to capture my sexual activities on camera, then later to share them with the world.

Not that she suffered much in terms of consequences, not the way I did. She wasn't banished to her bedroom for all hours of the day, no phone, no TV, no computer. It's like they wanted to reward her for catching me in the act.

Like they were proud of her because at least she knew what I was doing was wrong.

See, nothing ever changes around here. It doesn't matter how hard I try to show them, to help them see that she is the problem.

It's fucked-up, but sometimes I think about killing her.

There. I said it. I've been holding that in for a while now, but I can't do it anymore. I just can't.

It's...I dunno, weird, to think that way, right? I know it is, but it's true, and you're only supposed to write true things in a diary, so that's what I'm trying to do here. It's not like anyone is ever going to read this.

I think I could do it, though. Kill my sister. I never miss her when she's gone and wouldn't care less if she got hurt. One time she broke her wrist playing kickball in gym class. It was a few years ago, looked super gnarly, but also kinda cool. Anyway, she was a cry-baby about it, and all I wanted to do was break the other one, too. I mean, who breaks their wrist, of all things, playing kickball?

Those next few weeks afterward were a nightmare. Mom made me do everything for her, short of wiping her ass; luckily it was the other wrist that broke. But they even bought her a little bell, and fuck her for using it so religiously.

Fuck them for making me tend to her needs.

Here's the thing, I'm done playing nice. I can't do this anymore. I can't sit here and let her rule the roost forever.

I have to do something.

And I think we're all capable of something *big, something seemingly unimaginable. Maybe it's not as unimaginable as we think. Maybe society just wants us to think it is.*

Anger is normal.

Fear is normal.

Maybe the urge to kill is, too.

The decision to protect your own life above all others? It's primal. Instinctual. Animals do it every day; all the nature programs tell us that. So, if it's okay for animals, why can't it be okay for humans?

Maybe we just need to normalize it somehow—every he, she, they, them, and child for themselves.

The weak ones will fall first.

Like Erika.

She's my prey, and I'm the hunter now.

She won't even smell me coming.

SHIT STORM

Sawyer

I KNEW ABOUT THE DIARIES.

Of course I did. A man knows what goes on in his own home, even when it looks like he doesn't. It was a while ago, though, when I found them, probably a few years. I didn't bother to read them at the time—that was my mistake. I really could have ended this a lot sooner had it not been for my laziness. I was distracted with other things, what can I say?

I should have known there'd be something newsworthy within those pages.

Who in their right mind stumbles upon the innermost thoughts of *the* Ivy Rogers and doesn't bother to take a peek at those words?

An idiot, that's who.

Deep down I must have known. Maybe I wasn't ready to learn what she was hiding. I always knew there was something, but this? Definitely not what I imagined. All I knew at the time of my discovery was that those diaries would be useful someday. That's why I hid them under the floorboards in our room instead of returning them to her. She'd been looking for them for a while, was frustrated that she lost them, but I knew I'd give them a read eventually, maybe take a gander once things settled down a bit. I wasn't ready to give them back.

But I had other shit to do, like make nice with the leader of an organized crime ring.

I had a pay day to secure.

The diaries slipped my mind until recently, until this shit storm with Ivy started blowing in and I needed some reassurance, a way to make sure my wife kept her nose out of my affairs. It was Caramie who came through for me, though. Those diaries and proof of my ties with the Ehrens-Havenbrook Corporation were the smoking gun in that house after I left, the damning evidence I needed to regain possession of.

And my lover—the nanny to my wife's illegitimate son—was more than willing to retrieve them for me. She came in hot with the ace of spades in the last hand, she did.

I won't need her much longer, but part of me thinks I should keep her around, see what else she brings to the table. The thing is, I'm not sure what else she's good for yet, but she's loyal, I'll give her that.

The words feel hollow even as I say them. I know I'm a douche, but hey, I never said I was a nice guy.

Surely you know this, too.

But if this doesn't work, if I can't make Ivy go away and stay in Connor Ehrens's good graces at the same time, I may have to resort to more permanent measures, call in a few favors.

The last thing I need is my wife spilling secrets.

You don't mess with Connor Ehrens and his business, you just don't. The man has killed for much less, and let's just say I wouldn't want to meet him in a dark alley after crossing him, if you know what I mean.

Besides, the way I see it?

I've done my wife a favor.

With any luck, she may just end up right where she wants to be.

BUT WAIT, THERE'S MORE

Ivy

I'M uncomfortable with the knowledge that my diaries are now under a microscope, spread open for anyone and their mother to do with what they please. Detective Raylen has left the room and I sit here now with my lawyer, likely for another umpteen hours.

And Kelly Moon is fiery this afternoon, let me tell you. I knew she was scrappy before she even opened her mouth. The business suit she's wearing today looks like it was made for her, the way it's tailored to hug her curves without over-sexualizing her is impressive.

I don't want to need her, but I do. Raylen's claws are in deep, and I'm not sure I can stop the bleeding on my own.

Not to say that I like her or anything, but her services are necessary, so here we are.

"The State has brought forth some additional evidence, Ivy—can I call you *Ivy?* Mrs. Rogers still feels a little channel-two-ish."

I nod, careful not to chuckle and give her the impression that I'm enjoying our scheduled girl time. "What evidence?"

"I assume you were unaware you were being filmed?"

Her words cut like a knife to my gut. I can only assume she's talking about *before*—about my armature porn debut from high school, but the look on her face tells me otherwise.

This is something new.

"*What?* When?"

"Do you work for an escort service called Lady Ann?"

Oh no.

"Excuse me?"

"Do you?"

"What's it to you?" Her face softens at my rebuttal, and I almost feel bad for snapping at her, but to be honest, I'm getting a little sick of random evidence finding its way into our discussions.

"I'm your lawyer, Ivy," Kelly says. "That means I'm in your corner, and you should at least try to be honest with me. I don't care what you *actually* did, I'm just here to make sure you don't end up spending the rest of your life in prison."

Fair enough.

Kelly Moon: 1

Ivy Rogers: 0

"So, I'll ask you one more time. Do you work for an escort service called Lady Ann?"

"Yes."

"I thought so." She reaches into an oversize satchel and pulls out a stack of documents, sliding them over to me one at a time before leaning back in her seat and folding her arms across her chest.

It takes a moment for it to sink in, what she's showing me.

Pictures.

Surveillance photos.

Of me.

At Lady Ann's.

Where no cameras or cell phones are allowed.

"Look familiar?" she asks.

I nod with apprehension, but it's not the pictures that render me speechless—that increase my heart rate and threaten to send me into a full-blown panic attack.

It's the flash drive she's holding between her fingers.

There's more.

"This," she starts, waving it tauntingly in the air, "is your new worst enemy. Any guesses what's on it?"

It only takes me one.

But she's wrong.

These videos aren't my new worst enemy.

Kelly Moon doesn't know what's in those diaries.

"Were you aware you were being recorded?"

"No."

So, here I am, involved in yet another sex tape scandal. *How did this happen*, one might wonder. I can't overlook the irony; a sex tape started all this. I suppose it'll end it, too.

It's almost more unexpected this time around.

I had no idea these recordings existed outside of the ones I took part in willingly—the ones Sawyer and I made together—but these aren't from Sawyer's personal collection. I'd recognize those, and he's in them, too, so there'd be no point in sharing them since they'd ruin him, too.

These are new.

Recent.

Taken at Lady Ann's sometime *after* I resumed my employment. From the looks of it, just a few weeks ago.

And this time, there's more at stake for me. This time I have so much more to lose. And I wouldn't mind, really. If it weren't for my son and the trust fund, and the fact that I'm determined to get my hands on that money.

All this time, and Sawyer still found a way to back me into a corner.

I just don't know how.

Or better yet, *why* these videos matter in the grand scheme of things.

It has literally nothing to do with the fact that my sister is dead.

So why am I being questioned about them?

MOTHER DEAREST

Ivy

My first appearance is today.

In court, in front of the judge.

It's bittersweet, this formality, but in a way I welcome it. It's time to set things in motion, get this show on the road. I'm tired of sitting around waiting for what happens next.

First-degree murder.

It sounds so official, so permanent.

Like there's no way out of this, no matter how I spin it.

But all they have are my diaries, circumstantial evidence at best, right? What can they really prove with those words?

Anyone could have written them.

The videos of me at Lady Ann's mean nothing in relation to my case, merely a show of character I can easily talk my way around. Surely they won't do any damage when all is said and done, they're just a scare tactic. I'm a sex worker, so what?

That doesn't prove I'm a murderer.

It's simply an unfortunate coincidence.

I stand now, with Kelly at the defense table, my wrists shackled to my waist, hands shaking. The clink of the chains giving me away, despite the confidence I have that I'll be going home today.

It's all a bit unfair, though, in my opinion. How I have to sit here in this hideous orange jumpsuit, chained together like an animal, unable to scratch my own nose with ease. If we're innocent until proven guilty, why don't they at least let us wear our own clothes to these things?

I *look* like a criminal today.

Hell, I feel like one, too.

First time for everything, I guess.

"All rise...the honorable Judge John Waskey presiding."

Well, he doesn't look so bad, this judge. Just a regular old guy in a fancy robe, probably somebody's grandfather, a damn fine canasta player.

I like to think so, anyway.

The courtroom is seated, Kelly and I included, and I can't help but wish I had something to drink. She warned me about this, the scratchy throat and how nervous people get once they're in the hot seat.

"The Court will now call the State of Minnesota vs. Ivy Jean Rogers, case number..."

Judge Waskey clears his throat and shifts briefly in his chair. At the sound of his voice, he's no longer someone's grandfather, but rather the next man I aim to please. Not that I have any clue how I'll do that in this getup, but nonetheless, I find myself sitting up a little straighter, smiling, doing my best to look like an innocent offender. "Parties, please state your appearances," he says.

"May it please the Court, the State appears by Scott Pender."

"May it please the Court, Ms. Rogers appears in person and with her attorney, Kelly Moon."

So formal, they sound.

This is weird.

It hits me then, the seriousness of all this. The fact that everyone in this courtroom already thinks I'm guilty. There's a certain look in their eyes now, a distrust of sorts.

"We are here for a first appearance in this matter. In this complaint,

Ms. Rogers, you are charged with one count of murder in the first degree. Do you understand what you are charged with in this case?"

"Yes, your Honor," I state with as much conviction as I can muster. I want to say more, claim my innocence, but Kelly insists this isn't the time for that.

"Judge, we ask that my client be released on her own recognizance. Ms. Rogers has no prior criminal history, and is a pillar of the community. She and her husband donate thousands per year to the Minnesota Community Foundation, among other charitable giving. She has stable housing, financial means, and will be happy to await trial from the comfort of her home, where she can remain with her young son."

"State?"

"Judge, the State feels that Ms. Rogers is not only a flight risk, but a danger to the community. She is charged with murder in the first degree, which carries a life sentence, if convicted. We would ask that bond be set in the amount of one million dollars."

Fuck you, Scott Pender. A million dollars? Is he serious?

It's quiet for a moment, as Judge Waskey makes his considerations. I don't expect it, the words that come from his mouth next, and I sure hope Kelly's paying attention because once he drops the first bomb, I don't hear the rest.

"Given the nature of the crime, bail is set today at one million dollars..."

I find myself in the visitor's center the next morning, fully expecting to see Sawyer or even Caramie sitting in the chair across from me, preferably letting me know my bail is being paid and that I'll be released soon.

I can't wait to wash the stench of this place off, take a hot bath, and drink a bottle of wine.

But it's neither of their faces I see when I walk in there; it's not their eyes looking back at me when I reach for the phone on the wall.

It's my mother's.

That's right, *the* Cristina Lacey is here in the flesh, finally reuniting with the daughter she wishes she never had. And she doesn't look happy, not one bit.

Not that I blame her.

Sixteen years have passed since I last saw her face. Sixteen years since I've heard her voice, or felt the sting of the accusations in her eyes. I almost can't believe she's here, but then again, she'd go anywhere—do *anything*—for her precious Erika, wouldn't she?

So, of course she's here.

I suck in a breath and take a tentative seat across from her; I don't envision this going well, so I'm not sure how long I'll sit with her, or why I do at all. She hasn't earned the right to speak to me, not after all this time. I know I should turn around and head back to my holding cell, pull an Alisha and refuse to see her.

But for some reason, I don't.

For some reason, I suddenly want nothing more than to hear my mother's voice.

We reach for the phone at the same time, placing the plastic receivers to our ears, our heads unknowingly tilting at the same time, in the same direction.

Like mother, like daughter.

"Ivy."

She says my name, and it sounds weird on her lips. I imagine it tastes bitter, like an overripe grapefruit. I spot the tears in her eyes, but I know she wants to hold them back more than anything.

I don't speak, just look at her. At the age lines on her forehead, crows' feet around her eyes. The sagging of her chin, her neck. She looks old.

Not at all like I remember.

A single tear rolls down her cheek, and despite my resolve, I look away. I never could stand to see her cry. It's one of the reasons I left, why I never went back, despite the many attempts both of my parents made to get me to come home.

I couldn't after what I'd done.

The guilt only set in when they were around, and I simply couldn't live that way.

"Why'd you do it, Ivy?" she asks, and it's barely above a whisper, like she can't quite bring herself to say it. Like she doesn't want to believe what she's heard.

That's it, though—all it takes for me to break.

Two point five seconds.

She's not here for me.

This isn't a mother and daughter reuniting. This is a mother seeking answers—seeking justice—for a dead daughter she can't seem to let go of.

"How could you kill your own sister?"

I just don't have the words, certainly not the ones she wants to hear. This is *her* fault, *her* actions—Dad's actions—led to Erika's death, not mine.

But I don't tell her this.

She won't understand.

Instead, I stand and hang the phone back onto the wall. I nod to the corrections officer standing guard at the door and wait for him to approach. I watch my mother drop her head into her hands, I listen to her muddled cries, the long sobs with big fat tears that land in splotches on the dirty counter.

The same tears I remember shedding for so many years, while she doted on my baby sister and taught me the meaning of the word neglect.

My mother had two daughters.

And she lost one of them long before her favorite one was murdered.

It's true what they say, I guess: what goes around comes around.

So sorry to break your heart, Mother dearest.

SEX LIKE THIS

Sawyer

I USED to think Ivy was in control of her life, of her own destiny. She may have been somewhat crazy, yes—okay, a lot crazy—but she knew what she was doing and why. She had an explanation, a reason, for everything.

I loved that about her, the control she had on life.

Along with her free spirit, her desire to try anything once, and her ability to think outside the box. These days? These days that take on life is kicking her ass. Part of me feels guilty; I've played a role in her legal issues, as you know, but the logical side of me says she did this to herself, regardless of the role I played.

These are the thoughts roaming around my head as I fuck Cara for the second time today. I should really focus on what I'm doing here, stay in the moment, but my wandering mind won't settle. At least my dick is focused on the job. We're going strong, doggy style, so she can't see my face, how distracted I am.

I imagine that'd be an uncomfortable conversation.

Cara has surprised me, though. She's turned into a bit of a sex fiend and I love it, how easy she was to manipulate. I don't think she's all that different from the former women who've occupied my bed. If I didn't know better, I'd think she was born from their combined souls.

She has the curiosity of Ivy—the drive, and unfiltered thoughts, opinions.

But she carries the same unbridled ambition and force of nature as Alisha, too, the exotic beauty.

Alarm bells go off in my head every time I welcome her; there's just something about her. She's young, off-limits. A well-educated but sheltered mind hidden behind lingerie and closed doors, when all she wants is for the world to see her.

I can't let them see her yet, I can't.

And she knows it; she knows why our relationship is taboo, why it's meant to be kept in the dark. If you ask me, that's a small price to pay for sex like this. Yeah, yeah, I realize that makes me sound ridiculously shallow, but you and I both know I don't give a shit.

I'm a man.

With needs.

I won't apologize for that.

In the afternoon, Caramie and I drive back to the house—my former home, soon to be Ivy's former home when I move back in and stick all her belongings in storage. It's cold of me, I know, but I'm certain she'll be taking up residency elsewhere for the foreseeable future.

I hear her first appearance didn't go as she'd hoped.

Which is why the trip to the house is on the docket for today. There's a key fob in the safe I need to retrieve and encryption codes to recapture so I can finally move this money and get Connor Ehrens off my back.

The only real problem I seem to have now is that baby. Caramie is still caring for him while Ivy is away, which means I'm inadvertently stuck with him again. I need to find a way to remedy that issue, maybe suggest foster care or something, and make a mental note to discuss his custody with her. Today's not that day, though.

Today I have more pressing matters to tend to.

"Sawyer?" Caramie's voice interrupts my thoughts. "You're off in la la land…"

"Sorry, just some things on my mind."

"Anything I can help with?"

"No, beautiful, nothing for you to worry about."

"Are you looking forward to moving back home?"

"I am. It'll be nice to get out of the condo and back into the house. I've missed this place."

We pull into the drive and I enter the security code at the garage, grateful Ivy didn't get around to changing it, which is the first thing I'll take care of when we get inside.

She may be someone else's problem now, but I wouldn't put it past her to find a way to send someone over here to protect her agenda.

With the garage code changed, I head upstairs to my office, half expecting Ivy to have redecorated it but pleased to find it untouched. I remove the picture from the wall to expose the safe, entering the code with excitement coursing through my veins.

This is it.

The moment I've been waiting months for.

Time to put my life back together.

But the alarm sounds when I press enter, a warning signal indicating the code has been entered incorrectly.

That's weird.

Assuming I fat-fingered it, I try again, this time pressing the digits carefully, methodically.

A second warning is triggered.

I only get one more before the security company is called.

But I don't try a third time.

Because it's clear Ivy has already gotten to the safe.

And now I have a much bigger problem.

BLOOD-SUCKING LEECH

Ivy

SENIOR YEAR of high school is supposed to mean something. Every teenager knows that going into it—that it'll probably be the best year of their lives and until they get married and pop out a few kids, they'll have peaked.

I refused to peak.

Not that I had much choice in the matter after the sex tape incident, but still, I had plans. I wanted more from life, a chance to stand out from the crowd, make a bigger splash than the other fish in the pond. That's why I got into acting. My art was unique; it was special. I was talented, an above-average scholar with a knack for the arts.

But my wholesome image had been tarnished—obliterated. The new image I portrayed wasn't one I was ready to wear at first, but it grew on me, in a way. Or I grew *into* it. Even though my so-called "sex scandal" happened over the summer, before the start of the school year, the issue followed me into the halls. And trust me when I tell you, no one wants to walk into their senior year of high school with a target on their back.

But that's exactly what I did.

And instead of cowering and lowering my head, I wore that target as proudly as I could, pretended the condescending looks didn't bother me, that I didn't need the acceptance of my classmates.

Everyone in school knew what I'd done—saw the evidence—teachers and faculty, included. If nothing else, they heard about it. Personally, I didn't think it was any of their business, but I was used to my opinion being moot.

Now I was a slut, an impure young woman.

The judgmental stares, the sideways glances. The scoffs and down-cast eyes as they walked past me. I was practically a local celebrity.

And the fucked-up thing is, it could have happened to any one of them. I wasn't the only teenager having sex at that party; I didn't even know it was being recorded.

But none of that mattered.

The only benefit to my predicament was the newfound attention from the boys in school. A dick had been in my mouth, been inside me. Two dicks. Three. The list was growing because I allowed it to grow. The boys were finally interested in me, wanted to be with me to piss off their ex-girlfriends or write another name on their list.

And I was all for it. I was a legend among them, a conquest.

The game, despite my reasons for playing, was fun.

Sometimes I found myself watching it back, the video. There was something to learn from it, a desire to perfect my skills.

Erika caught me once.

She hated that I'd found a way to turn the ordeal into something positive, that it didn't appear to faze me as much as it once did. When she barged into my room that night, I didn't bother to pause the video, just let it play while she glared at it—and me—from the doorway.

"Can I help you?"

"Why would you let him do that to you?" she asked, her eyes revealing her adolescent ignorance. She wanted me to suffer, and I feigned the opposite just enough to piss her off more.

I shrugged, and because I wasn't sure what else to say, simply said, "I like it."

Erika folded her arms across her chest and diverted her eyes away from the screen. They kept creeping back though, just a split second here, a longer second there. She couldn't help but look, and I couldn't blame her. I looked good on screen—great, even.

Her jealousy was palpable.

At sixteen now, she was still a virgin, so I understood her curiosity. She'd probably never watched porn before, maybe even thought sex was only meant for birds and bees and didn't apply to human life forms.

She shook her head, denial still prevalent in her mind. "No... there's no way anyone would like that."

I popped up, rising to my feet and jamming a finger into the power button on the monitor. "Grow up, Erika. This is how guys are, how sex works. Don't act like you have a clue about any of it."

"It's not how they are, actually," she mumbled, her face settling into a pout.

"And how would you know that? You've dated what? Two guys? *Maybe* rounded second base if I'm giving you any credit. But not a step further, right? Do you even know what third base is?"

As much as I welcomed the argument, a chance to make her look as stupid as she sounded, as stupid as she always made *me* feel, she didn't take the bait, just moved on as if I hadn't insulted her. "Mom and Dad are still pissed."

"Yeah? Whose fault is that?"

"Don't kid yourself, Ivy. You're the one who had sex with your best friend's boyfriend."

"Why'd you do it, Erika?"

She shrugged, a smirk settling on her lips. "I guess I just felt like it."

Months before, Erika told our parents what she'd done and confessed to her discretion, as if she was disappointed in herself when really, she was nothing but proud. Pleased. She was the superior sibling, the one in control.

She ran to Mommy and told her just where to find it. How to watch it even. That's the worst part. She could have kept the information to herself, or at the very least, asked Mom to help her take it down before it went viral. But she didn't.

She purposely waited.

In that house, I stood alone. No one was ever in my corner.

My parents, of course, were livid, not so much at Erika, but at me. Their eldest daughter was a whore. It'd be sad if it hadn't been true.

I guess some things never change.

What bothered me most was that the video cost me the lead in the school play that year. The most important production I could've been a part of, on the last year of my high school acting career.

I wasn't even allowed to go to the show.

I knew that nothing I did would ever make my parents proud, for them to see me as more than just another body to clothe, a mouth to feed. I was a tax deduction with living quarters on the upper level of their modest, middle-class home.

Erika, on the other hand, had our parent's full interest.

She was a leech. A blood-sucking leech.

Not even a lobotomy could have saved her personality.

Still, they persisted. Rubbed my nose in her achievements, her success. It was worse after the tape, after I'd let them down so publicly.

"Ivy, did you hear your sister's good news?" Mom asked one night at the dinner table. I'd been pushing food around on my plate for the last ten minutes, unable to force myself to eat another casserole despite the grumbling in my stomach.

"Yep," I said without looking up.

"Isn't it wonderful? Second place in the tournament! As a sophomore!"

I dropped my fork, the metal clinking loudly against the porcelain. I didn't want to hear it anymore. I didn't give a flying fuck about my sister's tennis career. "Well, aren't you going to congratulate her?"

"Are you serious?"

"Ivy, manners," Dad chimed in.

"No! You guys missed *my* performances. All of them! *One* of you could have been there for *me*, but you always chose Erika instead. And now I didn't even get to participate this year and it's all *her* fault!"

"Your sister has a real chance at a scholarship, here, Ivy," Dad dared to say.

I shoved my plate away and got up from the table, my chair tipping and smashing against the wall, leaving a dent in the Sheetrock.

"Sit down, Ivy," Dad instructed calmly.

"Fuck you," I barked, the vein in my forehead about to burst.

Normally I wouldn't drop the f-bomb in front of my parents—I give myself a little credit there—but I'd had enough.

I didn't expect anyone to follow me upstairs, but it was only a few minutes later, after I'd thrown the contents of my desk onto the floor and flopped myself on the bed, when I heard a soft knock on the door.

It was Dad who tried to comfort me, despite my outburst. Dad who took a seat on the edge of my bed and rubbed my back like he used to when I was a child.

"What's going on, kiddo?" he finally asked.

"Nothing..."

"Doesn't seem like nothing." He nudged my shoulder, the gesture almost unexpected because of the infrequency of his affection toward me. I sat up, stunned, my expression stoic but likely leading him to the same realization.

That he wasn't good at showing me he loved me.

We sat in silence for a moment before he spoke again, inhaling awkwardly before the words spilled out. I'm sure he was desperate for a father-daughter teaching moment, but I think it's safe to say I didn't take his advice the way it was intended.

"You know, when life throws you a curve ball, you gotta hit it. Straight out of the park. There's no time to struggle with the curve, you just gotta swing and aim for the fences."

Dad and his sports analogies. I wish I could say that one went over my head, or that I fully understood the intention behind his words, but all they did was set everything in motion for me.

I didn't want to be second best anymore.

I didn't want to strike out on the curve.

I just wanted to matter.

To exist.

It's ironic, how my father's words ended up being the ones that took his precious daughter away, but hey…curve balls, am I right?

IVY ROGERS DIARY ENTRY

APRIL 12, 2005

LITERALLY *E V E R Y T H I N G is about Erika. She's like the Marsha Brady of our house. Stupid, nerdy, ugly Erika who gets all the attention, no matter what she does.*

I'm so sick of this shit.

Dad bought her a car. Imagine that, huh? For her sixteenth yesterday. Just gave her a car like it was a rite of passage for any sixteen-year-old.

Apparently, it is—for her, not me.

Because I never got a car from him when I turned sixteen. "We didn't have the money for one then, Ivy," Dad said. "Besides, you already have a car now."

She's rubbing it in my face, too. It's not brand new, no way Daddy could afford that, but it's nicer than mine—the one I bought and paid for my damn self—and that apparently gives Erika bragging rights.

He even filled up the gas tank for her, bought her some hot pink seat covers she can sit her pretentious ass on.

I want to take a shit on those stupid seat covers.

MAI TAIS

Ivy

IT TAKES a certain kind of person to do what I do, to seek revenge. I know this because I'm that certain kind of person. Hot-headed. Easy to anger.

Calculated.

Patient.

Filled with grievances and grudges I can't simply ignore, no matter how hard I try.

Like I told you before, I get it. I know I'm not normal in the eyes of society.

But remorse isn't really a word in my arsenal; I don't get that feeling in my gut like you do. I don't see the need to dwell on what I've done. What's done is done.

I deal with my shit.

And I deal with it the only way I know how.

Revenge.

Murder.

A new life.

That's what I need right now. A new life; a do-over. I don't think that's coming for me this time. I can't just pack up and move, run away to some foreign country and sip mai tais on a secluded beach with the best of them.

I *can* do something different, though.

I can shock them all, even you.

You'll see.

SHORT FUSE

Ivy

HIS HANDS MAKE *their way to my breasts and a shiver erupts in my spine. He's a gentle lover, more so than I could have imagined, and the pleasure, while welcomed, takes me a bit by surprise.*

When his lips meet mine, they're possessive, silencing me, and I welcome the intrusion by spreading my legs as he enters me.

"God, you feel so good." He moans against my neck and I relax into him, giving myself to him despite the alarm bells in my head.

This is wrong.

But it's so good, too.

Necessary.

"Aren't you going to arrest me, Detective?" I joke, and he smiles, the idea sparking something primal in him.

"Oh, now you like the cuffs, huh?" He winks and attaches a cuff to my wrist before securing the other end to the bed frame. I flashback to Dylan, to the sight of his body cold and lifeless, covered in blood. That morning with him was the last time I used handcuffs for sexual plea-sure, when I subdued him on his own bed, in his own home, and thought of his wife as I rode his cock.

This time will be different, I tell myself.

"*I know you did it, Mrs. Rogers,*" *Detective Raylen says. It stings, his words against my cheek, but he leaves them there like a permanent tattoo before he pulls away.* "*I have to take you in after this.*"

"*No, please. You can't.*"

"*I'm sorry, it's not my choice.*"

"*But…*"

I wake with a start, wet between my legs, anxious and longing for something that was never there after all. Something I can never have.

Detective Raylen. That's new.

How unexpected, this budding fantasy of mine. It's fitting, I suppose, considering the amount of time we've spent together lately. In such close proximity, no less.

It's still dark in my temporary cell, the lights dimmed in the common room on the other side of the locked door. My bunkmate snores softly beneath me, and without giving it another thought, I bring a hand to my clit and close my eyes.

This time Alisha will join us, and for the first time since they brought me here, I give myself just the release I need to keep fighting.

The object of this morning's wet dream sits across from Kelly Moon and me in the interview room several hours later. He's more unkempt than usual today, sporting a two-day stubble and a plaid shirt that's seen better days. Still, he looks good. Desirable. I have no doubt this man knows his way around the curves of a woman's body.

He runs a hand through his dark hair and I shift in my seat, my underwear damp as I watch the wheels in his head turn. When he finally speaks, he's laid out a legal pad, a pen resting alongside it, but he makes no attempt at note-taking.

"You were recently involved in a murder trial, were you not?" he asks.

"I was."

"The defendant in that trial seemed to believe *you* were the one who killed her husband, correct?"

"I'm aware of her claims, yes."

"And what do you make of her accusations?"

"I already testified on the matter, Detective. Perhaps you should request a copy of the transcripts? Save us both some time."

"I'd rather hear it from you."

"There's nothing to hear."

"My gut tells me otherwise."

"Sounds like you need some Tums."

He chuckles despite himself, as does Kelly, and I suppress a smile at the sight of it. He thinks he has me, that I'll cave and admit to the sins of my past. Surely, I must feel the need for repentance after all these years, right?

Wrong, next question, please.

"Tell me about your relationship with Alisha Thompson."

"There's nothing to tell; she no longer speaks to me."

"That's fine, I'm more interested in the past anyway. You two were involved romantically?"

"For a little while, yes."

"What happened?"

"She met her husband."

"And that upset you."

"That didn't sound like a question."

"It wasn't."

I see the challenge in his eyes, the desire to trap me, get me to stick my foot in my mouth. But I refuse to feed his ego. He'll need to try harder.

"Mrs. Rogers, did you kill her husband, Dylan Thompson?"

"Don't answer that," Kelly advises.

"No."

"Maybe you couldn't handle it, the idea of her with someone else."

"I was married myself, you know."

"Right. Yes, your husband—*Sawyer*—he's still in the picture?"

"No."

"So, he left you, too?"

"I wouldn't say *left*."

"No? That's interesting, considering he filed for divorce recently, did he not? That must have upset you."

"You seem to think I run on a short fuse, Detective."

"Do you?"

Yes.

"No."

"How did your husband's affair with Mrs. Thompson make you feel?"

"I'm sorry, I thought this was an interrogation, not a therapy session? Why all the questions about my former relationships?"

"I'm establishing a pattern."

"Of?"

"Jealousy."

"I don't get jealous."

"No? I wonder if Joy Braverman would disagree."

The mention of my former best friend sends my heart into my stomach, like a kick to the gut when I'm already down. It hurts, this reminder of what could have been. That the past can come back to haunt you even when you try to bury it.

"Why would—*what*? You've spoken with Joy?"

"Sure I have."

"Why?"

"She was a close friend of yours, yes? Of your sister's?"

"She and my sister were *not* friends."

"Joy seems to think they were."

"She's lying."

"I find that hard to believe."

"Why? You seem to have no problem believing *I* would lie. She's no less capable than I am."

"Again, I'm establishing a pattern here."

"You haven't caught me in a single lie."

"Perhaps I have."

"What makes you so sure?"

He slides a sheet of paper across the table. I know what it is, what the words are, and what sentences they make up.

It's a photocopy, but it holds the integrity of the original just the same.

IVY ROGERS DIARY ENTRY
AUGUST 4, 2006

I did it.

I killed my sister today.

I killed her and the only thing I feel is relief.

She's finally gone.

I have to call Joy. If I call her, she'll come to me. She'll hold me while I cry.

She'll forgive me.

Because who doesn't forgive someone after their little sister dies so tragically?

She has to.

I don't want to think about what happens if she doesn't.

SNAPPED

Ivy

EVIDENCE IS A FUNNY THING, isn't it? To think that we leave so many tiny traces of ourselves behind is kinda scary. But that's what we do; our DNA is everywhere, whether we leave it on purpose or not. A signature, if you will.

But somehow, in my case, they didn't need DNA to prove anything. They didn't need blood, or fibers, or hair, or even a verbal confession. I'd left them something much more damaging.

I don't remember writing the diary entry. Maybe I blocked it out, wanted to believe that I didn't do it, that I couldn't have possibly done something so stupid.

But it's a smoking gun.

A bullet that's reached its intended target.

IVY ROGERS DIARY ENTRY
AUGUST 4, 2006

She stole my best friend.

Right from under my nose. I've lost her, and she seems to have gone running straight to Erika. She had to know how much that would piss me off, right? Who the hell does she think she is?

Am I that replaceable?

We had plans, Joy and I. For life, the rest of high school, college. And now, all because I kissed her and ruined everything, she's nothing more than a stranger. A memory of the past.

I'm so fucking stupid.

I festered for hours, wallowed in nothing but my own pity, at the thought of my best friend and my only sister replacing *me* as easily as a weathered pair of sneakers.

I'm the chewed-up gum stuck to the sole at the bottom.

Joy's car trolled down the street and into our driveway slowly, like she wanted to scope out the place to make sure I wasn't there before committing to a parking spot. I watched from the shadowy bowels of the garage, my diary and pen in my lap as they pulled into the driveway and cut the engine.

I closed my diary and tucked it safely into the pocket of Dad's golf bag—it wasn't like he used it anymore—and stuffed the heavy tool behind my back, out of sight and into the pocket of my jeans before covering it with my shirt.

My heart ached at the reminder that I'd lost her, that she wasn't my best friend anymore. And now she was off gallivanting with my little sister, a girl she couldn't stand any more than I could growing up. A girl who put us in this predicament.

I've been telling her what she's like for years, how she'll do anything to protect herself. I was sure it was only a matter of time before she'd screw Joy over, too. I needed to help her, get her away from my sister.

The urge to pull her aside and talk to her was strong. To tell her again that I'm sorry, that I never meant to hurt her. But she didn't step out of the car, just used the crank to roll down her window and offer a tentative wave as Erika unfolded from the passenger seat.

Even that hurt, the sight of her looking so small, so afraid. I'd done nothing to give the impression that I was someone to fear, so the display took me by surprise.

"I don't bite, you know," I mumbled.

She pretended not to hear me, like my words were lost in the wind. I hated what we'd become: strangers in a familiar world.

"Oh, get over yourself!" Erika huffed with a flip of her hair. She slammed the car door behind her, slinging her purse over her shoulder and walking toward me. "Maybe you should've kept your legs closed," she whispered, shoving me in the shoulder before heading to the front door of the house.

I wanted to tackle her, shove her face into the concrete and make her bleed.

But I couldn't.

Not in front of Joy.

And Joy was finished with the conversation, I could tell. She rolled up her window, punctuating the act with a click of the automatic door lock. She waved goodbye—to Erika—and retreated down the driveway.

I huffed, muffling a scream, and stomped into the house and up to my room. I couldn't believe she had dismissed me like that.

And I didn't know what I'd done to instill such fear in her, it wasn't like my queerness—if that's even what it was, I wasn't sure—was contagious, and all I did was try to kiss her. There's no threat here.

Why can't she see that?

With the house quiet and Mom and Dad out for the night, I retrieved the tool from my desk and sneaked outside through the back door of the garage. To Erika's precious car parked on the street in front of mine. She didn't even take care of it, didn't appreciate it the way I would have. It was such a waste of Dad's money; she didn't deserve it.

It wouldn't be long now, before Erika emerged from her bedroom, gothed out in a mini skirt and black eyeliner, ready to attend a kegger at Kayla Fox's place.

Little did she know, she wouldn't be attending the party after all.

"You need Jesus, Ivy," she'd said to me earlier.

The last words my sister ever spoke to me, and I can't say she was wrong, but they're not words I dwell on. They certainly don't keep me up at night.

Our poor parents, huh?

IVY ROGERS DIARY ENTRY
AUGUST 4, 2006

I snapped.

It was bound to happen sooner or later.

Honestly, I'm surprised I was able to hold out this long.

I doubt she saw it coming, that she had any sense I was so close to losing it. It's unfortunate, really. She could have saved herself. Or tried to, but I doubt it would have mattered.

My mind was made up.

I looked down at my sister's battered body, at the thick stream of blood making its way through the cracks in the dirt, the tilt of her head unnaturally wedged in the ground, her leg folded beneath her. The jarring image did nothing but bring a smile to my face.

How lucky for me that she chose today, of all days, not to wear a seatbelt.

This couldn't have worked out any better.

I pushed to my feet and turned toward the vehicle a good twenty feet from the body, taking in what remained of the wreckage. Smoke from the engine polluted the air in dark plumes, glass sat littered in chunky shards on the ground around the base of the tree it had struck. It leaned to the left now, its massive trunk cracked at the base, the root unearthed.

Yet, the tree remained standing, erect and alive to see another day.

I couldn't say the same for Erika.

A head wound like that? Come on. Surely, she must've died on impact.

Such a shame, too.

Mom and Dad will be so heartbroken.

SEVENTEEN

Ivy

IT'S EERILY QUIET HERE.

I kinda thought it would be louder, in the county jail, but it seems the loudest thing in the room are my thoughts, all-encompassing and intrusive. There's a lot of time to think in here, to reflect, and I don't know what to make of that. I wonder how much they know, how much they think they can prove without any sort of confession on my end.

I'll go down swinging, though; it's what I do, thanks to my dad's great advice.

I suppose I had a good run. Sixteen years is a long time to get away with murder these days, if you think about it. In some ways, I always knew this day would come. Welcomed it, even.

I definitely wasn't expecting it yet, but shit happens.

All I can do now is keep my mouth shut.

Deny everything.

Although that didn't work out so well for Alisha, now did it?

I wonder if Sawyer knows I'm here, and how baby Dylan is doing with Caramie. I haven't called home yet. It's not like I can talk to a baby, and I don't really have anything to say to Cara anyway. She can make do without me until all this blows over.

She'll be fine.

Besides, I have a lot on my mind right now, especially today. I can't help but relive everything that's happened.

Erika was weak, in too deep with no way to paddle ashore. She thought she could take me on, but she was wrong. She should have been stronger, smarter. Her mistakes cost her everything.

If she would have just stayed out of it, minded her own business, left me alone. Things could have ended so differently for her. For us.

I remember the look on her face that day, how her eyes bulged, and her lips drooped. Her hair was slick and matted with blood, sprinkled with tiny pieces of glass. I knew I'd remember her that way forever, so I cradled her head in my arms for just a moment. I don't really know why, but I needed it.

It was nice.

Sometimes I wonder if she knew; if she had that moment of clarity.

I like to think she did.

I can't focus on her today, though. It's Dylan that's occupying my mind right now, Alisha's subsequent trial and conviction. I keep trying to forget, to move on and stop fantasizing about everyone, but I can't. *Something* in me knows what I've done is morbid and wrong.

It's murder.

Murder is illegal.

But it never seems to matter how many times I pretend I didn't do these things, that I didn't kill these people, it just keeps coming back to me, like a perpetual *Lifetime* movie on repeat.

I can't unsee it.

I can't un-smell it.

The flashes of red.

Wet.

Thick.

One.

The blood that splays on the wall behind me, on the ceiling, on my clothes. It drips in globs onto the carpet, sure to leave one hell of a stain when all is said and done.

My vision blurs, but still, I see red splotches.

I can't stop seeing red.

Two.

He did this to himself.

No, *she* did this to him.

She did this to us.

They did it to each other.

Three.

To me, to Sawyer.

Why didn't she love me?

Four.

She lied.

They both lied; we all did. It's in our nature, I guess, in our need for self-preservation and repentance. But how did it come to this? How did we get here?

Five.

"Why can't you be more responsible like Erika?"

Where's your precious Erika now, Mom?

Six.

My head throbs with tension, the muscles in my neck stiff and sore, but I can't stop now. I can't put this knife down. It just keeps going in and out of his body.

Seven.

I'll need to pack up the car.

She'll come with me, she has to.

What just dripped down my thigh?

Was that semen?

When did I have sex?

Eight.

My arm is so sore, the muscles tight, the veins bulging, but I keep stabbing because I don't know how to stop, and for some reason, this feels really good right now.

I see their faces: Alisha's, Sawyer's. I see the three of us together, happy.

Before he took that away from us.

Before he stole her for himself.

Nine.

Why would he do that?

He could've been a part of it. We would have let him in. Sawyer may be stubborn, but he didn't want to lose Alisha any more than I did. We could have found a way to make it all work.

A foursome.

Fun.

Ten.

No, not fun.

Stressful.

Stupid.

Certainly ridiculous.

Wishful thinking?

Eleven.

Definitely wishful thinking.

Ugh.

What happens now?

Twelve.

Why the fuck is it so hot in here?

I need some air. Some cool—no, *cold*—air. To breathe.

I feel like I've just run a marathon.

I don't even like running.

Thirteen.

Alisha loves running.

That's where she is right now, running.

I wonder if she gets that runner's high everyone always talks about.

Is it anything like actually *being* high?

Fourteen.

I doubt it.

Nothing beats that.

Fifteen.

Everything hurts.

Literally. Everything.

My arm…

I'm so weak, I could collapse.

I *actually* think I'm about to collapse.

I can't let that happen.

Just a bit more now…please.

Sixteen.

It's over, this pain. It's time for her to bear the brunt of it now.

I've carried this weight for us long enough.

Seventeen.

This is overkill, I know that. It didn't have to be this bad, this many stab wounds.

What a fucking mess.

I think I'm gonna puke.

Why did I stab him so many times?

I look down at the body. He's stopped breathing; I don't know when, but there's no way he could live through this.

There's so much blood.

Seventeen.

That's when everything changed, that moment I've been searching for.

The first time I saw red and never looked back. The age I was when my sister took it upon herself to singlehandedly ruin my life. The age she was when I ruined hers.

See, this is all Erika's fault.

It's *always* Erika's fault.

THE GOOD DAUGHTER

Ivy

I COULD LIE and say I never meant to hurt my sister.

I could do that.

But what's the point? How would that help? The simple answer is that it wouldn't. My intentions were impure, unnatural. Harmful. Lying won't change that. It won't bring her back—not that I want to—and it sure as shit won't fix things with my parents, not that I want to do that either.

But it's important for me to play the role of a lifetime here, to act the part. Pretend. Detective Raylen needs to think I love my parents, that I miss them dearly and would like nothing more than to welcome them back into my life. I need a poor me, a Hail Mary.

My mother used to call me her little peanut. She'd put one of those plastic barrettes in my hair, right at the tippy-top of my head, and those wispy ends would stick straight up just like Pebbles in *The Flintstones*. She doted on me. Loved me. Went out of her way to make me giggle, to play, and snuggle up with me to watch my favorite cartoons, even though she had a million better things to do than watch children's shows.

She did all those things. She loved me and I felt that love, that admiration.

We lost that somewhere. It was as if it dissipated as quickly as it had come.

But yes, there was a time before all this when things were fine, when I could be around my mother and not let her suck the life out of me. Now I have a hard time remembering those days.

If I were to guess, to try to point my finger at a timeline and say exclusively that *this* is when it all went to shit, the birth of my baby sister would definitely be the beginning of the downward trend.

Erika ruined everything.

From the moment she was born.

She was the new and improved epicenter of my mother's world, the one and only concern on her mind, and Dad simply followed her in blind ignorance. Almost like he didn't know any better.

It was like they'd forgotten they had another daughter.

They'd replaced me, and it was as if overnight I went from being their everything to a full-time babysitter for the sister I never wanted. I was the silent helper, the tiny tot whose sole purpose was to remind her parents that not all children are created equal.

My new purpose was that of a caregiver, the toddler version of a handy helper.

Ivy, grab Momma a diaper, will you?

Ivy, hand Momma that bottle.

The night it happened, I simply lost the will to fight it anymore. I wanted her dead since the moment I first laid eyes on her. Seventeen years was a long time to wait. A long time to plot and fantasize, to pretend.

I was done pretending.

Ivy, give your Dad a break and take out the trash.

Ivy, don't look at your little sister like that.

Ivy, stop pestering me while I'm holding the baby.

Ivy, grow up!

In fact, I was proud of myself for holding out, that I hadn't killed her the first time I'd thought of it, or the second, the third... I gave

Erika plenty of chances to do better. To not suck, to help me show Mom and Dad that I was *somebody*, too.

Instead, she did the opposite.

Ivy, why can't you be more like your sister?

She pitted them against me, showed them all the ways I was a disappointment. She was the good daughter, the one they *wanted* around, the one they'd do anything for.

To be honest, it was harder pretending to be sad about my sister's *accidental death* than it was to kill her. My parents were beside themselves, the community shaken.

She was so young, they'd say. *Her whole life ahead of her.*

Even in death, Erika had everyone's attention.

That's why I left.

Every time I saw my sister's face in pictures all I could think about was other ways to kill her. Less humane ways. But instead, I put on a brave face and did what I could to console my poor, sad, parents through the loss of their favorite daughter. And then once the dust settled, I would resume my role as the only child, and everything would be just like it was before Erika was born.

She'd be erased faster than a bad idea.

And *I'd* be the good daughter again.

And that's really the best way I can think to describe the way I feel anytime someone wrongs me; it never goes away, this desire to control things. First, it was Erika and my parents. Then Dylan and Alisha.

I wonder who will be next?

I'M FINE

Sawyer

Marriage isn't for everyone.

I've learned this the hard way, but I suppose all that matters is that I've learned it. Life's greatest lessons are often learned through trial and error.

I don't plan to do this again, not that I've shared that fact with anyone other than you. But I'm in a predicament because I see a spark in Caramie's eyes whenever we're together. I know the way she looks at me. I recognize the longing in her eyes. Like she knows I'm her future. It won't be easy letting her down, but I'll have to eventually, when the time is right and I no longer need her anymore.

I certainly can't put myself through this a second time; best to love and let go if you ask me.

This divorce has hit me harder than I thought it would. I was doing pretty well, keeping my heart and mind at bay, but at this point, I need closure. I need to see Ivy, to be with my wife one last time before she isn't my wife anymore.

So, that's why I'm going, why I'm headed to the county jail to see her.

I hadn't planned to, of course I hadn't, but somehow I'm behind the wheel and headed in that direction. She's like a force of nature, the way she manages to dictate my actions even when she's not around.

This is the last time, though.

After today, we're through.

I'll make sure of it.

Seeing her in the jumpsuit brings images of Alisha straight to the forefront. Ivy looks downright helpless in the faded orange getup, behind the glass where I can't even touch her or feel the warmth of her hand. Like she's on display at a museum.

I didn't expect to be separated by a partition.

The moment is brief, but I feel it, the guilt.

I put her here.

I did this to her.

The admission rests on my tongue, ready to take the leap from my mouth to her ears, despite my will to stop it.

But I do—I stop it because there's no other way.

I know what kind of damage Ivy could do with that kind of information.

Confinement within these walls won't stop her once she's set her mind to something, and the last thing I want to do is give her more ammunition.

No, I need her behind this barrier.

This is where she belongs.

"I miss you," she says into the phone, and I know my wife is a liar, but every other part of me knows she means it; she misses me and she can't help herself any more than I can. I want to say it back, because it's true, but I don't.

I can't.

"How are you holding up in there?" I ask instead.

"I'm fine."

"Ah, the classic, *I'm fine.*"

"Don't patronize me, Sawyer."

"I'm sorry. Just wasn't sure what to say."

"What are you doing here?"

"I wanted to see you. Make sure you're all right." And I did, it's true. Seeing her like this though, this isn't what I had in mind.

No makeup.

Hair piled like a bird's nest on top of her head.

This isn't my wife.

"Ah, so sweet of you," she says, and the sarcasm isn't lost on me. I hear it, feel it like tension at the end of an anchor.

"I'm moving back into the house," I admit, and her eyes light up. Her lips form a smile, but it's not the Ivy I remember. This Ivy is filled with hope—needy.

"You're waiting for me?"

"No, Ivy."

"Then you have no reason to be there." Her smile fades as quickly as it came, and she moves to stand, but I place a hand on the counter to settle her back down.

"It's my home."

"It was *our* home," she snaps. Tears well in the corners of her eyes, and it's almost heartbreaking to watch.

Almost.

"Not anymore."

"Why are you doing this?"

"I've drawn up a settlement agreement. There's some money set aside for you. Once the divorce is final, it'll be there. I'll have the accountant make monthly deposits to your accounts, keep up with your bills."

She shrinks against the seat, the plastic squeaking. "I guess you win then." She shrugs, and I can't tell if she's admitting defeat or demonstrating compliance. Either way, I take it. I didn't come here to argue.

"I think we have different definitions of winning," I say.

"What about Caramie? And Dylan? They live there now, you know. In the house. You're really going to put them out on the street?"

This is it. The moment I dreaded when I decided I was coming here today. Suddenly my throat feels dry; apparently, my conscience decided to join me for the trip.

"Sawyer?"

"Look, Ivy, Caramie and the kid will be fine. They're taken care of."

"What do you mean *they're taken care of?*"

"We're, ah…together. Cara and me."

Her face falls, and I see the fear in her eyes, sense the pain in her chest. I know I've hurt her enough already; this is just icing on the cake.

But she was going to find out sooner or later.

"How—*how* could you do this to me? You didn't want that baby to begin with!"

"No, I suppose I didn't. Things change, I guess."

And it's cowardly, I know, but I've said what I needed to say, delivered the news that I came here to deliver. "I loved you, Ivy."

I hang the phone up, press my hand on the partition as Ivy slams her end of the line onto the counter. She beats her fits into the Plexiglass as she screams.

The guards approach her, cuff her, and drag her out of the room.

I watch my wife disappear behind the locked door.

And I let her take my heart right along with her.

THE DARKNESS WINS

Ivy

LIFE IS AWKWARD. It's unfair.

Everybody lives and everybody dies.

Some of us lie down and take it, while others—like me—do something about it. We live life to the fullest, no matter the consequences.

It's human nature, really.

A never-ending cycle that we hope to go through with the support of family and friends. I, however, am more alone than I ever thought.

There's a darkness in me—mean bones, as Mom used to say. And when that darkness takes over, it's all-encompassing. The light is switched off. I'm overcome with emotions beyond my control.

But can you really fear what you can't see? The unknown? All the tiny monsters lurking in the corner?

I like to think there's something more out there, in that darkness. A higher power, maybe. Who knows? Maybe I'm wrong and just over-thinking this.

All I know is that the light doesn't always come back.

Sometimes the darkness wins.

And once again, I'm a lone bird in the sky, soaring against the blue.

I want to stand out, make my presence known without having to try so hard.

To be free.

That's why I pled guilty.

Despite my lawyer's advice, and the minuscule amount of evidence against me, I took the plea deal. I'll be an inmate for the next twenty-five years. I could be out with good behavior in much less, not that I'm likely to behave.

I know it's crazy, but I'm confident in my decision; standing by it proudly just as I did the day I watched my sister drive off down the street with her brake lines severed.

There's no reward without the risk, right?

Detective Raylen is under the impression I've pleaded guilty simply because I *feel* guilty; that I regret what I've done, who I've hurt in the process. It's good to let him think that for now, but I don't regret anything.

Not even a little bit.

That's not why I took the plea deal, though, why I waived my right to a fair and speedy trial, my day in court. I give a shit about a lot of things, but the opinion of this detective is not one of them. The truth is, avoiding a trial, taking it on the chin for a crime I'm well aware I committed, really is just a matter of self-preservation. A means to an end, sure, but a rather humane one at that.

Pleading guilty was the only way to make sure I'm never linked to Dylan's murder. He was onto me, Raylen, and I wasn't about to peel back the curtain when the show had already started, you know?

Surely, they won't reopen the investigation on Dylan's murder when the only two suspects are already behind bars, especially given our sentences.

So, this is it.

A moment of truth, a homecoming of sorts.

I'm off to see my girl.

HELLO, LISHA

Alisha

"HEY, BARBIE," Ronnie coos. She takes a seat next to me at the chow table and chomps into her sandwich, chewing it wildly, her mouth wide open like a cow in a pasture. A smirk plays on her lips as if the dry bologna sandwich she's scarfing down actually tastes good. I turn the page in the book I'm skimming and suppress the urge to moo. I'm fairly certain she'll take it as an insult to her build instead of her obnoxious chewing habits.

I'm not in the mood for Ronnie's shit today.

I'm never in the mood for anyone's shit.

And I hate myself for it, but I catch myself scanning the room for Tiffany. I wish I didn't look forward to her joining us, but I'm human, so sometimes the attention feels good.

It's been an interesting first year here at Smithson, starting with the borrowed use of the shiv that helped me take out Officer Marshall. I've been on edge ever since, somewhat of a bitch, even.

Tiffany's, that is.

I spot her in the chow line, nearly through with a full tray, and release a sigh of relief.

While it was never my intention to attach myself to Tiffany's hip, she's here and she keeps me off the radar, so for now, I'm playing nice and behaving. It's safe to say I eventually gave her the lead and let her drag me around with it.

I'm not sure how much longer it'll last, but I take advantage of it for now, her protection and what it affords me.

I take a bite of my own bologna sandwich, the cheap, white bread sticking to the roof of my mouth before it descends down my throat in a clump. Food is no longer a vice for me, but rather a means of survival. A necessary component to get through the day.

Not that I wouldn't kill for a plate of Lasagna Classico.

But I need the distraction today. My mind is elsewhere, my thoughts a randomized cluster of apprehension.

I saw her face on the news this morning, during rec hour.

She was right there, front and center, her mug shot like a lackluster glamour shot, but it was her. I'd know that mole anywhere, that dead expression in her eyes.

Suburbanite pleads guilty to sister's sixteen-year-old unsolved murder.

I'd give it less thought if I could, but alarm bells have been ringing in my head since the broadcast, since the admission of guilt I hadn't seen coming.

She didn't try to fight it.

As if by design.

I have a pretty good idea where she's heading, too, as I'm sure you do.

In retrospect, I should have done things differently. I should have looked out for myself, for Dylan. Maybe even for Sawyer, if I'm being honest.

I know that now.

But I can't change the past any more than I can hop the fence and skip out of here. I don't get a do-over. All I can do is go on living, eyes forward, with a can-do attitude—or some shit like that. There's not much else to do here, and right now my only goal is to get through today, to muster through work assignments so I can head back to my cell where I belong.

I close my book, one of the newer releases Chris sent me last week. I'm grateful for the distraction it provides but can't seem to focus on the words on the page, especially with Ronnie assaulting her food across the table. I pick up the trash around me and lock eyes with Tiffany. She smiles as she makes her way to our table. Lunch will only go another ten minutes, but it's still ten minutes I'm not in the mood for.

Not today.

"Where you off to, playmate?" she teases, her smile fading.

I force one in response, an attempt to ease her trepidation, I suppose, but it's weak and doesn't do the trick. She sees right through it.

"What's wrong?" she asks, setting her tray down on the table but not taking a seat. Ronnie stares up at her, and I savor the pregnant pause in her chewing.

"I'm not feeling the greatest," I lie, bringing a pointer finger to my head. "A bit of a headache creeping in."

"No time for headaches," she says, stepping closer. She snakes a possessive arm around my waist and gives my hip a squeeze. "There's a new girl coming in."

"Why do I care?"

"Rumor has it, she's a friend of yours."

My heart drops, the tension in my body suddenly stiff and intrusive. I smell her before I even turn around, my senses somehow heightened just because we're in the same room.

"Hello, Lisha," I hear.

I turn, so slowly I turn, certain I'm about to pass out. I didn't think she'd get here so soon.

Oh, but she is.

Right there in perfect porcelain flesh, no more than ten feet away, wearing the proverbial orange jumpsuit, the one with DOC in big black letters on the back of it that tells me she's fresh out of intake.

Tiffany takes a step forward before I manage to move my feet.

They're frozen to the ground; the ice always takes a minute to thaw when Ivy walks into a room.

"Oh, this is going to be fun," Tiffany says, drinking her in, a wide smile taking over her face.

Ivy smiles, too, and it reaches her eyes, bright and beaming.

For some reason, I smile back.

And then all I hear is music.

Because now I finally know how I'll kill her.

AYE, ME LUCKY CHARMS

Sawyer

HER FACE IS on the front page.

Ivy really is a looker, even in a DOC jumpsuit. But what makes me smile is seeing both of them together, she and Alisha; my girls. The spotlight always did them best; I should know. Ivy's sentencing has stirred up some renewed interest in Alisha's case. The media has exposed their history, and they know their story now. It made sense to share their unexpected reunion with the public.

Their faces are side by side on the front page, the headline sure to captivate even an outsider.

Former lovers reunited at Smithson.

I set the newspaper on the counter and grab a box of cereal from the cabinet—Lucky Charms today, because, well, I'm feeling kinda lucky. My wife is finally off to prison, I'm moving back into my house —where my mistress already lives with my wife's illegitimate son— and I no longer have to worry about her taking me to the cleaners.

The once damning evidence against me has been securely restored, out of reach to anyone but me. My ties to the Ehrens-Havenbrook Corporation will remain unnoticed.

I even found the missing account codes from the safe.

Life really is looking up for Sawyer Rogers, huh?

I scoop a few bites of cereal into my mouth, the marshmallows squishy and slimy and reminding me of my childhood. I usually prefer a fancier breakfast spread, but no one's here to cook for me this morning, and I just don't have the time to do it myself. It's fine, just a quick bowl before I shower and head to the office.

It'll be busy today, being my last…day in the office…before I move back. Home, that is. Sorry, not sure…why.

Wow, it's odd, the sensation swimming in my head right now.

Foggy…

A bit hazy…

I guess that's just a synonym for fog, though, huh?

Sorry, my mind is a little out of it right now.

Like I'm swimming under water…everything sounds far away.

It's bright in here…

Almost too bright all of a sudden.

Wow, my vision is seriously fucked-up.

I can't even read the words on the cereal box, and *oh, my fucking God*, what the hell is going on?

I'm warm, then suddenly freezing.

And now…I…can't…

…breathe, for…some…reason.

It happens then, the end of my life. How unexpected it was, too. I can't help but wonder if Dylan felt the same way when his life was cut short. Keeling over into a bowl of soggy cereal wasn't my ideal way to go out—it's really not very manly, I know—but I guess it beats seventeen stab wounds to the chest.

I always knew she'd come for me.

A bird certainly can't fly without its wings.

But what's most surprising, what I don't expect, is that it's not Ivy's face I see in that last moment. It's not Ivy who takes a predatory step into the room as I suck the last breath of air I'll ever take into my lungs.

It's Caramie's.

And she doesn't look the least bit concerned.

I guess I was wrong about her; she's a lot more like my wife than I ever imagined.

WHO WILL BE HER LOVER?

Alisha

THINGS HAVE a way of working themselves out, don't they? For instance, I've been convicted of murder, as you know, but I didn't commit murder until I ended up in this place, this prison. It's a crime, I must admit, I didn't think I was capable of.

Anywhere outside of here, one might be able to argue self-defense.

But nobody believes a convicted criminal. Hell, few believe any woman who'd take their clothes off for money. I was doomed from the start, blacklisted. And that's fine, I'm okay with that now.

The thing is, a handful of other women came forward with complaints about our fallen CO's conduct after I killed him. I think they hoped it would lessen my sentence, maybe help in some way.

It didn't.

Not when you kill a cop in cold blood; there's no leniency on a charge like that, even if he *was* a predatory psychopath. It turns out, the word of a few incarcerated inmates doesn't hold strong against a fallen officer, especially without proof.

But it's okay, really. I knew I'd be stuck here for the rest of my life even before I did it. Maybe that's *why* I was able to, why it felt right. I couldn't live like that, in fear, every day for the rest of my life. So, no, killing Officer Marshall isn't the heaviest regret I carry around with me.

Sometimes it makes me feel better knowing the other women who came forward can rest easy, though. That their stories were heard, even if not believed by those in power.

For me? It brings comfort. It wasn't easy to hear what those women had been through.

But Caramie's story hit me the hardest.

She, unlike the rest of us, had to live with that monster. For three years she stood beside him as his girlfriend before he met his current wife—now widow—blind to the fact that there were others out there, that his reign didn't exist solely behind closed doors.

She'd been in hiding.

Until the news broke that Officer Joshua Marshall had been murdered by an inmate.

She came to thank me.

And she had to wait a long time to do it.

I'd spent two months in solitary confinement before we met for the first time, locked alone with my thoughts, withering away to nearly nothing, questioning my life decisions and whether they were as necessary as they felt when I made them.

It was her voice that made it all worth it, her story.

Not that it's mine to tell. I suppose I'll leave that up to her.

Maybe she'll tell it to you one day.

WHO WILL BE HER LOVER

CRIMES OF PASSION BOOK 3

CLOUD OF DOOM

Alisha

THE DARKNESS HANGS *over me like a cloud of doom.*

It taunts me; forces me to hear things I know aren't really there.

Pounding.

Creaking.

Screaming.

There are voices littered in the background like specks of dirt—particles of white noise so loud I have to cover my ears just to drown them out. It never works, but I do it anyway because at least it means I'm trying.

That I haven't given up.

I cry, but only when the lights go out—when it's dark and they can't see what this is doing to me. That's when the voices grow the loudest. This psychological warfare exists solely in my head—I know this—but that knowledge does nothing to ease the anxiety that ping-pongs in my chest every time my world goes dark.

I am so very alone down here.

A prickle of fear crawls up my spine and raises the hairs on my arms; a reminder that although I'm still alive, my body and mind reside in hell. The concrete floor I'm lying on is caked in filth—dust, dirt, scraps of food, and dried urine. I, too, am coated in the muck, the putrid odor infiltrating my senses, burning my nose and watering my eyes.

There's no telling how long I've been down here, or how much longer I'll be forced to withstand this mind-numbing torture. They could leave me in here forever, and I wouldn't blame them. They did what they had to do—what they were trained to do—in the event an inmate were to murder a fellow officer.

The fact that he deserved to die does not matter.

It's not my fault they don't realize that, that I couldn't show them. But they don't have all the facts and they won't listen to me when I try to tell them. I've long since given up trying to explain myself.

There's no use.

I don't recall when I last had a sip of clean water, or when I last ate. What they serve me in this place is not food, anyway. There's no clock on the wall, no busy work to pass the time. I have nothing to write on or with, no books or letters to read.

No will to masturbate.

I am prepared to die in here.

So, this is probably it; the end of my story. And if it isn't? I don't want to think about what happens if they let me out of here. Because if they do, then this is just the beginning.

And in their attempts to punish me, they'll only have created a monster.

PART V

LOVERS' QUARREL

THE MURDER PART

Caramie

EVERYTHING YOU KNOW about me is a lie.

I suppose I can't say that for sure, not with absolute certainty. I don't *actually* know what you know. But I *do* know where you got your information from, which is why I'm so confident that it's wrong.

Does that make you mad, the fact that you've been deceived once again?

This may sound like an excuse, but it's really not my fault: it's *hers*. Well, *theirs*, really. Alisha and Ivy are the culprits here, not that I'm unashamed of my involvement in all this, of what I've done.

I am.

And more than a little.

I'm *a lot* ashamed.

I definitely should *not* have done the things I've done. That said, I'm not entirely convinced I had much of a choice. Ugh, that's a lie, too. Sorry, force of habit these days. Obviously I had a choice. We all have choices in this life. But sometimes we make the wrong ones, and that's what I seem to have done here: made a series of bad choices.

And now I'm paying the consequences; like I'm living with these demonic roommates that can't be bothered to pick up their dirty socks.

I killed a man.

Sometimes in those final moments before I fall asleep at night, when I'm all alone in the darkness, I say that out loud just so I don't forget. Not because I want to remember, but because I have to.

I killed a man.

And then I helped put his wife in prison.

It's messed up. I know this, and that reminder does nothing but play on a continuous loop in my mind.

Over.

And over.

And over.

Where would I be now if I'd have done things differently? If I hadn't listened to her?

I'd like to pretend I didn't know what's in store for Ivy Rogers. That when the time is right, she won't be forced to meet the same fate as the man I seduced and killed—her husband. But that would be another lie, and I'm trying to turn over a new leaf here, so I'm not going to say it.

The truth is I have a pretty good idea what will happen to her, as I'm sure you do. Which is why I'm doing my best not to think about my part in all this—the role I played in the downfall of Sawyer and Ivy Rogers.

The guilt tends to linger like a bad smell.

And this one's particularly rotten.

Alisha said it *had* to be this way; that Sawyer's death was the only way all of this would work. I listened to her—*because I'm impressionable like that*—and like a good follower, I did everything she asked of me and then some.

I'm not so sure I like the person I've become.

Or why all this was so important to begin with.

What I do know is that I can't live like this—in this perpetual state of regret—much longer. It'll drive me insane, and before you know it, I'll be occupying a cell right next to those crazy bitches.

Sorry, I don't mean to name call; I'm just frustrated.

There doesn't seem to be anywhere to go from here.

I know I need to press on, to figure out my next move before it's too late. Especially now that I have another life to think about, a child to look after. I can't let this little boy down.

I watch him now, Ivy's son, Dylan. His little lip trembles as he sleeps, and I'd give anything to know what he's dreaming of, what he sees when he closes his eyes. Does he long for his mother? To hear her voice? Crave the warmth of her skin against his own?

It's doubtful, considering the woman was never around for more than a few minutes at a time; he barely knew her. Hell, the little guy probably thinks *I'm* his mother. Which, may be for the best, all things considered.

So I cannot fail.

Not now.

Not ever.

But it's hard, you know? Having to do it all myself, with no support system, while I sit here marinating in fear. It's the unknown that kills me, that unwavering doubt that resides in the back of my mind. What will Ivy do once she figures out what I've done? Will she come for me?

She didn't scare me before. I mean, I certainly knew enough about her that I *should* have been scared. I knew what she'd done to get herself into this mess, and I know why Alisha chose to keep her on a tight leash, why she wanted eyes on her. But circumstances have changed, and I'm told I don't need to worry about her anymore, that she's being *handled*. Whatever that means.

I *do* worry, though.

Because Ivy knows about Sawyer and me—about our affair. He told her about us that day when he went to see her in county.

He wasn't supposed to do that.

And maybe he was just showboating a little. Maybe he wanted to prove to his estranged wife that he still had what it takes to bag a younger model. That he didn't *need* her. I think the news may have upset her more than he let on, that she couldn't possibly have taken it well, but I hate to make assumptions.

But it was that visit, that admission, that led Ivy to change her plea. As if she had nothing left to lose.

Guilty.

Of murdering her own sister.

After that, she was sentenced and hauled off to prison where she (arguably) belongs. And a woman like that is awfully dangerous once her whole world has been taken from her.

I *should* be safe now, with her behind bars. But I don't *feel* safe, and you never really know, do you? It's stupid, but sometimes I still can't believe she did it—that Ivy killed her sister. Call it denial, but how could she have done such a thing? Kill her teenage sister in cold blood like that? Over what? A little sibling rivalry? Forgivable acts is what they were, anybody can see that.

But not her; not someone with that many loose screws in their head. I think it takes a special kind of person to kill their own flesh and blood over something as petty as a sex tape. But what do I know? I've never walked in the woman's shoes.

And I don't intend to.

Still, I thought I *knew* her, this woman with whom I'd shared an intimate kiss—how unexpected *that* was! This woman whose home I lived in for months, sleeping just down the hall from her at night, looking after her kid every day... None of it adds up; she seemed so *normal*.

Her poor parents.

But Ivy wanted to re-write her own story, to start her life over and forget everything that happened up until that moment.

And she did.

The past had been buried.

Hidden away and tucked quietly into the darkest corners of her psyche.

I wonder if she knew it would come back to haunt her like this.

That she'd find a reason to kill again.

And I remind myself of this when the guilt gets to me, when it's too much to bear (kind of like now) and no matter how hard I try, I can't see the light on the other side of the tunnel. I *knew* Ivy was bad news, had been warned that she was a manipulator and not let her in too deep.

But that's how I knew I'd find that dark secret in her past if I searched hard enough. That was my job: to find the secret—something we could use against her when the time came to put her away for Dylan's murder—and expose it. I didn't expect to find what I did; those diaries, her dead sister's photograph. But Ivy is one of those monsters whose fangs can only be seen from up close. That's why she's so good at what she does, at making you feel sorry for her.

That's why I'm anxious.

Why I dread the day I have to face her again.

I haven't spoken with her; I have a new phone number these days for that very reason. I'm not supposed to have contact with her, and I'm damn sure not supposed to visit her at Smithson. Those were Alisha's instructions, her terms.

For your safety, and Dylan's, she had said.

Personally, I think avoiding Ivy only makes me look more suspicious, but like I said, she scares me now, so it's not like I *want* to see her anyway.

No, distance is good.

Distance keeps me and this child safe.

But she's a smart woman; I'm sure she'll figure out why she can't reach me sooner or later, if she hasn't already. I really don't want to think about what happens when she does.

I imagine she knows a lot of scary people.

So, no, I don't know *exactly* what will happen to her from here, but I don't think it's anything good. Whatever Alisha has planned for that woman will likely be brutal, perhaps even life-ending. Lesser people have been known to orchestrate some pretty fucked-up things from the inside of a prison cell.

There is no such thing as sunshine in a place like that.

But does she know about Sawyer yet?

That he's dead?

That *I'm* the one who killed him?

They assured me the poison would work fast, that just a little bit in his coffee would do the trick, and I'll be damned—it did. But I wasn't sure, so that's why I put the extra in his cereal, and some in the milk jug. And we don't need to talk about how I got my hands on such a toxic poison, but know this: it wasn't easy. I've met some very questionable characters in the months since my first sit-down with Alisha. Let's just say I hope I never see any of them again.

And maybe I'm an idiot.

Because Alisha told me to run. To grab baby Dylan and drive off into the sunset as soon as the job was done, to never look back. Make a fresh start somewhere far away, where I wouldn't be recognized by a single soul. The money had hit my account before I even left his condo —five million dollars, to be exact—and there was more coming: a deposit every year until Dylan's eighteenth birthday, as long as I did what I was told.

And I should've run, I know that.

I just wasn't sure I wanted to.

I'm still not sure.

That's why I've been hunkered down in Alisha's house in Buffalo for the past week. Why I can't seem to work up the guts to pack up and go is beyond me. I just need some time to figure things out, that's all. Get my bearings. But I kinda want to stick around long enough to watch it all fall down, too. To see Alisha come out on top.

And she wasn't happy when I told her I'm still here, that I've found refuge in her home. But I like to think that in some way, it brings her comfort—the thought of me raising Dylan here.

I know she misses this house and the memories of the life she had.

But the hard part is done—the murder part—and that's a relief because that kind of life isn't for me. All I can do now is count my blessings and focus my energy on raising this child, this beautiful boy.

Some days I think he's the only thing keeping me sane.

And I have to *get over* everything else. Because Alisha saved my life; the least I could do is save the life of her husband's son.

I'm just not so sure this was the way to do it.

BEYOND REPAIR

Alisha

THEY SAY all is fair in love and war.

I call bullshit.

Absolutely *nothing* is fair in love; nothing is fair in war. These battles we fight are far from equal, and most of us aren't even equipped with the proper armor, let alone mentally prepared for battle.

But we fight anyway.

It's all we can do when the only other option is death.

As for me, I am broken beyond repair. You can find my heart over there—the one abandoned on the battleground; left bleeding for all to see. This war has nearly killed me and certainly has taken everything from me. Now I have nothing left to lose, but so much to fight for.

That makes me a dangerous warrior.

I may have lost in love, but the strongest soldiers always win the war. And the last thing I'm willing to do now is surrender to the enemy.

So I will fight to the death if I have to.

When I was finally returned to my cell after nearly two months in solitary, dirty and weak from lack of proper nutrition and sleep, I found myself thinking of my mother. I didn't know why exactly, perhaps it was a sign. Of what, I don't claim to know, but these memories flooded my thoughts often, and I didn't know how to stop them.

They still come to me now, at night when I'm most vulnerable. It doesn't matter how hard I try to stop them, to move on; she still holds the reins. Reminding me—even from the grave—how she's won. That she was right all along, and I will never amount to anything more than what I've become.

I know she's high before she utters a word.

The whole trailer reeks of marijuana and other unidentifiable substances, and for a brief moment, I consider running over and asking Mrs. Maylen if I can crash on her couch for the weekend. But she has family visiting for the Fourth, and she's told me she's looking forward to spoiling her grandsons.

So, while she did extend an invite for me to stop by for the barbecue, I won't. Mrs. Maylen deserves some normalcy in her life—time alone with her actual family and not some trailer trash kid with a mother from hell who wouldn't know a holiday weekend from a regular Tuesday.

I'm stuck here whether I like it or not, so I drop my backpack onto the floor and close the front door behind me.

Mom's folded into the couch, the acne on her face freshly picked at so a spot of congealed blood rests above her right cheek. She takes a long pull from her beer and slams the can down onto the coffee table. It's coated with ashes and unpaid bills, like usual, and I find myself wishing she'd go out for the night just so I could clean the place up a little. Make it look more like a home and less like the dump it is.

I hate living in this filth.

"Doing anything tonight?" I try to plant a seed as I make my way

to the kitchen, doing my best to feign normalcy and pretend I'm in a decent mood. Sometimes that helps, and I can trick her into leaving.

I open the fridge, but there's not much in there, so even though my stomach is growling and I had to skip lunch, I close the door and take a seat in the recliner across from her in the living room.

"I thought maybe we could hang out," she says. "Ya know, like old times."

"And do what?"

"Fuck if I know...what do girls your age like to do these days?"

"I think I'll just read in my room for a bit if that's okay."

"Got some friends comin' over," she murmurs vaguely under her breath. The words are slurred, but that's nothing new.

"Why would you ask me to hang out if you already have plans?"

"Ron...he likes you, ya know," she say in response. I stand and take a step toward the hallway, but she grabs my arm with a loose hand, looking up at me with leering eyes. She wants something from me, and I already know I won't be giving it to her—or Ron.

"Here, have a toke," she says, extending a joint in my direction. When I don't react, she takes another drag for herself, settling the blunt between her fingers and exhaling dramatically. "What's wrong, baby? You too good to smoke a joint with your own mother?"

"Yes."

"Oh, fuck you!"

"Nice, Mom."

"Would it kill ya to do one little thing for me once in a while? I don't ask for much. Why ya gotta be such an ungrateful little bitch all the time?"

There she is folks...Darlene Hill, Mother of the Year.

"What exactly are you asking me for?"

"Ron's got a thing for you, ya know..." she repeats.

"What's your point?"

"Said he'll cut me a deal this week if I can get you to suck him off." She smiles like it's a form of currency, the smirk sinister and unnerving, but I tell myself not to dwell on it because she's my mother and this is what she does.

But the weight of what she's asking hits me like a freight train. This is what my life has come to: my own mother trying to sell my body for a discount on drugs.

"You're disgusting."

"Don't act like you're too good to suck some dick. I saw those condoms in your side table, Alisha. Before you know it, you'll be knocked up just like I was. At least ya can't get pregnant from stuffin' a dick down your throat."

I don't bother with another retort; just grab my bag and stomp out the door. Because the last thing I need tonight is to be home when Mom's "friends" show up. It's muggy as I walk, the air thick and mosquitoes nipping at my arms and legs. Not the ideal conditions for a night under the picnic table at Pulaski Park, but I guess it beats the alternative.

Because no matter how much she begs, there's no way I'm letting Ron anywhere near me— not after what he tried to do last time.

HUMDINGER

Alisha

SHE CAME to me on a Saturday.

I remember because it was the first weekend I was allowed visitors again after solitary—not that I had many lined up and waiting, but the option is always nice. I had no idea who she was, let alone what she wanted, and I can't say I was in the mood for her unexpected visit. I made a mental note to find out how she got on my visitor list in the first place, but I'd save that problem for another day; it was far too early to ruffle anyone's feathers.

I pegged her for media—figured she was a reporter looking for an inside scoop on my story. *Former porn star murders prison corrections officer.* Sounds like a good read to me, but what do I know?

She wasn't media.

"I'm not sure why I'm here," she said. We occupied a two-person table in the visitor center, surrounded mostly by families and couples who weren't even allowed to hold hands because the outsiders couldn't be trusted not to pass contraband to a prisoner.

I watched her hands shake, the anxious fiddling of her fingers, the motion of her leg tapping up and down. She was scared, as if it was her first time setting foot in a prison.

"Who are you?" I asked.

"My name is Caramie... Langley. I'm—"

She trailed off, like her name was supposed to mean something to me.

It didn't.

There was a sadness in her eyes; pain she couldn't hide no matter how hard she tried. Like she'd been stripped naked and exposed to the elements, only to have weathered a storm and lived to talk about it.

I liked that about her, that she was broken too.

"...he...he was—"

"Okay—Cara, is it?—you're going to have to finish a sentence here. We only have twenty minutes."

"Josh."

"I'm sorry, *who*?"

She leaned closer, cupped her hand around her mouth. "The CO you killed," she muttered through clenched teeth.

I drew in a breath and sat back slowly, waiting for the verbal beat down. Because, *of course,* CO Marshall's widow was sitting across from me. Why wouldn't she be?

Great.

I always wondered if she'd come by, demanding answers.

I waited for her to yell.

To scream.

Tell me how I ruined her life.

How I left her children without a father.

"I wanted to thank you."

"*Thank* me?"

"For doing...what you did. For saving those...inmates. Those women, I mean. His wife. For saving *me*."

"I'm not following."

She looked out the window to the rec yard, staring off into seemingly nowhere like she was lost in a memory. "His wife never told anyone, you know? She never saw that horrible side of him. Didn't believe me when I told her about it either. I warned her there would be others, but she wouldn't *listen* to me."

"Wait, *you're* not his wife?"

"God, no. Ex-girlfriend," she said, snapping back to reality.

I saw it in her eyes then, the damage he'd done.

It was a humdinger. Completely unexpected, to say the least—to learn I wasn't the only person who believed that man deserved to die.

It was convenient, her sitting there, the next words that came out of her mouth. "I just...I had to come. To meet you. H—how can I ever repay you?"

I looked around at the families then. Noticed the sad children sitting with their incarcerated mothers, the state-appointed social workers at their sides, the tattered clothes they wore and torn shoes on their feet. I knew without a doubt I didn't want this life for Dylan's son. He deserved better.

That *I* would never be enough for him, not while I'm in here.

And I couldn't let Ivy be the one to raise him either.

So, I asked her.

"Do you believe in revenge?"

HIS NEXT VICTIM

Caramie

I DIDN'T SET out to become Alisha's feet on the street, not in the beginning.

That's not why I sought her out, why I had to get close to her. That part just kind of...*happened*. The pieces fell together as organically as they could. But I knew from that first moment, felt it like an unexplainable pull—a force of gravity—that there was something special between us. We'd been through something, the two of us. We'd been ravaged by the same monster and crawled out the other side with matching injuries.

It was like our wounds had bled into the same bandage.

So, yes, I wanted to help her.

I wanted to *know* her.

Maybe even be a little bit like her.

So, when she asked if I believe in revenge, I knew whatever she had in mind would involve me, that I could help her, too. It was the way she asked the question, with this spark in her eyes as she spoke the words.

She'd been given a purpose again.

"Do you believe in revenge?" she'd asked.

"Yes," I said without hesitation. "Yes, I do."

And that was it, the start of the bond that led to all of this.

She didn't say much else during that first visit, not in terms of a plan anyway. I had no idea what she had in store for us—for Ivy or even Sawyer at the time—but at that moment it didn't matter.

Because I knew I would do just about anything she asked of me.

Josh was the thing that brought me and Alisha together, so I suppose it's fitting that I tell you about him, not that I want to. But you've been duped by fictional facts before, and I'd like to save you the trouble of false information this time around.

So, let me set the record straight: Joshua Marshall was, indeed, a rapist. The title wasn't erroneously given to him by some deadbeat inmate just to ruin his reputation; he had *earned* it. The man had a thing for putting women in compromising positions and taking advantage of them once their hands were tied.

He had somewhat of a God complex in that way, and rightfully so, I suppose. He *was* untouchable, and his word as a corrections officer held some clout, too. He was a master at abusing the system, at staying under the radar while he did it. A women's correctional facility was as good a place as any to do that, and he preyed on these women for years.

I hold the weight of that blame on my shoulders.

Because if I hadn't run, if I'd have just stayed, he would've had everything he needed at home. He wouldn't have had to hurt anyone else, and maybe he never would have put his hands on those women at the prison.

And that's where the blame comes in.

I know rape is never the fault of the victim—or even the one that came before them—and that I shouldn't harbor any guilt for being the one that got away. But that doesn't make me feel any less responsible for what he's done since the day I left him, for the scars he's inflicted on his victims.

But I'm getting ahead of myself here. Let me back up and start from the beginning like I said I would. My first encounter with Joshua Marshall took place nowhere near the prison. In fact, I met him at a bar. I know, it doesn't get more cliché than that, does it? You'd think I'd have had the smarts to take the free drink and walk away.

But, no.

He had this charm about him…this endearing quality guaranteed to render a woman like me defenseless just by breathing the same air. I was doomed from the moment those first words left his mouth, and he knew it.

He was there to ruin me.

His words rang in my ears, this soothing, deep voice that settled in beside me. "Buy ya a drink?" he had asked. Just a simple question. I turned to face him, mentally prepared to shoo him away so I could get back to watching my ice melt in peace.

He was handsome. Tall, seemingly well put together. Entirely unlike the guys I tended to attract, especially in such a seedy place.

"Who's asking?"

"Joshua," he said with an outstretched hand.

"Nice to meet you, *Josh*," I teased, ignoring the pretentious formality of his full name in addition to the floating hand he expected me to shake. He smirked and pulled his hand away, re-purposing it to signal the bartender. It was obvious he wasn't amused by my slight, but I pretended not to notice.

"Long island?"

"Yep," I replied, in spite of the fact that I didn't need his company. But it's rude to turn down a free drink, and since I only had enough cash left for the cab ride home, if he was willing to pay, I was willing to drink.

But I wasn't *interested*. Not after ending things so recently with Killian, my boyfriend of two years. College sweethearts, we were.

Or *had* been, I guess.

Until he decided to find out what it would feel like to stick his dick between my roommate's well-toned legs. The worst part was when he admitted it wasn't even good sex, that "she just laid there."

Poor guy.

After hastily stuffing everything I owned into garbage bags and hauling ass out of there, I'd been back home for four days, licking salt from my wounds that night at the bar. I know you're not supposed to drink alone, but at the time, nothing sounded better. It was either that or the sofa bed in my parent's basement, where I was currently sleeping while I figured out how to afford a new place to live alone on a college student's budget.

The bar gave me refuge; this way my parents didn't have to bear witness to the shit show that was my life.

"New in town?"

"No."

"Awfully chatty tonight," he noted after a couple minutes of silence. When my drink arrived, I picked it up, fished out the straw, and tossed it onto the bar top. I turned to the space invader beside me, "Thanks for the drink," I said before standing and slinging my purse over my shoulder.

"Whoa, whoa...you're not even gonna drink it with me?"

"I prefer to drink alone."

"I don't bite."

"I doubt that."

"...unless you like that sort of thing?"

I stopped then. Took a moment and drank in the sight of him before throwing my head back and slamming my free-to-me long island. And it wasn't the suit he was wearing, or the five o'clock shadow subtly outlining his jaw. It wasn't even the expensive cologne that left me in a stupor and turned my brain to mush.

It was the passion burning in his eyes.

He had this *look* in them. Like he wanted nothing more than to eat me for dessert—and I gotta be honest here: I let him.

We didn't chat long. Not at the bar, anyway. Maybe another ten minutes? My social skills had gone out the window in recent days; heartbreak will do that to you. I should've played hard to get, maybe made him work a little harder for it. But we're all young and dumb once; maybe he was *my* young and dumb.

And he was older than me, from what I could tell. It'd be confirmed several hours later when I finally asked him, but I knew it then, too. It was the sprinkle of salt and pepper in his sideburns, the smile lines on his face. I suddenly craved his aged experience, his desire to please a younger woman.

I wanted to let him take care of me.

Just for tonight, I told myself.

I didn't plan to see him again.

But he knew I would.

That I'd be his next victim.

VENOM

Caramie

YOU CAN TELL a lot about a man from his hands and how he uses them. If he's rough with you the first time, he'll be rough with you every time after. Josh's hands were soft, soothing. Gentle. He knew how to use them.

I used to think they were built purely for pleasure.

He used them well that first night. I wish I could say that was always the case, but I learned later that my hand theory was a crock of shit.

Everything I thought I knew about men was wrong.

And I was going to find out the hard way.

"What's your name, beautiful?" he finally asked *after* we had sex. And maybe that should've been a warning—the first red flag—but at the time, I liked that he didn't know *who* I was. That he somehow knew I needed to be someone else for the night. And he used his super-powers to make me feel comfortable and safe.

"Caramie."

"It suits you," he admitted with a wink. I rolled onto my stomach and watched him stand and pull on a pair of boxer briefs, admiring the tightness of his toned ass as he did.

"That was fun," I said with a relaxed smile, my heart still racing. It was good sex, *great* even, and I felt alive for the first time in days. Like maybe things would be okay, and my heart wasn't as broken as I thought.

"Stay with me."

"Hmm?"

"For the night."

"Oh, I—"

"Please. You look like you want to get out of here, but I think you should stay."

"I'm not sure that's a good idea."

"I'll make it worth your while."

"Oh yeah? How?"

He planted a kiss on my lips then. Before moving to my neck, my collarbone as his hands trailed down my chest and onto my breasts. "I make a killer pancake," he whispered in my ear.

"Mmm, that sounds dangerous."

"Yes, death by pancake. Tough way to go."

"Fine."

"Fine? As in…you'll stay?"

"Yes."

And that was it; all it took for him to sink his teeth in, to release the venom straight into my veins. I was high off him, so much so that my cab-ride-of-shame the following morning didn't even phase me. And I hadn't thought about Killian the Asshole in over fourteen hours.

A new world record.

Josh knew it, too; that he had me.

Some guys can really kick a girl when she's down.

FRESH MEAT

Ivy

PRISON LOG, Day One: Nobody likes the new girl.

Shocker.

Also, Lisha's upset with me—not that I blame her.

I hate when she's upset with me—can't stand it one bit. It's okay, though, I knew this would happen. That coming here wouldn't be a walk in the park, especially considering everything I've put her through to get us to this point. Nothing has gone according to plan, but that's why I'm here: to fix it, to give us a chance for a new start.

She needs some time, that's all, but she'll come around.

I'll give her all the time she needs, but I don't want her getting too comfortable, either. That bitch Tiffany Malone is a bit of a surprise. I must admit, I didn't expect Alisha to have shacked up with anyone in here, let alone someone like Tiffany, but it's obvious that's what going on between them. They're screwing, and that's unacceptable. Something tells me there's more to it, but I'll have to dig into that later. There's no time for this shit today.

433

Today I'm fresh meat.

And everyone wants a taste.

Eyes cut into me from every direction. I feel them like daggers in my back, stabbing me one by one. And I deserve that, I suppose. People can't help but be curious. Doesn't make it any less annoying. Still, it's only day one of my twenty-five-year sentence; I better get this under control—and fast—before I, too, become someone's bitch.

I came here for one person and one person only.

And I'm not settling for anything less.

Miss Tiffany, it seems, didn't get that message. I have no problem being the one to hand deliver it to her—just to make sure she gets it— but I'll be damned if she thinks Lisha actually wants anything to do with *her*. Surely she was just desperate for a temporary reprieve, and it'll be up to me to help her cut ties with the she-devil once I settle in.

I can read her better than anyone, and right now it's obvious that Tiffany has something on Lisha, that she needs my help to strip her of that power.

"What's your name, new girl?" Tiffany asks, approaching me with a side-eyed glance, her arms at her sides.

"Ivy," I say, my own eyes deadlocked on Alisha. I try to read the expression on her face, but it's unclear, and I have to say, I'm a bit surprised this woman doesn't already know who I am.

Alisha hasn't talked about me? In all this time?

There's a mask that wasn't there before; like she's hiding from something, trying to blend in. She never used to hide, not from anything.

"Your *last* name is Ivy?"

I give Tiffany a look, one she seemingly doesn't care for, judging by the way her eyes cross when I do. "Obviously not."

"We do last names here. Last names and inmate numbers, so pick one, Blondie. Nobody gives a shit what your first name is anymore."

"Rogers," I say, somehow managing *not* to roll my eyes at her.

"Easy enough. What's the charge?"

"Excuse me?"

"Jesus, are you slow or somethin'? What. Are. You. In. For?"

"You can watch your fucking tone," I snap, but my words are cut off, the punctuation lost as they're met with a sharp right hook to the face. My head whips to the side, and I feel the weight of her fist like a ball of fire. I swallow my rage and stumble to the ground like a rag doll, my pride wounded far worse than my cheek.

Tiffany—*or am I supposed to call her Malone?*—hovers over me and shoves a bony finger in my face. "You've got a lot to learn, bitch."

She stomps off in the other direction and the room clears, Alisha following her in a hurried step, not bothering to look back. Her message is heard loud and clear: I'm on my own here. Alisha is not the ally I expected her to be.

Not yet, anyway.

I'm the only one left in the dining hall when the COs come barreling in. With annoyance, they bring me to my feet, each of them hooking an arm through one of mine. "The pretty ones always gotta be startin' somethin', huh?" one of them mumbles.

"Welcome to the never-ending circle of bullshit," the short one says.

Other words are spoken, but I don't hear them.

I'm too busy fuming to give a damn.

ALIBI-READY

Caramie

Fᴇᴀʀ ᴀɴᴅ ʟᴏᴠᴇ can make a person do crazy things.

This perpetual cycle we find ourselves in can be exhausting. And just when we think we understand it, that we've figured things out, the wind shifts, and everything changes again; we're right back to square one. The worst part is that no one is exempt; we're all capable of falling down the rabbit hole and failing to find our way back out of it.

Sometimes we miss the warning signs—overlook the red flags and merely go about our lives like nothing is wrong. But when you know, you know, and by then it's usually too late to change course.

And knowledge by itself doesn't keep the crazy away.

No, of course, it doesn't; we still do that crazy thing because it's all we know to do, like second nature. Over and over again, we just keep doing it, no questions asked, no matter what the cost.

We do the stupid things.

Like stick around after your boyfriend slaps you across the face.

After he screams at you like you're nothing. Even when he apologizes, it won't settle the nerves in your belly, the uneasy feeling in your gut.

Afterward, you won't leave, but you'll flinch anytime you're around him.

And he'll laugh.

He'll make you feel like a silly little girl, remind you that even your own shadow can be terrifying. That *his* shadow is everywhere. He'll question your loyalty as if *you're* the one who's been sleeping with someone else behind *his* back. He'll make you feel guilty as if *you've* done something to hurt *him*.

He'll shame you.

Test you.

Try to figure out whether you'll tell someone; whether they'll believe you if you do. But he has a plan in place for that, too, so he's not worried. He'll have his alibi ready; a story that'll clear his name and tarnish yours just the same.

That's what they do, abusers.

That's why they always win.

They introduce you to the definition of insanity, and even then, once you've realized it, you'll still come back for more. Because they'll have made sure you're dependent on them, that you need them more than they need you.

And when you finally do get out? When, after months of abuse, you push past that fear and the persistent hammering in your chest as you gather up the few things you can manage to carry with you and sneak off in the middle of the night, as you run like your life depends on it—*because it does*—even then, you'll never stop wondering.

If he'll find you.

If he'll care that you're gone.

If he'll be upset.

If he still loves you; if he ever did at all.

What he'll do to you when he finds you.

So, you'll hide.

You'll leave your family and what little friends you have behind. You'll cower in the shadows, watching your back every time you leave the apartment. Watching your back even when you're still inside. You'll hear things. Little sounds here and there—*everywhere*—that have you convinced he's about to jump out from behind the curtain, an alleyway, the cereal aisle in the grocery store.

You'll stop leaving the house entirely.

You'll wallow.

You'll weep.

You'll talk to yourself because no one else will listen—and you're *obviously* losing your mind—and nothing will ever be the same because he's *broken* you, and there's no way to put all the pieces back together. The cracks will always be there, even once the glue dries.

But then you'll hear it.

You won't believe it at first, so you'll pick up the remote control and you'll rewind live TV, because there's no way you just heard what you think you heard and clearly you're delusional.

But you hear it again, so it must be true.

The words said on the news, delivered solemnly by the beautiful young field reporter on Channel 5, Lexy Dawson.

"Corrections Officer Joshua Marshall of the Smithson Women's Penitentiary was murdered today after a deadly run-in with well-known inmate Alisha Thompson. We covered her story earlier this year when the former adult entertainment star was tried and convicted for the brutal murder of her husband, Dylan Thompson."

You'll listen.

You'll sit closer to the TV, turn up the volume so loud the closest neighbors half a mile away can hear it, too. And the tears will fall slowly down your cheeks, then quickly, and before you know it you're spreading the curtains, opening the windows, and the birds are chirping, the sun is shining and it's *so nice* to feel its warmth again.

And it doesn't matter what happened before that day. It won't matter that someone took all the little parts of you and crumpled them into even smaller—more vulnerable—pieces, because today you get to pick them up and put them all back together.

Today you owe your life to a murderer.

You'll want to thank them one day, and maybe they'll even understand why. Maybe they'll be the one person who finally *gets it*. And it doesn't matter what they ask for in return, how impossible it may seem, how ridiculous it might sound.

You'll do whatever they ask.

Because they were a victim, too.

And no one should have to live like that.

But fear and love make you do crazy things, so you do it.

STREET CRED

Ivy

THE FOOD'S not so bad here.

Just kidding, it's terrible.

One star, do not recommend.

I suppose it'll work from a dietary perspective; at least I know I won't be trying to hoard the leftovers in my pants—which are sans pockets *for security reasons*—to binge later in my cell while I wallow in the depths of my sorrows.

Where's the Ben & Jerry's when you need it?

I make a mental note to check on my commissary funds in the morning—I'd kill for a box of honey buns right now—before stuffing the last of a dry peanut butter sandwich in my mouth. Wishing I'd opted for a carton of milk, I swallow it down with a gulp of water and drop my napkin onto the plastic tray.

Like I've been for the last three meals now, I find myself alone at a sizable table in the corner of the large room. Everyone else is clumped ten bodies to a table in case you're wondering. It's like *Mean Girls* around here; apparently no one wants to sit with me after what happened yesterday. Perhaps that's for the best, all things considered, but so far this prison thing isn't quite as easy as I'd hoped.

I spot Lisha a few tables down, her nose in a book while the founding members of her fan club mingle around her. She's made friends, much to my dismay. Malone sits closest to her, a leg draped haphazardly over hers, and I wish I could say it doesn't bother me, but it does. I don't like the way that woman looks at her as if she owns her.

My bruised cheek throbs, and I fight the urge to touch it, but also kind of dig the street cred it gives me. At least I didn't cry in front of them.

Didn't rat either.

Not that the whole ordeal played out to my benefit, but even the few inmates on our block who weren't in the room when it happened are looking the other way, as if I'm somebody they should avoid making eye contact with.

I'm not, for the record.

I actually rather like eye contact.

Which is why I'm annoyed that Lisha has been avoiding me all day. I can feel her looking at me, sense it even, but she breaks her stare every time I turn around to catch her in the act. At least she's curious, keeping a close eye. I suppose that's all I can ask for at this stage in the game.

"You the kid-killer?"

"Excuse me?"

I look up to find myself face-to-face with Malone's other bestie, not that I can remember her name. Bonnie or Connie or something like that. She's homely-looking, a bit like Miss Trunchbull from *Matilda*, but something tells me she's all bark and no bite. Must've drawn the short stick on the grunt work today.

I should have seen her coming, too, so shame on me. I'll need to do better at keeping my eyes peeled.

"I don't like to repeat myself," she says, "but I'll make an exception since you're new here. Are you the kid-killer?"

My sister.

"If you're standing here asking, you probably already know the answer."

Without warning, she produces an open milk carton and dumps its contents over my head. The white liquid sloshes down my shirt and finds its way into my prison-issued cotton bra. I jump to my feet and grab the Trunchbull-wannabe by the shirt collar, slamming her back against the table. Probably not quite the move she—or anyone watching out of the corner of their eye—expected from a petite woman like me, but if I don't start asserting myself around here soon, these ingrates will have made a mockery of me before dinner.

"Do that again, and *your* kid will be next," I hiss before rearing back and head-butting her. The shock of the impact knocks the lights out in my brain for a hot second, but the blood gushing from her nose makes it worth the power glitch.

Pain is only temporary, after all.

The alarm sounds and everyone but me drops to the floor with their hands on the back of their heads, but all I can think to do is cover my ears because that alarm is so damn loud. There's shouting behind me, and I can't make out the words over the deafening sound of the alarm. I'm still standing there like a newbie when the weight of CO Marin's baton comes down on the back of my knees. My body succumbs to the impact and folds to the floor.

I spend my second night in prison nursing my wounds in a solitary holding cell, closed off from Malone and her band of bitches.

Closed off from Alisha.

And I'm supposed to survive twenty-five years of this?

CLICK

Alisha

ONE DAY AT A TIME.

That's how you get through a prison sentence. One day. One minute. One measly step at a time. Today's step: counseling. As if there's any point in rehabilitating an inmate who's expected to spend the rest of their life in prison.

It kinda makes me miss Kristin.

Dr. Kristin Lindsay, I should say; we should really be on a more formal basis. Do you remember her? My former therapist. Not that we ever really *knew* each other; we weren't exactly friends or anything. Sure, she did kind of assist in getting my ass thrown in this dump, considering her testimony during my trial, but I try not to hold that against her. She was just doing her job. I can't fault her for that.

She knew me just enough to understand me, to see through the facade. I liked that about her. Which is why she's on my mind as I sit here now. This correctional counselor in front of me doesn't know shit.

Doesn't give one either.

Not one bit.

Even the fact that he's a male counselor in a women's prison says something about this place. As if a woman might be considered too soft to wrangle the herd.

As if I'd ever put my trust in a man like him.

But I'm required to meet with this jackass while I'm in here, at least once a week, more if deemed warranted. I'd rather not, but sometimes you have to suck it up and follow the rules; ignore the fact that he's here to do a mediocre job and collect his paycheck at the end of the week, maybe one day a pension, and nothing more.

It's evident.

"Any thoughts of suicide?" he asks, not bothering to look away from his computer screen. His pointer finger hovers over the mouse pad on his laptop, ready to morph my verbal response into a required check mark on the screen. We're nothing more than check marks to him, a monthly quota to reach.

"Right now?"

"Overall."

He still doesn't look up. I'm tempted to test him and throw out a yes, but all that'll do is extend my time here in his office today and that's really the last thing I want to do right now.

"No."

Click.

"Good. Any concerns I need to know about?"

"Does it matter?"

"Sure, it does."

"So, if I tell you I'm *concerned* about the quality of the food here, you'll do something about it?"

Click.

"The mattresses?"

Click.

He shakes his head, finally looks up at me. "This isn't a hotel, Thompson. You don't get to pick and choose the amenities."

"Then no, I have no concerns."

"Anyone giving you any problems? Considering…"

"Considering what? That I took out one of your beloved COs not too long ago?"

"Look, Thompson, I'm not here to go toe-to-toe with you. Just answer the question."

"No."

Click.

"Anything else you'd like to discuss today?"

"I wasn't under the impression this was a discussion."

He slams his palm down on the desk with an unnecessary force that makes me flinch. I hate that it does; I don't enjoy showing fear to an aggressor, so I can't help the scowl when it takes over my face.

"An attitude like that won't bode well for you anymore," he says with arrogance. "You know that, right?"

"It's working fine so far."

"Your stint in solitary leads me to disagree. Trust me, things can be a lot worse for you if you don't get that attitude in check."

We stare at each other in silence for a moment. He's testing me, I realize that, just as you probably do, but I'm not sure what his motive is. I can't say I care to find out either.

"I apologize that you feel I'm being less than cooperative, Mr. Garrison. What would you like me to say that would make this easier for both of us?"

He doesn't say anything, just turns back to his computer and clicks the mouse a few more times. The silence should be awkward, but it's not. When he's finished, he doesn't say anything at first, just closes his laptop and gets up from his rickety chair before motioning toward the door. I follow him like a lost puppy because that's what he wants me to do.

"We're finished?"

"For today. Have a lovely day, Thompson."

CO Carrie Shields, my new favorite authority figure, meets me on the other side of the door, because they don't let me walk the halls alone anymore. Her expression is unreadable as we make our way down to the day room in D block, my home sweet home for the foreseeable future. My counseling session ended early—*hurray for small miracles* —but even though there's time to spare before the next headcount and this is a minimum security facility, I'm escorted directly back to my cell.

I may be out of solitary, but I'm still very much on lockdown whenever the guards see fit.

As a precaution, they say.

They don't want me murdering any more COs, I guess. That's fair, and I can even forgive them for sticking me in a single-unit cell, but this however-months-long period of cruel and unusual punishment is getting old.

When the cell door closes and the lock clicks into place, I'm surrounded by a deafening quiet, left alone with thoughts that want nothing more than to eat me alive.

But I guess it's better than the basement; *anywhere* is better than the basement.

DON'T PLAY DUMB

Ivy

THEY'RE NOT TAKING my calls.

I don't know what's going on, but I expected to hear from at least one of them by now. It's been days—weeks—of radio silence from both Sawyer and Caramie; not a word from either of them since I left county lock up.

This is unacceptable.

During rec, I use five minutes of my tablet time to send an email to Caramie, and am only mildly surprised when it's immediately returned as undeliverable.

She's changed her email address.

And her phone is disconnected.

Something's definitely up.

I'd like to know what's going on with my son, whether or not Caramie is taking care of him like she said she would, and that Sawyer is still generously funding his care. How am I supposed to do that when I can't even get a hold of anyone in the short amount of time I'm allowed to use the phone every day?

Dodging my calls and refusing to let me see him is out of the question; I will remind Caramie of this if I have to. Just because she's sleeping with my husband doesn't mean she gets to avoid me. I make a mental note to add Penelope to my call list; maybe my former coworker and young confidant will run over to the house to check on her for me. We've spoken once since my arrest; in my book, that means we're close.

But I have bigger problems today, so for now, I table my aggression and mentally prepare for the unknown because CO Shields is escorting me to an interview room in the visitor center—and to say I have no idea what for would be an understatement.

There are two of them in there when we arrive, seated at the small table. They're dressed in cheap, wrinkled suits like they've been waiting impatiently for hours. I wouldn't put it past the prison administration to leave them sitting on ice for a bit, but my guess is they did their waiting elsewhere because it's not like my handler—whoever that may be these days—had a jam-packed schedule to work around.

CO Shields removes my cuffs—required on account of my newbie status any time I move between units—and instructs me to take a seat at the table. I do, and immediately rub my wrists like every inmate does as soon as their cuffs are removed. It's a natural reaction, I suppose; the skin gets itchy under there once you start to sweat.

"Mrs. Rogers, hello. I'm Detective Beck with the Wright County CID. This is my partner, Detective Nichols."

"Hello," the other one murmurs with a nod of his head. I've already forgotten his name because I don't actually give a shit who he is or why two criminal investigation detectives are introducing themselves to me like I'm a suspect. I'm already locked up; what do they need me for? I sit and cross my feet at the ankles, my arms folded over my chest, because as far as I'm concerned, all my skeletons are already out of the closet.

Of course, there's still the whole I'm-the-one-who-killed-Dylan-Thompson scenario they could've dug up.

It's doubtful, but…

"Mrs. Rogers, do you know why we're here today?"

Nope.

"I imagine it has something to do with my sister?" I say, because sometimes it's best to plant the seed *for* them instead of risking planting new ideas into their tiny brains.

The detectives exchange a look, and my stomach does a bit of a flip-flop. "No."

"Then what? Do tell, I'm on the edge of my seat."

I am not at all on the edge of my seat.

"Your husband—Sawyer Rogers?"

I shrug. "What about him?"

"He was found dead two days ago."

I am now on the edge of my seat.

His words suck the air right from my lungs, leaving me hollowed out to the point I could pass out right here and now. I can't possibly have heard him correctly.

"He…*what*?"

"Did you have anything to do with his death?"

"God! No. I would never…he's *dead*?"

"Spare us the act here, will you?"

"What act? No, I—"

"Who did you work with to arrange for your husband to be killed?"

"No one!"

"So you acted alone?"

"No! *I* didn't do this…"

"The thing is, the evidence is weighing heavily against you. Would you like me to walk you through it?" Detective Beck asks, and I can't say I care much for his tone.

"Look, Detective *Beck*, is it? Your intimidation tactics aren't going to work on me. I didn't kill my husband."

"Prison records indicate you made an outbound phone call three days ago, on the sixth, at 10:02 a.m., to a Michael Havenbrook. Does that ring a bell?"

"Yes. Look, my husband *works* for him. They're good friends, actually. Sawyer hasn't been taking my calls so I thought he might be able to get a hold of him for me."

Beck leans back in his chair, crossing his arms. "What did you talk about?"

I stare at him. "I'm sure there's a recording somewhere that you can get your hands on."

"Mrs. Rogers, I don't think you understand the severity of the situation here. Your husband's death is being ruled a homicide, so I suggest you start cooperating."

"I *am* cooperating, you're just too tunnel-visioned so realize it. So, let me say it a little slower for you. I. Didn't. Have. Anything. To. Do. With. My. Husband's. Death."

"You sure about that?"

And I say it then, the question I should have asked from the start. The one that sends these assholes packing and me back to my cell. "Shouldn't my attorney be present for this conversation?"

"We'll be in touch, Mrs. Rogers," Beck says as he pushes to his feet. Nichols gives him a look like he's not quite finished with me, but it's obvious who wears the pants here, so Beck wins.

For now.

When I return to my cell a handful of minutes later, there's nothing left for me to do but cry.

I really didn't think she had it in her.

It's the second visit I get later that week that unsettles me the most.

The one from Connor Ehrens.

Havenbrook must have sent him. And he looks pissed. I'm willing to bet that anger is meant for me, despite the fact that I'm not sure he has a reason to be upset with me.

Perhaps he misses me.

"Nice to see you, Connor," I say as images of our nights together back at Lady Ann's play in my mind. I find it hard to maintain a straight face, let alone keep my prison-issued granny panties dry as the memories swarm my mind, but I smile at him anyway.

He doesn't return the smile.

It's then I realize visits from men like Connor Ehrens don't typically happen behind the privacy of closed doors in a place like this; unless a guy comes in with a badge or a law license, they end up in the visitor center just like all the other commoners. It strikes me that he must have connections, ties to someone much higher up in the prison, to have managed to score this locked-door alone time with me.

I'm not sure how I feel about that beyond slightly alarmed. Maybe a little turned on.

"Is this a business call?" I ask, pulling my foot out of the knock-off rubber Crocs I'm wearing and running it up his leg beneath the table. "Or perhaps a more personal one?"

"Cut the shit."

"So, business then?"

"What'd you do to Sawyer, Ivy?"

"Excuse me?"

"Rumor has it he's a dead man, and I have a feeling I know who killed him."

"You're wrong."

"See, here's the thing: I *know* it was you. I know you poisoned him, took the money he owed my partner and me, and stuck it somewhere for safekeeping. So, don't play dumb. Where is it?"

"Sawyer was *poisoned?*"

"Where's my money, Ivy?"

"I don't have it."

"Then who does?"

"Look, I don't know! But it wasn't me, and I don't know who killed my husband." That *may* be a lie; I have a damn good idea who did it. I just haven't had a chance to figure out *how* yet, and until I do, my lips are sealed.

"Fine. Then you can pay off his debt another way."

It takes a second to sink in, but when it does, I immediately wish I never met this man. I expect him to unbuckle his belt and pull his pants down, and if he had, I could've lived with that. It wouldn't be the first time a man swung his dick around to show a woman who's boss. But what Ehrens has in mind for me is much worse than a load down the throat.

It's suicide.

"I'm not running drugs for you. Not in here."

"You *will*. Or you won't live to see the end of the week. Trust me, I can make your stay in prison a hell of a lot shorter if you'd rather join your husband in the ground."

Ehrens doesn't wait for a response, just stands and knocks on the door until the officer opens it. "An associate will be in touch," he says. "And Mrs. Rogers? You really don't want to find out what happens if you say no."

Less than twenty-four hours later, there's a prepaid cell phone waiting for me in the library behind a dusty stack of hardbacks that haven't been touched in years.

And I'm officially a drug dealer for the Ehrens-Havenbrook Corporation.

SOMEBODY ELSE'S WAR

Caramie

SOMETIMES I CAN'T UNSEE his face.

He's always there, like an old picture that hangs from a rusty nail in the back of my mind. It rattles when the trains go by, turns crooked if I stare at it for too long. Or maybe that's just my mind playing tricks again; it does that sometimes.

Maybe he's not really there at all.

It's the shame that eats at me, because of the look in his eyes when he saw me standing there, the moment he must have recognized my betrayal; that he was about to die.

And I know this will sound crazy—and maybe it is—but I think I loved him.

I can't explain it, this ugly truth that's stuck in the back of my mind like gum to the bottom of a shoe. And that's the saddest part; because I *know* Sawyer never loved me. I know what I was to him—a temporary piece of arm candy—and that knowledge alone should be enough to erase some of this guilt.

But it's not.

A tear rolls down my cheek, and I swipe it away because it doesn't make any sense. Another one follows right behind it—they always do, these tiny reminders of how weak I've become. I'm not sure this man is worth my tears, yet here they are, collecting for him like souvenirs.

And maybe it's the bottle of wine I'm sitting here drinking by myself, I don't know, but right now, in this moment, I don't think I can do this. I can't pretend to be someone I'm not anymore. But how do I stop? How do I go back to who I was before all this happened?

I almost called home tonight.

I know I'm not supposed to do that, not until all this is over. I can't risk putting my family in danger, not while I'm a foot soldier in somebody else's war.

And I wish I'd seen it sooner, this pattern of dependent behavior I seem to follow. I've never been the best judge of character; my mother once told me that—and not in a hurtful way, either. She simply saw my fault for what it was, knew it would kick me in the ass one day.

I wish I'd been smart enough to believe her.

I feel a pull in my chest at the thought of her, at the memory of her voice, the warmth of her smile. It'd be so nice to see her, even if just for a moment. I wouldn't tell her what I've done—I could never do *that*—but I'd let her know that I'm okay, tell her I'm sorry. That maybe I'll be able to come home soon.

Wishful thinking, I know.

I've been staring at the prepaid phone in my lap for twenty minutes now. It never rings when I want it to; only two people have the number, and Alisha only calls every few days as it is. I'm telling you, this loneliness is enough to drive a person crazy.

I will the phone to ring, for it to be my mother's voice on the other end. For her to tell me she's thinking about me. I'm sure she's worried after all this time. How could she not be?

It's been a couple years now, and I know that's wrong, that maybe it didn't have to be this way. But ask any woman who's been through an abusive relationship and she'll probably tell you the same thing: it's hard facing the people you hurt while you chose to love the wrong person.

In my case, it was easier to leave. To separate myself from my family in case Josh decided to go after them, in case he come looking for me. It's always been better that they not know where I am.

Not that it makes missing them any easier.

But that's why I lost touch, why I was in hiding, living alone in the middle of nowhere. When it was over, once I'd heard he was killed, I almost went back.

Then I saw the news.

And I met Alisha.

She sent me undercover—or some convoluted version of that—working for Ivy and manipulating Sawyer. It's Alisha's game I've been playing ever since.

Because I owe her *everything*.

And the moment I slipped that vial of poison into my purse, I knew any chance I had of ever living a normal life again was gone. That reconnecting with my parents will never be an option.

Because they're good people.

Great ones, really.

And they don't deserve to be the parents of a murderer.

My big brother, though, he's a different story. He's probably the only reason I'm alive today, that I got out when I did. We've always been close. He was my protector, the only person who knows the truth about Josh—about the monster he was.

That's why I ran to him the night I finally left.

Because I didn't know where else to go.

I still don't.

STRIKES A NERVE

Ivy

I GET IT NOW.

Why Alisha was so upset after Dylan died.

That must be what this lingering feeling is: sadness. I'd forgotten what it was like, this tightness in my chest, the overwhelming sense of dread hanging over my head. It must be, because my heart is heavy with the loss of my husband, at the understanding that not only the police but even Ehrens thinks *I'm* the one who killed him. As if I could kill my own husband.

I couldn't possibly.

Surely *you* believe me, right?

It dawns on me that with a homicide investigation on the table, it could be months or even years before I see a life insurance payout, and that's on the off chance that he didn't change the beneficiary after our separation. But maybe I'm focusing my energy in the wrong place; maybe I shouldn't worry about death benefits and finances right now.

What I *should* be thinking about is how she pulled it off.

How Alisha managed to orchestrate Sawyer's murder from inside these walls when I couldn't even get him to take a phone call.

And how could she betray him like this? Sawyer loved her, would've done anything for her if she'd given him a chance. She knew that; it's part of the reason she left us.

He was getting too close.

I briefly consider Connor Ehrens, that maybe he did this, but there's no way. He needed Sawyer as much as anyone, and Havenbrook never would've signed off on it—not when Sawyer was so good at cooking their books. Sawyer may have been a selfish asshole sometimes, but one thing he didn't suck at was making money for his bosses.

Confusion swims in my brain, but when it finally hits me why this had to happen, I'm a bit relieved. Of *course* she did this. Of course Alisha had Sawyer killed.

The logic is so simple.

Revenge.

I killed *her* husband, so she killed *mine*.

How could I not see this coming?

That this was her master plan? She wasn't after *me*; she was after my husband. To make me hurt the way she did. To take the same thing from me that I took from her. And I was so preoccupied with getting in here to be with her that I forgot she prefers to fight her battles with weapons that can't be seen.

She had this planned long before I walked through those doors.

But the joke's on her.

Because now I've got her right where I want her.

Now we're in this together.

I didn't think this through.

It seems Miss Tiffany—excuse me, *Malone*—had slipped my mind for a moment there.

Silly me.

I'll have to find a way to deal with her eventually, but that'll have to wait until I get these detectives off my back. I'm a little distracted here—trying to evade another murder charge at the moment—not that it matters all that much; twenty-five years may as well be life anyway.

But right now, I need to speak with Caramie, because she must know about Sawyer by now, and I can't imagine how she's feeling. I shouldn't care, but I do. She's the sensitive type, you know? Her poor heart is probably broken.

With ten minutes to spare of rec time, I hustle to the phones and dial home. The line rings; once, twice. Three times, but the machine never picks up.

Like the number has been disconnected.

Like the number has been disconnected.

Oh, no.

And that's when it hits me: I haven't spoken to Caramie since my arrest; that it's always been Sawyer, never her. Every email I've sent to her is undeliverable, the phone numbers aren't working.

She has my son.

And *she* must have killed my husband.

Not Alisha.

I slam the phone down onto the receiver and run down the hall toward the day room, where I find Alisha in the weekly Sex Addicts Anonymous meeting. Malone's appearance in the plastic chair beside her strikes a nerve I'm not prepared to play with today.

It's like she's become a permanent fixture on Alisha's arm.

"I need to talk to you," I whisper-shout to Alisha, taking her elbow.

"Not now," she barks, pulling her arm away.

"*Please*, it's important."

When she doesn't respond, I reach for the open chair beside her, but Malone kicks it away. "Seat's taken," she says.

"Ladies, let's play nice," the volunteer counselor singsongs. "Can everyone please take a seat?" The statement is directed at me; I'm the only person in the room left standing. I nod and find another chair in the back of the room. I don't belong here in this meeting, but I don't know where else to go, so I spend the next hour staring a hole in back of Alisha's head while listening to my fellow inmates tell stories about their former sex lives.

I'm sure she's pleased with herself, too—probably smiling like a crazy person at the thought of me getting pushed around like this.

And that's fine.

She can go ahead and think that.

But I'm done playing nice.

HER HORNS ARE SHOWING

Alisha

I LIKE to think I've tipped the scales in this game I'm playing with Ivy's emotions. Not to sound arrogant—you know that's one thing I'm not—but I do like to be realistic, to tell it like it is. And right now, I'm in Ivy's head, right where I should be. Like a marionette controlling the strings attached to the hands of the devil.

And her horns are showing.

I sure do love to see them.

To survive in prison you have to think like a criminal. When you're a full-timer like me, the best thing you can do is forget everything you think you are, every good thing you've ever done on the outside, and become someone you wouldn't care to run into on the streets.

It's like a rebirth without the celebration.

A birthday party without the fancy cake and balloons.

Because adaption is necessary.

So, whatever happened on the outside stays on the outside; except, of course, when your former lover frames you for your husband's murder. That kinda shit follows you anywhere. But unlike me—and as I suspected—Ivy isn't doing the greatest job of adapting to prison politics. She came in hot, thinking she'd own the place from the get-go, that her conniving mind would be enough to bump her right to the top of the food chain. Tiffany sure knocked her down a few pegs.

Someone had to.

I love it when she's wrong.

She hates it, that loss of control.

It's been a month since Ivy's arrival, and so far, avoiding her has been tougher than I expected. Last week it was SAA, and this week she's managed to get herself permanently assigned to a cell right next to mine. I don't care to know how, either, but she played a card I didn't know she had. And while you might think we'll barely see each other, that we're confined to our separate cells at all hours of the day, you would be wrong.

We have a lot of free time here, and much of it involves spending time with other inmates in the pod. Day room, rec, work, chow…it's not all steel bars, gray walls, and metal bed frames unless you're stuck in solitary or shuffled down to the max center for bad behavior. If you stay out of trouble, it's actually not much worse than a low budget retreat, minus the healthy food and full body massages—although I'm sure those can be arranged if you make nice with the right people, happy endings included.

Not to make prison sound inviting.

But back to my original point.

Establishing distance from Ivy hasn't exactly been a cakewalk, and now that she's right next door, I have bigger problems on my hands. She's too close, always talking to me through the air vents, following me when I leave my cell. And even when I do manage to slip away without her noticing, she's never far behind.

And that's why I find myself cornered by the temptress herself after noon chow when I make my way to the yard. I can tell she wants to chat, maybe have a quick heart-to-heart about where things left off, but as usual, I'd rather not. "Why didn't you tell me this place is so fucking depressing?" she whines when she strolls alongside me. I roll my eyes, but she doesn't see.

"Didn't think you'd notice."

"How could I not? There's nothing to *do* around here. Like ever."

"Yeah, well, last I heard, you did this to yourself."

"I did this for *you.*"

"Don't kid yourself."

"Hey, wait a second." She grabs my arm, stopping me in my tracks, and I fight the urge to kick her and run away.

"Get your hands off me."

"I just want to talk. We haven't had any alone time thanks to your *new friend Tiffany.*"

"I'm not interested in alone time with you, Ivy. Or should I call you Lila?"

"You can call me whatever want, baby," she says with a semi-seductive wink. The smirk on her face tells me she has yet to understand that she's in danger here.

"That's enough! Stop following me around like a lost puppy."

"Why are you acting like this?"

"Like what?"

"So...*bitchy*! Standoffish, snooty...take your pick."

"You're acting like you've done me a favor by getting yourself thrown in here."

"Haven't I?"

"No, you haven't. This is worst-case scenario for you. Trust me."

"Oh, I don't think so, Lisha. Sooner or later you'll realize we're better off together. As a team."

"What fucking world are you living in? Back *off.*" I shove her then, nearly knocking her to the ground and wishing I had.

"Wait! I really do need to talk to you."

"I'm not interested."

"Lisha, *please—*"

Her words are left unanswered when I veer off in the opposite direction. I expect her to follow, but to my surprise she doesn't.

Instead, she stands there with a sad look on her face as if I've hurt her feelings.

But that's good, that's what I needed. For her to feel like she has nothing.

No one.

Because when you're faced with an enemy, sometimes it's best to leave them on edge, to let that fear build up in the back of their mind and settle into the pit of their stomach.

You want them to know revenge is coming but have no idea when it'll happen.

Because devils disguised as humans do make the best predators.

LIKE HER

Caramie

I SETTLE Dylan in his new crib and tiptoe out the door, careful not to wake him as I close it softly behind me. He's usually a good sleeper, but nap time can be tricky, and he did his best to skip one today.

Not that I blame him.

Some days I don't want to nap either.

It's been hard these last few weeks, and maybe that's to be expected. But this wait has been long, this time in limbo. Everything is starting to feel normal—*intentional*. Like I'm an actual single mom staying home to raise my son on my own accord. I cook, I clean, I take care of Dylan. But at night, once he's asleep, I bide my time. I wait for the phone to ring, for someone to tell me what to do next.

But the call hasn't come.

Some days I wonder if it ever will.

So, I check for strange people outside, peering through the curtains like a crazy person. I jump at every sound, even the softest ones that don't carry the slightest threat. I can't shake this paranoia, this nagging

464

voice warning me that everything could still fall apart. That something has gone wrong and my services are no longer needed.

And what happens then?

What if Connor Ehrens finds out what I've done to Sawyer? What if he comes looking for me and wants to settle the score? Will he make it quick and painless? Will he kill this child, too? I've never met the man, never so much as seen him in person, but that doesn't make him any less threatening.

Not knowing only makes it worse…gives the fear something to eat.

Will he come for me?

These questions roam my mind, and before long, I find myself wandering aimlessly down the hall until I'm standing in front of Alisha's bedroom, the one she shared with her late husband. It's been over a month now, and I haven't had the guts to open the door. Sometimes I end up standing here, staring, and trying to convince myself that it won't be so bad if I go in there.

But what if the blood hasn't been cleaned up?

What if it's still there? All over the bed, the floors?

I've seen pictures of the crime scene, proof of the events that happened beyond this door. Those pictures won't compare to what I may be walking into, and I don't think I'd be able to get these images out of my mind if that room is still in the same condition.

Surely she'd have hired a cleaning service once the scene was cleared and released, right? Someone to come in and strip the room bare, replace the carpet, the furniture, maybe repaint the walls. Unless she likes that blood-spattered ceiling look.

I just want to go inside, take a look around. I've been dying to go through Alisha's closet, try on her clothes, see all of her most prized intimates, the secrets she keeps locked away from the world. Every woman has them—the secrets—even the ones who don't appear to be hiding anything at all.

And most of Alisha's have already been exposed; I'm not stupid. I know better than to think there aren't more. But I'd be lying if I said Alisha hasn't captured a lot of my imagination lately. She's not even here, and I still can't stop myself from thinking about her. And it's my own fault, really, this newfound obsession with her. I never should have brought emotions into this, but I couldn't stop myself from falling for the woman on the screen, the one who gave me this opportunity in the first place. All I wanted was to know more about her, get inside her head a little bit. Find out what once made this woman so special.

Find out if she still is.

I hadn't imagined she'd be so *good* at what she did.

Or that I'd be interested.

God, I'd give anything to look like that woman.

To not give a fuck like her.

That's why I find myself turning the knob on her bedroom door now. Why, despite my resolve, despite the crippling fear that there could be dried blood *everywhere* in there, I do it. I open the door and flick the switch to turn on the light.

It's not so bad.

The bed is gone. The carpet is removed, stripped down to the hardwoods. Sure, they could use a polishing, but they're in quite good condition, considering. I wish I could tell you the walls had been repainted, but they haven't. That's one chore I guess I'll have to do myself, a gift for when she comes home, I suppose.

Only a few minutes pass before I make my way to her closet.

Before I'm trying on her clothes.

I don't mean to; it just kind of happens. They're all so pretty, so fashion-forward. Expensive. Her heel collection is impressive, and lucky for me we're the same size. I feel like Cinderella the moment my foot slides into her Jimmy Choos. *My God, these are like little pillows for your feet!*

I find the camera in a box in the back of the closet, equipped with an instructional sheet on how to set it up and notes about her preferred settings, the best angles.

I can't stop myself from setting it up, from putting on the lingerie.

And now the camera is on, the red light an indication that it's rolling, and I'm capturing these moments in time as if I care to remember this transgression.

I don't.

But heat radiates between my legs.

I picture Alisha, in the few video clips I've seen, the photos, how she exudes such confidence and sex appeal, and I look into the camera the same way she used to.

Pucker my lips.

I know it's ridiculous, and I'm definitely not proud of it, but I can't help myself.

I spend the next hour masturbating in the woman's closet, hoping that when I come out I'll take a little bit of her with me. Because now that I've had a taste of what her life was like, there's nothing I want more than to live it.

RENT-FREE

Alisha

THERE WAS a time when I hated getting mail in prison.

I couldn't stomach the idea of this place being considered *home*, that I'd taken up a residential address here. The thought was disheartening, enough so that I despised that damn mail cart every time it came squeaking around the corner.

These days I embrace the postal service.

I look forward to the letters, the ones from my friend, Chris that come with books and pictures of him and his husband, Kevin, promises that we'll hang out again one day. The fan mail from creepy old dudes that still manage to get their hands on pirated content from my former website. But the letters I look forward to the most are the ones from my father.

I know it's weird, but it's true. My father writes to me, and while I haven't read a single one of his letters, I look forward to them. I simmer on the fact that my presence here eats him alive, feeds the guilt nestled in his belly like a bad habit.

He *should* feel guilty.

Because my father is a coward.

There's a new letter from him today and it's thicker than the ones he usually sends, but still, I don't open it. Instead, I pull the small box out from under my bed and stuff the envelope in there with the rest of them before moving on to the next piece of mail in my stack.

Caramie's name graces the top left corner of an otherwise plain white envelope.

What is she thinking sending me mail here?

The return address is my own—well, former—home, which is upsetting, yet comforting at the same time. I knew she didn't run; Kyle had mentioned as much when I asked him to find her, but I can't say I expected her to use *my* house either. Or that I approve.

I tear open the envelope and find a half sheet of paper in perfectly printed penmanship.

I found these in a shoe box in your closet. Please don't be mad at me for snooping. I just thought you might like to have them there with you, so I made copies and stored the originals in an air-tight container for safekeeping when you get home, whenever that will be.

All the best,
   Cara

I'm hit with a rush of facts: that Caramie is still staying at *my* house, and she had to be snooping pretty thoroughly to find this collection in my closet.

Which means she went into my bedroom.

I unfold the first letter.

My breath catches at the sight of Dylan's handwriting on the page, and I bring a hand to my mouth to stifle a gasp. I'd forgotten about these, that I'd saved them—the little notes he'd leave around the house for me, love letters he stuck in birthday cards.

I thought they were gone; like him.

My Dearest Alisha,

I'm ashamed of my behavior. I know I'll be apologizing for the rest of my life, but I promise you, it'll be worth it when you forgive me. I'm not proud of how we met, the things I've said and done to make you mine, but I don't regret us; not even for a second. I think you do sometimes, but the truth is, the only thing I wish is that I'd met you sooner, maybe in a different way.

But you're it for me, Alisha, that one true love they write about in books. The ones that make you cry when they end up together at the end of the movie. I'll spend the rest of my life proving that to you if that's what it takes for you to forgive me.

I loved you yesterday, I love you today, and I'll love you tomorrow. Even if you think I don't deserve to.

Yours,
   Dylan

His voice surrounds me as I take in the sight of his slanted handwriting. As I remember the way his mouth used to move when he spoke, the smile lines on his face that he hated so much. He's said these very words to me before, all of them. They are not new, but right now, in this moment, they mean so much more than they did before.

I feel like he's with me right now and I never want him to leave again. Like I want him to get into my head and live there rent-free forever.

No matter what happens tomorrow or the day after that, my only purpose left in this life is retribution, avenging my husband's death. Looking after his son.

Because it's my fault he's not here to raise him in the first place.

FISHING 101

Ivy

I NEVER IMAGINED I'd find myself fishing for drugs in a combination unit toilet. Then again, I never expected to be an inmate in a federal penitentiary either, yet here we are.

This is absurd.

And disgusting beyond the definition of the word.

But, I'm doing just that: fishing for drugs in a fucking toilet.

It's a *thing* in places like this, and I'll tell you how it's done while I sit here waiting for my turn to flush. There's a whole process, and it's quite clever despite the fact that it's unsanitary beyond belief. Whoever thought to do this must've been pretty desperate.

The Smithson Women's Penitentiary is unique in that it was built vertically, with a courtyard at its center; essentially it's a tower. And it's an old one, so what it lacks in width, it makes up for in height.

Eight wings, otherwise known as pods or blocks, divided into four stories, plus an extra for intake, medical, the (so-called) gymnasium, another for what's known as the basement dungeon (solitary confinement) and storage (for God knows what), and another for the parking garage.

That's eight stories in total.

Each of which are fitted with vertical plumbing.

It makes sense from a structural standpoint, but the whole design was flawed the moment someone realized they could send contraband through the toilets. It's really no wonder drugs are an ongoing issue in correctional facilities like these. And the sad thing is, everyone knows how to fish—whether they partake is another question—even the COs who want to make a quick buck, thanks to a lone rat or two throughout the years.

And while the COs are well aware of the of what goes on in these cells at night, unless the government wants to fork over a hefty chunk of change to redesign the plumbing in this dump, there's really no way for them to cut off the distribution channel.

Once those goods make it through the main doors undetected, there's little chance of interference from the prison staff unless you're stupid enough to get caught in the middle of a fishing expedition, but that's why we have conspirators and cellmates that double as lookouts, right?

The hardest part of the job isn't the fishing itself—it's not the fact that you have to siphon the water from the toilet bowl and stick your hands in there to send or receive the "rope"—it's *storage* once the goods make it into your toilet-water hands.

You have to hide the contraband in a way that guarantees it won't be found in the event of a tossed cell or raid, which the COs can invoke at any time but rarely do. Proper storage is still necessary because, let's face it, no one wants to catch extra charges just because they played in the toilet during recess.

There are plenty of places to hide things in here, but you have to get creative—in my case, when storing mass quantities of drugs—because the last thing a drug dealer needs is for their inventory to be confiscated. Tampon tubes, soap bars, toilet paper rolls, air vents—rookie mistake—mattresses, the list goes on. Basically everything has a nook or cranny—or a loose brick—that can be penetrated.

So, here, let me show you how it's done, I'd say if I were filming this for YouTube. After fashioning a "fishing" line from some shredded prison-issued white T-shirts, I wait for my turn to flush and hope these plastic spoons at the end of the rope intertwine somewhere in the pipe like they're supposed to so I can give it a good pull and retrieve a plastic bag stuffed to the brim with pills. Someone on the other side was even kind enough to make sure said bag would fit through the pipes. Thoughtful, I know.

Connor Ehrens is the asshole I get to thank for my newly acquired fishing skills. He's the one who taught me the trade—and told me to *suck it up and get to work* when I snarled at the idea of sticking my hands in a toilet.

I do, after all, have a debt to pay off, regardless of my culpability, and smuggling drugs through the toilets is apparently the way to do that. Once a week I get to prove to my "boss" why I'm worthy of this wonderful life I live, and unless I want to end up shanked and bleeding out in the middle of a dimly lit hallway during passing time, this is how I'll spend my Sunday evenings.

Why he can't find a better way to smuggle pills into this place is not my concern, so I'm told. So, I do my part, go through the motions as efficiently as possible to limit the amount of time spent hovering over the commode.

Don't worry, I cleaned it first.

Hold thy breath.

Siphon the water from the toilet bowl into the sink.

Tie the plastic spoon to the end of the fabricated T-shirt rope.

Meticulously watch the clock until it strikes the given minute and second.

Flush.

Pull.

But not so hard that the trusty T-shirt rope snaps and all the drugs get lost in Pipeville, Population: shit outta luck.

Who said you can't learn a thing or two in prison?

When it works, I fight the urge to perform a happy dance.

Drugs in hand, I use an undershirt—note to self: don't wear that tomorrow—to dry off the plastic bag and then double-check the contents to make sure all of the product is there and that none of the pills were contaminated in the great toilet bowl plunge.

Satisfied with the count and quality, I begin the process of stuffing the round pills into tampon applicators, repackaging each one with five pills and fitting them neatly back into the box they came in.

Throughout the week the fiends will come to "borrow a tampon" and Connor Ehrens will have made an easy ten grand, which I will see none of on account of the debt I'll be paying off against my will for the foreseeable future.

I suppose I shouldn't complain; at least he opted to use me instead of sending some crazy bitch to off me. And I guess it beats shoving the goods up the 'ole pooper.

At least there's that.

VIEWING PARTY

Alisha

THERE'S a secluded corner of the library off D-wing where inmates go to get laid. All the women in my unit know about it, and they speak about it freely, like it's as normal as a trip to Target, which actually sounds nice right about now.

I've been invited to the library more times than I care to admit, and if I'm being honest, I figured it was a myth for one simple reason: there are eyes watching us everywhere we go.

Cameras.

Literally everywhere.

At the beginning of my time here, I actually believed the COs—with the exception of CO Marshall—gave a shit about the rules. That they intended to enforce them, to keep us on the straight and narrow. I've since learned there are more corrupt officers in this dump than there are helicopter moms trailing behind their kids at the food court in the Mall of America.

And that's saying something.

There's one officer in particular—the one who transferred in from max after CO Marshall's departure—who especially likes to get his dick wet. They say he's the reason that secluded, camera-less corner of the library exists. The reason some of the inmates go missing at night without explanation, only to show up to breakfast the next morning looking satisfied and well spent.

They even go willingly—so they say.

I used to think these missing inmates were off in solitary or perhaps medical, maybe visiting the infamous psych ward. That they were troublemakers who managed to avoid the night count, only to suffer through agonies far worse.

I couldn't have been more wrong.

I got a good look at the space when I met CO Ryerson there last week. I was graced with his company thanks to my good friend and keeper, Tiffany Malone, who took it upon herself to drag me down there. And I'm only mildly embarrassed to admit I find Ryerson attractive as hell; that the thought of having sex with him does things to my vagina that haven't been done since my husband was killed.

"Should we be down here?" I ask Tiffany.

"Relax, we have special privileges tonight."

"What does that even mean?"

"Just...shut up. Don't make me break out the muzzle."

"Let's not pretend you have one of those."

She winks and pulls me further down the hall until we reach the library. The door squeaks as she pulls it open, but there's no one around to hear it so we move forward.

"The library? Really? There are cameras in here," I whisper, my heart ready to leap from my chest.

"Not tonight there aren't."

And I'll admit, a sex club in the bowels of a prison library was the least likely explanation for the inmates' frequent absences, but one of these days I'll learn not to let anything surprise me.

At least the inmates he fucks are consenting adults, I suppose. But only if you ignore the fact that his actions *technically* warrant felony charges, because an inmate can't legally consent to sex. In the eyes of the law, Ryerson's no less of a rapist than CO Marshall was, though I beg to differ. If anyone were to find out what he's up to, he'd lose his job and be sent to a federal prison faster than he can fill a condom with jizz.

That doesn't make him any less attractive.

"Hello, Alisha."

"I didn't realize we were on a first-name basis."

"In here we are, yes."

"Then what's yours?"

"Nice try, Thompson."

Shit.

"What's the catch?"

"It's a viewing party."

"Meaning?"

He nods to a handful of inmates making their way through the racks. As if on cue, they start removing their clothes, and it's incredible how much prettier everyone is when the prison uniforms come off.

"We play. They watch," Ryerson says.

Through *my* eyes he's a walking, talking dildo that I'd like nothing more than to play with on a daily basis, but I'm going to pretend I didn't just admit that.

It's hard being a sex addict in prison; give me a break.

And it's funny how far a person's standards go down when they have nothing left to lose.

I sit on his words for a moment before it sinks in, and I find myself shrugging with nonchalance; it's not like an audience is anything new, and at this point, I'm so desperate for a real-life dick that my inhibitions are pretty low. "That's fair," I say before trolling my eyes up and down his body.

He's still dressed, so he's not doing much for my libido just yet, but my spidey sense tells me there's an enticing package beneath that government-issued uniform.

"Are you clean?" I ask.

"Of course." As if proving a point, he reaches into his pocket and pulls out a strip of condoms. "I've got these, too. They're not optional,

in case you're wondering." And I gotta give Ryerson credit when I notice they're regulars. It's always nice when a man sets the proper expectations.

"I want you to perform for me," he says. "For all of us."

"Excuse me?"

"Like you used to. I'll give you a few minutes," he says before disappearing behind a rack of books. The women are watching, like they were promised a show even before I walked in here.

Tiffany passes me a zipper bag filled with red liquid and fruit peels. "Here, this should help you relax."

"What is it?"

"Pruno."

"The fuck is that?"

"Hooch? Juice? It's liquor, Thompson. Drink up." I don't bother asking how it got in here.

"I don't drink."

For her next trick, she pulls out a small baggie of white pills, holding them in her palm like a gift. "How 'bout this then? Rumor has it your girl is slinging oxy these days."

Ivy's selling drugs? In prison?

"I'm good."

"Really? You don't need somethin' to take the edge off a little?"

"Nope," I say, and the music kicks in. It's some pop song I've never heard, but it's as close to porn music as we'll get, so it'll have to do for my little strip tease. With a smile, I remove my top and swing it around my head before dropping it to the ground, and the action is met by whistles and applause.

It's rare I give these women what they want, but in here, tonight, I'm desperate enough to make an exception. I sway seductively to the music, letting it take over my body. With my hands tangled in my hair, I dance, my body exposed to the prying eyes before me. I bring a hand to my breast, teasing the nipple, pulling it taut and sending a shock throughout my body.

As the cheering ramps up, I hook my thumbs into my pants and slowly slide them down, dragging my hands along my thighs before kicking them off.

The fact that I'm now fully nude sparks a thrill of excitement, and I grab a chair and lean over it, shaking my ass and twerking just a little for the women. I sit, spreading my legs and pushing myself up with my arms, arching my back.

When Ryerson makes his way back into the room, he's naked too, his body tanned and toned and his cock fully erect, ready to play. A hush falls over the room as the women drink in the sight of him, and I try not to salivate myself, but the man looks damn good, and I can't help it.

I smile.

Because I get to be the one to devour him.

He stands in front of me, leaning down and bringing his lips to mine, our tongues tasting one another. As we kiss, the women move in, circling around us like hungry vultures, and I feel their hands on me—touching, caressing, as they explore my body. They're on Ryerson, too, but I can see that it's me he wants, and I nibble at his bottom lip to remind him of that.

I slide off the chair and drop to my knees at his feet, taking Ryerson's cock in my hands and stroking the shaft before bringing him in my mouth. With my eyes closed, he's not too far off from Dylan in size and shape, and I moan at the memory of my husband. But Ryerson moans too, and I'm brought quickly back to reality. This isn't Dylan's cock in my mouth, but at least it's there by choice.

"Get it, girl!" Ronnie coaches from the gallery.

Ryerson's hips thrust, rocking back and forth as he fucks my mouth, and I gag just a little before he pulls out and unwraps a condom. He rolls it on and leads me to an open spot of floor.

"On your hands and knees," he instructs, and I bend over before him, reaching back and spreading my ass cheeks so he can enjoy the view. He grunts before rubbing the tip of his cock on my wetness, pushing into me slowly, and I groan—because my fucking God, it feels so good.

I've missed this.

He thrusts at a rapid pace, and I feel him everywhere, his hands, his cock. And when the euphoria hits, it's like life is suddenly good again—like I can finally breathe in spite of being under water.

And I know you won't understand what I'm talking about, that this probably doesn't make any sense to you—how could it, when this picture I'm painting is so grotesque?

But this feeling, sex like this, is what makes me feel alive.

It's what I've been missing since I lost Dylan.

"You look so sexy when you get fucked," Tiffany whispers as she crawls to me. She's removed her clothes, and her tits drag on the floor as she makes her way over. Her mouth finds mine, and for the first time, I kiss her back like I mean it.

Because my body tells me to.

She lies down in front of me, spreading her legs and pulling my face toward her heat. I lick and suck then slide a finger inside of her as she bucks her hips against my mouth.

Ryerson fucks harder and harder...smacking my ass and then reaching around to rub my clit. My pussy tightens around his cock and I come hard, my body spasming from the relief of my orgasm.

When he doesn't stop, I'm grateful.

I come twice more before he pulls out and drapes himself across my back. His breath is hot on my neck, sweat slick on my shoulder as we breathe together, coming down from the high.

But the ecstasy doesn't last much longer.

"Tomorrow when you go to your Sex Anon meeting," Ryerson whispers, bringing a hand to my neck, "you're going to talk about how much you miss this feeling. How it makes you wet just dreaming about getting pounded like this again. Because this, Thompson? Never. Fucking. Happened."

He gives my ass one last smack before rising to his feet and turning off the music. "Fun's over, ladies," he announces as Tiffany slides out from under me.

"Does it always end like this?" I ask her, trying not to pout. She nods.

"Happy birthday, beautiful," she says with a kiss.

And I want to cry when the shame hits me.
Because that's what Dylan used to say.

Ivy's at her door pacing back and forth when I'm returned to my cell twenty minutes later. She's been waiting up for me, stressed about where I had run off to and why.

"Where were you?" she asks through the door.

But I don't answer, just step into my cell and let Ryerson lock the door behind me. And even though his final words tonight were a buzz kill, the fact that Ivy's beside herself with worry settles my nerves.

I sleep like a fucking baby.

LEADER OF THE PACK

Ivy

THERE'S a hush in the dining hall during breakfast; a lull, if you will, slicing right through the monotony of morning conversation. To the average inmate, this is nothing out of the norm: a typical morning in federal lockup.

To me, it's a warning.

A sign that one of us must be up to something, and I think I might know who.

Malone stares daggers at me from across the room, her lip turned up like that of a growling dog. I feel the weight of her stare in my gut, see the way her hand brushes against Alisha's thigh beneath the table.

She's showing her teeth—staking claim to someone who doesn't belong to her.

"All right, ladies, time to report for work assignments," CO Marin announces from her post at the double doors. Clipboard in hand, she makes a point of checking the roster to make sure we all head off in the right directions.

The grumbling floats throughout the room as I dump my tray and drop it into the wash bin before making my way toward the library. CO Marin catches my arm, stopping me in place before I can pass.

"Not today, Rogers. You're on janitorial duty the rest of the week."

"Excuse me?"

"Toilets, inmate. Let's go."

"Nuh-uh, no way."

"Are you refusing to report for your designated work assignment? Because that would be a strikeable violation."

"Of course not, but you can't be serious. Do I look like the kind of person who cleans toilets?"

"What you look like is the kind of person who *should* clean toilets," Marin barks with a snicker before folding her arms across her chest.

"How do you figure?"

"Because it's about time you say goodbye to the view from up there on your high horse."

"This is ridiculous."

"Take it up with someone who cares, Rogers. Toilets. Now."

What's a girl gotta do to get away from the commodes around here?

I sigh and stomp over to the supply cart, grabbing a plastic bucket filled with rags and cleaning products before making my way to the D-block bathrooms. My feet are heavy as I move, dread fueling every step. This isn't right, this midweek reassignment. I may still be new here, but even *I* know something doesn't add up.

It only takes another moment for my suspicions to be confirmed.

Because Malone's the one standing at the bathroom sink with a shiv in her hand.

"So *you're* the reason I'm on toilet duty today."

"Ah, five points for perception. Nothing gets by you, does it?"

"Fuck off."

Her posse appears as if out of nowhere, and I silently chastise myself for mouthing off to her in such a secluded space. I should have known she wouldn't be here alone, that her minions would be lurking in the shadows ready to do her dirty work. The leader of the pack rarely travels alone.

At the nod of her head, the women charge forward and take hold of my arms, their fingernails digging into my skin. I grimace and try to fight them off, but it's no use. They're stronger together, the lot of them, and I won't break free from their grasp no matter how hard I resist.

So I don't.

I'll be forced to accept whatever punishment is about to be brought down on me. For what, exactly, I don't know. But I don't see Alisha among the pack, and I take that as a sign of something, too.

Because maybe it bodes well for me that she isn't here.

They drag me into a stall and force me to my knees, pulling me down by my hair and shoving my head toward the dirty toilet. I know it's coming, but still I'm shocked when they push—when they hold me down and force my face into the water, my forehead smacking against the bottom of the bowl. A wave of pain flutters through me and I open my mouth to scream, but it's a mistake and I quickly take on water, choking as I fight the incessant urge to vomit.

This water isn't clean.

It tastes like piss and shit and yesterday's dinner.

My lungs on fire, I kick and try to punch but my efforts are worthless. I can't breathe…the water…

"Let her up," I hear faintly through water-logged ears before I'm yanked out of the muck.

I cough and burp and gag, and I don't know what the fuck is stuck in my throat, but I cough some more to rattle it loose. It takes several minutes to orient myself, for the cobwebs to clear and the shit to be wiped from my eyes before I can see again.

But it's her, like I knew it would be.

Alisha looks pissed, her brows folded into a scowl, locked into a staredown with Malone, who looks anything but apologetic. Her minions laugh at the sight of me, and I'm not so sure I blame them. I don't imagine I look my best after inhaling a toilet bowl full of shit.

"Out."

It hits me then, the smell, and it's enough to gag a maggot. It's everywhere, lodged in my nostrils, my mouth…my eyes. Surely, I've ingested the bowels of a fellow inmate, probably Malone's. And at that realization, I can't stop it from happening; I vomit all over the stall floor, my insides on fire as I heave.

"When are you going to learn, Ivy?"

"What…did I…do?" I choke out between coughs.

But Alisha's gone. They all are.

And I'm left alone to clean up the mess I've made.

GOOD MOURNING

Alisha

IN MY MOMENTS OF WEAKNESS, I wish I'd never met her.

That I hadn't given her the opening she needed to infiltrate my life the way she did. But that's what selfish people do: they find a way in. And then they take.

And they take.

And then they take some more.

That probably goes without saying, but I'm saying it anyway—putting it on the official record.

I don't know why I stopped Tiffany's band of misfits from drowning Ivy in that toilet. I don't. But then again, maybe I do. Because if anyone deserves to kill her, it's me. I won't let Tiffany or anyone else take that away from me.

It's *Ivy's* fault that I cheated on my husband in that library. *Her* fault that he's dead, because if I'd never met her, I'd never have met *him*, and maybe that would've been for the best. To be fair, I realize what I did last night *technically* wasn't cheating—you can't cheat on a dead man—but every part of my body feels this betrayal for what it is.

Last night my addiction got the best of me.

Because I let it.

And I don't think I would have if *she* wasn't here. I never should have brought her here. I guess maybe I wasn't ready to face her, not yet. In my defense, I didn't expect to see her so soon. Things moved rather quickly after her arrest, and I don't think anyone could have predicted she'd have plead guilty to a first-degree murder charge, that she'd bow down the way she did.

But that's exactly what she did, because apparently that's the life *I* deserve.

She's here because of me.

A fellow inmate.

And she's relentless in her pursuit, determined to get what she came here for, to stake her claim on me once again. But mark my words: I will not give in to her. She will *not* win this battle.

There was a time not so long ago when I could still look at her and smile. When I felt a slight tug on the 'ol heartstrings whenever she walked into a room.

She had gotten to me.

And I'll never forgive myself for it.

I've nearly forgotten what that feels like now—how not to hate her —because right now she's the only person who knows me from the outside. The only person here I've ever been excited to wake up next to.

She stares at me from across the lunch room now, her eyes red and clearly infected from her splash session in the bathroom, but they may as well have tiny red hearts in the centers of them because she looks like she's doing her best to cast a love spell on me.

Is it working? I imagine her asking.

Our souls are equally dark, hers and mine. Damaged. And that's what keeps us connected to this place. I feel like she knows that. Like she sees my weakness for what it is and will do what she can to use it to her advantage.

But there's no truth left for us, not in this life. Our husbands are gone now, their bodies left to rot in the ground, us—their widows—unable even to lie graveside in mourning.

So, there's no room for *good* mourning. Ours is not the kind that heals you and gives you the strength to move on, to continue living while you try to patch up the giant hole in your heart one measly stitch at a time.

This is the shitty kind of mourning. The unfair, stupid, and entirely preventable kind. No one should have to bear the loss of their spouse, not like this. Yet, we do.

I mourn every single day.

I will never stop.

Not until she's dead.

And it's coming.

I don't know what I expected from her arrival, but this isn't it.

Anger, yes.

Relief, probably.

But confusion? No. This is a surprise. I wanted her here for one reason and one reason only: she deserves to die for what she's done to me.

To Dylan.

And his son.

For ruining my life and setting me up to take the fall for it. Her betrayal was a power play; a chance to show her hand just because she could.

So I'll take her down with me—just because *I* can.

Not that it prevents the guilt from festering in my soul. Because maybe Sawyer didn't deserve the fate he was given, either, but let's not pretend his hands were any cleaner than Ivy's.

Let's not pretend her time in mourning is anything less than fair.

YOU SHOULDN'T HAVE

Caramie

THINGS ARE quiet on the home front.

They always are.

I suppose that's normal for a woman on the run, not that I consider myself one of those. I *do* leave the house sometimes—for the grocery store mostly, and sometimes I even take Dylan for walks to the park. So, I'm *not* running. In fact, most of the time, I'm very much standing still; like my life is on pause.

Just until all this blows over—not that I'm closer to figuring out when that will be.

With my morning coffee in hand, I pace the dining room because it's been one of *those* mornings. The kind where my mind races a mile a minute like it's competing in a marathon. I hate *those* mornings, but this is what the waiting does to me.

I'm a planner.

So you can see how being kept in the dark might be an issue for me.

There's too much time to think.

To remember.

"Is he out?"

"Like a grizzly bear," I say. "It worked, the stuff you said to put in his drink."

"Good, I'm coming to get you."

"No, you can't. I'll come to you. Just…can we meet at our spot? Down by the lake where Mom used to take us?"

"Thirty minutes, Cara. If you're not there I'm coming to get you myself."

I end the call and slide the phone into my back pocket before scooping up my go bag. There's not much inside, just a couple changes of clothes, shoes, and hygiene products, along with my purse and the small amount of cash in my wallet.

That's it, my whole life zipped into a satchel.

I peek my head into the living room one last time to confirm Josh is asleep—it's now or never. I tiptoe to the back door and slip outside, into the darkness.

And I run.

I run as fast as my legs can take me, the wind cold on my face, the tears falling down my cheeks. I cry for myself.

I cry for Josh.

For what we could have been.

And then I let it go. I breathe.

Because I'm finally free.

I'm startled by the sound of my burner phone ringing, and I spill my coffee in my hurry to answer it. If I miss this call, there's no telling how long it'll be before I receive another. "Alisha? You there?"

"Hey, yeah, it's me."

"It's been *days*, how are you?"

"Have you spoken to her?" she asks, ignoring my question. Her one-track mind annoys the hell out of me sometimes, but I suppose limited time to talk will do that.

"No, I haven't."

"You're sure?"

"I swear on it. Why?"

"Have you ever known her to use drugs?"

"Um, *yes*. Often, actually. Had a thing for booze, too."

"Really?"

"You didn't know that?" She's quiet for a moment, and I imagine her shaking her head in disappointment. "I think it started after Sawyer left her," I add, but the commentary is met with more silence.

"How's Dylan?" she finally asks.

"He's good. Getting big."

"Do you have everything he needs?"

"And then some."

"Good. When are you leaving?"

"What?"

"You shouldn't have stayed in town, Cara. You know it's not safe there."

"We're perfectly safe here," I argue.

"You're not. You should go."

"I—I don't want to go. *Please*. Let me stay here for a while."

She breathes into the phone, the weight of her frustration evident. And it's not that I mean to upset her, but Dylan and I are comfortable here. It feels like home. "Can I ask you a question?"

"Sure."

"What was it like? Doing your show, I mean. Being in the spotlight like that?"

"I wasn't in the spotlight until my husband was murdered, Cara. It wasn't like that before."

And I want to tell her what I've done—how I went through her stuff and what I found in that box. I *really* do. But the shame hits me before I can push the confession out, and I say nothing.

"Stay out of my closet," she warns through her teeth before hanging up.

And my heart drops at the sound of the call disconnecting.

Because now the waiting starts all over again.

STUCK

Alisha

THERE'S this recurring dream keeping me awake at night. I'm sure there's an underlying metaphor in it somewhere, a lesson I'm supposed to learn from it, but I don't have the mental capacity to give it too much thought.

In the dream, I'm running.

I run and I run and I don't stop. Not even when my chest burns, when my lungs are so heavy they could burst from the pressure and my legs are soft like jelly, the muscles weakening with each painful step. I keep running harder and harder, and it doesn't even matter because I'm not getting anywhere.

I'm running in place, and no matter how hard I try, I can't bring myself to move forward.

I'm just *stuck* there.

In motion, but unable to break free, like a dog on a leash.

And he's standing right there in front me, a hologram of sorts. I can see him, so I know he's *there*, but I can't touch him. I can't even reach him. Blood congeals around the open wounds in his torso, the deep lacerations on his wrists. *From the handcuffs*, they said. His face is forever frozen in pain, terrified.

I want to turn and run away from him, but I can't.

Because she's there, too.

And she's not going to let me out of her sight.

I'm hers forever now, she says.

And I believe her.

Because whatever Ivy wants, Ivy gets.

"Earth to Thompson. You all right?"

"Hm?"

"There she is! You daydreaming again, Barbie?" Ronnie asks.

"Shit, sorry. I was thinking."

"Must be painful," Tiffany jokes, nudging me in the arm.

"Hardy har," I mock.

"New work assignments this morning, ladies," CO Marin pipes in. "You have five minutes to report to your designated workstations. Posts are up on the board."

We gather around the bulletin board like actors trying to read a cast list, only with much less at stake. Work assignments change every few weeks to keep things interesting. They say it makes us more well-rounded inmates, leaves us better suited to rejoin society when our sentences are up, but if you ask me, it's just another way for them to punish us.

Because as soon as we get used to a job, they're pulling us away to start a new one, never quite giving us a chance to excel at anything.

Keeps us on our toes, I guess.

Not that it matters much to me; work is work. At least, it never used to. "The call center, Marin? *Really?*" She shrugs because she couldn't care less where we go as long as we go there and get shit done.

"How'd you get so lucky, Thompson?" Ronnie whines. "I got dish duty again."

"Trust me, the last place I want to work is the call center."

"Keep telling yourself that."

"Yeah, they probably picked you cuz they like your sexy phone voice," Tiffany teases. "I'm sure it's good for business."

"Miss Marin, what are we selling?"

"You're not. Market research only."

"Don't they have bots for that kind of grunt work these days?"

"Believe it not, Thompson, those fancy bot dialers cost more than you do. Gotta love outsourcing, huh?" And I laugh, because she's right. Seven hours of my time not even a couple years ago would've cost a hell of lot more than this place seems to think I'm worth.

I step away from the board, pushing my way through the crowd of women still waiting to see what work unit they ended up in for the next three weeks. I catch Ivy in the hall as I make my way to the call center.

"Hey, Ivy, wait up," I call behind her, taking her elbow.

"Hey, yourself," she says, pulling it away and picking up the pace. It's clear she doesn't want to talk today—how unlike her—but I persist, keeping up with her as we round the corner.

"How are the eyes?"

"They're fine," she huffs, and I use the moment to stop her with my arm, shoving her against the wall.

"What's this I hear about you selling oxy?"

"Why? You lookin' for some?"

"No. Are you selling?"

"Too bad," she says with a click of her tongue. "And what do you care?"

"Ivy, come on." But she pushes off the wall with her foot, the momentum enough to slide away from me.

"Gotta go."

"Stay off the shit!" I call behind her.

"Keep it down, inmates," CO Ryerson bellows from the end of the hall. With a sigh, I turn the corner and buzz myself into the call center, signing my name on the check-in sheet before finding an open cubicle in the back.

I take a seat and fasten a headset to the top of my dome, and because there's no point in dwelling on something that can't be changed—the fact that I'm stuck in here for the next seven hours—I click the first name of the list and dial the number.

"Hello, Mr. Faringer, this is Alisha calling from Tanson, Inc. Do you have a few minutes to answer some market research questions for me?"

BLOWOUT

Alisha

IVY DROPS two cards face down on the pile. "Two sixes," she says.

"One seven," Ronnie follows, and the fact that they're sitting next to each other, huddled around the day room table playing cards together, has my mind blown. They give each other the stink eye, but it looks harmless, just a semi-friendly challenge in a neighborhood game of bullshit.

But I know better than to assume Tiffany's BFF and her arch-enemy have kissed and made up. Especially considering Ivy's been avoiding me the last couple days. But there are pills beneath that pile, strategically placed there when Ivy's three cards hit the table, left on purpose for one of her regulars to swipe when she calls them out on their lie. Clever? Not entirely, but maybe the ploy is only obvious if you're me and able to spot a hand-off in your sleep. Seventeen years with a mother like mine will teach that to a person.

A trick of the trade, perhaps.

CO Shields and her posse walk the perimeter, their eyes scanning for anything amiss, signs that we're up to no good—but they won't notice Ivy's game. Sometimes it's best to make contraband exchanges in broad daylight on account of the many COs with a stake of their own in the game. I'm not sure I blame them, but if you want my opinion, there are better ways to make money in prison than to turn the other way while the trades go on.

Protection being one of them.

That's why I tapped into Ryerson when I had the chance. I'm not one to pass up a good opportunity, not in here, and a man like him will do just about anything if it guarantees he gets to screw a porn star on the regular. Not that a couple times a week is what I'd consider regular, but I don't have many viable options these days, so I'm not complaining about the new norm.

Nonetheless, Ivy is up to something. I can feel it.

Whatever got her into this pill trading mess isn't my problem, but if she's the one to go to for oxy, that means she's secured some protection of her own.

"Three eights," I say, dropping a ten and two threes face down onto the pile. My move won't be challenged, though, because I'm not the one meant to end up with the stash at the bottom.

I hate it when the game is rigged, but what can ya do?

"Malone, Thompson, you have visitors," CO Shields announces.

"Who?"

"Do I look like your secretary? Let's go, ladies."

I drop the rest of my cards face down on the table and push to my feet alongside Tiffany, annoyed that I won't be around to find out who was meant to pick up the stash at the bottom of that pile. There's a limited number of women at the table, and all I can do is hope like hell that it's not Ronnie's buy.

She's been clean for a few months now.

Shields escorts Tiffany and me out of the unit and into the visitor center, and my heart skips a beat when I see Chris's childlike smile gleaming at me as I walk in. I'd run and jump into his arms if I could; it's been much too long since we've seen each other.

"You look like shit," he says when we take advantage of our

allotted three-second embrace. Any longer can draw an officer's attention, and I'd like to keep them at bay today. I'd hate to see our visit cut short after flying him out here.

"Thank you," I say with a laugh. We sit, and he smiles again, reaching across the table and brushing my hand with his fingers. The gesture is brief since it's not allowed, but his warmth feels good. Human contact from the outside always does. I've missed him, and he's finally here— a body across from me at the table—even if just for a short time.

"Don't they have one of those, I don't know, hairdressers in here?" he continues, gesturing toward my hair. "Is that really a thing in prison?"

"It is."

"And?"

"And I haven't seen the point in wasting money on a blowout."

"Oh, honey, there's *always* a reason for a blowout. Have you forgotten everything I've taught you?"

"I'm taking that the wrong way. Are we still talking about hair?"

"You're terrible," he says with a chuckle.

"You love it." Chris looks around the room, his eyes settling on the table where Tiffany sits now with her daughter. I'd been surprised when she told me she had one; the girl had just turned sixteen and has been living with her grandparents in Chanhassen. If she keeps any pictures of her here, they're hidden somewhere safe in her cell, because not even I have seen them. Sometimes it's best to keep family out of this place, not to let the others know there's someone you care about back home.

Family makes women like us vulnerable, puts a target on our backs. Seeing them together now, I can't help but notice they look alike. Same smile, same demeanor. It's a side of Tiffany I've never seen before and doubt I'll ever see again.

"How's married life?" I ask Chris, changing the subject. For a moment, I feel a pang of guilt for letting him come here. He doesn't belong in a place like this any more than Tiffany's daughter does. But he's just about the only friend I've got and I need one of those right now.

"It's good! I wish you could've been there for the wedding."

"Me too," I say. "You'll tell Kevin hello from me?" He nods, and because we don't have much time, I move on. "Listen, I need a favor."

"Oh, boy…"

"It's nothing illegal, don't worry," I say, but it's obvious he knows better.

"Why do I doubt that?" he challenges.

"Because you know me well enough to know when I'm lying."

"Tell me."

"Do you and Kevin want kids?"

"Sure we do. Why?"

"What if I asked you to raise one for me?"

He gasps. "Shit, you're *pregnant*?"

"No, no. Nothing like that." And he pauses then, like maybe he's figured it out, and I wouldn't put it past him to be one step ahead.

"Wait…we're not talking about *Dylan's* son. Are we?"

"We are if you're interested."

"How?"

"I can get him to you."

"Why would you do that?"

"Because I trust you with my life. He's not safe with her, Chris. Cara didn't leave town like she was supposed to, and she won't listen to me when I tell her to leave. They'll find him, and I can't let that happen."

"Who's *they*?"

"Ivy's in with some dangerous people…the ones her husband was working for, I think. I don't know for sure yet, but they have her selling drugs in here, Chris. And that means she has connections on the outside and the inside. Eventually, they'll tie her back to Cara, and then what? They get their hands on her? On Dylan?"

"Attention visitors and inmates, visiting hours will conclude in five minutes. Please say your goodbyes and limit embraces to no more than three seconds. Badges are to be returned at the check-in desk."

"You know I'd do anything for you, Lisha."

"I'll get him to you, okay? When the time is right."

Chris nods, and it's enough.

He's the only person left on this earth I'd trust with that boy's life. I don't know what that means for Caramie, or how I'll make this happen, but it's really not my fault she can't follow directions.

During rec I find myself in the hairdresser's chair in the cell next to Ronnie's. I trade twenty bucks worth of commissary to get the damn blowout. Because with any luck, a good hair day will do wonders for my mood.

And I've been invited back to the library tonight.

JEALOUS LOVER

Ivy

WATCHING the woman you love getting eaten out by a piece of trailer trash is one hell of a kick to the jugular. I know this because it's happening right before my eyes. I'm feeling the gut-wrenching pain of that kick right in my throat as my breath hitches and anger bubbles up in my chest.

I was meant to witness this ungodly act, to suffer the sight of it.

Someone told me to meet her here.

Like an idiot, I assumed the kite—the small, handwritten note that was delivered to my cell this morning—was from Alisha, but I should have known better. If she had a message for me she would've delivered it herself.

I guess I wanted to believe she needed me.

That *she* had summoned me.

Malone lifts her head from between Alisha's legs and smiles, and while I'd love nothing more than to suffocate the bitch, I feign amusement and smirk right back at her as I shove my hand down my pants and start fingering myself instead.

Because it's the last thing she expects me to do.

And as much as I hate the sight of that whore pleasuring what's mine, I can't stop the memories when they come flooding back to me, seeing Alisha exposed like that. I know what that woman tastes like, what drives her crazy. How she likes her nipples pinched when she comes. What can I say? That knowledge manages to turn me on despite Malone's ill intentions.

That's what I focus on as I rub myself, as Malone stuffs her face back into Alisha's pussy and pretends she's not disappointed at my nonchalance. I'm tempted to join them, but doing so would only give Malone power she doesn't deserve to have.

I'd hate for her to think of it as an invitation, a form of acceptance.

Because she will *not* win.

I'll just have to do something about it before she gets the chance.

I leave before Alisha climaxes.

It's safer that way, leaves me feeling a little less vulnerable, albeit horny as hell. CO Ryerson stands at his post by the door when I exit the library, his thumbs hooked through his belt loops. I'd heard he was a softy, a pawn in this little game we inmates like to play with our sexual desires.

I guess the rumors are true.

I wonder how much their time in the library cost them today.

"Leaving so soon?" Ryerson asks, as if he actually expected me to be in there for a while.

"Do you know who sent me the kite?"

"What kite?"

"The one that told me to meet her here," I snap back. Annoyance has set in again, and if I'm not careful I'll end up in the hole punching concrete walls. But I play the card anyway; something tells me Ryerson will bite.

"I don't send the kites, Rogers."

"Who does?"

"You're a little too new around here to be asking questions, don't you think?"

"Maybe. Permission to ask another one, sir?"

"Granted."

"Do you ever join in?" I ask with a raised brow.

"Excuse me?"

"You can't tell me you do *this*—stand guard out here—just to help us get laid. What's in it for you?"

"You're out of line, inmate."

"I bet you go home and jerk off thinking about us, don't you?"

"What I do at home is none of your business."

"I suppose not. I could make a few other things my business though."

"Meaning what?"

"Well, you'd have to answer my question first. Do you ever join in?"

He smiles and it's the confirmation I expected. "All the time."

"How?"

"Not your concern."

I can't help but think he's playing me, that there's no way this man, this decorated corrections officer, is involved in anything unorthodox that takes place in that library.

Or is he?

Could it really be that simple? That the COs are *always* in on it? That they encourage it? Condone it? Without another thought, I drop to my knees to find out, my hands quickly working Ryerson's belt. I can feel his cock through his pants—see it, too—hardening as I rub him through the fabric.

"That's enough," he says.

"Please? I'll make you feel so good," I promise. He pulls me to my feet, forcing me to stand in front of him. We stare at each other for a long moment, and I don't know whether to take off running or simply stand here and wait for him to back down.

But he doesn't.

"You *will* make me feel good. Tonight. Before count. Be ready, and be clean." He kisses me then, full-on tongue, and I don't know what the fuck is going on, but he pulls away and shoves me down the hall before I can say another word.

Prison just got a lot more interesting.

THE QUIET ONES

Ivy

MY ASS SLAMS into the metal baker's rack behind me.

Ryerson lifts me off the ground, and I wrap my legs around him as he carries me to the prep counter and sets me down. His mouth finds mine again, and I don't know what we're doing or why, but I don't complain when he reaches under my shirt and tugs on a nipple.

The sex is quick—desperate, in a way—but it's exactly what I need to get my mind off what I witnessed in the library.

Alisha and Malone going at it wasn't my idea of a good time.

I learned a few things, though, so it's safe to say the trip to the racks was worth it. Ryerson's crooked, and that's the kind of CO I need in my corner. One who's not afraid to play dirty.

When he pulls out, he shucks the condom off and stuffs it into a plastic bag he pulls from his pocket. He's prepared, like he's done this before, and maybe I need to rethink my game plan, that Ryerson may be too obvious of a choice.

"Here, take this in the morning," he instructs, dropping a small pill into my hand. I stare at it for a moment longer than necessary, dumbfounded.

"The morning-after pill? Really? We used a condom."

"Can never be too safe," he admits with a wink.

And I hate it.

Why do men think it's sexy to wink at a women after looking disgusted at the thought of impregnating her? I get it; in this situation a pregnancy would be less than ideal, but for some reason Ryerson didn't seem the type to point it out so flippantly.

But I haven't decided yet if I'll be using his services, so I ask, "Same time tomorrow?" as I fasten my bra and stuff the pill into one of the cups.

"I'm off duty tomorrow."

"Then when?"

"This will probably be the only time." He shrugs, like he couldn't care less how insulting that sounds. Once and done. Hit it and quit it.

"Bailing on me so soon?"

"Priorities, Rogers. I hear you're a bit of a loose cannon—and you know what they say about those."

I'd take offense, but he's not wrong. My morals wouldn't stop from me from blabbing about our illicit affair if the opportunity presents itself. Blackmail can come in handy in a place like this. "He got to you, didn't he?"

"Who?"

"Ehrens."

"No idea who that is."

"You know exactly who I'm talking about," I say with a threatening finger. It's useless, arguing with him. Because if I'm right and this guy's on Ehrens's payroll, then I'm the one with the problem.

"Get dressed, count's in ten."

Ryerson's gone before I even have a chance to pull up my pants.

There's chatter coming from the unit as I make my way down the hall and around the corner after breakfast the next morning. A pack of women hover near the opening of my cell, precisely where they *don't* belong, and all I can think is that they've found my stash.

Which means I'm screwed.

I shove my way through the mob, surprised to find Ryerson inside my cell—*day off, my ass*—with an inmate I've never seen before.

And it looks like he's doing an orientation of sorts.

"What's going on? What the fuck are you doing in my cell?"

"Calm your tits, Rogers," Ryerson says with a wave of his hand. "Finally got a roomie for you."

Wink.

"I didn't ask for company."

"Neither did she." He laughs like his joke is funny, but the punch line falls on deaf ears.

"There's been a mistake. I'm supposed to have a private cell."

"Not anymore."

"Why not?"

"Let's blame it on overcrowding. So many offenders these days," he says, shaking his head like he thinks it's a shame. "Mulligan, meet Rogers. Rogers, Mulligan. Try not to kill each other, ladies." He chuckles to himself again when he turns to leave, heading back to his post where he'll start the headcount in two minutes.

I want to plop myself on the ground and throw a tantrum, but such behavior won't help me establish dominance in this cell once the door closes, so I stand with my back against the brick wall, my new cellmate next to me doing the same.

"This is a dick move, Ryerson!"

But he waves me off with a flip of his hand.

After count, Mulligan and I return our cell, the door latching behind us as the locks kick in. My new cellmate breathes loudly because apparently, she's under duress at the notion of bunking with me, *of all people.*

That's good.

I can work with that.

But what the fuck is up with Ryerson screwing me over like this?

"What's your name?" Mulligan asks, as if she didn't just hear Ryerson introduce us. I can practically smell the fear on her, see the tension in her shoulders as she stands there like a lost child in the grocery store.

"Don't."

"I can't ask a question?"

"You just did."

"Where can I put my stuff?"

"What stuff?"

"Aren't I supposed to get one of these shelves?" she asks, pointing.

"Can't you see they're in use?"

"Look, I'm sorry they sprung me on you. I'll stay out of your way, if that's what you want, but there's no need to be a b—"

"Don't you dare finish that sentence," I bark, cutting her off and taking a hard stance in front of her before pushing up in her face.

"I don't want any trouble," she whines, her arms up in the air defensively. I consider hitting her, just once to set her straight, but sometimes fear is best instilled through words.

And I don't feel like getting my hands dirty today.

"You see that panic button on the wall over there, Mulligan?" She nods uneasily. "Doesn't work. Don't ever push it."

"What happens if I do?"

"You'll be dead before help comes through the door."

During outdoor rec, I make small talk with a couple of the women from SAA: Henderson, Schoener, and Wetzel—a pill-popping regular that must've transferred in from C-block along with my new buddy, Mulligan.

"How's the new cellie, Rogers?" Schoener jabs with a snicker.

"Quiet."

"Ah, the quiet ones are usually the most problematic."

"Yeah, she probably has a strap-on fetish or some shit like that.

Wants to 'get to know' ya," says Henderson. The women cackle, and I almost do, too, but Wetzel's question leaves me on edge, so I don't.

"You worried she's gonna rat on ya?"

"She doesn't know shit."

"Not yet, but you won't be able to fish with her breathing down your neck," Schoener warns. "You've got customers to please."

"I'll bring her up to speed. It'll be fine."

"Yeah, good luck with that," she mutters.

It's then that I realize Mulligan isn't outside, that her absence probably means she's up to no good. "Chat later," I say, pushing my way through the group and speed-walking toward the door. I scan my wristband and shuffle quickly back to the unit, stopping abruptly when I reach the pod.

Our cell is closed.

Which can only mean one thing: she's in there.

I stand behind a support beam in the day room and peer through the door, watching as she rummages through my stuff. She's frantic, looking under my mattress, then hers, and dropping them back down in a huff as she tucks a loose strand of hair behind her ear. She probes every cubby—not that there are many—and crevice she can find, and she does it quickly, as if she knows I'm coming.

She's looking for something she seems to already know is there.

"The quiet ones are usually the most problematic."

It's clear then, why she's here and why I'm being forced to share living space with her: she's a plant. A looky-loo with a hidden agenda.

She's here to find the stash.

And that means my fishing privileges may very well be going out the window.

Because now I have no choice but to put her ass in medical.

BODIES DROPPING

Alisha

THERE'S A WELL-WORN trail of grass surrounding the courtyard in the center of the prison where rec takes place. Months of walking along the thin, patchy grass will do that, even though less than one percent of inmates with rec privileges actually utilize the space, not to mention it's covered with snow four to six months out of the year. I've asked, but Warden Cadell refuses to put in an actual track—it's not like I ask for much, but whatever. Some days I drag my feet on purpose to wear it down a little faster.

I like it here.

Not nearly as much as the walking trails back at home, but the quiet—that slight echo of voices overlaid by the birds chirping in the few trees planted throughout the years—makes it feel like I'm some-where else. Like I can escape the chaos of this place for just a little bit. It's why I find myself walking here every Monday, Wednesday, and Friday. It's a good place to go when I want to forget where I am and how everything fell apart.

Or at least, it was.

Until today.

I spot her now on the other side of the track, invading my sanctuary, her blonde hair flipping back and forth in its elastic pony tail holder as she strides. She knows this is *my* space.

But that's why she's here.

Sometimes it's hard not to let her push my buttons.

Today's one of those days, I guess.

I pick up the pace to ward off the rush of anger festering in my belly, my eyes flicking back and forth between her stupid hair and the trees swaying in the breeze behind her. But she starts walking faster, too. Like she'd kill for a chance to join forces and form a neighborhood speed-walking alliance.

I huff in frustration and find myself veering off the "trail" and making a beeline for the door. Rec time is almost over anyway, and if I can avoid a one-on-one with Ivy this afternoon it's worth cutting my walk short. It's not like I can't make up the steps by pacing back and forth in my cell later while I try to figure out what to do with her.

There's commotion in the lunch room when I scan my wristband at the door to get back inside. Raised voices, COs shouting, inmates shoving one another so they can get close to the action.

Something has happened.

I'm not close enough yet to know what, but I'm expecting the alarm will sound at any second, so I stop moving and stand in place, my eyes darting back and forth among the disorder.

That's when the quiet comes.

It's a hush so loud I can hear my own heartbeat.

I find Ronnie on the other side of the room, and I see it then—the look of despair on her face.

She's crying.

I've never seen her cry, but she's full-on sobbing; just standing there all by herself with her arms loose at her sides like jellyfish, and the only movement coming from her body is the shaking of her shoulders with each erratic breath she takes.

Against my better judgment, I cross the room quickly and stand shoulder to shoulder with her. I wait for her to look at me, but it's like she doesn't even know I'm here. I'm not prepared for what she says when she finally speaks, because it can't possibly be true.

"What happened?" I ask when I reach out and take her hand. She's sees me then, notices me for the first time, and the pain in her eyes is nearly unbearable to watch.

"It's...*inhumane!*" she says, mumbling the words. I nudge her a little more, try to coax it out of her while she's still lucid.

"Ronnie? What's going on?"

"...she...she's *gone*..."

"*Who's* gone?"

"Tiffany!" she wails as the alarm finally sounds and bodies start dropping to the ground. I lie flat on my stomach with my hands on my head, turning it uncomfortably from side to side to see what's going on around me. Ronnie is still on her feet when COs Ryerson and Shields reach her. I'm not sure what Shields says to her, but her baton is out and her words are threatening enough that Ronnie drops to the ground beside me.

I want to grab her and tell her everything will be okay, but I know that's not true, so I don't. Instead it's Ivy's eyes that meet mine through the chaos of the room. I watch her lips move, hear the words in the back of my mind as if she actually says them out loud.

She didn't, but they haunt me just the same.

"Tell me you love me."

It's the warden's voice that reverberates throughout the room, slicing through the sound of the alarm and everyone's screams, along with Ronnie's incessant crying.

And that's a problem.

Because Warden Cadell *never* comes out of his office.

"I want this prison on lockdown. NOW!"

PART VI

UGLY PEOPLE

SCRAPPY

Ivy

SURE, I did it.

Of course I did.

I won't bother justifying my actions to you; there's no point. See, when I want something badly enough, I get it. You know this about me, so why sugarcoat things now?

Malone was a problem.

She needed to be dealt with, so I dealt with her.

And no, I don't regret it.

Sometimes people just deserve to die, it's as simple as that. And I was going to wait, you *know* I was, because right now, I'm supposed to be laying low; I'm still a suspect in my husband's murder investigation. That, and the whole cellmate situation I've found myself in have made it difficult for me to run my operations. But given the escalation of Malone's hazing—and her desire to flaunt her affair with Alisha—it was time to put that bitch in her place.

I don't have time for her childish games anymore.

And when opportunity comes knocking, you have to answer the door.

I've been working in laundry for the past week, my first time on the gig, and one thing I learned right out of the gate is that the laundry room may as well be a damn steam room. Those dryers run hot, and they run all day long, without any windows or air conditioning.

Which means the COs are just as upset to stand post in there as we are to work. So, despite the warden's strict instructions, aside from the couple do-gooders on staff, they tend to stand watch elsewhere, on the other side of the door. Because with their uniform and all the gear they get to wear on their belts, those suckers would be dropping like flies from heat exhaustion. So, they post in the hall, popping their non-sweaty little heads in every once in a while to make sure everything's hunky dory on the wash and fold front.

Shame on them, huh?

Lesson number two: the dryers here have a handle latch from the outside; there's no way to open them from the inside, not even a safety release. Clearly, this is a flawed design if you ask anyone who's ever been trapped in an industrial dryer, but here in prison, our budgets are even lower than our standards, so we make do with what we've got.

In this case, what we've got worked in my favor.

All I had to do was stuff her in there after the shift change and wait to get my hands on her again right before clocking out. Of course, I had to bust my ass in the meantime, doing the work of two people because, you know, gotta keep up with the status quo around here.

Fold, stack, fold, stack.

Repeat about umpteen times until the numbness settles in.

The day flew by, never mind the fact that I had several sets of eyes on me at any given time. Fellow inmates and members of the *I Hate Tiffany Malone Fan Club*, waiting to see if I'd actually go through with it.

They wanted me to, I know they did.

And these things are so easy to get away with when you have certain COs in your pocket like I do. When you have just enough on them to guarantee they'll keep their mouths shut and their feet on the other side of the door.

Surely, Ryerson saw this coming; he had to have known. And aside from threatening to hang him out to dry, there wasn't a whole lot of planning involved, just the usual cohorts to butter up with promises of cash and pills, a couple sexual favors. They had a little stake in the game, too.

With apprehension, Ryerson did his part—the hall cameras were turned off long enough for me to skedaddle away from the crime scene when the deed was done. And everyone else would be none the wiser until Malone missed count after lunch.

The bitch put up a hell of a fight, I'll give her that. I hadn't expected her to be so scrappy. My arms are littered with catlike scratches that I'll need to keep covered for a while, but I'll make do, I suppose. It's not like anyone will be looking at me for this.

Did I stick around to listen to her screams for help?

To watch the panic set in as she begged and begged to be let out?

No.

Those dryers do get awfully hot, though.

It's too bad no one got to her before it was too late. Now, I know what you're thinking…you're thinking I turned that dryer on and watched her burn, right? But is that really what you think of me? That I could be *that* ruthless? Give a girl some credit, why don't you? That would've been loud; her body tumbling around in there. On top of her muffled screams, surely *someone* would have come running, despite having Ryerson on lookout.

No, that would've been hard to explain even with the help I had.

I didn't burn her.

Never even turned on the dryer, although it *was* still hot from the cycle I'd removed from it before putting her in there, so maybe it *did* burn her a little. How unfortunate.

Okay, fine, I'll admit that I *considered* it.

It certainly *was* the easier option. But I could never do that to a person. Plus, the smell of burning flesh is enough to make me puke my guts out, and I had to ride it out in the laundry room until the end of work duty.

Pass.

I did, however, hit her with a sedative before I shoved her ass in there. Didn't even take all that long for it to kick in, either. But the only reason I stuck her in there was to make sure she couldn't overpower me and find help before I could hit her with the good stuff: the hot shot that guaranteed she'd never wake up again.

Not my typical drug of choice, but that's why it was the perfect murder weapon.

It doesn't tie back to me.

I suppose that just goes to show that money can still buy you anything you need here in prison. Especially if it means agreeing to be someone's mule even after you've worked off your debt, but I'll worry about that later.

See, if you play your cards just right, they'll even find someone else to pin the murder on. Lucky for me, this one was written off as more of a *careless accident* than anything, no culprit to take the fall other than the deceased.

Who knew Malone was a heroin junkie, they'll think.

Gosh, it sure is frustrating when those closet addicts sneak off to the laundry, climb into a dryer, and shoot a bunch of heroin, isn't it? As if that tiny bubble were a portal out of here.

If only she'd realized how much she'd taken…

Poor Tiffany.

GROWING LIMBS

Alisha

MY ANGER IS GROWING LIMBS.

I get that things happen; that people die every day. And Tiffany was no angel. But she didn't deserve to get caught up in all this, and maybe I should have warned her. Maybe I should have told her to stay away, to stop hazing Ivy.

But it was fun to watch Ivy's torment; I didn't *want* to stop her.

So I can't help but feel responsible for what's happened to her now, and I'm not even sure why the hell I care so much, but I do. Tiffany's is another death on my hands, an unnecessary sacrifice for the mission.

I don't have much time to dwell on it today, though, because at the moment, I'm being questioned by DOC officials—as is anyone who can be tied back to her crew. You don't take out the top dog and expect there won't be consequences.

And maybe there won't be.

Ivy did set this one up quite nicely, but you and I both know she's had practice. Either way, I have nothing to hide, so I don't balk at the

fact that Kyle isn't here—that he *should* be here for this line of questioning. But it's not like my sentence could get any worse, and because
I didn't kill her, I'm not worried I'll say anything self-deprecating.

Not that innocence saved me before.

"Did you see what happened?" the DOC officer asks, clearly
reading from the list of questions in front of him. I'm no expert on
reading people, but Officer Titan looks like he couldn't give two shits
about what happened here.

"No."

"Were you involved?"

"No."

"You and Ms. Malone were close?"

"I wouldn't call it that."

"Well, you were seen together often. Daily, according to several
inmates. Were you not?" He looks up for the first time since I walked
into the room, his expression pained, like he has to poop. Perhaps it's
his thinking face.

"So? There aren't a lot of options around here. We were in the
same pod."

"She cared for you."

"Okay," I say, crossing my arms over my chest.

"Perhaps a little *too* much?"

"What are you implying?"

"I dunno…maybe she kept you a little too close to the hip? And
that bothered you a bit."

"I'm not a dog."

"Of course not."

"No, she didn't."

"So you enjoyed spending time with her?"

"Look, am I free to go? I don't know anything. You're wasting
your time."

"Sure, fine," he says flippantly, making a few notes on the page. "I
expect you'll keep us informed if you hear anything?" I nod since it
means my cooperation will get me out of this room.

I don't intend to share what I know.

No one will.

Because narcs have a hell of a short lifespan in places like this.

And I still have so much work to do.

CO Ryerson escorts me back to the unit and into my cell, not uttering a word before locking me inside again. The whole damn prison is still on lockdown, thanks to Ivy's antics, and Ryerson hasn't been the same since that day; he's not talking much.

Probably because he's one of two COs who was posted to the laundry room that day. Not to point fingers, but I don't imagine that sat well with the warden.

Either way, it's been four days of this. Of three meals a day served through a slot in the door, of lingering whispers and accusations echoing off the walls every time the lights go out at night.

Everyone knows who killed Tiffany; they're just too afraid to talk, and no one can force them to. Even the guards are quiet, and not just the ones involved. It's what Ivy wanted, what she planned.

Everyone is afraid of her now.

I'm sure she's basking in the glory.

"How'd it go?" she asks through the air vent at the base of the floor that connects our cells. I roll my eyes, well aware she won't see the gesture, and take a seat on the floor with my back to the wall. I used to ignore her when she spoke to me this way, but after so many days of little interaction, I can't help but give in.

"Fine," I admit.

"Give them anything?"

"Nope."

"Me either."

Shocker.

"I miss you," she says softly, and I picture her pressing her hand to the wall, hoping I'll do the same, that we'll be connected somehow.

"I'm going to bed," I announce, not taking the bait. I stand and strip out of my clothes before climbing into bed, because despite the fact that I'm not about to crawl into a swoon-worthy California King right now, I still sleep in the nude.

My last bunkie hated it; said it was a sin not to cover my body, that she'd pray for me. Clearly, she hasn't prayed hard enough. I lie back on the mattress, my arms over my head, and stare at the ceiling.

I breathe, slow breaths in then out. I count backward from 100, closing my eyes halfway through. But nothing is working. And even though I tell myself not to do it, that it wouldn't kill me to skip it for just *one* day, I can't stop myself.

The urge is too strong.

It's always too strong.

I bring a hand to my breast, my fingers grazing the nipple, and the other to my center, sliding slowly down my stomach to the wetness between my legs.

"Are you touching yourself?" Ivy whispers through the vent. I shudder at the thought that she's been listening, her ear pressed to the fixture, waiting for this moment. For the heavy breathing, the rustling of the scratchy blanket.

The faintest moan.

Because she knows me better than anyone now. She knows I can't resist, not even when my only friend in this place has been murdered and I should be lying here crying myself to sleep.

But I'm not ashamed.

This is who I am.

And a vice is nothing if not a crutch to lean on when you don't have the support of anything else.

ALMOST

Caramie

THERE'S scuttle on the news tonight. I don't usually watch it, and I didn't exactly mean to now either, but it's been *days* without word from Alisha. I'm starting to worry, pacing the house at all hours of the day, double-checking the locks on the doors and the burner for messages— waiting for proof of life.

Something has happened.

And now I know what: a prisoner at Smithson has been killed. I panic, the air sucked from my lungs, and thank God it's short-lived because a text pings on my phone a few minutes later:

It's not her.

I whoosh out a breath, the tension in my chest lifted, my heart rate nearly through the roof. This is good, this feeling of relief.

But how did he know I'd be watching?

With Dylan down for the night, I turn off the TV and grab a bottle of wine from the kitchen. I'm not sure why I bought it when I stopped at the store earlier today—perhaps I'm taking a page out of Ivy's playbook?—but I needed a little something to calm my nerves.

I pour a generous glass and take it with me to the living room, dropping down on the couch with a file folder in my hands. It's the information Alisha had sent over weeks ago; the contingency plan for if something happens to her.

I don't want to read what's inside this folder, and in light of the unanswered text on my phone, I don't have to yet. But I can't help it.

I open the folder.

Look through the printed photos, the dossier of information inside. My stomach does a flip-flop, goosebumps rising on my arms as I read.

I know why she did it, why Alisha put all this together, and I don't want to do any of it.

But I will.

Because I promised her I would.

My head swims from the alcohol, the dizziness disorienting me as I fumble my way up the stairs and into Alisha's bedroom. I close the door behind me and strip out of my clothes, standing naked in her closet, my fingers trailing along the fabrics on their hangers. The box is on the top shelf, the label taunting me like a piece of chocolate cake I'm not supposed to eat.

I don't want to open it, but I know I have to. The file says so, the instructions she left made that clear. I pull the box down and dump its contents onto the floor.

There it is.

I scoop the lace teddy off the floor and pull it over my head, settling my breasts into place before giving myself the once-over in the floor-length mirror. The garment falls mid-thigh, and it's perfect—flattering even—with just enough cleavage and ass cheeks to draw the attention I'm looking for. I slide my feet into the red Louboutin heels to complete the look, and with my hair down, in this dim lighting, I almost look like her.

Almost.

I smile at the thought, my confidence boosted for the first time in months, but it quickly fades because I know it's just the alcohol making me feel this way. And tomorrow when I have to walk into Lady Ann's with this outfit on beneath a trench coat, something tells me I won't be able to go through with it.

That I won't be able to face my next victim.

LIKE A DRUNK COLLEGE GIRL

Ivy

I CAN'T FISH.

Can't even move the product I have on hand—which isn't much—while we're in lockdown like this, and certainly not while Mulligan is occupying the bottom bunk and consuming half my air supply.

The choice between her and Malone wasn't easy, but there comes a time when compromise is necessary. That's the only reason Mulligan's still breathing. But her time will come, and she knows it.

I refuse to let her forget.

The poor woman has hardly slept the last few nights.

Still, my inability to work is a problem. I'm behind on my quota this month, and I have a feeling Ehrens won't give a shit no matter what excuse I give him when the time comes. I can't even say it's not my fault, so there's that.

The good news in all of this, the silver lining if you will, is that I got a chance to test out my nifty nook during yesterday's cell raid. Not even the dogs could smell what I have stuffed behind the brick above my sink. I'd celebrate the creativity of my deceit, but there's no point, because it's *my* wallet that's dwindling with each passing hour.

I mean, what good is a product you can't sell?

And did you really think I could sit here for days on end and *not* tap into that supply myself? The answer is no. No, I could not. I'm high, all right? There, I said it. It is what it is. Some days being clean isn't worth the effort.

Not in here.

And the fact that I'm going a little stir-crazy isn't helping either. I keep forgetting I'm giving Mulligan the silent treatment, and *because* I've been high for nearly four days, I'm finding it increasingly difficult to ignore her. She's a chatty Kathy, let me tell you. Must be the nerves; she probably thinks if I let her get close, I'll be less likely to kill her.

But ignorance is bliss, so you know, mum's the word.

The problem is, my personal stash is officially wiped out, gone. And I can't risk exposing my hide-a-nook to Mulligan, so all I've done for the past two hours is lie in bed and stare at that brick above the sink.

"Got kids?" Mulligan asks, breaking the silence.

"One son."

"How old?"

It pains me that I have to think about it. "Eighteen months."

"Shit, that's rough."

Is it?

"How do you figure?"

"Being away from him." She sits up in bed, her legs draped over the side, shuffling along the floor. I open my mouth to respond, but CO Marin's baton raps on the bars before I get a chance to.

"Rogers, you've got company."

"During lockdown?"

"Your guests have badges. Get dressed."

This ought to be good.

I hop down from the top bunk, a little woozy on my feet, and pull on my last clean pair of pants. Feeling like I could puke at any moment, my mind races as I consider what I'm about to walk into.

Did Ryerson fuck me over?

Throw me under the bus on account of his guilty conscience?

Do they know I killed Malone?

CO Marin and I round the corner to the visitor center, the lock on the door clicking as she scans her swipe card. For a moment I'm relieved when she opens the door for me to step inside the interview room, because I recognize the detectives at the table.

Beck and Nichols, back for another verbal tennis match. But to my surprise, and unlike last time, my attorney, Kelly Moon, sits across from them. So, they're prepared today, and that's a little concerning.

Kelly doesn't look too happy either.

"Mrs. Rogers, thanks for joining us," Beck says.

"Didn't realize it was optional."

"It wasn't. I'm sure you recall, but I'm Detective Beck, this is my partner, Detective Nichols."

"I'd say it's a pleasure, but…"

"I'd like a moment with my client," Kelly interrupts with an air of authority I forgot she had.

"We figured as much," Nichols says, and the detectives get up from the table to wait outside the door. Kelly sighs and rubs her temples.

"What's going on?" I ask.

"Hi, Kelly! How are you? Nice to see you again. Thanks for driving two hours in traffic to join me for this last-minute meeting."

"You done?"

"You're still on retainer, but if you'd prefer someone else, just say the word. Otherwise, you're welcome."

"Thanks for being here," I state with nonchalance. *And gosh, I'm so sorry you have to do your job,* I don't add.

"The lab results from your husband's autopsy came back. They have a few questions."

"That horse shit again? Really?"

Kelly looks at me sideways, her face morphed into some sort of confusion. "Ivy…are you *high?*"

"Of course not."

"Bullshit, you *are!*"

"Okay, fine, but it's not my fault—"

"Listen to me. Sit up straight, hold your head up, and don't say a damn word. I'll do the talking. You're slurring like a drunk college girl."

I suppress the urge to giggle at the thought, instead sitting up straighter as instructed. "Someone's salty today," I say.

Kelly stands and knocks on the door and the detectives are let back in. They sit, each of them eyeing me with more suspicion than necessary, but I don't say a word because Kelly Moon will send me back to my room if I do.

Can't have that.

"Mrs. Rogers, your husband's toxicology results indicate he had TTX poisoning in his system. What can you tell me about that?"

What the fuck is TTX poisoning?

"Detective, my client has already stated she had nothing to do with the murder of her husband, Sawyer Rogers. She was incarcerated at the time of the murder and hadn't even been given phone privileges yet."

"Do you know anyone that would want to kill your husband?"

I shake my head.

"Let me run a scenario by you then, draw you a quick picture. We've got two theories on this. One, *you* killed your husband. Plotted it long before you got yourself arrested, and simply sat back to wait for it to happen. Or two, you arranged for someone else to do it."

"What makes you so sure I'm involved at all?" I ask, and Kelly shoots me a warning look.

Oh yeah, not supposed to be talking.

My bad.

"He had a new girlfriend, did he not? I hear she was young."

"And hot," Nichols adds.

"And hot, yes. That must've upset you? Brought on some feelings of jealousy?"

"My client's feelings about her estranged husband's romantic affairs are not of concern, gentlemen. She wasn't there and had never even been to his apartment. He always came to her, or they spoke on the phone."

"I mean, just a *little* bit of that stuff, trace amounts really, in his coffee could've killed him within a few hours," Beck continues, as if he didn't hear Kelly. "Another hit in his cereal *maybe*, and he would've been a walking dead man right up until his heart stopped."

My blood runs cold at the thought, and I'm nagged again by the idea that Caramie could have done this. That she might have been the only person close enough to Sawyer to even have the opportunity. But what motive could she possibly have had?

Why would she have killed my husband?

"You're barking up the wrong tree, pig," I state, and I don't know why, but the words come out more nefarious than intended.

"Enough," Kelly barks under her breath. She closes the folder she had open on the table and stuffs it hastily under her arm before rising to her feet. "My client will be returning to her unit now, Detectives. You can direct any further inquiries on this matter to my office."

"Just one more question, Ms. Moon? If you don't mind."

She nods, not bothering to sit back down.

"Ask your client why Penelope Kingston was arrested two nights ago with a vial of the very same—*very rare*—substance in her possession."

Penelope?

"No...not Pen, she wouldn't have. She's—"

"...a former associate of yours, yes? From Lady Ann's?"

"Don't answer that, Ivy. This interview is over."

I drag my feet the whole way back to my cell, every muscle in my body aching as if I've been tackled by a sumo wrestler. None of this makes any sense. Penelope never would've done this to Sawyer; she didn't even know him.

And we're friends; she'd never...

"You okay, Rogers?" Mulligan asks after the locks engage.

I want to tell her to fuck off, to pull her hair and punch her in the face for sticking her nose where it doesn't belong. But all I do is climb back into my bunk and go to sleep.

Because if Penelope had anything to do with my husband's death, then I am—without a doubt—going down for his murder.

And that means Connor Ehrens may have supplied the substance that killed him after all.

TAKE OUT THE TRASH

Alisha

WHEN THE LOCKDOWN IS LIFTED, there's a hush in the pod. The locks disengage, but the women don't come rushing out like you'd expect. It's like they're worried it's a trick, that they'll be stepping into an ambush if they set foot on the other side of their cells.

That's why I'm the first to do it. The others follow right behind. Ivy, too, but I find my way over to the CO's posting station before she —or anyone else—has a chance to speak to me.

"Miss Marin, can we use the phones now?"

"Yes, you can—walk, please!" she adds when I almost take off in a sprint.

I make it to the phones and snatch the receiver off the wall, dialing Cara's number from memory. It's been a week of radio silence, of lost privileges and mindless boredom. She'll have no idea why, and that means she's probably been worried.

"Hello?" she says into the phone with a heavy breath.

"It's me…"

"Oh, God, Alisha. Where the hell have you been?"

"We were in lockdown."

"What for?"

"Someone was murdered."

"I saw on the news…"

"You did? Never mind. I don't have much time, but I need you to do something for me."

"Anything," she says, like I knew she would.

"Take out the trash."

And she knows what it means, what I'm asking her to do. I just don't know if she has it in her to do it. Not this time. But if she was listening at all before, she'll realize she doesn't have a choice; that she *has* to do it.

"Alisha…"

"What? I have to go. Did you hear what I—"

"I already did it."

"Wha—you did? When?"

"When I didn't hear from you. You said before that if anything happened—"

"I know what I said. Good. That's *good*, Cara, thank you. I have to go."

I hang up the phone, a herd of prisoners behind me ready to pounce at their chance for contact from the outside. But I'm relaxed for the first time since hearing Ronnie's cries a week earlier.

Because the rest of that poison finally ended up in the right hands.

And that means Caramie may be trustworthy after all.

YOUR MOVE, THOMPSON

Ivy

SHE'S SAD, and I guess I understand why, to a point. She's lost a friend, and that's on me. But she'll get over it eventually. It's not like they were in love, not the way *we* are. Malone's death should help her realize that. The woman was simply clouding her judgment, weakening her armor.

Making her forget who she is.

But she's over there sulking because of *her* and now I'm annoyed —it's been a week. Surely, enough time has passed for her to stop feeling sorry for herself. The Alisha I knew would never shed a tear over a woman like Malone, but prison seems to have softened her a bit; she suddenly cares about people, and I don't know what to make of it.

When she crosses the yard, stomping like an angry toddler, I try not to chuckle. She looks so cute when she's mad. What's *not* cute, however, is the fact that—now that she's close enough—she looks like she's about to take a swing at me. I take a quick step back, surprised when she doesn't clock me. I don't particularly care for being hit, so I exhale a sigh of relief.

She stands before me, her arms crossed and a scowl on her face. "Why'd you do it, Ivy? Why'd you kill her?"

"I don't know what you're talking about."

"Don't lie to me!"

"Why do you care so much? Miss your trashy *girlfriend*?"

"I care! All right? Is that what you want to hear? You want me to admit that I care whether people live or die?"

And it hurts, her admission. I guess I asked for it, but I can't say I expected it. "Why *her*?"

"She helped me. With the CO. It was her shiv before it was mine."

"So that's why you've been so buddy-buddy with her all this time? Because you *owed* it to her?"

"In a way, yes."

She's quiet, somber. Like she really believes she's lost a friend. "She grew on you, didn't she?"

"She was the only person who gave a shit about me when I first got here, Ivy," she admits. "So, yeah. She did."

"What'd he do to you anyway?" I ask. "Why'd you kill him?"

But she doesn't answer, just shakes her head.

"Don't you see, Lisha? I won't let anyone come between us. Not again. Not ever."

"She has a daughter."

"And?"

I'm a mother, so I'm supposed to care?

"You're delusional if you think there won't be blow back for this."

"Keep telling yourself that."

"I'm serious. The women will come for you," she warns. And it almost sounds like she cares.

"Is that supposed to scare me?"

"It should, yes. Tiffany had a lot of them in her corner."

"Yeah? Where are they now?" I ask, my arms spread out. There's no one else here, no one close enough to touch me even if they wanted to.

"So what now? What happens next?" she asks, ignoring the point.

"I suppose that's up to you. Your move, Thompson."

I pivot on my heels and walk off toward the dining hall, my blood boiling at the fact that I still haven't had a get a chance to talk to her about my suspicions; that my son's nanny may have been the one to kill my husband.

And that Caramie may be involved with some very dangerous people.

I don't know what that means for my son, but it can't mean anything good for Caramie.

Not that I give a shit about her.

PUNCH HIM IN HIS UGLY FACE

Alisha

I WAKE to a loud bang on my cell door, the sound of a baton clanking against metal. She'll never admit it, but we all know it's CO Marin's favorite way to wake a prisoner, me in particular. I suppose there could be worse methods, but she knows how much I hate it, so she does it every time she catches me snoozing when I'm supposed to be elsewhere.

"Thompson, you're due for your counseling session. Get dressed."

I pull on a fresh pair of pants and a plain white T-shirt before scraping my hair into a messy top bun; the go-to prison look no matter the day of the week, joyous occasion, or federal holiday.

Fashion has no meaning in a place like this—not that I'm complaining.

When I'm ready—and as if she has nothing better to do—CO Marin escorts me to the counseling offices. She presents Garrison with a nervous smile before sauntering off in the other direction, and any cool points she earned before this moment go right out the window. Because, of all people, my favorite CO has a crush on Mr. Garrison.

I expected more from her.

Mr. Garrison motions to the chair for me to sit, and I do, already aware that he's in rare form this afternoon. He greets me with a half-cocked smile; a step up from the usual head nod, and I can't say I care for it.

"How are you today?" he asks, taking a seat at his desk.

"Fine."

"You're always *fine.*"

I shrug.

He sighs, continuing on as if he's decided not to let me ruin his rare dandy mood. "I'm hearing rumblings of a beef between you and another prisoner, Ivy Rogers. I think we should talk about that."

"People still refer to conflict as beef?"

"Sure they do."

"You might want to read up on current lingo."

"I'll keep that in mind. So, you're admitting there's something going on between the two of you?"

"No."

"You and Ms. Rogers seem to have it out for each other. Does that have anything to do with Tiffany Malone's death?"

"You shouldn't put words in people's mouths, Mr. G."

"So the rumors aren't true?"

"What are we, twelve? Aren't you too old to listen to rumors?"

"None of you women ever want to talk to me, so what else do I have to go on?"

"Ah, are you feeling left out? The girls still won't let you play in their sandbox?"

Then out of left field, he says, "Tell me what broke you." Like he's so sure a defining moment sits right there on the tip of my tongue, begging for a chance to spring free at the rarest of moments.

"I'd rather not."

"You saw a therapist previously, yes? Before your arrest?"

"Nice work, Nancy Drew."

"All right. So you know what to expect here. That these sessions can be valuable to your overall mental health."

"*Really?* Gosh, I hadn't thought of it that way."

"That's how you want to play it today, huh?" he asks with a click of his tongue.

"Didn't you read my file, Mr. Garrison? I'm pretty sure there's a note"—I point to the file on his desk—"right *there* that says 'doesn't play well with others.'"

"If you're not going to take this seriously, why are you even here?"

"Quotas, sir. I'm required to grace you with my presence, remember?"

"Showing up is only half the battle, Thompson. If you put in the work, you might find that our time together can be quite valuable."

"I highly doubt that."

"How do you figure?"

"I'd never sell my soul to a man like you, Mr. G. Can I go now?"

I *do* remember the moment.

The one he's thinking of. He's taunting me because he wants to hear what it was like. He wants to know that I remember, that I still think about it.

Because sometimes when the darkness comes, it's Ron's face I see. The memories of my mother often lead me back to him. As her on again-off again boyfriend, he was around our trailer all the time. And he was *always* hungry for something.

So, it's *always* Ron that I think about on days like this, when I have to see Garrison and I have no choice but to shoot the shit with him. Because at his core, Mr. Garrison is no different from Ron. In fact, I think they're two peas in a pod, and Mr. Garrison knows it, too.

That's why he pushed me today; just to see how far I'd let him take it.

To see if it still hurts.

.   .   .

I feel him inside me—not that I want him there. His presence in my bedroom is not my choice, but rather my mistake. Mom died two days ago; I wasn't expecting company, certainly not a drop-in from her drug dealer and frequent fuck of the week.

I'm supposed to be safe now that she's gone.

He grunts as he thrusts in and out, sweat from his forehead dripping onto my chest. I want to wipe it off, but I don't think I should.

He might take offense, and that may be the last thing I need right now.

I want to fight him off—to kick and scream and punch him in his ugly face—but his friend is waiting for him on the other side of the door, and I think he'll come for me if I do anything stupid.

Will he want a turn, too?

Ron says my mother owes them for that last stash, the one that already cost her life. I think she more than paid the price for their product, but what do I know?

I'm just a teenager.

He's still inside me when the first tear finds its way onto my pillow.

It's dark, so at least he doesn't notice.

I'm numb by the time he finishes, and that's good, because I don't want to remember sex like this, not when I know it can be so much better. Ron's wanted me for a while now, so he didn't exactly wait patiently before claiming me as payment tonight.

When he pulls out, he's out of breath, a smirk on his face that I can see even through the darkness. He's proud of himself, like he's finally taken home the grand prize at the fair. He says nothing as he stuffs his limp dick back in his underwear and pulls up his pants. He wipes his brow on his forearm and turns to leave, but with his hand on the doorknob, when it's so quiet I can hear myself breathing, his threat echoes in the air around me.

"See you soon," he says.

Only he doesn't realize that "soon" this trailer will be empty, that I won't be living here anymore. And if I ever see this piece-of-shit again it'll be the last day of his fucking life.

Jon Garrison's, too.

Because what kind of man guards the door while a teenage girl gets raped?

The same kind that grows up to become respected corrections counselors in an all-women's prison, that's who. And fuck the universe for putting me in the same room as that man again.

KEEP UP

Ivy

I RUN into Alisha on her way back to the unit after our scheduled counseling appointments. She doesn't look happy coming out of Garrison's office, but that's nothing unusual. She's not a fan of his from what I've observed.

"Alisha, wait up," I say as I jog over to her, only mildly surprised when she doesn't sprint off in the other direction. "I really need to talk to you."

"Not now, Ivy."

I grab her by the arm and shove her against the wall with more force than intended, but this conversation can't wait anymore, and I'm tired of her giving me the cold shoulder. "Yes, now! Listen to me!"

"Fuck, okay, *fine*! Get off," she pushes back, shoving off the wall and rubbing her arm after I release my grip and take a step back. "What do you want?"

"I think I know who killed Sawyer," I say, and my announcement is met with a less-than-enthusiastic eye roll.

544

"I'm pretty sure that person is *you*. Are we done here?"

"No, *no*, it wasn't me. You *know* that," I argue. "It was Caramie! I think *she* did it, and then took off with Dylan—with my *son*. It's the only—"

"Who?"

"The nanny, Lisha! Keep up!"

"Why would your nanny want to kill Sawyer?"

"I don't know, but it's the only thing that makes any sense right now."

"It doesn't, actually, and you sound ridiculous."

"But it *had* to be her. She was the only person close enough to him to have *poisoned* him. They were *fucking*. Can you believe that?"

"Yes, I can," she shrugs. "Have you met your husband?"

"Whatever. Look, I haven't been able to get a hold of her since I was in county. Her cell number has been disconnected, she's not picking up at the house, and her email address isn't working. I don't know what to do."

"Ivy, this is ridiculous. You realize that, right? That your nanny—the person you *purposely* left your son with—could have killed your husband—the man she was sleeping with?"

And it takes me a moment to answer, for the shame to dissipate long enough to form a coherent thought. Because she's right; I'm being ridiculous. Grasping at straws.

For all I know, I'm standing in front of the person responsible as we speak.

"She's not taking my calls," I finally say.

"Do you trust her?"

"I mean, I *did*. I'm not so sure anymore."

"Then what's changed—other than the fact that you can't get a hold of her?"

"I...I don't know," I admit. "But something doesn't feel right."

And for a moment, neither of us says anything. We just stand there looking at each other, trying not to remember what it felt like to be in love, to be together.

"It hurts, doesn't it?" she finally says. "Knowing your husband fucked another woman behind your back. That he's probably dead because of you."

"The circumstances are different, Lisha."

"Do you really believe that?"

"Sure, I do."

"Then you're even dumber than I thought," she says before turning and walking away like she always does. And once again, I'm left standing alone in the hallway, unraveling one measly stitch at a time.

SHOO FLY

Alisha

IVY'S ANNOUNCEMENT comes out of nowhere, smacking me in the face like an adult-sized fly swatter. She isn't supposed to suspect Caramie of a damn thing. But she does, and now here we are. None of it matters though—not really—because the plan is already in motion. Caramie took out the trash, and if my negotiation skills are still worth a lick, I've even managed to talk Ivy off the ledge.

For now.

And that's all I can hope for because currently I'm sitting in the warden's office trying not to lose my lunch. I'm sick to my stomach with the news he's just shared: my father has died.

"It was an accident," he says. "A split-second decision on a winding road in the middle of the nowhere."

"How did you find out?" I ask.

"Got a call from his wife just a bit ago."

How thoughtful of her, I think. The new wife was kind enough to give *the warden* a call to let *me* know my father is dead. She couldn't be bothered to tell me herself, but I guess I can't say I blame her, all things considered.

It still would've been nice.

It's weird, though, this feeling of helplessness. Like I've lost something, but I never had him to begin with. Still, the loss hits home, like a knife to the heart. Because now we don't have a chance. "I'd like to request a day release to attend his funeral," I tell Warden Cadell.

"Not happening, Thompson."

"Why not?"

"You know the rules. You're a Class A offender. That means no day releases for you."

"That's bullshit."

"Is it? You're here on two counts of murder, Thompson—one of them for our own CO. Hell, you're lucky you're not in max as it is. Besides, you weren't even close to your father."

"How would you know?"

"Did you ever once respond to his letters? Give him a call? The man wasn't even on your call list."

I hate that he's right, that he feels the need to remind me, and that I'm fighting tears as he does it. But I refuse to give in, to cry for this man who had a chance to save me and chose not to. This man who left me alone with my mother and replaced us with a new family—daughters, even, if you can imagine that.

What kind of man does that?

And now it's too late.

"Miss Marin, can you escort the prisoner back to D block for lunch, please?" Cadell says through the intercom. I want to fight him, to prove to him that I deserve to attend my father's funeral, but there's no point.

Just like there was no point in my father sending a single one of those letters.

Because it's all for nothing.

"Thompson? You all right?"

"Uh-oh, she's spacing out again…"

"There's a fly in my soup," I say softly. I watch him struggle in the liquid, flop around between two noodles. He's drowning, and I'm doing nothing to stop it from happening.

"A fly?"

"Yeah."

"Scoop it out then," Ronnie says, making a spooning gesture with her hand. She laughs to herself, not understanding that this poor fly's life is about to end.

"I can't eat it now."

"Why not?"

"There's a fly in it."

"What, are you afraid he pooped in it? Left ya a little surprise?" The table laughs, and several eyes roll.

"He's dying."

"Shit, Barbie, it's just a fly. You want to switch?"

"No."

"Thompson? You okay?"

"Soup day is my favorite." I look Ronnie in the eye as I say it, but she doesn't get it. She doesn't care about this fly; not the way I do.

"So eat the soup."

"I can't, there's a fly in it."

After lunch, I make my way back to my cell, skipping rec entirely because I'd rather not run into Ivy today. I just want to be alone, so I lock myself inside and hang a sheet over the door before grabbing the box of letters from my father.

Fifty-two envelopes fill the void, but the one in my heart remains.

I tear open the first one and unfold the letter. It's short, but it's the most words he's spoken to me my entire life, so for now, I cherish it.

Alisha,

I know I screwed up. I should have done more for you. Come back for you or something, I don't know. I'm sorry that I didn't, but I can't change the past, I know that. I hate the thought of you being alone in that place. Let me come see you.

Love,
   Dad

It hurts, to see his words on this page.

The fact that I had a chance to know him and didn't take it. Some days I swear the universe is messing with me. Trying to see just how much of this torture I can take before I crack.

I didn't think I would.

But I'm starting to believe this facade just might, if given the right amount of pressure. And like the fly drowning in my soup, all I can do now is keep swimming.

SMARTER THAN THAT

Alisha

I DON'T KNOW why he's here or what he wants from me.

It's been a while since I've seen him, let alone received a phone call, so his presence here is alarming, to say the least. I'm racking my brain trying to figure out why he'd schlep all the way down here, but nothing comes to mind. I'm pretty sure my name hasn't been linked to any new incidents—not even Tiffany's murder, despite the fact that I was questioned like everyone else. And I'm not saying a word to him about Ivy's suspicions toward Caramie. The way I see it, there's no reason for him to be here right now.

That doesn't change the fact that he is.

That his expression is unreadable.

"Hi, Alisha."

"Hi yourself."

"How are you doing?" he asks, and it almost looks like he cares. "Holding up okay?"

"Why are you here, Kyle?"

"Just checking in on ya."

"You never check in on me. What's the catch?"

"No catch. Just here to show my support. As your attorney, of course."

"Cut the shit. What's going on?"

"Okay, fine. You're right. I do have ulterior motives today. I'd like to run something by you."

"No."

"Just...hear me out," he says with an eye roll. "*Before* you say no."

"I already said no."

"Yes, and I'm pretending not to have heard you." *Wink.*

I swear, sometimes it impresses me how well Kyle can hold his own in conversations with me; few people can. He slides a folder across the table, opening it to reveal a stack of pages and a bold headline that catches my eye: **APPEAL**

"What's this?"

"*This* is a motion that I'd like to file with the Federal Court of Appeals."

"For what exactly?"

"To overturn your convictions."

And I can't help it, it just slips out: I laugh. I laugh harder than I've laughed in months, maybe years. My abs hurt as if I've done a ninety-minute workout alongside Mark Wahlberg. Several minutes pass before I can summon the breath to speak again. "Are you *insane*?"

"You done?"

Like a shamed child, all I can do is nod.

"I have a credible witness willing to testify on your behalf that corrections officer Joshua Marshall was a sexual predator. That you acted in self-defense. Her testimony will corroborate your story, help flatten his character, make him more one-dimensional. And it probably won't matter all that much, but I think we could get a couple of your fellow inmates to say the same—assuming others were raped as well?"

"Why are you doing this, Kyle?"

"Doing what?"

"Putting me through this...this dog and pony show. No judge gives a flying fuck why I killed that CO. All they care about is the fact that I did, and that I had a weapon showing premeditation."

"Right. In self-defense. Because no one in this prison would listen to you when you tried to report him. Your complaints never even made it to the warden's office, but we still have copies of them because *I* helped you write them, remember? We can show negligence at the very least. Not to mention, you were clearly under duress having just been convicted of a murder you didn't commit."

"Exactly. There's still that fact, Kyle. You can't overturn *one* conviction with this, let alone *two*. I thought you were smarter than that?"

"Try me."

Fine, I'll bite.

"How would you do it?"

"I think *you* can find a way to get a confession out of Ivy Rogers."

"And how would I do that?"

"Her testimony in your trial is contradicted by the diaries confiscated in her sister's murder investigation, right? That means she committed perjury, which is grounds for a new trial at the very least. Tell her that. Get her to retract her statement and come clean—take the rap for Dylan's murder. Bonus points if she signs a full confession with a detailed account of the murder."

"There's no way she'd go for that."

"That part's on you. Let me work my end, you work the Ivy piece. Make her think it's a matter of principle. Even if she confesses to your husband's murder, she'll think you're stuck here based on your conviction for the CO. Make sure she doesn't find out otherwise. She won't expect you to appeal *both* convictions."

"Right. Because nobody would."

"Touché."

"So, who's the witness?"

Kyle eyeballs me for a second, not wanting to share his source, but knowing he'll have to eventually if he expects me to hop on board his crazy train. I'm about to call his bluff when he finally comes clean.

"Caramie Langley."

"Absolutely not," I argue, shoving the file across the table.

"Come on, you've heard her story, Alisha! You know it's convincing."

It's quiet for a beat while I wrap my head around everything Kyle's telling me. It's a lot to digest, and I almost hate to admit it, but he may be onto something. In some fucked-up way, this almost makes sense, not that I think it could actually work.

I shouldn't get my hopes up, but I ask anyway.

"Caramie agreed to this?"

"She did."

"Fine. I'll see what I can do."

And I will.

Because I think Kyle just stamped my ticket out of here.

NOT HER SEXIEST PLAN

Caramie

IT'S NOT her sexiest plan, but I think it could work.

I've been expecting this call, the one that sets part two of the plan into motion. Part one is done. Checked off the list with time to spare, even—and while I can't say I particularly enjoyed my time at Lady Ann's brothel, I also can't say I didn't. The task itself wasn't too tough.

Get inside, find Penelope Kingston, plant the vial of poison on her, and get the hell out of Dodge. Finding her was the easy part. She has a favorite room, apparently; most of the members do. So, I went there, got myself an honorary gawker pass (because you don't get to join in on the fun unless you're personally invited by a member), and made my way upstairs to the dark room. I walked in to find her sucking off some well-dressed nine-to-fiver with his dick hanging right out the zipper of his pants, his hands pressed to the top of her head as he pumped in and out of her mouth.

It was hot.

I wish I could say otherwise.

I took a seat in the viewing lounge—with my legs tightly crossed on account of how turned on I was—and spent the next fifteen minutes watching her work her magic on this guy's dick like what they were doing was *normal*.

And because the woman was practically naked all night—*and* a hot commodity—it was hours later, sometime after four in the morning, when the opportunity I'd been waiting for finally happened—when I followed her outside to the parking lot.

"Excuse me," I said, trotting behind her in my heels. She turned, on high alert at the sound of someone following her. But her eyes softened when she saw me and she realized I wasn't a man about to rob her or stuff her in the trunk of my car.

"Yes?"

"Hi, I'm—Tara—hi. *Sorry*, I don't usually do this," I started, stammering on my words. She was even more beautiful up close, and after seeing her perform, I was a little tongue-tied.

"Do I know you?" she asked.

"No, I'm new here. My first night actually. I was in the gallery—the *lounge*, I mean."

"Oh, sure. That explains the nerves, I guess, huh?" She smiled, and touched my arm, and it was such a sweet gesture that I almost didn't go through with it.

"I just wanted to say, you're very, um…talented. It was a pleasure watching you tonight. It was fun, I mean. God, I'm so sorry. I must sound like a blabbering idiot."

She laughed, and it was that moment—when she tipped her head back and shut her eyes for just a second—that I dropped the vial into her Michael Kors bag. She invited me back, said she'd love to show me around the following night—and I told her yes. That I'd be there.

But I wasn't.

And neither was she.

Because the following afternoon, Penelope Kingston had already been picked up by the cops.

And "Tara" was nothing more than a ghost in the wind.

I dab the roller into the tray, allowing the excess paint to drip back into the pan before rolling the sponge onto the wall. The soft beige is nice, complimenting the overall color scheme in the room, but even with two coats of primer it's clear I should have gone with a darker color.

Even someone with bad eyes would be able to see the splattering of blood stains beneath these layers. I guess it'll need another coat, but I don't mind.

Painting is oddly calming.

It's mind-numbingly boring, sure, but that's the kind of hobby I need to occupy my mind right now. Something to keep me busy while Dylan's napping, since I can't seem to sleep myself these days.

And I think she'll like the color.

Alisha needs me now, and I'll come through for her just I like I have the times before. Because I'm not going to lie; the idea of watching her walk through the front door is pretty damn exciting.

So, I'll put in the work.

I'll do what they're asking.

And I hope they know I'll want something in return.

I mean, nobody does something for nothing, right?

JUST LIKE THAT

Alisha

THERE'S no way any of this will work.

Kyle can't pull this off; it would take a miracle, perhaps an act of God. Not that I'm unwilling to try; there's no reward without the risk, right? But this won't come easily, and I'm well aware it'll take some planning—not to mention coercion—to make it happen.

But Kyle *has* let me down before.

Maybe it'll all be for nothing.

With ten minutes to spare before work duty, I find Ivy in the common room and grab her by the arm, dragging her into the corner of the room and away from the cameras—and prying ears.

"Ow, stop it," she says, snatching her arm from my grasp.

"Shh. We need to talk."

"What do you want? A quickie? My cell or yours?" she winks, and it takes everything in me not to slap the grin off her face.

Deep breaths, Alisha. You need her right now.

"I have a proposition for you."

"I'll bet you do," she says, snaking her arms around my waist and pulling me close. I resist, scraping her hands off me and straightening my shirt.

"Shut up, I'm serious."

"Well? What is it? Don't tell me you're finally crossing over to the dark side and looking to score some oxy?"

"No, never," I say, recoiling at the thought.

"Enlighten me, then. What can I do for you, my love?"

"Recant your statement."

"My what?"

"You heard me. Recant your statement in my case. Tell the truth."

"I *did* hear you the first time, yes, but you're insane if you think I'm going to change my statement. Why the fuck would I do that?"

"For me."

"You're gonna have to give me a better reason than that, don't you think?"

"Look, you already contradicted yourself in those diaries, right?" —*thanks, Kyle, for the tip*—"You lied during your testimony. That's perjury, and could get me grounds for a new trial. Is that what you want?"

"So?"

"So, my lawyer wants to appeal."

"Oh, give me a break!"

"Please."

"Why would I do that, Lisha?"

"For *me*. You'd do it for me. For *us*."

She's quiet for a moment, pondering, and I don't expect her to give in, but the fact that the wheels are turning—that she's considering it— gives me a glimmer of hope.

"They'd give me more time," she says.

"Maybe," I agree.

"And then what? You'll get out, and I'll be stuck in here forever? All of this would be for nothing. No. No, I'm not doing it."

"I think you're forgetting something," I say, taking her hand and caressing it softly with my fingers. I'd be lying if I said it didn't feel nice, so I won't.

"What's that?"

"The CO I killed? Because of him, even if Kyle can get this conviction overturned, I'll still be a convicted murderer; I won't be getting out."

"So why even ask? What's the point if it doesn't get you out of here any sooner?"

"I just want to clear my name, Ivy. I *loved* Dylan, you know that. I *need* people to know it wasn't me who killed him. His parents...they... his mother keeps writing me. I can't take it anymore."

"*Betsy* is writing to you?"

I nod.

And it does the trick, despite the fact that it's not true. Ivy shudders at the mention of Dylan's mother; she knows how ruthless that woman can be.

"You never told me that."

"I don't like to talk about it."

"What would I get in return?" she asks, because she knows there's a catch; there always is. And I've prepared for this—as best as I could on short notice.

It pains me, but I say it. I make the only offer she wants to hear. "Me."

And her face softens, the features I once loved and dreamed about suddenly finding their place again, as if they never went away in the first place.

"Just like that?"

"Just like that."

She crosses her arms, but quickly uncrosses them and reaches out to me, taking my hand in hers. It makes me question everything.

But maybe that's the point.

"Why, Lisha?"

"Because I need a reason to wake up tomorrow. Don't you?"

BUYING FRIENDS

Ivy

MY, how the tables have turned.

Who would've thought prison life could be so simple? That the politics aren't all they're cracked up to be? It turns out, I was right.

All I had to do was get rid of Malone.

If I'd known that, I would have done it sooner, but hey—you live and you learn, right? I should have trusted my instincts and stuck to what I know: love, kill, repeat.

It's worked for me thus far.

And Lisha has softened up; she's finally coming around and using her head like she should have been doing all along. She needs me. I *knew* she would, that she couldn't survive this place without me—her muse—and the only person on this planet who would do the things I do for her.

It's about time she realizes that.

And maybe I'm being obtuse, jumping the gun by letting her back in at the drop of a hat, but I don't care. I need that woman as much as she needs me, and that's all that matters right now.

Us.

A team.

Partners.

Just like it's supposed to be.

I slept well last night for the first time since arriving at Smithson. Perhaps all I needed was Lisha in my corner, but nonetheless, it's nice to feel rested again. To think with a clear head, a sound mind.

A person can get lost in here without it.

With Mulligan in medical thanks to an appendectomy, I make a quick cup of instant coffee—courtesy of yesterday's commissary— before pulling my prepaid burner from its hiding place and powering it on. Overnight lockdown won't be lifted for another hour or so, which gives me time to do today's wire transfers.

The drug game has turned into a lucrative business ever since the lockdown was lifted, which means my debt to the Ehrens-Havenbrook Corporation is officially paid in full. I'm earning my keep and taking a cut of the profits now. I knew I wouldn't be let off the hook entirely— you can't know what I know and expect to walk away unharmed. I won't be heading off to the mall anytime soon, but I'm definitely bene- fiting from the commissary funds and extra protection.

The notoriety.

Don't get me wrong, I'm not foolish enough to assume none of this comes at a cost—a favor here or there, an extra oxy every once in a while—but the thing is, I don't care. I'm not opposed to buying friends, not in a place like this.

I'm the popular one for once in my life.

It's nice not having to watch my back anymore.

And with the exception of Ronnie, Malone's former wolf pack is even playing nice.

It helps that I have something these women want, something they need. And that means I've done my job well; they're hooked. Because if there's anything federal inmates can't seem to live without, it's opioids. A chance to escape from the madness of this place every once in a while, to numb the pain. And right now, I'm the only one who has the supply to meet their growing demand.

And that makes me untouchable.

Thanks, in part, to Warden Cadell.

Ehrens' now-identified right-hand man inside, the one turning his cheek just far enough to make sure the drugs have a way of getting inside, that the COs up on 4C that are stupid enough to risk their careers bringing it through the doors have a way past the body scanners.

It's interesting, their little operation. The agreement Cadell fortuitously found himself in. I guess that's what happens when you're a public authority figure with a habit of frequenting certain underground brothels.

I recognized him.

Couldn't figure out where from until I questioned Ehrens about it, not that he came right out and admitted it. Lady Ann herself did that for me, but we'll keep that between us.

With the day's wire transfers completed, and the evidence stuffed back into the wall, I sit down on my bed and sip my coffee while I wait for the lockdown to be lifted. I think about Lisha and the fact that she's asked for my help—that we can finally be together if I do what she's asking of me.

She knows as well as anyone that no matter how hard you try to run away, fate often has other plans.

And it's our time now.

Because the offer on the table is exactly what I've been waiting for, the sole reason I'm here.

How could I possibly say no?

SHIT-EATING GRIN

Alisha

I WAKE COVERED IN SWEAT, *my heart pounding against the walls of my chest. The nightmares wake me from a cold sleep sometimes, but they've been fewer and farther between lately, so it takes a moment to reorient myself.*

To realize that I'm not at home, in my own bed.

I see her now; she's here at my side, watching me sleep, staring. "You were having a nightmare," she whispers.

"Did I wake you?"

"No," she says, and it's obvious what she wants now that I'm awake, that she's been watching me for a while. But I'm not sure I'm quite as prepared to give in to her as I was last night.

"Lisha," she whispers, and she's moaning as if I've done anything that warrants the sounds that are coming from her, but I haven't even touched her yet. She brings a hand to my chest and tugs at the covers, pulling them down slowly to expose my breasts. The air is cool, sending chills down my spine and hardening my nipples.

And I feel her mouth on them before I realize what she's doing, her hands roaming my body, her fingertips soft as they caress my skin, her leg brushing against mine.

It's nice, this attention so early in the morning.

Especially after a night of the most incredible sex of my life.

Lila tugs on my nipple with her teeth, just enough to send a wave of pleasure to my core, and I realize right here and now that I want her to keep going, that I need her to.

She slides her hand to my center and pushes a finger inside me, and that's when I see him. Grant stands in the corner of the room, his erection pressing hard against the seam of his slacks. He's dressed for work, fastening his tie with a shit-eating grin on his face as he watches his wife pleasure me.

"Good morning, ladies," he says.

"Morning," I say sheepishly.

"Would you care to join us, my love?" Lila teases before flicking my clit with her thumb. I moan and bring a hand to her cheek, staring into her eyes as she flicks her thumb again. And again.

"I'll watch," Grant says, but he comes closer anyway, leaning over and pressing his mouth to my other nipple, his tongue teasing and tasting. They're trouble, the two of them.

Lila and Grant.

And for some reason, I suddenly want nothing more than to be in trouble all the damn time.

The memories come flooding back to me often now.

I wish I could say they didn't, but they do, and I don't know how to make them stop. How to forgive myself for letting them ruin me the way they did. For overlooking all the warning signs with Ivy and her obsessive behaviors.

It's because of her that I'll spend the rest of my life torturing myself like this. In agony over the loss of my husband, and the fact that I let her get close enough to hurt him.

The fact that I can't get her out of my head.

That I want her, too.

This is my fault, I know this.

But I couldn't stop, I couldn't.

There was something about them, and I did nothing but lie down and take it as they drug me deeper and deeper, until I had no choice but to let them have me, to lose all control. But it's not Ivy's fault; it's these demons inside me—the ones that feed my addiction—they're the ones to blame.

The source of all this evil.

If I'd never given in to the temptation, I wouldn't be in this mess.

And I'd never have met Dylan.

Maybe that would have been for the best.

BECAUSE OF YOU

Alisha

Y<small>OU CAN TRY NOT</small> to break—to fight it when it inevitably happens—but sometimes there's no way to stop the cracks from forming. We all walk in here with scars, some of us with open wounds. But the ones we leave with often hurt more than the ones we brought with us.

Places like this suck the soul; they chew up what we have to offer and spit it right back out at us. And it's all we can do to come out on the other side to pick up the pieces. But that's life, really. Just a world full of opportunity that most of us spend a lifetime pissing away no matter how hard we try to avoid it.

There's no telling where we'll end up.

Who we'll be at the end of this life.

But in here, in this prison, time is in our side. We have so much of it, and that's why this works. This thing with Ivy; that's why it makes sense for now. Kyle's antics sent me to her with this idea in my head. It's blurred my vision and led me astray once more, but if I can get her to do this *one* thing—to tell the truth—this can all be over.

It's my heart that keeps me here, entangled with her on the floor in the library, as if our limbs grew from the same body. She pulls me closer now, kisses my forehead, smells my hair.

"I've missed you," she says, and for some reason it's nice to hear because I think she's the only person who ever does. When I don't respond, she brushes her fingers along my cheek before trailing her thumb over my lip.

"So what now?" she asks, and her words are so soft I hardly hear them. And maybe the question is rhetorical, but I answer anyway.

"I don't know."

"Will you ever forgive me?"

"I can't," I say softly, and it's true.

"I bet you want to forget, though, right? Move on with your life?"

She's right, I do. I want to forget *everything*, to make it all go away, because I'm so tired of hurting. I'm tired of being reminded of what I've lost, what she's taken from me.

What could have been.

But she doesn't wait for an answer this time.

Her lips meet mine, and I know I should stop this kiss, that I shouldn't be here with her. I *need* to reject her; fight her off like I've been doing since the day she got here.

But all that does is make her want it more.

And when Ivy wants something, she *always* gets it.

So I *have* to give in.

Because it's the only way out.

And when the enemy is standing right in front of you, it's best to strike first.

After rec, Ronnie shoves her way into my cell, her hands balled into fists like she'd love nothing more than to use them to break my face. "The fuck are you doing talking to her?" she barks.

"Calm down, Ronnie."

"No! Tell me why you're talking to her!" She backs me into a corner, and I raise my arms, resting them on her shoulders.

"Hey, shh, stop it. Keep your voice down," I say.

"Not until you tell me what's going on!"

"It's not like that. Just...hold tight, okay? I promise whatever you saw is not what it looks like."

"Well, it looks like the two of you are *friends* again." She spits the words like they're sour, shoving me hard against the wall. "Are you *fucking* her?"

"No."

The PA system beeps twice, alerting us that it's time to report for work duty, and I see the confusion on Ronnie's face. She wants to believe me, but doesn't know how to. "Ronnie, listen. Find me tonight after dinner. I'll tell you everything, okay?"

And I do.

I tell Ronnie the plan—all of it.

Because she needs to hear it.

And right now, I can use all the help I can get.

AWFULLY SPOTTY

Ivy

SHE'S TOYING WITH ME.

I can feel it.

Not that the attention isn't nice, to hold her like that.

To kiss her again.

But something doesn't add up here, and I can't put my finger on it. It's like that feeling you get when you know you're about to do something you'll regret, but you go on and do it anyway because the pull is so much stronger than you'll ever be.

I don't know where Lisha's loyalties lie these days, but I'm not sure we've crossed over enemy lines just yet. This woman has every right to hate me for the ways I've betrayed her, but when you look close enough, you can always see the holes in a person's armor. And right now hers is looking awfully spotty.

You find their weak spots, learn what makes them tick.

And if I've learned anything about Alisha Thompson, it's that all she wants is for someone to love her.

To be seen.

To be heard.

It's only a matter of time before she realizes that I've loved her all along, that all of this is just a way for me to show her that.

"You okay?" Mulligan asks, interrupting my thoughts after I've paced the cell for several minutes. "You're gonna wear out your shoes if you keep that up."

"I'm fine," I say. "Fuck off."

"If you say so…"

I'd hit her, but she just got back from medical today, and I'm not one to prey on the wounded, so I go back to pacing instead. Back and forth, one foot after the other, over and over.

Because even though I woke up this morning thinking of Alisha, right now it's Caramie that I can't get off my mind. The thought that she's involved in all this somehow is nagging at me, that maybe she's more than *just a nanny* and I've made a terrible mistake trusting her.

Because the Caramie I know never would have slept with a married man.

She never would have left me hanging or skipped out on me like this.

And that's why I've called Ehrens.

"Rogers, visitor," CO Shields announces, and they're the words I've been waiting for. It's time to hash this out, to put our grievances aside and start working together to find out who killed Sawyer and where the hell all that money went. Because right now, my bet is on the nanny—and that damn smirk she had on her face back when I was arrested. As if she had some kind of vested interest in my incarceration, a reason to be smiling like that, other than having my son all to herself.

I made the call yesterday to Ehrens from the burner phone while Mulligan was still away. Not that the conversation went smoothly, but the fact that he's here now, not even twenty-four hours later, says something.

That maybe he's on my side after all; we can work together to figure this out.

He's intrigued, at the very least. Perhaps enough to do something about it. He sits across from me now and clears his throat, a look of contention on his well-groomed face.

"Why am I here, Mrs. Rogers?" he asks once we're alone.

"It's Ivy," I remind him.

"Very well. Why am I here, Ivy?"

"I need your help."

"With?"

"My son is missing, and—"

"No, he's not."

"Then where is he?" I demand, my fist hitting the surface of the table. Ehrens takes a breath and adjusts his tie, as if my outburst unsettles him.

"My sources tell me he's safe with your nanny. The one *you* signed his custody over to," he says as if he's stating the obvious. And he is, I suppose, but not entirely, because my son's nanny—from what I can tell—is nowhere to be found.

"So you've checked in on him? Seen him with her? You know where they are?"

"Of course I have."

"It was meant to be temporary," I say quietly. "Her taking him."

"Yes, twenty-five years by my latest calculation, right?"

"Don't be a dick."

There's something else on his mind, I can see it. Perhaps my coercion isn't the only reason for his appearance here today. "Just say it."

He shrugs with nonchalance, like nothing I say will change the outcome of what he's about to tell me—the fact that he's here with an agenda of his own. "You're moving product well. Think you can handle more?"

"No."

"I disagree."

"They gave me a cellie," I tell him, and that hits a nerve; it's news he wasn't expecting.

"When?" he demands, sitting up straighter.

"I dunno, a couple weeks ago. I can't work with her in there, and even when I can, the guards are limiting flushes anyway. They figured out the system, and they're cutting us off at five per day. So I can't move any more product than I'm already moving—not with Mulligan hanging around, and not unless you expect me to shit in a cup."

"We all have our fetishes, don't we?" he says with a wink.

"Can you get her out of there?"

"Give me a couple days."

"Fine. And anyway, I think it's time I start getting something out of this for myself, don't you?"

"What is it you'd like?"

"A favor."

"No."

"I haven't even told you what it is yet."

"Do I need to remind you, Ivy, that *you* work for *me*, not the other way around?" And his tone is back, the one he uses when he wants me to know how powerful he is.

"I can make it worth your while," I tease with a smile, because just like any man, Connor Ehrens has his weaknesses, too.

"You seem certain you have something that I want."

"Maybe I do."

"Perhaps you're mistaken then, because last I checked, you have nothing to bargain with."

"Try me."

"Fine. What it is?"

"I know where your money is."

And that gets him, it does the trick. "If that were true you'd have already told me where it is."

"I wasn't sure yet. But I am now. I know who has it."

He shakes his head in disbelief, the admission hitting him where it hurts. "You've already worked off the debt. What makes you think I'm interested?"

"Let's not pretend you aren't motivated by money, Mr. Ehrens. I know you want it back."

"Go on, then," he says, amused.

"I think my son's nanny killed my husband," I say. "She's the one with your money."

"And what do you expect me to do about that?"

"Find her."

He stands then, pushes his chair under the table. "You know," he says with a grin, "it's awfully timely—your accusations—don't you think?"

"What do you mean?"

"They're charging you today. For your husband's murder. I'm sure your attorney will be by later to share the news. I'd hate to see you go down for something you didn't do."

Shots fired.

ON THE LINE

Alisha

SHE SIGNED. I can't believe it, but she did it: Ivy recanted her statement.

And against her lawyer's advice, I hear.

"I don't know what to say," I tell Kyle after he shares the news.

"You did it, Alisha!"

I smile, only slightly though, because I have no idea what this means or what I actually *did*, aside from fall into bed with the devil. "What happens now?" I ask.

And he tells me.

But I'm not sure it'll be enough.

"Warden wants to see you," CO Shields announces as she escorts me from the visitor center.

"What for?"

"Why do I have to keep reminding you that I'm not his secretary?"

"Because you're always the one telling me where to be and when. Sounds kinda secretarial, don't you think?"

"Move it."

Warden Cadell doesn't look happy when I step into his office, but I think I know why. "What's this I hear about your lawyer filing this bogus appeal?" he asks, slamming a file folder down onto the desk.

Confirmed.

"I'm not at liberty to say, sir."

"No? Why's that?"

"Because it doesn't look like my lawyer received an invitation to this party," I say, looking around as if in search of Kyle, who's probably still in the building.

"You don't need your lawyer present to have a *casual* conversation, Thompson."

"This doesn't feel casual, sir."

"Take a seat."

I do, but he doesn't, and the fact that we're not eye-to-eye for this conversation doesn't exactly sit well with me. "Do you want to tell me how the hell you convinced Ivy Rogers to sign a statement admitting to the murder of your husband?"

"She did?"

"You should brush up on your acting skills, Thompson. That wasn't very convincing."

"Noted."

"You'll be due back in court the end of the month," he says with annoyance, as if I've inconvenienced him.

"My lawyer mentioned that."

"Ya know, I gotta say, I'm concerned that you think it's okay to walk around murdering COs and expecting little more than a slap on the wrist. What possible grounds could you have to appeal that conviction?"

"With all due respect, sir, as I said, I don't feel comfortable having this discussion without my attorney present."

"I'm not a detective," he barks with more bite than necessary.

"No, but anything I do or say in here could be used against me in court, so..."

"Get out."

"Sir, I—"

"Now!"

Cadell's afraid to admit the truth: that Joshua Marshall was a disgrace to the corrections system. And to *his* prison. But that's not a problem I care to solve for him.

And with any luck, it'll be *his* crooked ass on the line when the hammer falls.

MONSTERS

Caramie
Nine Weeks Later

WE WALK DOWN the hall side by side, Kyle and I. He's here on Alisha's behalf—and mine too, I suppose. Legal representation at an appeal hearing is always necessary, and it's safe to say I need him for a number of reasons today, moral support being one of them.

The modest heels I've borrowed from Alisha's closet click loudly on the floor, the echo prevalent in the open space in the foyer of the federal courthouse. At least it covers up the sound of my heartbeat; the organ feels like it could jump out of my chest at any moment.

I don't want to do this.

I don't want to tell this story.

Not to that room full of important people.

Not to anyone.

I want to turn around and run, pretend this isn't happening and that the rest of Alisha's life doesn't depend on me not to fuck this up. But it does.

Her son's does, too.

And Kyle says this is the only way.

I've spent months believing in him, going over this testimony and trusting that he knows what's best for this case; for all of us, really. I have no choice but to walk into that courtroom and face those people, I know this. But now that I'm here, mere minutes away from spewing my soul out onto the floor, I'm not so sure I can do it.

We stand just outside of the courtroom, surrounded by men and women in suits, people much more important than me. An itching feeling in my chest tells me they all *know*, that they're watching me and they can see right through me. That what I have to say isn't important enough to fix things. I feel their eyes on me, looking right over my head without a care in the world, like this is just a regular Tuesday and nobody's life is in my hands.

They have no idea what this kind of pressure can do to a person.

I feel their judgment, their preconceived notions that perhaps the statement I'm about to make holds no value after all. That those judges in there already know how they'll rule even though I have yet to open my mouth.

But if Kyle is right, and this is all I have left to do, then maybe I *can* do it. Maybe I can summon the courage to tell my story. That it'll bring Alisha home, and there'll be a place in her life for me when this is all over.

So, I do.

"Joshua Marshall was a rapist," I tell them.

When his fist connects with my jaw it rattles my teeth.

I collapse to the floor, my body in a state of shock, its defenses immobilized. I hear him behind me pacing the room, his breaths shallow and jagged as he does. When I find the strength to look up, it's his fist I notice first. It's still curled into a ball.

Like he wants to hit me again.

The veins in his forearm bulge.

Sweat beads on his forehead.

His chest rises and falls rapidly.

I don't know what to do or say, so I do and say nothing, just hold my jaw like I'm afraid it'll fall off my face if I don't. It pulses from the pain of the blow.

There's so much hate in his eyes.

It's ravenous and dark, and it hurts my heart because it's everything I thought he wasn't.

I no longer know who he is or why it's me cowering in fear in the corner of our bedroom and not some lesser woman. I'm stronger than this, smarter.

I don't belong here.

"Get up," he says through gritted teeth.

And I hate those words, how they make me feel so stupid and worthless even though I'm sure I've done nothing wrong.

I didn't mean to upset him like this; I didn't know. So I listen anyway, follow his commands, and like some broken girl I push to my feet and stand in front of him. I wait for an apology that never comes.

I don't want to need it, but I do.

"Take off your clothes."

"Wh—what?"

"I said, take off your clothes."

I should hesitate, but I don't; there's no point. With shaky hands, I unbutton my blouse and then remove my bra. His clothes come off quickly and he waits for me to finish, until we stand in front of each other, naked and vulnerable.

But he's turned on; his dick is hard like he's enjoying this.

And I don't know why or if it even matters, but when he lunges forward and grabs my arm, when he drags me over to the bed and shoves me face down into the mattress and climbs on top of me...when he pushes into me and starts fucking me even though I'm not ready, I don't even make a sound.

I don't push him off me or try to gouge his eyes out like I want to.

I don't scream.

I don't cry.

I just let him.

Because sometimes it's easier not to fight the monsters that scare us.

It's hard to hear myself tell this story. It's hard to relive it, to remember the shock I felt that day. But I know I have to.

At least it's better than living it.

At least I'm not doing *that* again.

Josh is gone now, and remembering what he did to me won't kill me anymore than it already has; as long as I keep telling myself that, I'll be okay. I swipe at a tear, the moisture thick on my finger.

And I wonder if maybe that's all it takes to erase the past, just the swipe of a finger and it's gone. Obliterated. Because once I've told my story I suddenly feel like I can breathe again.

"What happens now?" I ask Kyle in the car on the way home. He looks about as somber as I feel—quiet, oppressed. Like the shock of my words has set in and left a permanent mark on him, too. What I shared today was more than I've ever told him before.

But I'm glad he listened.

I'm glad he was there.

"We wait," he says.

BED AND BAGGAGE

Alisha
Six Weeks Later

NOTHING IS EVER EASY.

I have only two options today: exact revenge on Ivy and spend the rest of my life in here, or get the fuck out of this prison.

That's it.

I certainly can't have both, and I suppose that makes sense, because when has life ever been fair to me? If I leave now, if I go and refuse to look back, then Ivy wins. She will live and my soul will die instead.

And I'll have failed once again.

I would walk out of here a coward.

Or I can end all of this.

Right here, right now.

I can make it all go away.

I can let myself love her.

Or I can choose to continue hating her.

It's unfair in a way, this suffering. But it's not like anyone ever said the space between a rock and a hard place was comfy.

If only I'd known it was possible to love and hate a person so equally. You'd think my mother had prepared me for this lesson, but my hatred toward her outweighed any love she managed to squeeze out of me. Her true colors were a rare shade of gray in the colorful world I wanted to live in, but at least I *understood* them. They made sense to me.

I can't say the same about my feelings toward Ivy.

Those tell a much different story, evoke a different kind of lesson I'm not yet sure I understand. I loathe her, but I crave her, too. It pains me to admit, but hers would be a loss of epic proportions. Much like Dylan's has been. Because this line between love, lust, and hate is mighty thin.

Faded, but still visible, even in the dark.

I know this is not a healthy love. It never has been. It's not a fair one either, but none of that matters anymore. Our time is up, and for the rest of my life I'll be left with nothing but regret when I think of Ivy Rogers. Not for my actions or even lack of, but for everything it took to get us here.

For everything I've lost and how little I've gained.

Because I'm running out of time.

I'm going home today, they say.

Perhaps I'll believe it when I get there, but in this moment I can't say that I do. It hasn't quite sunk in yet, not even when the familiar boom of CO Ryerson's voice echoes through the day room. "Thompson! Bed and baggage, let's go."

I'm sure it killed him to say those words, to know he has to let me go. And even though I'd rather have heard them from someone else, it's a moment I want to remember.

Because this moment was never meant to come.

I stand from my place at the table and tuck my paperback under my arm, making eye contact across the room with Ronnie, who's hovering by the D block bathroom. She gives me a congratulatory nod; the kind you take with you when you leave because even though no words are spoken, that nod says everything. Our goodbye doesn't warrant a hug, but her unexpected friendship will never be forgotten.

We have Tiffany to thank for that.

Inmates mill about around me, but their voices are drowned in my thoughts, and although I know they're saying their final goodbyes, and I know I'm supposed to say them back, I can't do anything but nod.

Because it says something that I'm getting out of here and they're not.

See, so I'm not in the clear quite yet.

I still have to walk through those doors, and any one of them could decide that today's not the day I'm going to do that. That maybe my exit from this place is unjust, that I deserve to be here as much as they do. Jealousy does run thicker than molasses in here, but I do not fear my life any more or less than I did when I first walked in. At some point, you have to leave things to chance.

To fate.

If I am to be shanked before I make it through outtake, then so be it.

Not that it wouldn't suck.

I go through the motions: pack up the few contents of my cell that I wish to take with me—the box of letters from my father, the photos of Dylan and me, of his son—roll up my mattress, and meet Ryerson at the door. He escorts me down the hall and to the right, then to the left, and down a long corridor. He leaves me in a locked room with two other inmates expected to return to the real world today, and we say nothing to each other, just stare off into proverbial space; none of us can believe they're actually going to let us out of here.

Ryerson gives me a curt nod as he turns to leave.

With any luck, it'll be the last time I see him.

And I'm reminded that there's still one loose end in all of this...

that you can't win them all. So, as much as it pains me, I sit on the image of Jon Garrison. The way he waved goodbye when we strolled past his office, the arrogant way he smiled at me. I lock that image into my brain, store it away for another time, because—for now—he will live to see another day.

But maybe I will come back for him later.

Only time will tell, I suppose.

Minutes pass, not hours like I recall from intake, before I endure one final strip search—one last intrusive bend and cough—before I'm handed an air-tight plastic bag containing the clothes I walked in here wearing. They are nothing special; an old pair of faded jeans and a torn T-shirt—one of Dylan's—but I feel like a new woman as I put them on.

Like I'm no longer someone's property.

I sign a handful of papers and my ID bracelet is cut off and tossed into a shredder. My wrist feels naked, exposed, but it's nice to be free of my branding.

I'm escorted through the processing center and to the main door where CO Shields wishes me well and tells me with a smile how she hopes to never see me again.

It almost makes me reach out to hug her.

The automatic doors open and I'm hit with a chilly gust of wind and a pattering of snowflakes that melt when they land on my cheeks.

It's fall here in Minnesota, and I'll be the only idiot walking through the lot without a jacket, but I don't care because the sun is shining despite the seasonally low temperature.

I take a step forward and I'm outside, on the right side of freedom for the first time in the better part of nearly two years. I walk to the far end of the sidewalk, far enough away that if they change their minds I may still be able to make a run for it. A dark sedan pulls up next to me, the engine purring softly, and I know that car is for me, and that I should get in, but I need a minute to *feel* this first.

And freedom gives me the right to take my time; I'm on *my* schedule now.

When he opens the door and unfolds from the car, he takes my bag of possessions from my hands and looks at me like he's seen a ghost. Like he can't believe I'm actually standing *here.*

Outside.

Free of handcuffs and ankle chains, no officer at my side.

I can't quite believe it either.

It must be the smile on my face that's throwing him off; I'm not sure he's ever seen me smile like this. But it's okay; I can be vulnerable in this moment because I've earned the right to be. So, I'll stand here smiling like a lunatic in the freezing rain all afternoon if I fucking want to.

Because I *can.*

He stuffs my belongings into the trunk of the car before opening the passenger door and motioning for me to get in. I do, because I'd much rather enjoy the fresh air from somewhere far away from here, and he's the one with the getaway car.

"Hey, jail bait," he says once we're both inside.

And I can't help it, it just kind of *happens.* I lunge across the center console and hug Kyle Lanquist for the first time. The words feel insufficient, but they're all that come to mind so I say them. "Thank you."

Kyle shrugs and tries to hide the tear in his eye, but I spot it before he manages to swipe it away. He buckles his seat belt and then shifts the car into gear, and off we go, out of the parking lot and onto the highway.

The open road.

I can't help but turn and look back as the prison that once felt so huge becomes smaller and smaller. I roll the window down even though the air is chilly, and stick my head out like a dog to watch that place disappear. And when we're up over the hill and I can no longer see it, I pull my head back inside of the car and listen.

Because it's nice to hear the sound of the alarm echoing in the distance.

It's nice not being the one down on the dirty floor with my hands over my head while the COs make their rounds and do whatever it is they do when an inmate is found dead in the bathroom on cell block D.

We drive further down the road, but the blare of the alarm still slices through the air; it's fierce and nonthreatening, and for the first time ever I kind of like the sound of it.

"We good?" Kyle asks.

And I nod.

It's time to go home.

SQUEEZE

Alisha

WE ALL HAVE those demons that can't be fought.

The ones so well-hidden in the shadows they sneak up on you when you least expect it. They are the silent killers; the voices in our heads that tell us it's okay to do that horrible thing we know we're not supposed to do.

They encourage it.

They come to us first as whispers, so faint you hardly even know they're there. But they grow louder and louder the more we fight them off, until eventually, they're so loud it's all we can hear.

They take the reins and lead us into the darkness.

And we may never return, but even if we do we will never be the same once we give into their demands. Because the demons always win, whether we want them to or not.

Even when what they want us to do seems impossible.

. . .

"Ronnie, I can't let you to do this."

Her hand brushes mine, and it's motherly despite the fact that Ronnie is anything but. *"And I can't let you keep servin' time for somethin' you didn't do."*

"What are you suggesting?"

"You've got money, right?"

I nod.

Because money is her vice, the root of her evil. She's killed for it, not that I heard that from her.

"You scratch my back, I'll scratch yours," she says. And I play dumb, just a little bit, because she likes it when I do that. She likes to be the smart one sometimes.

"I'm not following."

"Commissary, woman! Maybe a little extra on the side, too. You keep my accounts nice and fluffy for the rest of your natural life, and I'll make sure none of this falls back on you."

"Why would you do that for me?"

"For Tiffany," she says. *"I miss her."*

"I know you do. I'm so sorry, Ronnie."

"She loved you, Barbie."

"She loved you more."

We sit in silence for a moment as it sinks in, the weight of what she's offering. What it means for me, and even for her. *"You never did tell me what you're in for,"* I say.

"I won't, neither," she says with a half-cocked smile. *"Alls you need to know is I've got life. Ain't nothin' more they can do to me that hasn't already been done."*

"They'll send you to solitary."

"Honey, I been down there more times than you've been fucked since you got here. I can handle it."

"Then you're a better woman than me..." We laugh, and it's the reassurance I need.

"Your lawyer...he got special connections or somethin'?"

"He says he doesn't, but I'm not so sure I believe him. None of this makes any sense."

"Take it and run, love."

"You're sure you can do this?" I ask one more time. Just be sure.

"I won't let you down, Barbie."

After rec, I find Ivy in the showers and watch from the door for a moment as she lathers her naked body with a melting bar of generic soap. The suds are paper thin, but they still look good rolling off her breasts, her nipples erect because she's cold and the showers here are never warm enough.

I can't wait not to dream about hot water.

This will be my last shower at Smithson, and officially, the first time I've ever looked forward to a shower in this hell hole. I slip out of my pants, then my shirt and bra, and stand naked at the edge of the shower awaiting the invitation I know will come. Ivy sees me then, a smile on her face because somehow, I've managed to keep the fact I'm leaving a secret.

She doesn't know that this will be the last time, that I'm going home within the hour.

"Join me?"

I make a show of canvassing behind me for a CO, but my efforts are for nothing because I already know none are coming. We have fifteen glorious minutes of privacy, and I intend to utilize every single one of them.

"Come on, no one's coming," she coaxes, pulling me to her. Our lips meet as our bodies come together, wet and slippery, and the kiss is filled with longing. With a passion I never used to believe in, just like every other kiss we've shared since the night we met.

But I feel it then.

The moment the hate fills the void in my heart.

Like a thirsty sponge, it takes over every crevice, every hole, and tiny wrinkle inside of me. This is the moment my love and hate for Ivy finally come together.

And they mix like oil and water.

I see it then, that fiery rage, and I remember what it was like the first night I laid eyes on her. How she had this aura, this air of mystery, that hovered around her like a halo.

I remember wondering how crazy and beautiful could look so good on someone.

This hurts, the knowledge that our love will live on forever whether I want it to or not. I don't, but I've accepted that it will, that even though I loved Dylan with every part of my being, I might love Ivy just as much for entirely different reasons.

I pull back, our lips breaking apart, breath hitched. Ivy looks at me and brings her fingertips to her lips as if she's lost in thought. I know what she's doing, what she's trying to remember, because it's the same thing I keep remembering, and it almost stops me from doing what I'm about to do.

Almost.

My hands graze softly down Ivy's torso as she wraps her fingertips into my hair. She tugs on the wet strands, and I kiss my way down her stomach before licking her slit. She moans audibly, riding my mouth like it's her job, and the friction is nearly too much to bear.

The movement is slow, and I know she won't see it in her current state, but my fingers reach out and find the drain cover, the thin line of string secured to the metal in a tight knot. I slide a fingernail under the string and pull it up before pushing to my feet and bringing my lips to hers again.

I think she's crying, but I can't say for sure, because maybe it's me.

Maybe it's both of us.

I rear back and jam the sharpened point of the toothbrush into her torso.

Once.

Twice.

Ivy's eyes go wide, and I feel the warmth of her blood on my skin as she bleeds.

I won't let her go out this way, though, not this easily.

Because it needs to hurt.

"Wh...y..."

A tear slides down her cheek when I drop the makeshift weapon onto the ground and bring my hands to her neck. She inhales sharply when I press my thumbs to her throat and squeeze.

"Because you're too good at wanting what you can't have."

And I squeeze.

Her body fights against mine, but I won't be fooled into thinking she cares what happens from here, that deep down she doesn't want it to end this way just as much as I do.

She knew this was coming.

Her misery, after all, is the kind best worn on the sleeve.

It takes all the strength in my body, every muscle and bit of energy that I have to fight her, but I squeeze...I squeeze so fucking hard until her body goes limp and slides down the wall.

Until I feel the crack of a bone.

I stand over her and cry as I wash her blood off my hands. Because this isn't just the end of Ivy's reign; it's the end of us.

Of our pain.

Of our suffering.

They say everyone has a breaking point.

I guess this means I've reached mine.

And her death has always been imminent; forgiveness was not. So, the law of war wins again.

REASONABLE DOUBT

Kyle

I USED to think I could spot the guilty ones.

That their lack of innocence would be so glaringly obvious that my ability to read people would never come into question. That I'd never met an innocent client. Then again, as a criminal defense attorney, I don't think the innocent ones graced my office too often.

And it didn't matter.

Because the law doesn't work like that.

It's not about whether they did the thing they've been accused of doing or not; it's whether it can be proven beyond a reasonable doubt in a court of law in front of a jury of their peers.

It's about finding the loophole and pulling on all the loose strings around it until the prosecution's entire case unravels before their eyes.

I screwed up with Alisha by not tugging hard enough on those strings the first time.

Instincts aren't always right, what can I say?

I used to think I was good at what I do. That while, admittedly, I've

lost more cases than I've won—nature of my profession, unfortunately
—there would always be some wins mixed in to even things out. I'd be
able to give some falsely accused person their life back, keep them out
of prison, get them into rehab or reunited with their families, their kids.
Something.

At least every once in a while.

That was good enough for me.

But I haven't taken on a client since I lost the Alisha Thompson
case.

Not that I sleep any better with fewer clients on the books. There
was still work to do with Thompson, appeals to file and whatnot. I
owed her that much, so I did it. I had to get creative, bend the rules
a bit.

I fought hard for her.

I couldn't get her face out of my head, the look in her eyes when
they removed her from the courtroom after her first sentencing hearing.
Her case is the one that changed things for me, one riddled with life-
altering mistakes that needed to be rectified.

They haunted me, so I did what I had to do to make it right.

A lesser man might have swallowed a bullet over this shit, but not
me. I don't roll like that. Not when I hold the power to right the
wrongs.

Because at the end of the day, there's always a system to work and
manipulate—and until I'd done that, until I saw her walk out of that
hellhole, her case was my only priority.

My sole purpose.

That's why I called my sister.

Caramie has always been a sucker for charity work, and despite the
fact that she almost blew it by sharing her last name with Alisha the
first time they met—she was nervous—in some ways I'm surprised she
was able to pull it off.

But she did, and thank God for that, huh?

Of course, this job came at a price. My sister's prior involvement
with CO Joshua Marshall came in handy—not to glorify his actions by
any means. I knew it'd be hard for her to testify, to share her story and

put herself through the wringer like that, but that's why her services came with a nice stack of cash. There had to be something in it for her, a chance to start over, live a new life, and I knew she'd agree. It really didn't matter where her motives stemmed from as long as she followed through on her end of the deal.

And she did.

Aced the assignment with flying colors.

This shit took some planning.

I'd tell you more, but you and I both know I can't do that—attorney-client privilege and all.

But you're smart; I'm sure you'll figure it out.

I'm just glad this shit is finally over. And I'm happy to say, now that Alisha's off running free in the wild, I can move on with my life, relax for a bit. Maybe even take a vacation for once. For now, I'm taking the night off—introducing my new girlfriend to my sister for the first time. Treating my leading ladies to a nice steak dinner, so they better not order salads.

I just *know* Cara will adore Penelope.

I'm sure of it.

HELLO, CARAMIE

Caramie

SHE'S COMING HOME.

I won't play coy and try to hide my excitement; there's no point in pretending I'm anything but tickled pink that Alisha will be walking through the front door soon. And it doesn't matter that the nerves festering in my belly are a sure sign that I've taken more than just a liking to Alisha Thompson—I'm not ashamed of that. Mutual or not, this will be good for me. A new start, a chance to do things right for once, maybe I can even reconnect with my family once the dust settles.

One step at a time, right?

There's so much to do before she gets here; I made a list. Some light cleaning, organizing, food prep. Some shopping, too. Don't get me wrong, I wanted to be there with my brother—with Kyle—at the prison to pick her up, but he said they have some things to discuss and that I should wait at home.

I'm so tired of waiting.

That's why I need to stay busy.

The idea of slumming it around the house all day, of losing my mind while I do nothing but sit and wait, is just too much. So for the first time since taking custody of Dylan, I've hired a sitter.

And I'm off to the mall for some me time.

Once inside, I take my time picking out a new outfit—dark skinny jeans and a low-cut green top, a new pair of boots. It'll be nice to have a reason to dress up again, to do my hair and put on a bit of makeup.

At the home store, I find some new bedding for Alisha—bathroom necessities, too, some new towels and stuff. All of hers were thrown out long before I ever arrived here; they must have reminded her of her husband, so I don't blame her. I'd want new stuff, too. I figure I can help her settle in, give her a chance to find her new normal again.

And today I feel safe outside for the first time in a long time, like I did in those first moments after I learned of Josh's death. She gave me that, you know? Alisha did. And now that I know the Rogers are out of the picture—that they can't hurt me—that feeling has finally returned.

I needed this.

Back at home just after dark, and with my shopping bags looped on my arm, I turn the key in the lock and step into a quiet house, dropping my purchases onto the floor. It's not supposed to be this quiet, though, and a strange feeling washes over me.

They must be upstairs.

Instinct tells me otherwise.

That something is wrong.

Where's Dylan?

"Hello? Anyone here?"

I set my purse on the kitchen counter and flick the light switch on the wall, but the light doesn't lift the darkness I feel inside. My gut settles inside me like an anchor.

I should have known.

The baby is gone.

The note on the counter tells me so, along with the deed to the house, signed by Alisha herself. She's already been here.

Thank you for everything.

And maybe this was all a dream, too good to be true. A journey that's reached its natural end. I've fallen victim once again, been just dense enough to trust a criminal. I'd sit here and cry, but I'm not sure I have the energy to let it hurt right now.

I cannot look for them, I know this.

She's already a ghost.

And it hits me now—how you can know so little about a person even when you've walked in their shoes. When you think you have them all figured out. There's just no telling what they're capable of— what they'll do to survive. Who they'll be willing to harm to get what they came for.

But I've kept her secrets, the ones I found hidden in her closet.

The ones no one knows about.

Will she keep mine?

There's a knock at the door, a sturdy, hefty one. Like there's power behind that banging fist, unwavering control. Kyle, I'm sure. Here to tell me he's sorry for manipulating me into thinking I had a chance with a woman like Alisha. That I could keep that boy. That he knew all along none of it was really possible.

And I'd give him an earful if I truly believed he was the person on the other side of that door.

I breathe; in and out, in and out, but the panic rises in my chest and I can't calm down. *Don't answer it*, I tell myself. *Just go, run, and don't look back.*

But what if it's them?

What if it's Alisha and she's locked out, holding Dylan in her arms as the cold air hits them? Surely, everything must be fine, right?

This isn't really happening.

I'm safe, and so is that boy.

Except I'm not so sure.

What if?

What if?

What if?

The doorknob turns behind me, and that doesn't make any sense because I know I locked it when I came in. But maybe it *is* her. She's come to say goodbye, to tell me she'll take me with her wherever they're going. I feel the presence in the room, the looming threat behind me, but still I can't move because it's not her, and none of it matters anymore.

I should have known.

"Hello, Caramie."

This is all my fault.

I suck in a breath when I turn around and see him, and I know I shouldn't be surprised that it's *him* standing there, but I am. Even though a part of me expected this all along.

That he'd come for me.

That there would be no room for mercy when he did.

Because the man standing in my living room is Connor Ehrens.

And he's wearing gloves.

I was never supposed to take that money from Sawyer's apartment.

"Which one of them sent you?" I can't help but ask. Because I *have* to know.

"Ivy," he admits. "And I believe you have something that belongs to me," he says.

It's a moment; just a small one seemingly frozen in time, but it's *the* defining moment of my life. The calm before the storm. Not that I'll have much longer to dwell on it.

The damage has already been done.

I expect a gunshot, perhaps a horrible beating even.

But he's a fair man, and it's a sharp needle to the base of my neck, a strong arm pinning me against his chest as the tip punctures my skin. I'm relieved when it doesn't hurt.

That he holds me until the end.

UGLY: AN EXTENDED EPILOGUE

Alisha

THE KEY to getting away with murder is in the details.

It's those deceptive seeds you plant long before the kill.

The manipulation has to begin early on. It starts small at first, with tiny, manageable lies, each one gradually evolving into something bigger, until it builds and builds, and before you know it, you're in the eye of the storm and debris is falling all around you.

But you can't quit; it can't all be for nothing, so you keep going.

You tell the story.

Because you've invested the time—*so much time*—to make them love you just enough that it'll be hard for them to hate you when the truth comes out.

You'll have told those lies for years, like they're the only truth you've ever known. You'll have lived and breathed those lies, nurtured them and never given up on them. Even when the evidence doesn't add up, and you find yourself on the wrong side of the holding cell for something you didn't do.

And maybe you deserved it because of all those lies you told.

Maybe you weren't the one wielding the knife on that fateful morning, but it's still *your* fault that *she* was.

They never checked the phone records.

But you didn't have a choice when you called her; not after what he found out about you. And that's when you really start to panic, when the fear kicks in and nothing you do or say will stop it from happening because the damage has already been done.

And now he's gone.

But it wasn't supposed to go down that way.

She had *one* job.

And she fucked it up.

Seduce him.

Get caught in the act.

So you could make him feel as little as he made *you* feel.

That's all you really wanted.

Just a chance to start over on an even playing field, maybe find a way out of your marriage eventually, if it came to that. But that choice —that option—was taken from you. All because you asked the wrong person for help and put your faith in someone who wasn't operating on all cylinders.

Ivy had other ideas; a different way out of the mess I created.

And Dylan still breathing after she got her hands on him wasn't part of those plans.

See, so I screwed up, too.

Because I didn't know it was Ivy that I was letting into my house— that she and Lila were one and the same. And that's why it was *me* who left the back door unlocked when I went for my run. It was *my* fault she had the motive and the opportunity. But maybe there's still room for sympathy in all this; because everything I've done since that day has been in his honor, for Dylan.

To make things right.

Because I loved him so damn much it hurts—*it always hurts*—and I would make her pay for taking him away from me like that.

And when you're a warrior like me, the solider in you always comes back to fight. She puts on that armor again so she can protect those lies she once lived by, so that impenetrable person she once was can go back into battle.

And you say all the right words, at the right times, to the right people. And you find it in yourself to take out the *one* person you know you can still reach while you're stuck in a cage. The person who ties you back to the outside.

Corrections Officer Joshua Marshall, rapist extraordinaire.

And you wait.

Until your accomplice—your predetermined fall guy—shows up to thank you. Because you remembered what Kyle told you about her, about his little sister who had history with that CO. The one he ruined.

You knew she'd come to you, because you're her hero now, and she'd do anything to show you just how much she appreciates you. She might mess up and deviate from the plan, but even then, she whole-heartedly believes that she did what she did to protect *you.* To protect your dead husband's son. That the man you asked her to kill was part of the solution, and *she* was the only person who could get you out of this mess.

So you'll assure her that everything will be okay, and that when it's all said and done, you'll find a way to be together. Just the two of you, raising a young child together, like she asked. That's all she wanted in return: a chance to matter to someone. And she loves you more than enough to do what she's told.

You saved her life, after all.

That means something to her, and to her brother, who's been obsessed with you since the day he took on your case. He even under-stands you now, knows he fucked up the first time; he's in it for *redemption.* So you'll use your body and mind to work your way so far into their heads that it messes with their wiring—until they do what you asked of them.

You'll make all the promises, give the necessary reassurances.

Then you'll sit back and watch as they dig their own graves, as she cracks under the pressure even though she assured you she could keep a level head. As he works his voodoo magic with the law. And it won't matter that a small part of you feels guilty for dragging them into this, because deep down maybe they're horrible people, too. I mean, just *look* what they've done.

She's killed for you.

He's lied for you.

And surely, it wouldn't have stopped there.

In the end, it might be hard to see them go—you may even shed a tear or two—but that's okay because the fall guys never get out alive, and you're emotionally prepared for this. How were you to know Ivy would figure things out? That she'd send her goons after them?

They never had a chance, not really.

But that's why you picked them.

And sometimes collateral damage is a good thing; sometimes the act is bigger than the sum of its parts. And now that your husband's son is safe—sent off to Florida to live a happy life with the only person left in the world who's never let you down—you can go, too. Because Chris will take care of him.

So you can stop fighting and just *be*.

Start over like you wanted to.

But you know that when you do, that guilt, and the reality of what you've done—the lives you've ruined—will stay with you. Over and over it'll fester in the depths of your soul, and you'll never be able to escape it.

Because you did something terrible all those years ago, not thinking of the consequences.

And, my friend, I know you think CO Marshall was the first life I've taken. I *know* you do, because that's what you're supposed to think.

That losing Dylan, seeking revenge for his death, was *the thing* that turned me into this person: a murderer. See, I shared that with you because I felt comfortable telling you about him, about what I did to him. Because Joshua Marshall *deserved* to die.

You *know* that.

And I'm not so sure you would have been so willing to talk to me if you knew that someone else came before him. That he *wasn't* the first.

That's what Dylan found out; what led to my panicked phone call to Ivy the night of our big fight. It's why I asked her to break him, to give *him* a reason to feel as guilty as he made *me* feel. Because the truth behind that lie I told for so long was too much for him. And unlike me, he could see right from wrong, without all the gray space in between.

That's why I never told him, why I never told you.

Because it would have changed the narrative, you see?

I can hear him up there, in our bedroom, throwing things, breaking them. As if he has a reason to be upset with anyone other than himself. He's betrayed me; taken my trust and stomped on it like a cigarette butt on the sidewalk.

He knew who I was, that I was connected to his stepbrother, to his ex-girlfriend—and he went after me just to hurt them back for what they once did to him.

That's why he wanted me.

He used me, just like everyone else.

And now he's judging me like them, too.

I stomp up the stairs to our bedroom and find Dylan on the floor in the closet, my high school storage bin beside him, documents and keepsakes strewn about, not that there are many. But it's my diary he's holding in his hands, the damning words I wrote so long ago, much like Ivy had at that age.

I'd always meant to burn it, but I couldn't bring myself to let it go.

"Dylan?" He looks up at me from the floor, pain pinching his face into a grimace, his cheeks wet from tears, because now he knows the worst thing there is to know about me. "What are you doing?"

"Is this true?" he asks, motioning to the pages. And I can't say anything; I can't lie to him again.

Because it's a diary, not a fiction novel, so of course it's true.

I killed my mother today.

And there's so much anger in his voice when he says his next words. He believes them with every part of his being. "My father was right—you'd make a shit mother."

"You don't mean that," I say, feeling the sting of his words in the depths of my soul.

"What kind of person kills their own mother?" he asks, rising to his feet.

"It wasn't like that. You don't understand."

"I do understand, Alisha. I get it. Your mom was a narcissistic drug addict, and she did a shit job raising you. But you had no right to do what you did."

"Dylan, please. Don't say that. I—"

"Just stop! I can't even look at you right now. This...I can't do this anymore."

"Give me a chance to explain!"

"I don't think I can have a child with you. Not after this...I...fuck! I don't even know who you are anymore."

"No, please don't say that."

"This changes everything. You know that, right?"

And I did; I knew it.

My husband would never love me the same.

Because my mother was a rotten woman to her core, and she taught me these things. That people are nothing if not predictable—that everyone has something to hide, and there will always be someone who will stop at nothing to find it. I mean, how well do you ever really know a person?

And when you're just a kid trapped in their sordid world, listening to this kind of bullshit for seventeen of your most impressionable years, and the cop who comes by to tell you that your mother has died assumes you're better off without her, that it's *for the best*, you just nod and go along with it.

Because damn it, he's right.

It doesn't matter that *you* laced her bottle of vodka with a concoction of legal substances and left it there on the table for her to find. It simply doesn't, because on principle, what you did was the right thing to do, and nobody gave a shit about your mother anyway.

Just as she didn't give a shit about you.

So, no harm, no foul.

Another junkie dead and gone, another child orphaned at the hands of an addict.

But you'll wonder if she knew.

In those last moments as she choked on her own vomit, as she drew her last breath, you'll hope she figured out that it was you who took her life.

That in some convoluted way, she was proud of you for finally growing a pair.

The tears will come easily for you because they're real.

And you're finally free.

It feels so good to get these lies off my chest, to be honest with you after all this time. But I imagine you feel pretty duped, don't you?

For that, I apologize.

But some things just aren't what they seem; it's all about perspective in cases like this. And I wonder what you might think of me now that all is said and done—not that I care. But I find myself wondering, nonetheless. Do you agree with my actions or see them for the mistakes they are?

I've never claimed to be perfect, as you know, and this path I've chosen to walk was never well lit; it hasn't been easy navigating in the dark. There was no arrow at the curve to point me in the right direction, no caution sign to warn off the wrong one, either.

I like to think I've done the best I could with the information I had.

You are the one person who knows everything there is to know about me. I do hate that, but I suppose it is a weight off my chest, too; I sleep just fine at night knowing my secrets are safe with you.

And I think we're good for each other, you and me. You've served a purpose in my life, just as I have in yours. We've shown each other how a good, solid bond can withstand anything. How an unlikeable person can spark that reasonable doubt, leave you questioning everything.

Did she do it? Is she innocent?

I know this blood on my hands will never wash off.

That the pain surrounding my heart will never subside. But I can find a way to live with the damage if you can. Because that's what humans do; we adapt. We screw up our lives at every possible twist and turn and always seem to find a way to keep on keepin' on.

My time at Smithson was not for nothing, I assure you. Because I emerged from that dreary dungeon with more grace than I went in with.

I've accepted loss.

I've made peace with it.

And you may disagree, but I think I've served enough time.

Because I lived in my mother's prison for long enough.

Today, on her birthday, I'm reminded of her. Of the unwarranted maternal advice that often rained upon me with the subtly of volcanic acid. Her highs and lows were her perfect ruin, and now they are just as much mine as they once were hers. I've spent my whole life trying to escape her, trying *not* to be like her. But it never mattered in the end, did it?

One could argue I have fared far worse than she ever did, despite the fact that she's dead and I am not. But her words echo in the back of my mind as I sit here in front of my husband's headstone for what will likely be the first and only time. There's a pang in my heart, a tiny tug that tells me my mother is watching as I mourn, as I cry for him. That she knows what I've done, and for some reason, she's beaming down on me with ill-advised pride.

Because, surely, my actions—these lies that are now truths—mean she was right all along. That I had no real chance in this life. That I will forever be held captive to this broken mind of mine, the choices I made when I was too young to understand the consequences.

And she's won; she had me figured out from the start.

Did you?

"You are the end product of two broken people, Alisha. It doesn't matter how beautiful you think you are; there will always be ugliness inside of you. One day you'll see it, and you'll realize you're no different from me. You just feed a different addiction."

See, even beautiful people can be ugly when you paint them in the right light.

But the way I see it, there's beauty in the darkness, too.

You just have to find it.

ACKNOWLEDGMENTS

When I started my writing career in 2020 I had myself convinced I was a stand-alone author and never expected to find myself writing a series. Now, nearly two years later, here we are: I've completed a trilogy! They say writing is a lonely business—and while I don't disagree—I have some people to thank who have helped along the way.

To my husband, daughter, and son for their support, encouragement, and understanding. None of this would be possible without you!

To my editor, Kiezha Ferrell of Librum Artis Editorial Services for taking on this project with me! I'm incredibly lucky to have you in my corner.

To my beta readers for their endless support, suggestions, and for always talking me off the ledge every time I was ready to toss this thing into a dumpster fire. Sawyer Cole Hobson, Chris Shaneck, Erika Bucci, Danielle Renee, Ashley Heck, and Caramie Malcolm.

To the many friends I've made in the #bookstagram community since the start of this journey—the best gift you can give an author is not just to buy their books, but to review them, to tell your friends about them, and then ask them to write another one. For that, I thank you profusely, and in return, thought it'd be fun to use your names in these books. Featured in this series:

Alisha @alishareadsgoodbooks, Sawyer Cole @colesbooknook, Chris @analyzedbychris, Jen @inkdrinkerjen, Danielle @dani.reads.1225, Lexy @lexy_attemptedmystery, Erika @erikalaceyreads, Caramie @memyshelfandwine, Cristina @frosty-ourshelf, Sebastien @seb.reads, Bethany @bethanyburiedinbooks, Krissy @books_and_biceps9155, Kelly @dearbooks_iloveyou, Kristin

@read.it.and.sleep, Carrie @carriereadsthem_all, Lisa @mokwip8991, Laura @laurasnextchapter, Cody @codyloud5.

To every member of the Jump Street Team—thank you for your unwavering support and excitement for this series! I can't tell you how great it is to hear, "I've seen this book everywhere!"

Lastly, to you, dear reader. Whether you loved this series, liked it just a little, or loathed it entirely, thank you for giving it a read.

Until next time…

ABOUT THE AUTHOR

Shannon Jump is an avid reader and writer of multiple genres, with a passion for storytelling. She refuses to start the day without the perfect cup of coffee and is a die-hard Minnesota Twins baseball fan and Food Network junkie. She lives in small-town Minnesota with her husband and two teenage kids.

If you enjoyed this series, please consider leaving a review—even just a sentence or two will do. Who knows? Your review could be the reason a future reader says "yes" to one of my books! To sign up for my newsletter, shop official merchandise, and stay up to date on my next project, visit my website at www.shannonjumpwritesbooks.com.

facebook.com/shanjumpmnauthor
instagram.com/shannonjumpauthor
tiktok.com/shannonjumpauthor

Made in the USA
Middletown, DE
10 November 2022

14385321R00345